CLOCKWISE

A GHOST STORY FOR AUTUMN

SUSAN BORDEN

ISBN: 978-1-7349709-1-3

Leerie Lights Press

*To the readers who are creating an Act Two
for their lives, by choice or necessity.
I'm cheering you on from the wings.*

I'm so glad I live in a world where there are Octobers.

— L. M. MONTGOMERY

CHAPTER 1

*W*hen she thought about that summer day
months later, Claire realized that if it hadn't
been for the papier-mâché jack-o'-lantern in the window, she
would never have entered the antique store at all. The jack
was so odd-looking that it snagged her attention and
brought her footsteps stuttering backward. Apparently
enjoying its pride of place on an overturned flowerpot, it
grinned among the foggy bottles, curling issues of *Life*, and
wooden farm implements that surrounded it. Claire blew her
damp bangs off her forehead and leaned forward to examine
it through the glass. The large round eyes under arched
brows, snub nose with flared nostrils, and downward dip in
the lower lip gave it the look of a festive frog—Kermit's
ancient, autumnal cousin. And it was utterly impractical,
even for a Halloween decoration. That chapped papier-
mâché must be decades old, so lighting a candle in the jack-
o'-lantern's dusty innards would be pure folly. Halloween
was over two months away, and she knew that she shouldn't
be spending money on needless purchases right then. She

1

frowned. The jack-o'-lantern smiled. She turned with a sigh and entered the shop.

Instead of the expected chime of a bell, she heard an electronic chirp, incongruous amid the bric-a-brac and furniture staggered before her. The interior of the shop was dim and cool, and it smelled of must, dust, and olden times. She paused just past the threshold, doubt rising in her, and half turned to head out into the August morning again, regretfully leaving the jack behind.

"Hello," a sandy voice called out. "May I help you find something? Or is there anything you'd like to take a closer look at?" A man emerged from behind the counter. The ring of gray hair around his head stood out in tufts, and a V of concentration connected his wild eyebrows. His hands jingled coins in both pockets of his khakis, a sound that Claire found soothing because it reminded her of Gus, her grandfather. This man was not as old as Gus, though—sixty-five, maybe seventy. Claire found it difficult to estimate people's ages. So many things beside years could bring on the loose skin, rounded shoulders, and somber eyes of this gentleman.

"Yes, thank you. I'd like to see that jack-o'-lantern from the front window, please." She stopped while she was ahead. Often now, her words came out in a jumble, drawing confused looks from the person she was speaking to. The other day, she'd said "sixteen" instead of "Thursday." These mistakes were so embarrassing that she'd become quiet with others. And honestly, the quiet suited her just fine. She wiped her palms stealthily on the front of her jeans, then ran her claddagh pendant on its chain. Nothing to worry about here; this was just a simple interaction that involved no commitment or energy from her. She was browsing—that's what she would say next. She wouldn't take much of this man's time.

The shop owner nodded before padding over to the

window and beginning the process of shifting a rocking chair made of twigs and bent wood, a coat rack holding women's feathered hats, and a disreputable steamer trunk, all of which were blocking him from reaching the display window.

Claire let her eyes sweep around the shop. It held so many items that they melded together in her view, like chunks of rock that had gradually hardened into conglomerate. She waited amid the rough scraping noises of furniture being moved, noticing some other small sounds that were much more pleasing: a gentle ticking and a regular "skee, skee, skee" that was so faint, she could barely hear it. Mechanical sounds, but also warm and regular, they reminded her of quick, light breaths. They emanated, she realized, from a clock that hung in the dimness behind the counter.

It must be a cuckoo clock—it had the whimsical house shape and the curved door tucked under the roof's peak—but the design was unfamiliar to Claire. Were those owls perched on top? She felt a tickle at the nape of her neck: sweat drying, probably. She lifted her hair with one hand and let it fall again, but the prickling sensation continued. Weren't owls the natural enemies of cuckoos? And didn't they also prey on those sparrow-type birds gripping twigs on either side of the clock's dial? Yet the owls, with their round heads and soulful eyes, looked to Claire as if they meant no harm, and the sparrows had the perky, confident air of the birds that swooped and picked at her front yard feeder. The clock sighed internally, the curved door snapped open, and a tiny golden cuckoo popped out, bowed for each of its eleven cuckoo calls, and then leapt back into the house. The door clapped shut again, leaving Claire gazing.

A high wave of longing washed through her. She wanted that clock.

"Here's the jack-o'-lantern, ma'am." The man laid the papier-mâché decoration to one side on the counter. "This guy's from the forties. Has a few dents and scratches, but he's in pretty good shape for his age. A customer brought it in a month or so ago, saying that it had been stored in her grandmother's house in Germany for decades. Don't know if I believe that, since I doubt that Germans were celebrating Halloween in the forties. But it's definitely of that era. Unmistakable if you know a thing about this type of decoration." Claire felt she had to at least pretend to consider the jack, even though she had completely forgotten its existence during the last few minutes. Close up, it looked bizarre rather than intriguing, with its leering, downturned grin and empty eyes. The crackled surface was a neon-bright shade of orange that hurt her eyes. What had she been thinking to ask after this monster?

"Hmm, yes. Well, it is…unique. Now that cuckoo clock. What do you know about it?" Claire gestured vaguely at the wall, noticing that her heart was thudding in her chest.

"Ah, the owl clock. Pretty, isn't it? I've never seen another like it. Hand-carved, Black Forest—the real deal. Keeps good time, but you have to adjust the pendulum when the humidity changes dramatically. Just nudge this"—he pointed to the carved leaf swinging steadily on the flat wooden pendulum—"if the clock needs help. See, the leaf slides up and down; move it lower if the clock is running fast and raise it if it's running slow. Just a tidge, mind you. A tiny adjustment will do the trick." He paused. "I don't know how old this clock is, to be honest with you. Seventy-five years? A hundred? Clocks aren't my specialty, you know, and I haven't had this one long enough to get my buddy Clark in to look at it. But I liked it right off. Cuckoo clocks are kind of companionable, I think. I have one at home that plays music. This one just cuckoos." The man coughed lightly, as if embarrassed at having revealed something personal.

Claire considered. You're in no position to spend money frivolously, she told herself sternly. The bungalow needs a lot of work, and soon, there will be no paychecks coming in for a time. She should be sensible, buckle down, watch every dollar.

"So, how much does it cost? I mean, what will you take for it?" She scarcely recognized the rickety voice as her own.

The man plucked briefly at one of his eyebrows before turning to gaze again at the clock. Claire wondered if this were part of a shop owner's performance, meant to increase suspense in her. If so, it was working. Disliking the suspicious thought, she tipped it out of her mind. But it immediately crawled back up again, along with the knowledge that whatever price he named, she should dicker with him. That's the way these transactions were handled. Claire hated to dicker.

"Well," the man drawled. "I'd say that eighty-five dollars would be fair since I don't know its provenance aside from who owned it last." He paused, then continued in a softened voice. "It seems like you've taken a shine to it. Some things just belong with certain people. That's what my wife used to say, and the idea seems to have taken ahold of me, too." He shrugged self-consciously and twisted a low button on his summer-plaid shirt.

"Sold," said Claire, and began to fumble for the wallet in her canvas tote. "Do you take credit cards? Or would you rather have a check? Either one is fine, really." She drew in her breath, surprised, not at herself for buying an antique, but at the lack of guilt she felt for doing it. In fact, she felt wonderful, buoyant, exhilarated. A beam of clean light swept through her mind, immediately followed by the hollow sea-sound of applause. Well, someone's happy about my getting this clock, she thought, and I guess it's me.

SHE MADE her way gingerly up the front steps of the bungalow with a sealed cardboard box, feeling with each foot before shifting any weight onto it. Impatient scrabbling sounds reached her through the double set of doors. "Lute, stop that; I'll be right there." She tucked the box onto a porch chair and shot the door's deadbolt with her key, noticing for the first time that the varnish had bubbled around the door-knob. Old homes, she was learning, were not for perfection-ists. Or worriers.

Inside, she was met by chilled air that smelled like the back of the freezer and by terrier Lute, who bounced and leapt and shimmied as if Claire had been gone for days instead of an hour or two. "Yes, yes, I see you, buddy. Where are the girls, hmm?" She set the box carefully on the dining room table and let Lute out the back door into the fenced yard, watching as he streaked for the raspberry bushes, a skein of brown and white energy. The fence was new, and it had been expensive, but both she and the dog were thankful for the freedom it gave him. Her pets' pleasure in their new home was as great as her own, she thought. Maybe greater, since they didn't have any worries about upkeep.

When she returned to the dining room, she found a tiger-striped cat rubbing her cheeks on one of the box's corners, claiming it for herself. "Kipper, get off the table! You know better." Claire scooped the cat up and settled her against her shoulder, kneading the nape of Kip's neck until she broke into a confident purr. Another cat, gray-blue and leopard-slim, sat atop the wardrobe and surveyed her realm. She stared fixedly at the box even after Claire let Kip leap to the floor, her golden eyes watchful. Claire reached up to trail a hand over the cat's soft head, pleased to see that Tamsin's flinch at being touched was only a slight one. She was gradually getting used to Claire, to the other animals in "her" house, and to life without her previous person.

Claire scuffed off her shoes and stood in front of the window air conditioner for a calming moment, blouse pulled out like a sail to catch the cool current, then fetched a pair of scissors, anticipation causing her fingers to shake lightly. "Stop that," she told them, just as she had chided the terrier.

Even in its current nest of cardboard and packing peanuts, the clock called out to Claire, reminding her of home, childhood books, and Old Countries. Like many American families, hers was a blend of nationalities, English and Irish on her father's side, and Czech and Polish on her mother's. Why, then, did this German clock feel like part of her own past?

She reached out to stroke one of the stylized maple leaves that decorated the face of the clock. The leaves sprang up energetically, as if frozen in mid-twirl. The dial, with its white Roman numerals and dainty wooden hands, was set into a carved diamond pattern, reminding Claire of a jester's suit. From the peak of a shingled roof, owls kept watch over the plump sparrows, clutching pine cones with their talons. Claire admired the range of color in the wood, from golden honey tones, through acorn tans, to the smoky browns of autumn. A wisp of October curled up from the box.

She scanned the room for the proper place to hang her beautiful clock. Ah, that was the spot: the narrow wall between the front door and the entry into the sunroom. She would be able to see the clock from the living room, dining room, even the doorway to the kitchen. She fetched the measuring tape and hammer, laid them on the dining room table, and moved pesky Kipper to a safe perch on a windowsill, resulting in some scratchy meows of protest.

Tamsin had hunkered down on top of the wardrobe and was watching the proceedings narrowly, her tail flipping with studied nonchalance. Both cats seemed to be finding this project engrossing, as if awaiting something particular.

The shop owner had told Claire the height at which the clock must be hung to allow the chains and weights their full length. He had also supplied a special picture-hanging nail that would anchor it to the wall. The thought of the clock crashing to the floor due to her own ineptitude with the hammer caused a sharp intake of breath. She measured with care, made a small mark on the cream-colored wall, and then measured again, horizontally this time, so that the clock would look balanced between the front door and sunroom. A few taps with the hammer, and the job was done. Almost done.

Claire lifted the clock deliberately, trailing the wrapped chains. The cats, she noticed, were sitting side-by-side now, faces tipped upward at the same angle, watching her, watching the clock. Claire fitted the clock to the wall and then just barely took her hands away, leaving her fingers curved protectively around the case without actually touching it. It held. She unwrapped the chains, fitted the pinecone weights to the S-hooks on their ends, and set the pendulum swinging. The steady ticking and "skeeing" sounds commenced immediately. Claire glanced down at her watch. Twelve twenty-seven. Up at the dial. Twelve twenty-seven. A spark of excitement and anticipation skipped through her chest. "Hey, you," she whispered, "Welcome home."

As THE LATE afternoon sun angled in through the west windows, Claire stood at the sink, her hands in lukewarm, sudsy water. The bungalow had a dishwasher, but she didn't trust it with her favorite ceramic mugs: the two-toned, peachy one from the Lunts' country home, Ten Chimneys; and the brown one with "Gunflint Trail" lettered in gold on its side. Enjoying the steady ticking that pattered into the kitchen, she set the Gunflint mug in the bamboo dish rack and dried her hands. Maybe some gardening next.

Maybe not. She caught her breath and froze, hoping that the sensation beginning to nudge into her brain would just go away. The space immediately in front of her vibrated slightly and formed itself into jiggling dots that grew larger as she watched. Then, the crown appeared, sparkling, scintillating, cruel in its brightness. Claire shut her eyes and rotated her thumb-tips hard into her temples, knowing that it would do no good, that the dots and the sparkling crown would be with her whether her eyes were open or closed.

Sighing, she drowned a handful of ice cubes in cold water and pressed the sweating glass against her forehead as she walked toward the bedroom. The familiar sense of distance from her surroundings set in, as if she were gazing through lens after lens that separated her from the world. Bars of black now blocked her peripheral vision on both sides. The oak floor seemed to rise to slap against her tingling bare feet with each step. Numbly, she set the glass on a bedside coaster, pulled the window blinds down with as little clatter as she could manage, and wended her way to the bathroom, dreading what was to come. Shards of bright metal wedged suddenly through her skull, making her gasp in pain. She was able to raise the toilet seat in time. Bile slid up her throat and she lurched forward in response, one hand automatically holding her hair back, defeated once again by the migraine.

There was nowhere to be but in bed. Finding her nightgown in the midst of this onslaught was not possible, but she could remove her jeans before slipping between the cool sheets. Flat on her back, tears sliding out of the outer corners of her eyes, she humbly met the migraine. Every movement, bit of light, and scrap of sound brought on fresh, cutting blades of pain, and the deceptively beautiful aura cartwheeled majestically through her brain, trailing its comet-tail of black dots. She lay still, despairing of ever being free of this torment. Even though she knew that these headaches were not fatal and did no damage to her brain, her faith in these facts faded each time she was in the vicious clamp of a migraine. Time slowed to a crawl.

From the living room, a mournful cuckoo sound reached her, as sad-sounding as a night train's whistle through the darkness. Strangely, it did not pierce her head with new spears of pain, as most noises did. Claire re-arranged her head slightly, seeking a fresh patch of pillow.

Little by little, she became aware of a new bundle of sensations. Although the headache still rampaged through her skull, someone was offering a slim comfort. Cool finger-tips tenderly brushed a strand of hair from her cheek, and a breathy sigh—full of sympathy and regret—blew gently over her face. Among the shrieking sheets of metal, she now felt ripples from a northern lake, shadows from a swaying pine, their twilight tones of blue and gold sliding through her battered mind. Gratefully, she reached out for this comfort.

Maybe there was some hope for her after all.

CHAPTER 2

*T*he wall phone rang in the kitchen the next morning as Claire was listlessly pouring cereal into a bowl. She started violently, although the phone's ring tone was a cheerful, old-fashioned "brriingg" that she usually found charming. Setting down the cereal box, she lifted the receiver that was heavy enough to serve as a weapon and answered with a cautious, "Hello?"

"Hi, Claire; it's me. How're you doing?" said a familiar, welcome voice.

"Marguerite." Claire exhaled with relief. "I'm so glad it's you. I'm doing—well, better than yesterday. I had another migraine." Her palm felt slick on the receiver as she remembered the nausea, the pain, and then the sensation of hands touching her face that was surely imagined, but lovely, nonetheless.

"Oh, sweetie, I'm sorry to hear that. How long did this one last?"

"About four hours, I think. The cats joined me after a while, even Tam. I think she's getting used to me. And to Kip, too. Lute is another story. She still hisses and swats at him if

11

he comes too close." An image of Tam in a pose of pleasing symmetry, front feet together and tail curled around to cover her toes, floated serenely across her mind.

"And what did Lute do while you were suffering?" Marguerite's voice was warm and concerned, with a hint of amusement that made Claire smile in spite of herself.

"He can't stand the sight of someone in pain. I found him under the couch this time. He'd brought his favorite carrot toy with him."

Marguerite laughed. "Poor guy. He's so empathetic."

"How are you?" Claire felt a niggle of regret that she had let this conversation go on even this long without asking about her friend. Her right eyelid began to twitch, and she put up her free hand to massage it.

"Good. Busy." She paused as if considering whether to say more, then hurried on. "Hey, let's get together today. Would you like to?"

"Oh, Margo, I don't know. It's so far to drive. And I'm always wiped out after a migraine." She scrambled for another reason. "Plus, it'll be hot." Desire to see her friend struggled against the sluggishness that often pulled her down these days.

"Claire, it's August in Minnesota—what do you expect, chilly breezes? It'll be fun. I tell you what; I'll come to you this time. I don't venture into the big city often enough. And I bet you've been in that house practically twenty-four seven since you moved in. Listen, how about this: you rest during the day, and I'll come by at about three. We'll get a cup of coffee at Kiffles and go for a walk with Lute afterwards. Coffee is good for headaches." In response to Claire's chuckle, she spoke with mock indignation. "Seriously! Closes up the blood vessels or some such thing. I read it a magazine."

Whenever Marguerite had some tidbit of information or

advice to pass along to Claire, she defended it by saying that she had read it in a magazine. The fact that she subscribed only to *National Geographic* and *Smithsonian* didn't faze her one bit, and she said this each time with conviction, no matter if she were talking about the benefits of Internet dating, new car tires, or classic fondue.

"Okay, okay! That plan sounds great—honestly. Thanks, Margo. You're the best."

"So are you." Her friend's voice was serious, then suddenly surged with feeling. "And don't you forget it! See you at three."

Claire hung the receiver carefully in its cradle, wetted her cereal with milk, and carried it slowly to the kitchen table. Kipper trotted in from the dining room and began weaving around her feet in a figure-eight pattern, chirping encouragingly. The fur that brushed against her bare ankles was warm from the sun of an eastern windowsill. "You and Marguerite," Claire said, bending down to give the cat a stroke, "always cheerleading."

The clock cuckooed nine energetically as she was putting the bowl and spoon in the dishwasher, and Claire jogged over in bare feet to stand beneath it. How did this thing run so neatly with just weights, chains, and pulleys? If the power goes out, she thought, I'll still know what time it is, and felt greatly reassured by this. Instead of buyer's remorse, I'm experiencing buyer's jubilation. How odd.

She checked her watch and found that the clock was keeping time so far. The pinecone weights were already over halfway to the floor. Despite knowing that the clock wouldn't run down until early afternoon, she decided to wind it. A superstitious belief that she should always keep it running formed in the back of her mind, and she knew instinctively that it was there to stay. The playful growling sound of the chains whirling through the clock's interior pleased her. "Here's another thing to take care of," she told herself aloud, but she stayed to admire the clock's rich, autumnal colors in the morning sunlight and its steady, small voice, anyway.

CLAIRE DECIDED to forego working on the house today and instead take Marguerite's good advice about resting. So after the quotidian activities of scooping the cats' litter boxes, starting a load of laundry, and throwing a dingy tennis ball for Lute from the back steps, she settled on the couch with the newspaper. A glance at the dreadful headline made her decide that today's paper wasn't for the low-spirited. She tossed it on the hardwood floor and approached the built-in bookcases that formed the lower part of the archway between the living and dining room. Scanning the hard-backs' spines, she felt a familiar pleasure in the presence of old books. Although she'd moved in almost two months ago, she hadn't investigated these shelves much, leaving them for the time when she felt more like herself and in the meantime, reading paperback Agatha Christie and Dorothy L. Sayers mysteries when she read at all.

Her gaze lingered over a book that had once been black, perhaps, but was now dark grayish-green, like a man's suit left in the closet for far too long. *Puck of Pook's Hill* by Rudyard Kipling. She plucked the book from its shelf and smoothed the cover with her palm, enjoying the full-sailed Viking ship embossed under the book's title. Inside the front cover she found a bookplate, black and cream, showing the silhouette of a seated child leaning her back against a tree, holding an open book in her hands. In the sky above, a towering summer cloud held the spires and ramparts of an airy castle. The printed words "My Book" ran across the top of the plate, and along the bottom, the inked signature "Kate

Bendik" appeared in rounder, larger letters than she had seen her great-aunt's name before. Kipling wasn't exactly in favor with academics these days, but who cared? This was her great-aunt's book, saved since childhood, so it must've been a favorite.

Claire settled back down on the couch, noticing that Kip had taken possession of the newspaper, eyes half-closed, ears still alert. The clock ticked and breathed, adding its wistful presence to the room and to the house. Claire had turned off the air conditioner and opened the windows earlier, and a faint breeze now stirred outside, bringing the morning scents of foliage and sidewalks into the room. Preparing to abandon herself once again to the time travel and nostalgia of old fiction, she tucked her legs under her, opened the book, and began to read.

Some time later, she glanced up in surprise as the cuckoo came bowing out of the clock, each call accompanied by a confident chiming sound. Ten o'clock already? She marked her place in *Puck of Pook's Hill* and laid the book on the dining room table as she passed it, thinking that a glass of lemonade would be just the thing. Lute trotted at her heels, detouring widely around Tamsin, who was snoozing on the chair that Claire never used, curled as neatly as a spiral shell. As she lifted a glass from the kitchen cupboard, she became aware of a slight thump from the dining room and also of a change of some sort—maybe the weather was rolling over from sunny warmth to something more dramatic? She set the glass on the counter and returned to the entryway between the kitchen and dining room, mouth suddenly dry.

Puck of Pook's Hill still lay on the table, but it was no longer closed. The book rested open on its covers, splayed and vulnerable, and as Claire watched silently, several early pages curved upward of their own accord, paused at the midway point, and then gently tipped over to the left, as if someone were reading a few lines, considering them, and idly turning a few more pages.

Claire glanced toward the window, wondering how the breeze could be doing this, knowing with certainty that it could not. The curtains hung still. Through the screened window, she could hear the neighbor's small granddaughter randomly striking notes on a toy xylophone. Lute was whimpering. Tam sat ramrod straight, whiskers fanned out from her cheeks and eyes moon-round.

The prickling sensation from yesterday returned, stronger than before, raising the hair in a strip from the nape of Claire's neck over the top of her scalp, misting her forehead with perspiration, electrifying the skin around her lips. Her breath stuttered in her chest, and her hands drew up into icy fists. Several more pages turned part way, deliberated, and then continued on their trip to the opposite side of the book. The air above the pages fluttered lightly, tantalizingly.

Tendrils of coolness reached out for Claire, touched her wrists and shoulders and face. Sadness and longing that were not her own seeped through her, like spring water welling up through porous rock. Images of tiny white lights in bare tree branches, exotic purple flowers, and twisted locks of sun-bleached hair flashed through her mind, accompanied by a spiraling flute melody. The tangy scent of lime drifted past her. She was, she realized, trembling with fear—definitely *her* fear rather than this other's.

"Who are you? What are you?" she croaked.

At the sound of her voice, whatever was in the room withdrew. The coolness, the charged air, the contagious sorrow, the mysterious images—all were gone.

Trailed by a subdued Lute, Claire emerged from the doorway, unclenched her fingers, and pressed them deliberately on the table, one hand on each side of the book. It looked perfectly ordinary now. Bending over it, breathing as if she'd been running, chilled now from the clamminess of her t-shirt, she noted that the visible pages were numbers 62 and 63.

The clock's steady ticking sounded like tiny feet marching.

"Hey," she said shakily to the empty room. "Don't you know that it's hard on the binding to leave a book splayed open like that?" And she shut her aunt's volume with a snap.

CHAPTER 3

When Marguerite arrived in the waning afternoon, Claire beckoned her through the doorway and then hugged her tight, breathing in her scent of almond soap and sporty perfume. Marguerite returned the embrace, but Claire could feel her confusion.

"Hey, sister, are you all right? You're not feeling sick again, are you? That wasn't an 'I'm-sorry-I-can't-go-to-the-coffee-shop-with-you' hug, I hope." She stepped back to examine Claire's face until her attention was pulled away by Lute, who was dancing on his hind legs and waving his front paws wildly. Marguerite knelt down to smooth his ears, her wavy brown hair falling forward over the sides of her face.

"No, I want to go," Claire said, unintentionally dropping her voice. "I'm just...well, I'm glad to see you. And I have something to talk with you about. Something to, to get your perspective on. But not here." She already had her sandals on, although normally she never wore shoes in the house, and her pouch-like leather bag was slung over her shoulder. She twisted her fingers together and smiled nervously, willing the younger woman to accept what she was saying and not argue.

"Okay," replied Marguerite cautiously. "Is there someone else here? You sound so mysterious." She arose from her tête-à-tête with Lute just as the clock began its three o'clock performance, sounding particularly harmonious and full, Claire thought. Her friend stepped forward to admire the clock. "Wow, this is fabulous, Claire—I love it! It reminds me of a German restaurant I used to go to with my family when I was a kid. It had a cuckoo clock in an upstairs sitting room, and I was crazy about it. Used to hope that we'd have to wait a long time for our table so I could hear it cuckoo. I've never seen one with owls, though. When did you get this?"

"Just yesterday. Yeah, I love it, too, although it cost more than I probably should have spent. Ready to go?" she asked a shade too heartily. And sending a backward glance at the quiet room, she gently shooed Lute away from the door, ushered Margo onto the warmth of the porch, and engaged the deadbolt emphatically with her key.

Kiffles Café was just a little too far away to walk to in the summer heat unless you wanted to arrive sweaty and cross—if you were Claire, that is. They ordered at the counter: a cappuccino with a double shot of espresso for Marguerite, a whipped and frozen coffee and caramel confection for Claire, and cinnamon biscotti for both. When their drinks were ready, they slipped into a booth and immediately leaned toward each other. The café was cool and quiet, and Claire felt herself relaxing. Here, her experience of watching the pages turn by themselves seemed—well, unlikely. Yet she still felt unnerved and puzzled by it.

"So," said Marguerite casually, but she shot Claire a look with her dark eyes, "How are you doing? Aside from the migraine, I mean. Have you been working on the house much? Does it feel like home yet? Tell all."

Claire chose the easiest of these questions. "Well, I haven't gotten as much done as I'd like to, but some. Mostly, I've been cleaning. You know, the house was left closed up for months after Aunt Kate died, and so everything seemed—I don't know, begrimed when I arrived. I take it a room at a time. That must sound like drudgery, but it's satisfying in a way, and simple. My job is to clean a room. That's all."

"Believe me, I understand that," Marguerite responded. "After I submitted the grades for spring semester, I went over to my mother's house and dug dandelions for two hours. It was a beautiful day, I remember, and I felt perfectly happy. I probably should have asked myself, 'Am I supposed to feel so happy about digging dandelions?' But I didn't ask. Just enjoyed being outside on a perfect May afternoon doing something utterly mindless."

Claire nodded. "Yes, it's exactly like that. And I love the house. It's old and charming and it was Kate's. It makes me happy to clean it and fix it up without changing it too much. She loved it, too, but she couldn't take on big projects herself in those last years. She had a lawn service take care of the shoveling and raking—outside jobs like that. But the inside was hers alone. She told me that she hired a cleaning service once—just once—and she was so appalled by the harsh chemicals that the staff used that she never called them again. Said that it took two days to air the house out."

"But you helped her, I know, and Greg, too." Marguerite protested gently. "She couldn't have stayed in her home 'til the end if her life without you."

"Yes." Claire sighed. "We both helped. And Dad and Gus when they were in town. And now Greg is mad because she left the house to me. I mean, I guess he is. It's hard to tell *what* he's feeling; I think that even he doesn't know. But something's wrong." She drooped a bit at the thought. At least Greg still allowed Scott, her six-year-old nephew, to visit her, as usual. Of course, Greg got some valued free time out of that arrangement, but still...

"Wait, I thought that Kate left Greg money in her will? And doesn't he have a nice house of his own? He wouldn't have wanted a bungalow from the twenties, would he?"

"No, he wouldn't have wanted it. He would've sold it as soon as he could, I'm sure. That's why Kate left the house to me and extra money to Greg. But it still sticks in his craw somehow. Maybe he thinks that the house is more personal than money." She shifted uneasily and started folding the paper wrapper to her straw into a neat accordion with her slender fingers. She hated strife, and strife with her friends or family was by far the worst kind. She'd heard people talk airily about family bonds and about how they could fight with siblings, knowing that all would be forgiven soon. Her family wasn't like that, and besides, conflicts with the people she loved the most hurt her deeply. Being biologically related to someone was no excuse for inflicting casual injuries on him or her.

She sighed lightly and turned the conversation. "How are you, Margo? How's Jason?"

"Good. We're good. Jason likes his new boss, and I can see him growing more confident in his work. And I'm—just getting ready. You know." She ducked her head to take another sip of her cappuccino and tap the handle of her wide, white cup with one fingernail.

"Yes, it's that time, isn't it. Tell me again what you're teaching this semester. I'm not sure that I remember every-thing." Claire's mood started to waver and sink. God, she didn't want to hear about classes and schedules and syllabi. Not now. Not yet.

"Oh, the usual, plus one new class. But Steve Haugmeister gave me his syllabus, so I have something to go on. If it weren't for colleagues, the job would be—." Marguerite paused and blushed, evidently embarrassed.

Claire finished for her, voice flat. "Impossible. And it was impossible for me, even with the great colleagues." She smiled to let her friend know that there was no harm done.

"How do you feel about school starting without you? You've been a teacher a long time. Is it weird, not to be gearing up in August for the new school year?" Marguerite spoke in a rush, and Claire recognized that she really wanted to know, from compassion and curiosity both.

Claire considered, smoothing the condensation from the icy drink around on the surface of the plastic cup. "It's a relief. I know that I need this break, and I want so much to be healthier. I'm grateful to Kate that the house and the money that came with it have given me a chance to take a leave of absence without needing to find some other way to support myself. And I have my own savings, of course." She drew in a breath and went on with the hard part, the unrehearsed part, the part she hadn't even fully articulated to herself. "But it *is* weird. To step out of a career I've been in all these years, and before that, I was a student myself, of course, like everyone. I'm forty-two, Marguerite, and since I was five, I've gone to school in the fall. I loved being a student. It's being a teacher that I'm having trouble with now. All that craziness." She swallowed hard, not wanting to think again about the students' disappointment, despair, frustration, and rage that had battered her and her colleagues at the suburban community college where she had worked since she was twenty-seven. She felt bruised by it still. Her bones felt bruised.

Marguerite reached out and covered Claire's chilled hands with her own, squeezing gently. "You've got it worse than I do, sweetie, because you're an English teacher. All of those essays, so personal. People put their soul into writing.

Geography isn't like that." She paused and lowered her voice. "Maybe it's time for you to be a student again."

Claire's throat tightened with grief and gratitude. She nodded hard, just once, not trusting herself to speak.

"So," said Marguerite, narrowing her eyes with interest, "what did you want to tell me? I'm eaten up with curiosity. You sounded so cautious earlier. Like you were afraid someone was listening."

Claire's breath caught with surprise. "You're right! I was afraid of someone else...being there." She stammered in agitation, not knowing how to describe what she had witnessed with *Puck of Pook's Hill*. "I had a, a...very strange thing happen to me this morning." She launched into a description of the pages turning so purposefully, of the scintillating quality of the air above the book, of the tendrils of coolness that had reached out hesitantly for her. "It was so spooky, Margo! Nothing like that has ever happened to me before." She picked up a napkin to wipe her palms, which felt sticky now. "What do you think?" Her heart was hammering, she realized, as she waited for her friend to speak.

Marguerite sat back on the bench and crossed her arms, hugging herself in the lightweight cotton cardigan she had brought against the café's overzealous air conditioning. "I think you were haunted! What're you going to do?"

Logical Marguerite's complete faith that Claire's experience had been supernatural elicited a snort of surprise from Claire, but yet...she felt an internal nod of agreement and certainty, a sense that yes, that incident was definitely beyond the pale. "I don't know. I guess I'll see what happens next. If anything." She swallowed down the fear and anticipation that flooded suddenly through her, mingling with the certainty of a moment ago. "After all, I've lived in the house for six weeks with no problems. Maybe it was just a passing thing. A one-off."

"Just a ghost who happened to be in your neighborhood and decided to drop in on you? Seems unlikely to me. I think you need to be braced for that." She picked up her biscotti, dipped it in her coffee, and took a tiny bite from its corner. "Honestly. Would you like to sleep over at our place tonight? We have that sofa that converts into a bed. You could even bring the critters." She raised her brows encouragingly. "It would be fun."

Claire's smile in return was genuine. "Thanks, Margo, but I think I'd better stay at Kate's. See what's going on there. Take a stand." She slowly spread her hands on the scarred table. "After all, it's my home now, too. At least, I have to make it mine. And if that includes chasing off a ghost, so be it."

Suddenly, Claire was visited by a memory of yesterday: hands smoothing her hair as she lay locked in pain, the cool fingers stroking her cheek. The calming images in her mind that were not hers. A rational person might suggest that these experiences were just new manifestations of her headache; certainly her addled brain did conjure up perceptions under the influence of the migraine: the glittering crown and the bands of black. Yet Claire knew this did not explain what had happened yesterday. Oh, God. She definitely had a guest in Kate's house. And it wasn't Kate herself —of this, she felt sure.

THAT EVENING, Claire fed the animals and then made some rye toast and scrambled eggs with dill for her own dinner. The warm food tasted good to her, and she promised herself to prepare real meals from now on, banishing the habit of eating peanut butter and jelly sandwiches or Life cereal with a cut-up banana for dinner. Her touchy stomach tolerated the eggs and toast well, for which Claire was grateful. No twisting pain from acid reflux made her wince and head for the large, economy-sized bottle of Tums in the medicine cabinet. The rate at which she was going through these bottles lately had begun to worry her. Another thing to drag her down, make her feel vulnerable and weak. She pushed this thought aside for now and turned to face the evening head on.

Even with the elderly window air conditioner running, the house seemed too quiet for comfort, so Claire dropped *Pride and Prejudice* in the DVD player. Jane Austen seemed so staunch. She wouldn't countenance anything supernatural, Claire was sure. Kipper settled down in her lap, awfully warm on an August night but a comfort, just the same. Tamsin leapt lightly from the end table to the built-in book-case to the wardrobe, and then began a thorough bath, relaxed and absorbed in her work. Lute flopped at Claire's feet and was soon having action-packed dreams, if his twitching paws and intent expressions were any indication. Claire resolutely pinned her attention to the movie, watching for the thoughts traveling behind Darcy's eyes and the growing respect he felt for fiery Elizabeth.

As the living room grew soft with twilight, apprehension began to clench in Claire's chest. Nothing's going to happen, scaredy-cat, she scoffed to herself as she smoothed Kip's head, paying special attention to the rivulets of black fur that ran across the top of her tweed-colored head and down her neck, spreading over her shoulder blades. The cat lapsed into a purring doze. Claire doubted that Kip and the others would be so content if there were anything—well, uncanny—about. She let her glance land just once on the bookcase that held *Puck of Pook's Hill*, securely wedged between other volumes now. Claire wondered if she'd ever find out how it ended; she was hesitant to even check it out from the library after what had happened this morning.

There had been nothing accidental about the turning pages of Kate's book. Someone had acted with purpose and deliberation. She hesitated to think about ghosts, especially at nine thirty, with the newly arrived darkness pressing in at the windows, the shadows pouring out of the room's corners, and Darcy and Elizabeth coming to an understanding of each other at last.

Claire clicked off the DVD player and TV from afar when the film ended and arose, setting the protesting Kip down in the warm spot on the couch and calling Lutsen, who leapt up as if embarrassed at having been caught napping. As she walked toward the back door, she snapped on every wall- and lamp-switch she passed, welcoming each burst of light. She had never been afraid in her aunt's house before, and sadness crept on top of the fear, as if she were losing something precious just as she became aware that she had possessed it at all. She let Lute out, then hastily served the cats their last ration of kibble while he was investigating the raspberry bushes by starlight.

After letting the little dog back in and locking the door, she headed for her room, leaving all the glowing lights on. Just for tonight, she told herself. Tomorrow, everything will feel normal again. Yet she had to admit that life in her aunt's house, during a stretch of time that included no paid work, had not yet seemed "normal" to her in the first place.

In her favorite nightgown, a pale pink knit garment that was softer than her oldest t-shirts, Claire examined her face in the bathroom mirror. The dark, shoulder-length hair seemed more flyaway than usual, and the gray eyes over high cheekbones, more wary. She reached up to tuck a few white strands under their dark counterparts and touch the notch that had mysteriously appeared in her forehead, near the inner edge of her right eyebrow. When had a scowl of concentration become her default expression, and would that notch go away in time? The white hairs, she knew, were here to stay. When she had pulled them out, they'd just regrown, but wild and crooked this time, more noticeable than ever.

Steeling herself, she looked not at her reflected face but at what appeared behind her in the mirror. Although she had always avoided frightening movies and books, she knew enough about the supernatural to mistrust the mirror. Spooky things were attracted to mirrors like moths to candlelight. But Claire saw only the back cabinet where the shampoos and bars of soap resided and part of the butter-yellow wall. From the living room, the cuckoo called the hour of ten. Claire rolled her shoulders, which were strung with tension, and smiled at herself in the mirror, her fear momentarily replaced with a shy sense of confidence. Whatever was to come, would come.

CHAPTER 4

*C*laire placed her hands on her hips and leaned back, rotating her head and wondering how the crunching and popping noises emanating from her neck were actually produced. Resolutely, she squared her shoulders. How many times had she caught sight of herself in a shop window and been appalled at the stooped reflection with the head pressing forward, like a turtle's? All of that time bent over essays as she graded had certainly done its evil work. Even now, she found herself thinking, how many essays do I have to grade today? A question she had asked herself every day of every semester since she was twenty-seven. The answer still astounded her, as if there must be some mistake, and one day, she would open a file drawer to find essay after essay, implacable rows waiting for her. The English teacher's nightmare. This was the first summer that she had not taught a summer session, and now the fall term was approaching and she would sit that out, as well. And the spring term after. The freedom from essays had not percolated yet into the deepest regions of her mind. Well, maybe in September, it would.

The idea of "nightmare" snagged a memory from the previous night's sleep, and the dream returned to her, not in the shattered state that most of her memories of dreams took, but whole and clean, like a clamshell. Rather than her usual nightmares of students crawling out the windows, she had dreamed of reading the pages of a loosely-bound book and being frustrated at the task of memorizing its contents. In the dream she had paced furiously, repeating sentences and then realizing that they were wrong, all wrong. Remembering, Claire felt a puzzled tension. This had not been her experience as a student or a teacher, not even in the dream world that twisted and exaggerated life's events, and no associations presented themselves to her, either.

She reached back to squeeze the back of her head with one hand, trying to soften the knobs of aching muscles that lay beneath the skin. When was the last time she had felt fully relaxed? An image of diving into a swimming pool when she was ten arose in her mind. Mentally chastising herself for self-indulgence—certainly her life hadn't been that bad—she turned back to her task of removing clothes from Kate's closet and laying them on the bed. Flowing blouses in shades of russet, gold, sienna and turquoise; fitted woolen blazers as sharp as those worn in old black-and-white movies; trim Oxford cloth shirts, their cuffs fuzzy with wear; A-line skirts in navy and tan with pockets on the side hems; and last of all, a summer robe in clean, bird's-egg blue. Kate had not worn most of these clothes for years before she died, yet they were still imbued with her presence somehow, a wisp of her character. What could be more personal than someone's own clothes? And how could they exist so calmly when their wearer was dead and buried?

Claire startled at a movement behind the mounds of clothes. A smoke-colored face appeared, sniffing daintily at a paisley blouse. Kate's cat. Claire eased herself around to the far side of the bed and carefully picked her up. "Oh, Tamsin. I miss her, too." Sudden tears stung her eyes as she cradled her aunt's pet.

Tam drew back in her arms, stiff and affronted, her eyes green with accusations. "You're right; I'm sorry." Claire set the cat gently back on the bed. Her heart ached for Tam, who had lost her beloved Kate, been taken to Claire's apartment and made to live with an enemy cat and boisterous dog, and then brought back to her own house, which still lacked the person who made it home. The hurt and bewilderment that Tam must be feeling, Claire thought, lay behind her stand-offish behavior. Tamsin had always been a one-woman cat, attached to Kate with a fierce love like that of a wild animal —a hawk perched on its handler's shoulder. Claire gave her a lot of leeway and hoped that in time, her attitude would soften. If it didn't, Tam would live out her life as an alien in this bungalow, and she was only four years old.

Tam jumped down from the bed and stalked away, and Claire began packing the clothes into large, clean garbage bags to take to Goodwill. She wished that some of these clothes, at least, would fit her, but Kate had been inches shorter and pounds lighter than Claire, a whip-thin woman with a dancer's gracefulness and prominent cheekbones that always reminded Claire of another Kate: Hepburn. The association went way back, when the child Claire had come to Kate's downtown apartment and the two of them had whiled away summer afternoons with Kate's collection of 40s screwball comedies on videotape, recorded from Public Television airings. Claire smiled at the recollection. Those movies had hinted to her that life possessed an undercurrent of merriment—joy, even—if only it could be tapped.

Claire and Kate would sit on the couch with lemonade, popcorn, and Twizzlers (Claire's choice) and laugh together over the black-and-white films, the forty-plus years that separated the two people forgotten in their shared enjoyment of this vanished world. It had never existed in the first place, in reality, but what wondrous escape hatches those movies had been for Claire.

"I wonder what happened to those old tapes?" she muttered aloud as she closed the garbage bags with twist ties. Neither they nor the VHS player were in the house now, as far as she knew. But then, the basement still held stacks of bins and cardboard boxes, all unlabeled, holding who knows what. She didn't have the strength to tackle those yet. The closets were proving hard enough. The only thing that kept her working was the knowledge that Kate would want others to make good use of her blazers and blouses and slacks, most of which had the timeless quality that meant they were always in style. That, and the desire to unpack more than the few of her own clothes that she had already hung in the closet and folded into a single dresser drawer. Kate had given her this house, so she must have intended for Claire to do more than merely tiptoe around its fringes.

ON THE DRIVE home from Goodwill, with Lute pressing his nose against the crack in the window, Claire noticed that the local community center's marquee was offering a three-month membership for the price of two. She slowed and pulled into the driveway. The center had been built into a hill, and its lower parking lot around the back was partially shaded by lollypop-shaped maple trees that rustled in the morning's dry wind. Claire found a shady spot and parked the Toyota. Accompanied by Lute, who pranced delightedly at the end of his gold- and red-striped lead, she walked toward the entrance, feeling the heat rise up in waves from the asphalt.

Thinking morosely that August was definitely her least

favorite month (worse than the begrimed snow banks and cold mud of March), she approached the windows, three stories high, that dominated the back of the building. She'd have to wait for another day to make a proper visit since she had vowed to herself when she'd gotten Lute as a squirming, grunting puppy that she would never, ever leave him in her car in the summertime.

An elderly couple carrying gym bags strolled toward her, prompting Lute to sit up smartly, cock his head, and make a warbling sound that she'd never heard come out of any other dog's mouth. Every stranger he met was treated as a long-lost friend. Claire dipped her head, wondering how an intro-vert like her had ever gotten paired with such an outgoing canine. The couple paused to stroke his shoulders, giving Claire scant attention. She glanced surreptitiously through the window and was rewarded with the sight of the pool. Pools, actually, for there were three.

Ah. Claire felt a yearning toward that dancing blue water that surprised her in its strength. The pool farthest from her had clearly been built as the splash-down site for a tall, twisting yellow slide, along which children shot in quick succession, spaced by a lifeguard standing on its upper plat-form, her silver whistle held at the ready in her hand. The children's squeals of excitement and fear reached her even through the thick window glass.

The next pool, linked to the first by a narrow channel, provided a safe harbor for the youngest folks in the aquatic complex; she saw toddlers, their suits puffed by the swim diapers they wore underneath, clinging to adults' hands while they waded in as they would a shallow lake. Older chil-dren crawled over a many-portholed ship situated in the center of the shallow pool, or ducked and laughed under the spray from fountains that rose and fell with delightful unpre-dictability.

Fully half of the last and largest pool was divided into lanes for the adult lap swimmers who propelled themselves up and back with touching determination, no matter what their skill level. The same sunlight that was baking Claire's shoulder blades streamed into the nearest sections of this pool, creating disks of wobbling silver on the blue. In the undivided section, the participants of a water aerobics class bobbed and swirled in response to their instructor's calls.

Claire closed her eyes briefly, still seeing the hot summer light as smooth orange-red behind the shelter of her lids. No doubt, the din in that aquatic center was terrific. The floors would be slippery from scampering wet feet. The artificially clean water would sting her eyes and stiffen her hair, even after a thorough shampoo. And Claire felt that she needed the water more than just about anything at that moment.

AFTER THE CUCKOO clock struck one, Claire steeled herself and dialed her brother's cell phone number, shifting from one foot to the other as she waited for him to answer.

"Claire, what's up?" She jumped at his sharp tone. It still surprised her when people knew who was calling before they answered.

"Nothing," she stuttered, anxiety rising in her chest, chilling her fingertips. "I mean, everything is fine here. How are you?" She frowned in embarrassment.

"Busy. Always way, way too busy." He launched into an involved story about a troublesome client that Claire struggled to process, but at least he was talking and not expecting her to answer.

"Hmm, sounds tough," she ventured during a brief pause. "How's Scott?" She needed to turn this conversation before it got any farther away from her own, familiar shore.

"He's good, looking forward to visiting you." Suspicion

sprang into her brother's voice. "You can still take him, can't you, Claire? Because I've got plans, really important plans, and his mother is out of town for a wedding." Greg seldom called his ex-wife by her first name, which was Grace, and they shared equal custody of six-year-old Scott.

"Sure, sure, I'm happy to have him," Claire rushed to reassure him. Here was the tricky part. "Say, could you pack his swim trunks?"

"Well, yeees, I could do that." He drew the words out, like he was doing her a big favor. "What's your plan, though? You know that she doesn't like Scott to swim in those city lakes. Says that they're full of goose crap. And he burns so easily…"

"It's an indoor pool I'm thinking about. The one at the neighborhood community center. I thought he'd enjoy a dip since it's been so hot and dry out lately." Claire cleared her throat, which felt raw and scratchy. She realized that she'd been talking in lower tones than her natural register called for. "Women do that, often without realizing it, to sound more authoritative," an older teacher had told her once. Purposefully, she raised her voice, refusing to press. "He has a suit, doesn't he? I mean one that fits? He's been growing so fast lately, it seems." Stop talking! she instructed herself roughly. You sound like a sap.

"The community center? The day passes there are kind of expensive there, aren't they? Scott can't swim for very long, you know; he gets cold and his lips turn blue. Then he starts to whine about going home. So you probably won't get your money's worth."

"No, it's fine, Greg, really. It'll be fine." Claire drew in a deep breath. "I bought a three-month membership today, actually, and it comes with some free passes. I'll use one of those for Scott, and we can leave when he's ready. They have a great kids' pool there, with a yellow ship in the middle. Or maybe it's a submarine. Yes, I bet it is, just like the old Beatles song. So I'll see you both at three. Gotta run. Bye!"

She heard Greg's voice, tiny at this distance, during the arc of the receiver traveling toward the body of the phone. "A community center membership? Can you afford that?" it squawked. Claire closed her eyes gently, her hand still gripping the receiver as it hung in its cradle. When did her relationship with Greg get so out of balance? Big brother or no, he was overstepping her boundaries. And what boundaries are those? The question formed in her mind as if someone else had spoken it. I don't see any boundaries.

GREG AND SCOTT arrived a few minutes before three. Claire ushered them in and shut the door against the blast of hot air that threatened to follow them. Scott came up shyly to hug Claire around the waist while she patted him on the back with one hand and smoothed his hair with the other. It had been weeks since she'd seen him, and he looked taller than she remembered, his thin legs taking up little of the cargo shorts that he wore, his white Cubs t-shirt hanging loosely on him. He turned and grinned up at Claire as if they were sharing a secret already. She felt a rush of love for him, her only nephew, most probably the only child whose life would ever mingle with hers. And he was such a nice person, too.

Greg stood nearby, holding Scott's little blue duffle bag, a solid man in jeans and a striped golf shirt who looked like it would take a hurricane to move him. He was smiling as he watched Scott, though, his light blue eyes crinkling in his sun-darkened face. Scott was the only person who brought out some softness in Greg, and even then, it appeared only sporadically. When had Greg become so impervious? After his divorce, Claire supposed, with the change setting in gradually. Now, she thought of rough rock every time she saw him. The two siblings had sidled past each other in recent years, neither understanding much about the other. Kate's will had only pushed them further apart. Claire saw little chance for this dynamic—or lack thereof—to change. She could cope with it, as long as they had Scott in common.

Claire had put Lute in the backyard because Greg complained that Lute scratched him when he jumped up, so Greg stood unmolested. The cats, who generally preferred women to loud-voiced men, were hiding, as usual. "Okay, sporto," he boomed out. "Be good for Claire. I'll see you tomorrow at two." He squeezed Scott's shoulder, handed him the duffle, and strode toward the door. "Oh, Claire." He turned on his heel. "You might want to consider getting some ducts put into this house so you can get central air. Less trouble than dragging window units in and out every spring and fall, you know? And it would increase the re-sale value. Thanks for taking Scott. Call me if you need anything." And he shut the heavy oak door behind him.

"Scout," she said, using her private name for him. "Look what I got. What do you think?" And she drew him under the cuckoo clock and then carefully set the stilled pendulum swaying. Almost immediately, the little door flung itself open and the golden bird careened out, cuckooing energetically. Giggles bubbled up in Scout. He bounced in his sneakers and pointed first at the cuckoo, then at the owls, and finally swung his arm in a circle to encompass the whole clock.

"It's great, Claire—I love it! How does it work, batteries?"

Since Claire didn't understand the details of the clock's innards herself, her explanation was rather general. But she was able to convey that the pinecone weights were crucial to the clock and that it had to be wound, without fail, at least once a day. Without that attention, it would stop. "Almost like another pet," Scout commented astutely. "Where's Lute and the cats?" He trotted toward the back door, answering his own question in regard to the dog. There were no pets in either of Scout's households, and Claire was happy to fill in this gap with Lute and Kipper. When Scout came to visit, Tamsin surveyed their activities from large pieces of high furniture, not wanting to be touched by a child but too curious to make herself completely scarce. To Claire's quiet joy, Scout accepted this amicably, saying of Tamsin, "She's just shy. I get it," before kneeling to stroke Kip from head to tail and receive Lute's ecstatic greetings, complete with whimperings and cheek-washings.

Claire followed Scout into the kitchen. "How about a snack and then a swim, pal? I got some of those Ranger cookies that you like."

BECAUSE CLAIRE WASN'T sure of how the locker room situation would work for a forty-two-year-old woman and a six-year-old boy, she and Scout arrived at the community center already wearing their swimming suits, with a shift over the top for Claire and the Cubs t-shirt for Scout. She had packed extra towels, too, and was relieved to see that there were tiny lockers for keys and wallets opposite the check-in desk; she wouldn't need to use the locker rooms today. As the customer service person had promised, her new ID and the passes for guests were set aside for her at the desk. She asked about the family locker rooms for future reference while Scout jigged up and down in anticipation, then locked her wallet and car keys up before opening the door to the aquatic center and ushering Scout in like a magician introducing a glorious trick. He trotted through and began shucking his t-shirt immediately. Claire walked decorously to the banks of cubbyholes and snugged the rolled towels in one before unobtrusively slipping off the cotton shift.

The air she breathed in was warm and, as expected, chlorine-scented, but gloriously moist. She wondered if her lungs were surprised at the tang of water and chemicals that they were being exposed to. The shouts of excited children caromed off the high ceiling and walls that had been painted with undersea scenes of dolphins, humpbacked whales, and sunken ships. Scout came to her, grinning, taking her hand in his small one. "Could I use one of those?" he asked quietly, gesturing with his free hand toward brightly-colored swim noodles in a bin alongside the wall. She didn't know for sure, yet in a burst of confidence, told him yes. He chose a bright blue one, and they approached the small pool with the gently-shelving sides and the yellow submarine in the middle.

Wading into the warm water with Scout, she resolutely put questions about the efficacy of swim diapers out of her mind and prepared to enjoy herself by witnessing Scout enjoy himself. He handed her the noodle and reached down to twiddle his fingers in the bright water, then trundled thigh-deep to the submarine and stuck his head under a spouting fountain. Let the fun begin, she thought, remembering how much she had loved summertime swims when she was his age, and all the way up through high school, really. The activities at the pool had changed over the years, of course, but the sense of release had remained. An image of her hair swirling while she turned her face upward to see the sunbeams slant into the water came to her, as clearly as if that swim had taken place recently instead of thirty-odd years ago. She had pretended to be a mermaid, she recalled, and wished that Kate would never call her from the pool for dinner and home. Why had she given up swimming for so many years? As an adult, she had taken the occasional dip in hotel pools only, not realizing that this community center had offered a blue refuge anytime she'd needed one. And she had often needed one.

Well, better late than never. She walked slowly toward the channel that connected this pool to the deeper one with the slide, wearing the noodle around her neck like a scarf, calling to Scout, "I'll be right here, buddy." Scout was already playing with the other children, creating some tag game around the submarine, his mahogany hair plastered flat and his torso sleek with water. A little girl with a ponytail that curved between her shoulder blades tapped him on the forearm and then fled around the other side of the submarine, silent and determined. Scout took off in pursuit, laughing as he flailed after her. He didn't need Claire, and she felt buoyed by his independence. She took a few more steps, still keeping her eye on the boy as he dodged and splashed. Suddenly, the life-guard's whistle rent the air; she called to some teenagers in the largest pool to get off the ropes. Scout and his playmates froze momentarily and turned toward the lifeguard, impressed by her authority. Seizing this opportunity for herself, Claire fell backwards in the waist-deep water, gasping at the shock as the waves rose up to envelop her, reveling in the joy of the plunge, thinking to herself, I get to come here as often as I like for a whole three months. Freedom. Play. Joy. She certainly had a lot of catching up to do.

CHAPTER 5

*L*ater that evening, Claire and Scout sat on the cement steps out back, watching the cats in their figure-eight harnesses and long leashes as they high-stepped through the prickly grass, hunting for moths. The cicadas whirred in concert, the invisible presence to mid-August, reminding Claire again that school would soon be starting. Scout was poised on the brink of first grade. Like most children in the area, he had attended all-day kindergarten, but still. First grade was the real deal, as he had told her over his chosen dinner of frozen corn, broiled hot dogs, and macaroni and cheese. He looked so small as he bent over on the step, drawing a picture of Lute with yellow sidewalk chalk, the loop of Kipper's leash encircling his thin wrist, his hair falling in a C-shape over his forehead.

Even if he were to drop the leash, Kip would hardly notice and certainly not take advantage of the situation—in contrast to the wily Tamsin. When Claire didn't watch her narrowly, she would swiftly turn in her harness and begin to wriggle out of it, and if successful in that escape, she would lurk in the shadows of the roses and hydrangeas near the house, refusing to heed Claire's wheedling, then increasingly desperate, calls. She pulled her mind back to the boy and cleared her throat.

"So, do you have your school supplies yet, Scout?"

His face still tipped down, he shook his head slowly and began a chalk picture of an alien spaceman on the step's riser. "Mom is going to take me when she gets back from the wedding. She's in Wisconsin." Silence flowed from Scout as he worked industriously, drawing antennae that poked through the alien's helmet. Several robins alighted on the overhead lines and scoffed at the cats in between offering their evening "tweedle" calls to the warm, fading sky.

"Would you like to call her when we go in?" Scout nodded, a short, sharp, double nod. Space creatures appeared alongside the humanoid.

"Okay then. We'll call from the kitchen. That's the best phone in the house." Claire had a cell phone, but she had never bonded with it, so it could usually be found in the bottom of her bag, seldom used and often forgotten. The idea of being constantly available to others, no matter if she were walking by the nearby lake or mowing the patchy lawn or choosing lemons from a display, appalled her. The wall phone, with its old-fashioned ring and secure attachment to the house, was better. She glanced at her watch. "But she may not be able to answer right now if the reception is in full swing."

"What's a reception?" He had finished his artwork for the time being and was returning the fat sticks of chalk to their handled bucket without Claire having to ask.

"That's the party after the wedding, and it can take a long time. Hours and hours, especially if there's a dinner before the music and dancing." She felt a tiny curl of anxiety in her chest, even though the party was far away and had nothing to do with her. How much nicer to be sitting here with her nephew and the cats, admiring his creative output and feeling the sun-warmed cement on the backs of her legs and derriere, right through the fabric of her shorts.

"Claire, when will I read the book that has Scout in it? You know, the one about the mockingbird? Will I read it in first grade?" His brow was scrunched with uncertainty.

"No, sweetheart, that one won't come till later. In first grade, you'll read wonderful books with pictures, like *Minn of the Mississippi* and *Mike Mulligan and His Steam Shovel*." She paused, suddenly worried that what she'd said would prove to be untrue. After all, it had been a long time since she was in first grade, and she had been taken aback by how serious kindergarten seemed now, based on Scout's occasional comments about it. *Mike Mulligan* had been a big hit with him last month when she'd read him the copy she'd found on Kate's shelves, but maybe it was too easy for first grade. She added hastily, "At least, that's what I remember reading. Your teacher might choose different books."

"Can we read *Mike Mulligan* after I call my mom? And then make popcorn. You promised!" He held out the bucket of chalk to her as if to seal the bargain.

She smiled in relief. Whatever first grade brought for Scout, it would be only a part of his education. Especially his relationship with books. "Okay, big guy. We need to remember to wind the clock, too. Let's go. I bet if you open the door, Kip will scamper right in." And she slowly picked up Tamsin, easing her fingers into the cat's plush fur under the harness, thinking that this time with Scout was doing her a world of good.

After Scout's conversation with Grace and a session with *Mike Mulligan* and a bowl of popcorn, which he tried to eat kernel by kernel until he realized that Claire's handfuls would leave him with a short portion, it was time for bed. He had already taken a bath when they had returned home from swimming, so all there was left to do was put on light summer pajamas and brush his teeth. "Wait, the clock!" he shrieked as she held out his toothbrush with strawberry-flavored paste, and he took off into the living room, showing a flash of heels. Sighing, Claire set the toothbrush down on the edge of the sink and followed him.

It was true that the clock had almost run down, its bronze and black pinecone weights hanging near the floorboards. Scout stood beneath the clock, gazing up appreciatively. "You know what, Claire? The owls remind me of nighttime and the other birds of daytime. Will the cuckoo come out to sing at night? Or will an owl come out?"

"The cuckoo, buddy. The one that you saw before. The owls on top are just for decoration. They don't move."

"I don't know. Maybe it's a magic clock. I think it is! It looks kind of—bright to me. Does it look like that to you?" He tugged on the hem of her shirt, his expression hopeful and somehow younger than usual.

He had spoken with such energy that Claire glanced up again, too. Scout could pull out quite a few gambits to delay bedtime, and this might be one of them. She took in the swinging pendulum, the flourish of carved maple leaves springing from the clock's case, the chipper little birds perched on either side of the dial, the owls with their soulful eyes at the roof's peak, all appearing burnished and warm in the evening lamplight.

"Hmm," she said. "Time will tell, right?" She nudged Scout's thin shoulder. "That's a pun. Get it, chum?" And she led a chortling Scout back to the bathroom.

"How do you like this bed?" she asked him a few minutes later as she helped him settle under the sailboat sheet and blue flannel blanket. "I got it just for you. But the cats get to sleep on it when you're not here."

"They can sleep on it when I *am* here," Scout offered. "Do

you think they will? Or Lute?" He waggled his shoulders against the pillow.

"Lute's got his own bed, in my room, remember? But maybe a cat or two will join you. Do you want the fan on?" He nodded and then repeated the gesture even more emphatically when she asked about the nightlight. The proper guestroom was upstairs, not ideal for a six-year-old sleeping in the bungalow for the first time, so Claire had ordered a wooden mission daybed with a trundle shelf and assembled it in the study, with oaths, a simple set of tools, and Marguerite's invaluable help several weeks before.

A new idea occurred to her. "Do you think the cuckoo clock will bother you, Scout? I can turn the cuckoo part off for the night if you want." She thought about the times she had heard the clock singing in the deeps of the night, as poignant as the call of a loon in the dark. It had never pulled her out of sleep, and she had found the cuckoo calls reassuring, but maybe they would startle Scout.

"Nah," he replied stoutly. "I'll like it." He held out his arms for a hug, which she gave him, thinking how wiry and lithe he felt, like Kip when she was being extra alert—but with strawberry-scented breath. At the doorway, she blew him a kiss and waited for the other part of the ritual, hand on the switch to the overhead light. At the moment he blew her a kiss in return, she flipped the switch, as if the kiss had blown the light out. Chuckles erupted in the dimness.

"Night, Scout. Sleep tight. But be sure to give me a wee shout if you need anything."

"Okay, Claire. I will." His drowsy voice reached her slowly.

Claire made sure that a nightlight was glowing in the bathroom, too, and then trailed into the living room and dropped down in the rocking chair near the fireplace. She felt soothed by the clock's ticking and by her impression that the day with her nephew had gone well, that he had enjoyed it. She rocked half as quickly as the clock ticked, stretching her bare feet out and rotating them at the ankles experimentally. She leaned her head back and allowed her eyes to drift shut for a moment. Then something niggled at her sense of well-being, and she sat up again and opened her eyes, deliberately seeking out the source of her worry, as if she were flipping through a deck of cards, looking for the ominous ten of spades. Money? Returning to her job? Her health? Hmm.

The turning pages. Of course. Kate's house, her house now, was haunted. And tonight, Scout was sleeping over, and she was responsible for him. What if something terrifying happened and he was scarred for life by it? Her fingers tightened on the rocking chair handles. As soundlessly as she could, she tiptoed across the living room, turned right, and paused at the threshold to the study.

Scout was already asleep, one arm thrown backwards over the pillow, the other crooked by his side. Kipper was nestled between his bent arm and torso; she gazed up at Claire with faint reproach, as if to suggest that Claire was interrupting a private moment that should be shared only by cat and boy. Claire smiled, trilled her left-hand fingers at them both, and turned away, leaving the door wide open.

THE NEXT MORNING, she made pancakes for breakfast, enjoying the sight of the golden rounds, speckled at the edges in darker brown and rising lightly in the electric frying pan. She had opened the windows early and turned off the clattering window unit to exchange the air in the house. Currently, Tamsin sat in a window in the breakfast nook, the sunlight streaming through her delicate ears and brightening her gray fur to blue. The cream-colored curtains billowed gently outward and then were suddenly sucked against the screen by the morning breeze. Out in the yard, Lute barked, a short bark of warning to some other animal.

Sunday. Claire used to dread it because it bore such a freight of teaching angst ahead of Monday, but lately, she had felt less suspicious of it. Breathe, she reminded herself. Breathe in and out and enjoy this moment with Scout. The pancakes are lovely. The breeze smells like the clipped grass from a hundred lawns being mown at this very second. You have a house to live in that's paid for, a few more paychecks coming, and some money in the bank. You are very, very fortunate. And she knew deep in her bones that this was true, regardless of migraines and panic attacks and fears for the future.

"Did you sleep all right?" she asked Scout as he sat facing her at the small table in the nook, his back to the windows. He nodded energetically, his mouth full. She had asked him to put one of her old t-shirts on over his own shirt, which bore the logo of the Minnesota Twins this time, guessing how much Greg had paid for that jersey and wanting to avoid strife if Scout got blueberry jam on it.

"I think you should tell Dad that you don't need a better air conditioner." He casually licked a stray bit of jam off his thumb. Claire experienced a frisson in her lower backbone despite the warmth of the frying pan and the August morning. She flipped another pair of pancakes neatly over, one after the other, and spoke up, hearing the wobble in her own voice.

"Why is that, Scout?"

"Well, last night, I kept feeling these waves of coolness washing over me." He continued calmly eating his pancakes, running a forkful around the edge of the plate to pick up more of the jam that had ended up there.

Claire's set the spatula down on the counter patterned with little boomerang shapes. "From the oscillating fan, you mean? From the fan turning back and forth?" She translated quickly, chiding herself for using "oscillating" with a six-year-old at a time like this.

"No, I mean really cool, not from a fan. Refrigerator cool. December cool." Scout nearly shouted, "Iceberg cool!" He grinned, his hazel eyes curved into crescents of happiness. "It felt great. I had to snuggle my whole self under the blanket, and Kip came under, too."

"Oh. Well, I wonder what could've caused that," Claire said weakly.

"Beats me, but I liked it. This is a great house, Claire. I mean, I remember coming sometimes when Aunt Kate lived here. Before she died. But it feels different now. Lighter. You know?"

"Yes, it feels different to me, too. I'm glad that you like it, buddy." She spoke with more firmness, in case anyone was listening, and dropped a protective hand on Scout's shoulder. "Because it's my home now. Kate gave it me." She couldn't help casting her eyes upward a bit. Are you listening to me? she asked silently. It's my home. So take off, okay?

GREG SHOWED up at two on the dot, and she had decided not to stop the clock before he arrived, so the cuckoo bird was calling merrily as she opened the front door. If Greg were surprised, he refused to show it. Instead, he smiled down at Scout and patted his back briefly as the boy hugged him. "Hey, sporto, how's it going? Did you have a good time with your Aunt Claire? And did you behave yourself?"

"Of course he did," Claire responded firmly. "Good as gold, like always. Right, Scott?" She shared a quick private glance with him, his expression hinting at the amusement he felt over the switch in names. "Did you pack up your Legos and your jammies? And *Mike Mulligan*; don't forget to take that. Your folks can help you read it until you can handle it completely by yourself." She didn't mention school in case that was a sore point today. Two weeks of summer could feel like a very long time to a small child, she thought, a little wistfully.

"Go check your room to make sure you didn't forget anything," Greg commanded. As Scout ran off to obey, Greg turned to her. "So." A pause ensued. Claire gestured toward the couch and took a seat herself in the rocking chair, folding her legs underneath her as if to avoid crocodiles on the living room rug. "How are you, Claire? Doing okay? Had any migraines lately?"

She frowned, knowing that there was no way to lie about this and no reason to, actually. "Yes, I had one a couple of days ago." She shrugged and showed her palms as if to add, "No big deal."

Greg leaned forward, his large, sunburnt hands on his knees. "There's medication for those, you know. New medication. I read about it on some website while I was waiting for the car to be fixed. What were the names now? I made a note." He stood up again to begin extracting the smartphone from the back pocket of his slacks.

"It's all right," she said quietly. "I know all about those medicines. And I've tried some of them, including a few of the narcotic ones. But the side-effects..." She let her voice trail off, realizing that she didn't *have to* go into the details. Once Greg had ahold of information, he tended to keep pushing with it or use it as a prop for his own opinions about what was good for her. Telling him the most important kernel—that the migraines were caused by work stress— would be the worst thing she could do. And she felt that he didn't deserve to know that, really. "Thanks anyway, though."

"This isn't about the cost of the prescriptions, is it? You must have some kind of insurance." Man, he was insistent.

Yet she knew that he did genuinely care for her. He might even be trying to protect her, in a clumsy, big-brother way. If only he weren't so certain that he always knew best.

"Yes, Greg," she replied gently. "I do. Please don't concern yourself." Oh, that was the wrong thing to say. She watched as he drew himself up and set his face in a patient, forbearing expression that masked the anger underneath.

Scout came trotting in, his duffle bag bouncing against his thigh. "I'm ready, Dad. I even remembered my swim suit. But, Claire," he turned to her, "I want to leave *Mike Mulligan* here. I think this is where it should stay. Is that okay? Can we read it together the next time I come to visit?"

"Sure, we'll read it next time. I had such fun with you, pal. Thanks for coming." She knelt to give him a quick hug, not wanting to embarrass him in front of his father.

"I had fun, too. Will you say goodbye to Lute and Kipper and Tam for me?" Greg was tapping his fingers on the arm of the couch, as if sending a signal. "Thanks! Thanks for everything!" Scout piped up. "I loved the pool and the clock and the pancakes. So long!" Once he and Greg were out on the porch, he turned to wave frantically one more time. Claire returned the wave and watched them drive away in Greg's silver SUV before reentering the house.

She leaned against the inside of the door, hearing the button lock click. In the past, her rather anonymous apartment had felt empty when Scout had left. The bungalow, though, seemed to be humming with anticipatory energy, similar to the atmosphere she had experienced at a theater recently while waiting for the play to begin.

The slabs of sunlight coming in through the west windows held swaying dust motes, and a beam in the ceiling creaked experimentally. Claire again caught a whiff of a scent comprised, she thought, of lime and spices. Perhaps it was Greg's aftershave, although she had never noticed it before.

She picked up *Mike Mulligan* from the dining room table, ran her first finger down its battered red spine with the loose threads, and then carefully shelved it near *Puck of Pook's Hill*. This house was developing more personality by the day, she felt. Maybe an outing was called for. A fun, summery, Sunday activity to give her a change of scene. She checked on the snoozing animals, retrieved her purse from the closet, slipped on her tennis shoes, and exited through the back door, closing it gently behind her, not wanting to disturb.

HER AFTERNOON OUTING ENDED up lasting longer than she'd anticipated. First, she'd caught a matinee at the nearest movie theater, and then, she'd had an early dinner at a Mexican chain restaurant, splurging on a container of guacamole to go with her burrito. On her way home, she'd stopped at the pet supply store to pick up some cat litter and canned dog food, studiously avoiding the part of the store where puppies and kittens from local shelters were bouncing and napping and pining in wire cages. Kipper and Lute had come from shelters, and she knew how difficult it was—heartbreaking, really—to look when you already had as many pets as you could take care of.

Standing outside her own backdoor and searching for the proper key on the ring, she chuckled briefly at Tamsin's outrage if Claire were to bring yet another interloper into *her* home. Then she forced herself to sober. Poor Tam didn't deserve to be laughed at, even from afar. She was Kate's cat, and Claire admired her loyalty to the absent one. If only she would soften her attitude a little, Claire thought, as she stepped through the mudroom in back and set down the bag of canned dog food and cardboard container of leftover burrito on the kitchen counter.

She halted immediately and stayed still for a moment, uncertain. Lute crept up, laid the side of his face near her shoe, and whimpered, while Tam swaggered through the kitchen on her way to the dining room, studiously ignoring Claire. "What's up, Tam?" she called out, and bent to reassure Lute with a few strokes along his muzzle. The anticipatory feeling that she'd noticed in the house before and forgotten about while she'd been out was gone. In its place, she detected—what was it, exactly? Tension. Frustration. Anger.

She pressed her lips in a firm line and paced to the center of the kitchen, following Tam. Her tennis shoes squeaked with every step, giving her away. The individual hairs on her arms arose, each one in the center of a goose bump, and her mouth felt numb again, yet she walked on, not wanting fear to quash her spirit. Lute streaked past her, stuffed carrot toy in his mouth, making her jump straight up. "Geez, Lute!" She watched as he dived under the couch, his haven from unruly human emotions. Or inhuman emotions, as the case might be. She didn't believe that whatever here was evil, but it *was* seriously miffed.

Kip was curled on the couch, but her head was up and her eyes opened wide, as if assessing the situation. Tam had evidently left Claire to her fate. "What? What?" Claire found herself mumbling, her tongue feeling thick in her mouth. Behind her, the yellow checked cloth on the kitchen table flapped suddenly, just once, tossing pens and receipts and grocery lists up into the air and onto the floor. Oh, God; this was worse than the turning pages! That had been idle curiosity; this was dark and red and furious.

Then she saw.

The clock was silent, its pinecone weights almost touching the floor, its pendulum still.

She had let the clock run down. Yesterday evening, Scout had wound it at his bedtime, holding each weight while gently drawing the chains, one at a time, through the clock's house-shaped case, but he was too short to hold the pine cones up close to the base, so the clock had run down in fewer than its usual twenty-four hours. She exhaled a long, shuddering breath, aware of the chilly perspiration across her chest and sides.

Somehow, she found herself underneath the clock, reaching up with shaking fingers through layers of cold air to wind it and then re-set the wooden hands, risking a quick glance at her watch to find out the current time. The clock had stopped only twenty-three minutes ago, she noted automatically. As her hand drifted toward the pendulum, it started swinging by itself. The patient tick-tock sounds resumed, and after a moment, the clock made its preparatory clicking noise, like a person clearing his throat before singing, and struck eight, as cheerily as ever.

The loops of coolness became less intense and receded. "I'm sorry," she whispered. "I didn't mean to be careless. And I'm learning. Honestly." Then she thought about Lute hiding under the couch, and a surge of anger roiled up in her, struck, crashed down. How dare this spirit, or whatever it was, behave this way in her house over an honest mistake? Scout was just a child, and she couldn't think of everything. She was sick of people pushing her, sick of being the recipient of others' frustrations. Now she was being accosted in her own home? Outrageous.

She called out in a strong, clear voice, "Please don't scare my dog again."

Then she took a seat deliberately on the couch, crossed her arms, still bearing their burden of goose bumps, and waited. Nothing. Not a wisp of January air touched her, not the slightest sense of another's presence reached across the room. The clock's pendulum swayed steadily. The scuffling sounds she heard were created by Lute crawling on his belly from under the couch, his carrot toy hanging by the green, leafy top from his front teeth. He dropped the carrot at her feet, hopped up on her lap, and snuffled affectionately in the vicinity of her left ear. "It's nice to be in somebody's good graces, buddy," she said to him softly, and gave his athletic, fuzzy body a firm hug with both arms.

CHAPTER 6

That evening was blanketed with uncertainty and disquiet. Bolstered by that wave of anger that had surged through her, she stayed up several hours after the tablecloth-flapping incident, watching her DVD of *The Music Man*, thinking that no one could possibly be more reassuring than Robert Preston as Harold Hill. Underneath her calm exterior, she felt knotted with anticipation. The animals wandered in and out of the room as usual, the cats becoming more alert as their witching hour of ten approached, and Lute eventually dropping with a sigh to snooze at her feet. After the earlier drama over the stopped clock, Claire had sensed no more frustration directed at her. On the contrary, the atmosphere in her living room was now comfortable, companionable, even. She wondered if ghosts liked Robert Preston, or perhaps they favored musicals, in general. Or maybe she had scared this one. She smiled inwardly at the idea of mild-mannered, soft-spoken Claire Bracken scaring ghosts.

She pondered the possible causes of the ghostly anger. Was this a particularly conscientious spirit, and so had flown into a rage because she had let the clock run down? And I thought I was hard on myself, she mused. The ghost has higher standards for behavior than I do. Or was the ghost simply looking for an excuse to scare the dickens out of her? Claire considered these possibilities, colorful cards in a Tarot deck. When the answer came to her, she experienced a "snick" sensation —the internal certainty that this answer was correct, like the glossy lid of a wooden music box shutting snugly over the lower part.

The ghost had come with the clock. Everything pointed to that conclusion: the timing, the anger, even the comments Scout had made about the clock's appearance. She cast a glance up and sideways, trying to be casual. The clock looked just as it always had, yet Scout had said that he thought it looked "bright." Well, "haunted" was close to "bright." In the same ballpark, Claire decided.

It was difficult to fall asleep after such a supernatural snit, and even more difficult to stay asleep. Claire found herself dozing more than truly sleeping, dreamlike images flicking through her mind: lights nearby but cavernous darkness ahead; plank boards underfoot; rustling sheets of tattered paper; faces alight with laughter, shadowed with grief. A person who really needed a full eight hours of sleep to function well and who had been chronically deprived of this rest for years now, she dragged herself up at dawn to let the dog out onto the shadowy back lawn and feed all three animals before plunging onto her tangled bed again, chasing more sleep. No more dreams came to her, but no more sleep, either.

The migraine struck at mid-morning, making Claire groan with despair. Refusing to spend any more time in her bed no matter what her condition, she laid her beaten mind in its exhausted body down on the couch after the obligatory trip to the bathroom and pulled a lightweight throw over herself. The ominous crown rolled across her field of vision, tossing off silver sparks and agonizing bolts simultaneously. The windows were open, and Claire retained just enough consciousness of her surroundings to feel air moving over her face and arms—natural currents, for a change. She huddled against the pain, hoping for respite. None came. Her fingertips and left elbow vibrated with the "pins-and-needles" zings that sometimes invaded a limb or two during migraines. She knew that if she were to speak, gibberish would come out. There were some advantages to living alone, she thought mournfully. No one would hear her nonsense, the result of a mind gone temporarily haywire.

Then, gradually, she became aware of a new sensation. Someone was stroking and gently pulling her toes under the throw. Next, she could actually feel the tasseled end of the blanket being pushed back so that whatever it was—whomever it was—could pull some more with small, cool, impatient fingers, paying particular attention to her big toes and pinkies. Claire gasped in surprise and instinctively yanked her feet back under the throw, kicking the blanket wildly over them so that they were covered again. The pause that followed was brief. A portion of the fringe flopped back and the fingers gave her left foot a decided squeeze. It wasn't painful at all—more playful and perhaps sympathetic. Claire sighed and gave up. There was no way she could interact with another person during a migraine, never mind with a ghost.

As before, the glittering crown was supplanted by other images. A flashlight illuminating a midnight cavern of trembling canvas walls. A hand extracting a quart of orange sherbet from a freezer. A fountain of water leaping up around the curled body of someone in the classic cannonball position. Damp, deep-summer grass marked by long slide marks, like otters' trails at the riverbank. Claire turned over each image in her mind deliberately before letting it go. Her perplexity relieved her of some of the pain, it seemed; usually, the migraine demanded her full attention until it retreated again.

Retreats. She realized that the toe-tugging had ceased and the cool fingers were gone. It was as if they had been drawn firmly away. The mysterious images slid away with them. She detected a whiff of lime.

With a twinned blow, the two phones in the house, one on the kitchen wall and the other on her bedside table, shattered the gentle sounds of the clock ticking inside and wild birds tittering outside. Oh, God, was there any interruption of a migraine more agonizing than the shrilling of a telephone? Claire cautiously pressed her hands over her ears and prayed that it would stop soon, which it did. Three rings only had driven their spikes through her ears. Her hands subsided once more over the throw that covered her, and she surrendered another fight.

After she had dragged herself off the couch several hours later, limp and shaking, she slanted a look at her watch, holding her wrist high so that she wouldn't have to look down and risk a pounding head if the blood were still pooling there. One twenty-seven. That made her pause. Was the cuckoo clock broken? It should've sung five times or so during the migraine-saturated session on the couch, yet she hadn't heard it at all.

She began slowly folding the cotton throw, mulling over the clock's apparent silence. What was she going to do if the clock were broken? Complain to the man who'd sold it to her that this dang haunted clock had stopped cuckooing? Just as she was arranging the little blanket over the back of the rocking chair, the miniature door flipped open and the cuckoo popped out, as merry as ever. But softer in its call than usual. Or perhaps her thoughts and senses were still scrambled from the brain storm she had just gone through and she was imagining the low, flutey quality of the call.

She trailed into the kitchen, arranged some saltines from the battered white tin on a plate, poured Canada Dry ginger ale into a tumbler, and eased herself into a chair at the kitchen table. She was aware of her bones at the core in a way that she wasn't normally aware of them. Migraines changed perceptions for hours after their disappearance, making her recognize fully her tenancy in this forty-two-year-old body, reminding her that freedom from pain was not an inalienable right. She appreciated the smallest, simplest graces after each one. A little food and the ice-cold ginger ale, for example, would taste wonderful right now.

The hand reaching for a cracker paused in midair.

Instead of the wall phone's receiver hanging securely in its cradle, it was completely off the hook and lying on the table. Claire stared at it, feeling her cheeks go white and chilly. Gently, she set her outstretched hand on the table alongside the receiver, noticing the nubby texture of the yellow tablecloth under her fingertips, wondering what in the world she should do. Because now the ghost was answering her phone when she was indisposed herself. Or perhaps just taking it off the hook. She reached up to set the receiver gently back in its cradle before nibbling the corner of the first saltine. I need some help here, she thought as she chewed. This situation was not one to face alone. She swallowed with difficulty, her mouth dry from cracker and fear.

By LATE AFTERNOON, she felt able to drive. Praying that the antique shop would still be open, she left the car parked along the street and walked as quickly as she could manage without jostling her still-fragile brain. She halted before the shop door and tried the handle, which looked brassy in the slanting, four o'clock light. Unlocked. Thank goodness. She slipped into the shop without opening the door very wide, catching the strap of her bag on the inside knob as she sidled in. Stop acting like you're sneaking, she told herself. He's the one who sold you a haunted clock. Therefore, he's the one who should be embarrassed.

The owner was chatting with another customer at the front counter as he deliberately wrapped a pair of telegraph insulators, the bubbled glass amber in one, sea blue in the other. Claire hung back, waiting, breathing in the scents of furniture polish, dusty fabric, foxed books, and recycled, artificially cool air. Stealthily, she ran her pendant on its chain and then hid her hands in the back pockets of her slacks. She was going to have to be firm here. She hated conflict, wished wildly that she would never have to argue with anyone again, felt an illogical urge to flee the shop and face the ghost on her own rather than confront this man with his air of deliberation and competence.

"Ghost?" he would sputter. "What nonsense. If you don't want the clock, you'll have to sell it on eBay yourself. Don't come back here with weak excuses about it being haunted. It keeps good time; that I know. If you have invented a ghost, that's your problem. Ghosts, really, in the twenty-first century!"

The customer paid for her insulators with a credit card and gave Claire the forced, U-shaped smile that Midwesterners use to acknowledge strangers as she walked past. The alarm chirped to mark her departure.

The owner carefully placed his fleshy hands on the counter, reminding Claire of the pudgy pink sea stars she had seen affixed to the wet rocks on the Oregon shore, and leaned forward. "Hello," he said pleasantly. "May I help you? Are you looking for something special?" His impressive eyebrows rose interrogatively. He hadn't recognized her,

Claire realized. The man's smile faded. "I think maybe you are."

"Well, I have some questions. I was in the other day, you see." Claire sometimes lapsed into these formal expressions that made her sound like she'd escaped from one of her favorite British television serials. She hurried on, hoping not to stutter or fall silent as she cast about mentally for some crucial word. "I bought a cuckoo clock. With owls on top. It was hanging right there on the wall." She pointed to the wall, which now had a black cat clock with googly eyes that swiveled with each tick and a tail for a pendulum. The owner turned to look at the spot, as if her cuckoo clock were still there.

"Yes, of course. My memory for faces is not good, I'm afraid. But I remember now. You were interested in that pumpkin from the front window display originally and then saw the Black Forest clock. What can I do for you? Is there anything wrong with the clock?"

Claire's left eyelid started to twitch, and she interlaced her fingers to keep from pressing on it and giving herself away. "Well, not with the clock itself. Not exactly." She was bouncing on her heels slightly, she realized, and forced them down to the floor. "I'm just wondering…Was there anything strange about it while you had it here in your shop? Anything out of the ordinary?" Lord, she must sound like a wacko to this decent, straight-forward man.

He frowned in perplexity. "Out of the ordinary? Nooo, not that I recall. Of course, I didn't have it very long." He paused. "Maybe if you were more specific, I could be of more help." His voice was gentle, but Claire didn't get the impression that he was humoring her. She licked her lips and laid her cards on the table. Bluffs and hints would get her nowhere in this situation.

"I think that the clock is haunted, and I was hoping you

could give me some information about who might be haunting it."

The man's face was slack with surprise, his pale eyes round. "Haunted?" he whispered. "Are you sure?'

Claire almost laughed out loud—his response was so different from the aggressive one that she had imagined. "Well, not absolutely certain, but pretty confident."

"Tell me. We can have some tea while we talk. I'm Walter, by the way. Walter Henson." Claire introduced herself, and they shook hands over the counter. His palm felt dry and slightly rough in hers—another reminder of sea stars. He led her over to a beautiful dining room table the color of rich maple syrup and gestured toward one of the five high-backed chairs arranged around it. "Please have a seat. Just rest yourself while I make the tea. This late, I doubt that we'll be interrupted."

Claire settled herself and watched Mr. Henson lope away toward the back of the shop, hiking his slipping trousers up by the tooled cowhide belt as he went. She told herself to relax, and truly, she felt an odd sense of relief, even though nothing had changed and she had no information yet. Just the thought of sharing her uncanny experiences with Mr. Henson calmed her. He dealt with old things, so he would probably know what to do. She sat up straighter and pressed her back into the chair's, arranging her feet flat on the floor as if she were going to have her blood pressure taken. Maybe this had even happened to him before. It could be an occupational hazard, even. She swept her gaze over the tangle of chairs, knick-knacks, books, lamps, framed pictures, and dressmaker's dummies that surrounded the table on three sides, shivering lightly in response to the dummies. Man, she would never have one of those things in her house. A wire person who had no head and could be expanded and contracted—what a nightmare, even if it weren't haunted.

Mr. Henson returned with two matched mugs, the teabags still steeping in the steaming water, their strings neatly looped around the handles. Claire didn't drink hot tea often in August, but she reached out eagerly for her mug, set it on a nearby coaster, and smoothed its matte-brown side with her fingertips. Mr. Henson took a seat in the chair to her left. "Tell me. Please," he said again, and handed her a spoon.

For someone who often struggled to speak coherently these days, Claire thought she did a good job of telling the story of the days since she had purchased the clock. She left out the parts about Scout, feeling that she needed to protect his privacy even though, of course, Mr. Henson could have no way of knowing who Scout was. She also stuck to the narrative of actual events: pages turning, tablecloth lifting, feet being squeezed, phone receiver removed from its hook. The unfamiliar images that had flashed through her mind, she did not describe or even mention. In that choice, she felt like she was protecting *her* privacy.

Mr. Henson listened carefully, not interrupting, taking a sip of tea once in a while. Occasionally, he asked a question when she paused to collect her thoughts, or breathed, "Go on, please." When she finished her tale, they sat motionless for a moment. The ticking of the googly-eyed kitty clock and the air conditioner's hum kept the quiet between them from being uncomfortable.

"Well, Ms. Bracken, I don't know what to say." Mr. Henson shrugged. "I certainly didn't notice anything like what you've described while the clock was here. But I had it less than two weeks. And I'm busy with customers, inventory, repairs...dusting. You wouldn't believe what a never-ending job that is. I go through three or four Swiffers a week!" Apparently realizing that he was getting off the subject, he hurried on. "You know, a person would think that

I'd be crowded with ghosts, living with all of these objects from other people's lives. Mostly dead people's, since a lot of my stock comes from estate sales. The relatives go through the house, take what they want—and I bid on what's left. Stuff that belonged to a person who died just a month or two before, usually. You'd think that some of those spirits would be hanging around their personal possessions—the comfortable chairs, for example, or the wedding china. But what do I experience? Zip." His head drooped, as if in sorrow. "Maybe I'm just not sensitive enough to pick up on subtle things. Supernatural things. You know?"

Claire felt an absurd desire to say something comforting. "I'm sorry," she offered, patting Mr. Henson's wrist lightly— just over his cumbersome silver watch. "I'm sure it's nothing personal."

"I wish I would experience something—hear a voice when no one is here, or see a chair rocking by itself. Or pages turning, like you did. Me? Not even a little cold spot on the stairs." He pinched the bridge of his nose and closed his eyes. When he opened them again, they were unguarded and beseeching. "You see, Ms. Bracken, I lost my wife this year. Helen. She passed in February. Forty-four years we were married. God, I miss her. I miss her every day. I would *love* to see a ghost, even if it wasn't hers. Just to be reassured that she's not...gone forever. Snuffed out, spirit as well as body." His voice was as dry as cracked leather, and his chest seemed suddenly concave.

Claire whispered again, "I'm so sorry, Walter. Please accept my sympathy over your loss." This man's yearning to experience some shred of his wife's presence again washed over her anxiety about being haunted, dissolving it for the time-being. She hadn't thought as he had. She had viewed the haunting as an infestation rather than as a gentle touch from beyond the grave. It's not mice we're talking about moving into Kate's house but a soul, she thought. I need to bear that in mind. Be more respectful.

When he spoke again, Claire could tell that they were compatriots now. "I tell you what, Ms. Bracken; I'll call the person who sold the clock to me and ask if she will contact you. Will that be okay? That's the best I can do, I'm afraid. Confidentiality and all."

"Yes, of course, that's fine, Walter. Thank you. I'll give you my e-mail address; that way, there won't be much personal information divulged on either side if we communicate. And please, call me Claire."

SHE HAD PUT the bag with her swim gear in the trunk before leaving for the antique shop, thinking that a dip before dinner would feel good. Actually, she thought, as she stepped down the broad stairs of the pool and lowered her body into the water, it felt fantastic. Buying the community center membership was the best idea she had had since—buying the clock. That answer popped into her mind spontaneously, without sarcasm attached to it. She began a slow breaststroke in the edge lane, keeping her head up and dry for the time being, relishing this immersion experience. Lights glowed alongside her at regular intervals, creating wavering cones of bright gold in the intense blue. She stroked through them majestically. How could she still welcome the clock after all of the trouble it had already caused her? Why didn't she get rid of it and see if the ghost went, too? She could take it to another shop to sell, lock it in the garage, throw it in the trashcan minutes before the lumbering yellow truck pulled up in the hot alley. Smash it with a hammer until the wooden case was reduced to splinters and the springs to flattened coils like the ones in abandoned spiral notebooks. Even the birds crushed...

Claire gasped in pain, shocked that she was capable of thinking such a thing, and stopped swimming, her feet finding the rough floor below her and her hands, the curled edge of the pool.

The clock was beautiful. It had been crafted by hand in Germany decades ago and brought to this alien land of corn and pine trees and skyscrapers. It had the look of a fairytale clock. It reminded her of childhood, home fires, and contentment. Whoever had attached himself or herself to it was temperamental, perhaps, but not wicked or harmful. Maybe the ghost had not ventured out into the antique shop because it didn't belong there. A small fountain of pride rose in her. It came to me, she thought to herself and resumed her slow breaststroke. It came to me, and it's up to me to figure out how to deal with it. She pondered this idea for a moment, her hands parting the silky water methodically and her feet frog-kicking. Although I could use some help while I wait to see if the former owner contacts me. Who could she trust with this paranormal situation? Margo, of course. Her grandfather, Gus. She would start with them. And who knew? Maybe some other people were, unbeknownst to her, in the wings waiting to play some unscripted part in the haunting of Claire Bracken.

CHAPTER 7

"*A*re you calling from a cell phone?" Claire's father asked, his voice accusing. She shifted her weight uneasily from her seat on the back steps, drawing her knees in toward her chest.

"Yes, Dad, I am. I'm out with the cats and I thought I'd, you know…" She sought in vain for the phrase she was looking for and settled on an alternative. "Feed two birds with one hand." Ha! That was a good substitute. She'd read once that people who stutter often end up saying something a bit different from what they intended because they mentally veer away from a word or phrase that they think will cause them problems. She was developing a similar strategy in learning to find another way to say what she wanted: paying no attention to the word that had skittered away from her like a playful pony. Experience had taught her that the desired word only returned to her when *it* wanted to, and chasing it only drove it farther away from her grasp. She could feel the up-coiling of acid reflux in her throat and swallowed deliberately.

"Claire, there's no such thing as multi-tasking." Multi-tasking—that was the elusive word! Her father continued on, using what Claire thought of privately as his sententious voice. "Only people doing several things badly because they're switching from one to the other. And you know that I don't like talking with people on cell phones. You sound like you're calling from a distant star! I can't hear you properly. And there's that weird lag time. First no one talks, and then we both talk together!" Her father snorted and fell silent. He owned a fairly new iPhone and used most of its functions regularly except the calling feature, saving that for emergencies. She sympathized with him in these criticisms, actually, but she couldn't very well explain that she was calling on her cell from the back steps because she was afraid of being overheard by a ghost if she used her tethered kitchen phone. He would never understand that.

"I know what you mean, Dad, and I'm sorry—truly. Listen, I'll call you back from the landline tomorrow, okay? We'll have a good talk then." Here came the difficult part. "Say, Dad, is Gus available? I have a quick question to ask him." Her father wouldn't like being passed over, but she could make amends with him tomorrow. She shifted the phone by her face, trying to find a natural place to hold it. Kip had returned to roll indulgently on the warm step, and Tamsin was stalking a miniature grasshopper through the parched grass. The evening felt baked by the gathering August heat and by weeks with only an occasional sprinkle of rain.

"What time will you call tomorrow?" he asked, not answering her question about Gus. When she suggested ten o'clock, he replied. "No, that won't work for me, sweetheart. I'm volunteering at the nature center in the morning. Better make it two." How typical that he wouldn't ask if that time were convenient for her, Claire thought, but she let the observation go. He *was* volunteering, doing useful work for others, which was more than she could claim right now. "Are you all right, Claire? Is something wrong? Aside from the obvious, of course," he spoke abruptly, his voice sounding suspicious across all the long miles between Missouri and Minnesota. She had an image of his words zigzagging from one cellular tower to the next, as jagged as lightning.

"I'm fine, fine." This wasn't a lie, actually, even a white one. Compared with the past year, she *was* doing fine, migraines, clumsiness, acid reflux, forgetfulness, and all. Being haunted by a high-strung ghost was preferable to the terrors of teaching—the students screaming profanities, the students writing her messages soaked with grief, the students looming threateningly over her in the hallway. Now that says something about my situation, Claire mused to herself. But not anything that I want to share with my father at present. She felt certain that if she brought up these incidents, he would talk about his own experiences as a teacher, and they were a decade old and attached to an entirely different kind of person than Claire herself was. She had heard his exhortations to toughen up and knock the students back into their place a number of times already.

"Hmm," he rumbled. "Well, okay, daughter; I'm glad to hear it. I'll get Gus. He's building a birdhouse in the basement, so it may take a minute for him to get here. Talk to you tomorrow."

"Bye, Dad." The softening of his voice at the end of the conversation created a knotted twig of remorse that twisted in her chest. Don't be so hard on him, she told herself sternly. He's trying to understand and support me, the best he knows how. She heard him shouting, "Gus. Gus!" and then the clumping of heavy shoes on the stairs. Her father's phone hung near the door to the basement, too.

"Claire-Bear," her grandfather said into the phone, wheezing lightly from his hurried trip up the stairs. Gus still occasionally used that childhood endearment, making her feel about eight years old for a moment. What did people who had no living parents or grandparents do to feel young again? She suspected that there was nothing to breach that solid sense of middle age once those folks had passed. A gust of longing for Kate swept through her.

"Hi, Gramps. Building another birdhouse, eh? Is every bird in St. Louis going to have one eventually?"

"Listen, if I had my way, every bird that needed a house would have a house. Period. Same with people. And dogs!" He chuckled at his own mild joke, but there was a hint of seriousness in what he said, Claire thought. Gus was kind. And generous. And, he was Kate's younger brother.

"Hey, Gus," she began slowly, and then realized that there was no way that she would be able to describe over the phone what was happening in her house and in her head. She needed his expressions, his body language, the light in his bright eyes, to tell this tale. She changed tack. "Have you thought about coming out to visit soon? You could see Greg and Scott. Grace. Your old friends." Pause. "Me." She hurried on. "It's probably cooler here than in St. Louis, too." She remembered that the high temperature in St. Paul tomorrow was predicted to hit ninety-two degrees and that the heat had never bothered Gus. "A little bit cooler, anyway," she amended.

"I'd love to come, little'un. Is your father invited, too?" This last in a whisper.

"Of course, Gus—Dad, too." Gus was eighty, and he'd never liked to drive long distances by himself, anyway. He could fly, of course, or the two men could drive together. And she didn't want to cause conflict between them by inviting one without the other. She could extend the invitation to her father tomorrow, with due formality. She remembered that there was supposed to be a question she wanted to ask her grandfather. From her living room, the sound of nine cheery cuckoo calls wafted through the glowing screened window and door behind her. Lute yipped impatiently at being left inside for so long and scratched vigorously from his side of the door. The growing darkness wrapped stealthily around her, shot through with fireflies and cricket songs. "Um, do you know anything about antique clocks?"

AFTER A LONG DISCUSSION with her father the next day, the date for the visit from both men was scheduled to begin the weekend after next, which would give Claire some time to prepare. She'd had the inspiration to ask Greg if he would like houseguests, too, and suggested that Gus visit her first while their father was at Greg's, and then the two men would switch places, spending a few days at each abode. This would give Claire the chance to talk privately with Gus about her unusual situation. Greg was initially skeptical about the plan but acquiesced once he'd thought it over. He had met Claire's ideas with suspicion for so long that it had become his default reaction. Both father and grandfather agreed without a murmur. Maybe six days apart sounded wise to them, as well. And Greg was willing to use his expansive, unadorned backyard for a cookout, during which the entire family would gather. Claire rashly promised to contribute home-made baked beans to that feast. She'd never made them before, but she could find a recipe on the Internet.

And now for the preparation for her first houseguests, excepting Scout. And Scout was so easy to spend time with, so eager to be happy. Older people would be harder.

Claire's new home, like many bungalows, was a story-and-a-half structure. This meant that on the upper floor, the walls came straight up from the floor only to about shoulder-height, and then they started to form a curving, tunnel-like ceiling through a series of angled panels. Tall people could stand with confidence only in the center of the floor. Both her father and grandfather were tall people, so Claire decided to give over her bedroom temporarily and sleep in the upstairs guest room herself. Once the plans were set and this decision about the sleeping arrangements made, she trudged up the steep, narrow steps to the second floor, muttering, "Worse than a danged sauna" as she plunged into the hot, humid air that had been trapped under the roof.

The guest room was in the front of the house, facing north and shaded by the enormous Norway maple that dominated Claire's front yard like a duchess, so it was fractionally cooler than the stairway and open room to the south, through which the stairway emerged like a trapdoor. The first thing she had to do, she thought gloomily, was to get another window air conditioner for the guest room, and this wouldn't be easy because the windows were tiny. The room held a hardwood bedstead with a fairly new mattress and box spring, a matching dresser, and a peach-colored rug with seashell motif rucked up on the dark oak floor. That was all. Claire revolved slowly, mouth pursed slightly in distaste as she surveyed the walls, painted an unfortunate pale, Band-Aid color that made her spirits drift downward like leaves on a November lake. Sweat prickled her arms and face, and she felt her face flush with the packed heat. "Okay, I know what I need to do now," she said aloud. "Paint! But only with an air conditioner running."

Surprising even herself, Claire launched immediately into her project, measuring the guestrooms walls, making numerous calls to appliance stores, and considering color swatches with names like "Melba Morning," "Sunday Sorbet," and "Mayonnaise." She found that this burst of activity kept her mind off of the supernatural and the recent lack of contact from the clock's previous owner. Having a deadline moved her right along, and she felt more focused than she had in months. Her first triumph was finding a tiny air conditioner that fit into either of the twinned north windows in the guest room. She twisted the knob to "low cool," reveling in the sound of first the motor and then the compressor running, and bending low so that the cold air washed over her nose, brow, and cheekbones. Why did this feel so good while the ghost's chilliness made her hair stand up and her heart stutter? Context.

She smiled to herself, thinking about the discussion of this important term in her lit. classes. What, she heard herself ask, is the context for this event? Burnt-out teacher takes a leave of absence from her job to make the bungalow inherited from her great-aunt into her own home. And find new purpose in life. Ghosts may be involved. Claire sputtered with laughter at how flat and pompous this all sounded. "I need to get out more," she whispered, and then departed from the guest room, closing the door carefully behind her to keep the cool air in before clattering down the stairs. Time to buy paint.

THE NEXT MORNING, she bent down to stir the paint, being careful not to slop it over the sides of the can. Her feet slithered on the plastic drop cloth that lay across the entire floor. Claire had told Greg yesterday that this wasn't a good day for her to babysit, but he had been desperate—or so he'd said. "Scott's no trouble, Claire. You know that. He can even watch TV while you paint. Please. I wouldn't ask if I had anyone else to turn to today."

"So, are you saying I'm your only hope?" Claire had asked with a mock-plaintive quiver in her voice and been rewarded with a chuckle from Greg. They both loved *Star Wars*.

"I owe you big time now. And I'll pick him up by six, so

you won't even have to worry about dinner." He'd said goodbye hurriedly and hung up before she'd had a chance to protest or even answer his request, really. And to be fair, he had stopped by that same evening to help her move the bed and wardrobe into the center of the room and cover them, as well, taping plastic loosely around the legs of the bed and the lower reaches of the wardrobe with blue painter's tape. She had done the easiest part of the painting—the ceiling—last night and early this morning before Scout had arrived, and been pleased at the fresh, creamy transformation.

She had no intention of parking her nephew in front of the TV while she tackled the rest of the job, though. Instead, she'd dragged an easel that she'd found in the basement up the steep stairs and set it up near the window, complete with a large, stiff pad of pristine paper, and on a nearby milk crate, a glass of water and a set of ten watercolor paints in cakey ovals. Just like she remembered from her own childhood, even down to the brush that shed bristles, she'd noticed as she'd picked up the larger one from the easel's front rim and run the soft tip along her thumb. Scout could do his painting at one end of the room while she did hers on the opposite wall. A large part of this wall was taken up with the room door and closet door, so it seemed like a good place to start.

She just hoped that Scout's attention span for painting was as long as hers. He stood in front of the easel wearing an old striped Oxford shirt over his own clothes that came down nearly to his knees, watching her stir. Unable to resist the lure of new paint, he walked over to her and knelt down, too, breathing through his mouth in concentration, exhaling the scent of sour apple. "Wow, that paint is thick!" he commented. "Like the frozen custard Trevor had at his birthday party." A pause to consider. "Well, almost that thick."

Claire had to agree that the paint was lovely. "Always buy good quality paint!" she heard her father's voice in her mind.

"The cheap stuff looks terrible and will need to be painted over in a matter of a year or two. Remember, your time is valuable." Maybe not so much right now, Claire mused, but she agreed with her father's principle of buying good quality items—whether they be cloth napkins, a pair of boots, or a set of steak knives—and taking care of them so that they would last.

"What do you think of the color?" she inquired as she poured the smooth paint into a tray and approached the pool with a tentative roller. Deciding to be bold with this room, she had chosen a luscious, intense peach color with golden undertones, which had the extra advantage of not requiring primer to cover the pale Band-Aid shade, according to the paint salesman. She who dares, wins, she exhorted herself as she saturated the clean roller in "Burnt Sage" paint.

"Now honestly, Scout, would you call this color, 'Burnt Sage'?" The roller cover made mild sucking sounds as she revolved it by its handle up the tray, picking up more paint.

"Well, I don't know. It doesn't look burnt to me. And what is sage?"

"Sage is an herb, a plant. A grayish-green herb. I would think that 'Burnt Sage' would be green. Or possibly black. Not this gorgeous color." Scout watched as she stood up and created a wide swatch of golden-orange on the wall, magically transforming the drab expanse into a bank of sunlight.

"It's okay, I guess," he said doubtfully. "For girls. It doesn't look like a color that Grandpa or Gus would choose." He skipped across the plastic-covered floor, picked up his own brush, and plunged it into the glass of water, swirling it so energetically that some of the water curled over the rim and plopped onto his bare foot. He shook it off lightly, his back to Claire. He looked so small in that huge Oxford shirt.

"What, you think only girls like beautiful colors and boys get the dull ones? Hey, I'd keep that in mind while you make your picture, Scout. Use the red, the orange, the purple! Dare to be confident, buddy! And remember," her tone became exaggerated, teasing, "this is my house, so I get to pick the colors. If you get a house someday, you can paint the walls any color you want. 'Pancake Batter!' 'Guest House!' 'Fiery Poppy'!"

Scott giggled and applied his small wet brush to one of the cakes of paint. "'Cherry Popsicle!' 'Pumpkin Pie!' 'Squished Grape!'" He was warming to this game and almost shouting now. "'Pool Blue!' 'Peashooter!' 'Nightlight!'"

He may have a career ahead of him as a color namer, Claire thought to herself. I think there's definitely some talent there...

Her chuckles were interrupted by a series of tiny popping sounds behind her. She turned quickly back toward the wall that she had just begun painting to see what was causing them.

An erratic line of "Burnt Sage" drops smattered onto the drop cloth and slowly spread. Automatically, she looked up at the ceiling to discern where this paint could possibly be coming from. There was nothing there, of course, except for the cream-colored surface of a ceiling that she had already painted. Yet on the drop cloth, the drips were advancing away from her, deliberately. One hit the strip of protective newspaper that she had taped to the baseboard and ran downward, a streak of gold obliterating the black print. Claire sucked in her breath sharply. The drops were emanating from flat disks of wet paint that hovered horizontally above the floor, looking like small, golden-orange lily pads.

The disks approached the wall, paused, and then sprang forward. Four ovals appeared in a loose arc on the dry section next to the tacky apricot-colored swatch. Claire realized immediately what they were—fingerprints. A slight swishing sound attracted her attention next. The paint in the tray on the floor was being agitated by something. More lily pads of paint arose from the tray and then bounced in mid-air, advancing purposefully toward the wall. As she watched in stunned silence, a personified crescent moon, complete with gently closed eyes and up-turned mouth, appeared on the tan expanse as if someone were drawing it. Silence hummed while the unseen artist considered the image. Then the paint in the tray erupted again and stars began to join the moon, simple round spots that were teased outward to include blunt points, presenting the illusion of light.

Claire felt cool currents that had nothing to do with the tiny AC unit wafting over her, lifting the individual hairs on her forearms and the back of her neck, thickening her tongue and constricting her chest. Her breath rasped in her throat. Oh, lord, the ghost had followed them upstairs and was experimenting with the paint. She should have told Greg that she absolutely could not babysit for Scout in this house until she figured out what was going on with these haunting events. He must be terrified. Traumatized. And it was all her fault.

Ignoring the cheerful designs on the wall, she revolved to face her nephew, ideas about how to deal with this bizarre situation tossing wildly in her mind. Grab the boy and run? Yell at the spirit? Paint over the moon and stars as quickly as she could and hope that Scout hadn't noticed?

He was staring past her to the snoozing moon on the wall, his hazel eyes round and freckles bright. His gaze shifted to meet hers. She braced herself for a shriek of fear or a croak of utter horror. Instead, she saw an amazed smile overtake his childish face, a smile that she had never seen on him or anyone before. He began chortling, his hands below the rolled sleeves flapping delightedly. His bare feet did a little jig on the drop cloth. "Claire, did you see that? Did you see that? It was…it was…" he sputtered, spraying a little in his excitement. "It was *amazing*! It was *magic*!"

Claire's shoulders dropped in relief. These were not the words of a traumatized child.

Suddenly, she recalled with great clarity a video she had seen on YouTube the year before. Two teenaged girls canoeing on the River Shannon had unexpectedly encountered a murmuration of starlings, and the video showed the skeins of flying birds in the overcast sky, hundreds of thousands of them, twisting and tossing, joining and separating, rising and sinking, and then retreating into the distance as mysteriously as they had appeared. The glory of this vision had been captured in the video, and tears had risen in Claire's eyes as she'd watched it, but the last part, after the birds had headed downriver, was moving, too. The girl in the prow of the canoe had turned to face her friend who held the camera and had laughed from sheer joy at what they had just experienced.

Scout's laugh had been like that.

CHAPTER 8

*T*hey sat in the creaking wicker chairs on the front porch, woman and boy, eating raspberry chocolate chip ice cream from brown crockery bowls. Tamsin perched on her favorite window ledge, as composed as that statue of Bastet that Claire had purchased at a King Tutankhamun exhibit, years ago. The leaves of the maple tree just outside were tossing fretfully, and the porch was dim. Puffs of cooler air swept in through the screens. Rain coming, Claire thought. Maybe a storm. Thank goodness for that. She put those ideas aside and turned to Scout. "Well, buddy, that was quite a show upstairs, wasn't it?"

Scout nodded energetically, his eyes still round with amazement. "It was terrific, Claire, wasn't it? Have you ever seen anything like it?" He popped another spoonful into his mouth, shaving off only the top layer in order to make it last longer, and then withdrew the spoon with its smooth mound of ice cream remaining. Claire had taken a few moments earlier to change out of her ragamuffin painting clothes with hands that shook, but Scout still wore the Oxford shirt over his neat shorts and t-shirt. The Oxford worked equally well for ice cream drips or paint splotches.

"Well, now that you mention it." She set her bowl down on the faded little table that she'd found in the basement last week. "I've never seen anything *quite* like what happened up there, but during the past few weeks, there have been a few, a few strange events in the house. I'm not sure what they mean or what's causing them," she added, "but I don't think that anyone means us—I mean, me— any harm. Were you scared?"

"Heck, no!" Scout piped up. "I knew that the...person was just playing. Just having fun with the paint, like I would do if you let me." He stirred the last of his ice cream into pink pudding with dark flakes of chocolate and dropped his voice conspiratorially. "Who do you think it is?"

"I wish I knew," Claire sighed. "I'm trying to find out, but it's going to take a while. I think, though, that while I'm working on this mystery, you and I had better spend our time outside of the house. I mean, I can pick you up and take you to parks, the community center, movie theaters—places like that. We'll still have plenty of time together," she hurried on at the sight of his outraged expression. "And school will be starting soon, anyway." Her voice faded as she searched his face, holding the bowl of ice cream loosely between her palms. "I've got to think about what's best for you, pal."

"What's best for me is to keep me from the most exciting, awesome thing I've ever seen? I can't believe this! I'm not afraid, Claire. There's nothing to be afraid of." His mouth was pinched with frustration at his own powerlessness in this situation, and he was breathing hard. The pause lengthened. She could see him shifting to another strategy. "Please, Claire," he wheedled. "Please let me...see the magic with you?" He cocked his head in a charming, attentive attitude that had first made its appearance when he was two.

The porch had grown dusky from the rain approaching from the west, marching down the street as she considered his request. Mingled scents of dust and damp pavement whisked in through the screens. The tossing maple was keeping the rain from coming in at the porch windows, so there was no need to slide the glass panels down over the screens. Tamsin tensed. A squirrel had climbed a few feet up the maple's trunk and was now in the process of plastering herself against the rough bark. As the welcome rain pattered through the heavy canopy of leaves, rivulets began to wend their way down the trunk, but because the squirrel had wisely chosen the south side of the tree to take shelter, she was staying relatively dry.

"Look at the squirrel, Scout," she pointed. "I think she's the one who bundled up all of the purple yarn I'd put out for the birds and made off with it for her babies last spring. Have you ever seen a squirrel flatten herself against a tree trunk like that?"

He crossed his arms over his small chest and tucked his chin down. The hair over his forehead had arranged itself in pointed spikes, giving him a jagged, determined appearance. "No, I haven't seen that before." His stare challenged her. "There are a lot of things I haven't seen. And you're keeping me from them. Just like my dad does."

THE REST of the afternoon did not go well, needless to say. Scout refused to soften toward Claire, and for the first time ever, she felt a solid barrier rise up between them. Or rather, Scout had erected and was maintaining that barrier, obviously believing strongly that Claire was the one at fault. She looked at his set face, with the chin forward and the eyes narrowed, and remembered that same expression on Greg's face when he was a child. She felt sadness spreading through her, as gray as the rainy skies outside. "Okay, buddy, we're going to the bookstore. Please use the bathroom and remember to wash your hands. And use soap this time." Once he'd slammed the bathroom door shut, she snatched up her camera from the study closet and sprinted up the stairs into the unreleased heat as quietly as she could.

The guest room was still closed up, just as she had left it, and she could hear the little air conditioner unit running, running, through the oak door. Cautiously, she slipped into the chilled, paint-scented room, flipped on the overhead light, turned, and saw—the same nightlife scene as before: moon and stars, clear and simple and radiant. There was something pleasing about the smiling moon and rudimentary stars, and Claire felt a gentle smile curve over her own mouth as she looked at it. After shaking herself out of her reverie, she snapped a few photos, making sure that the flash worked and that the painted images were showing up in the pictures. "Nicely done, whoever you are," she whispered. "But I hope you realize that I'm going to have to paint over it." As a last thought, she pulled an ancient umbrella off the hook in the closet, twisted the knob on the air conditioner to the "off" position, and returned downstairs to find Scout waiting for her on the couch in accusing silence. The Oxford shirt had been flung on the floor.

"We're going to share this," she countered, waving the furled umbrella. "Isn't the rain great? We need it so badly. And rainy afternoons are perfect for bookstores. Did you make sure Tam was in before you shut the front door?" Noticing that Tam was curled up on the nearest dining room chair, she continued as if Scout had responded to her questions. "Good man. Pick up that shirt, please, and then we can go."

. . .

IF GREG NOTICED the frostiness between Scott and Claire when he came at six, he didn't mention it. Sometimes, unimaginative, practical people are the best kind to deal with, Claire thought as she watched her nephew and brother drive away in the steady rain. But she couldn't shake the mental images of Scout, so excited and wonderstruck in the guestroom this afternoon, and then later on the porch, furious at what he perceived to be her disloyalty. If this ghost's actions had driven an on-going wedge between her and Scout, she'd, she'd… What would she do? How could she express her frustration to a playful spirit? "Just watch it," she growled to the empty living room. "Do you hear me? I won't have you disrupting my life. It's totally…" she searched for the proper word for a beat and then seized on it triumphantly, "disarrayed, anyway!"

She stamped into the kitchen, Lute skittering at her heels, and called Marguerite's number, hoping that she wouldn't be interrupting her friend's dinner with Jason. Marguerite picked up on the third ring, sounding breathless. "Hello?"

"Margo! I'm so glad you're home. Is this a bad time?"

"No, it's fine, Claire. I don't answer if it's a bad time." Her voice sounded far away, just the quality that Claire's dad had complained about. "How are you?"

"I'm fine," she returned automatically, then realized that this was not the occasion for polite misrepresentations of the truth. "Actually, I'm, I'm—still haunted! Haunted big time! And now Scott is mad at me because I told him that he couldn't hang out at the house until I get this thing figured out. Oh, you should have seen the look he gave me, Marguerite! I've never seen that expression on his face before. Not directed at me, anyway. It was like I'd betrayed him. It felt like a blade between the ribs, that look. Geez, kids can be tough." She found that her throat was tightening painfully, so she swallowed hard before a sob could escape. Scout. Her Scout.

"Oh, Claire, that sounds awful. And you're right about kids. My sister Andrea's son told her that he would rather have any other person in the world as his mother, including Darth Maul! I know; that doesn't make a lot of sense, but Andrea was crushed. Darth Maul, with that crazy double-bladed lightsaber…And Corby's a sweet little boy, really. He was just lashing out. Adults do that sometimes, too, unfortunately. Anyway, I tell you what. I'll pick up some dinner for us both, and then we can spend the evening together. We'll talk." She drew out the "a" in "talk" to sound like a dolled-up Mike Myers in an old *Saturday Night Live* sketch. Taken off guard by this, Claire snorted lightly instead of sobbing.

"What about Jason?" She pitied herself, suddenly, because Marguerite had a special someone, and she had a ghost. As well as an uncertain future. Now really, whose future is certain? she asked herself sternly. And I also have delightful pets, and lots of great people in my life, even if I can't count a partner or spouse among them. Even if Scout has stopped… Margo's voice interrupted her wallowing.

"Jason has been waiting for the evening when I leave him alone so he can have nachos and two beers for dinner. I'll be there shortly. Do you want to put in a request for take-out food or should I surprise you?

"Surprise me," Claire almost whispered. "Hey, Marguerite, thank you. Thanks for rushing to my defense. You're a rare gem."

"And you are the only one I know who says things like that. I'll be there in forty-five minutes. An hour, tops. Don't let anything spooky happen until I get there, okay? Bye!"

While Claire waited for Margo, she first turned on several lamps, then gave the animals their dinner, and finally ended up at the dining room table under a pool of light from the chandelier with a fresh notebook and her favorite Dr. Grip pen (the purple one). The Dr. Grips had helped alleviate the pain she'd experienced in her right hand and arm from all the notes and comments she used to write in the margins of student essays, and although she no longer wrote by hand much, she still used the special pens because five minutes with a traditional Bic would bring on that familiar clench of pain. She brushed her fingertips over the mottled black and white cardboard cover and then flipped it back. The clock's door swept open and the cuckoo announced six thirty without incident. Fresh, rain-scented air was making its way through the windows that Claire had not been able to resist opening.

"I should've done this a long time ago." She spoke under her breath as she wrote, pausing to glance over first one shoulder, then the other, every now and then. Kip settled down over Claire's foot under the table, and she could feel the cat's purring right down to her arch. She wrote swiftly, not stopping to make corrections or consider a turn of phrase. This document was not for anyone's eyes but hers. And possibly Marguerite's. Despite the traumas of the day, she found herself warming to the task and enjoying the flow of words that appeared on the pages of the college-ruled notebook. Writing has always been a pleasure. When did it stop being a pleasure? she pondered. When did it stop altogether?

She heard the porch door open and sprang up to reach the front door before Marguerite forgot and pushed the button for that God-awful buzzer that sent the cats into deep retreats that could last for hours. A glance through the porch told her that it was still raining, just gently now.

Marguerite was dressed in a yellow slicker that looked vaguely nautical, jeans, and Birkenstocks with wild striped socks. Her exuberant brown hair was spangled with raindrops. She carried an object that prompted a jolt of anticipation: a white pizza box, only lightly spotted with rain. Claire took it reverently, feeling its comforting heat in her hands and bending to sniff deeply. Melted cheese, oregano, Italian sausage, and something earthy and enticing. "Mushrooms? Sausage and mushroom pizza? Oh, my gosh, Marguerite, there must be a special place in heaven for people who bring sausage and mushroom pizza to their friends on rainy nights."

"Do you know this from personal experience?" Margo asked as she shrugged out of her coat, revealing a black Renaissance Fair t-shirt, and draped the slicker over a chair back, wet side outward. "Did someone tell you this who has —shall we say—first-hand experience?" She raised her eyebrows at Claire mischievously.

Claire laughed and carried the pizza into the kitchen. "Bring some plates from the buffet, will you, please? No, I just know this to be true, in my heart. So, do you want to eat first or see the artwork that appeared spontaneously on my guestroom wall first?"

"Oooh, that does sound spine-chilling. You can tell me about it while we eat. No guarantees that I'll want to see said artwork at all, sister. After all, it is a dark and stormy night. Well, dark and wet, anyway. I do want to hear about it, though."

They settled at the tiger-oak table with plates of pizza and glasses of Coke. Between bites, Claire told the story of her encounters, including the visit to the antique shop, and ending with a thorough account of the painting episode earlier that day.

"Wow, Claire, that *is* spine-chilling. And honestly, I don't want to see the moon and stars picture tonight. Maybe another time. When it's broad daylight. Maybe." She wiped her mouth gently with the one of the deep red cloth napkins that Claire had laid out for them both and returned it to her lap, twisting it unconsciously.

"How about a photo?" she asked triumphantly, handing the camera over to Margo, and scooching her chair over so that she could better note her friend's reaction.

Marguerite gazed at the photo on the screen for a long moment, bending forward over the camera that she held in both of her squarish hands. "This is amazing, Claire. Just amazing. If it weren't you telling me this story, I would be scoffing." She glanced up. "What are you going to do?" Her voice quavered a bit. Lute yipped, and Claire dropped a hand on his furry head under the table.

"Well, it's only been a few days since I saw the antique shop owner, and he might not have contacted the clock's previous owner right away. So I haven't given up hope that I'll get some information from her. And just before you arrived, I realized that I should be writing this all down, with as much detail as I can, including dates and weather and such. Luckily, I remember it very well! But I need to record it as soon as possible. Maybe I'll see an explanation in what's been happening, or a pattern, at least." She continued petting Lute, smoothing the springy curls back from his muzzle, feeling the coarse whiskers there. He licked her fingers, whether to comfort her or taste the pizza sauce on her fingertips, she wasn't sure.

"Were you terrified when you saw the painting appear on the wall? I would've been!" Margo leaned in and planted both elbows on the table, her turquoise pendant swinging out past her collarbone.

"It was scary, sure." She was finding her way, not only with the words but with her own thoughts and impressions as well. "It's really, really weird to see something happen that could not be happening—that should not be happening in a rational sense." She paused and brought both hands up from

Lute's tousled head, spreading them over her crumb-strewn Fiesta plate. "But I feel sure, with all of these…" She searched for a word and settled on one. "These happenings, that no harm was meant. There was no feeling of ill intent or evil or anything like that. Even when the kitchen tablecloth flapped, it seemed like an act of frustration or annoyance, not meanness. So yes, I'm spooked, but not terrified. Does that make any sense?"

Instead of answering the question, Marguerite said, "Wow, Claire, you're brave. Very, very brave. You know that?"

Claire expanded inwardly at her friend's praise, realizing that it was true but feeling unable to accept the compliment without demurring. "How can you say that? Remember that student who threatened me in the hall, when Annette DeVere from Sociology hid in the bathroom with her phone, ready to call 911 if the situation escalated? I didn't sleep for two nights after that. I was a wreck. I wasn't brave at all."

"Well, you're brave now," Margo countered. "And it was smart to be scared in that other situation with the student. Didn't the dean bring him back to your class the next day, even though he'd been suspended for threatening another teacher?" She drew her shoulders up. "That kind of thing—don't the headlines flash through your mind afterwards? 'College Teacher Slain, Student Arrested at Murder Scene.'"

"Yes, they do. They still do, sometimes," Claire agreed. "Hey, you be careful when classes start, okay? Be sure that there are other people around when you meet with students. Any students. Because you can never tell when one is going to go ballistic." She sighed, feeling more worried about Marguerite going back to work than she did about the uncanny situation in her own home.

They sat in silence for a moment. Marguerite was the first to speak again. "When I was a little girl staying at my grandmother's house and was sure that Dracula was hiding in the closet, Grandma used to tell me that it was the living we need to be afraid of, not the dead." She paused. "That didn't help me much, needless to say. Especially because everyone knows that Dracula is the undead rather than the dead. Anyway! What do you say we watch some TV? Something fun and comforting?"

"Sounds great. You know, I haven't been reading much this summer, but I've sure been giving that DVD player a workout. Jane Austen films, comedies, musicals—as long as it doesn't make me cry or wince in embarrassment, I'm there. Why don't you look through the DVDs while I take care of the leftovers and the dishes. Remember," she warned, with a plate in each hand, "there's no cable or streaming here, and the antenna isn't even hooked up, so all we have to choose from are the DVDs. An eclectic collection, to say the least."

She heard the muted click and slide of the plastic cases near the small, flat-screen television as she walked toward the kitchen, mingled with Margo's voice that trailed after her. "'Eclectic!' You know, I always feel smarter after spending time with you. Do you use words like that when you talk to yourself?" Claire let that go.

When she returned a few moments later with Baileys liqueur in two juice glasses, Marguerite spun toward her, waving several DVD cases triumphantly. "Let's watch these! Talk about comfort. I had no idea you were such a fan of eighties television."

Claire set the glasses carefully on the flat arms of the futon couch, hoping not to spill. "Eighties TV? I don't know what you mean." She reached out for the cases, a puzzled frown on her face.

"*Partners in Crime, Remington Steele, Scarecrow and Mrs. King*…you can't get any more eighties than those," answered Margo. "God, I loved those last two shows. Saw them in reruns on Pax and Lifetime. Pierce Brosnan and Bruce Boxleitner. Both as hot as can be. But Pierce had that glorious Irish accent, and that tipped the scales in his favor for me. How about you?"

"Where did you find these?" Claire fanned out three of the cases like cards. "They're not mine."

"Really? They were in this tall case in the sunroom, with the CDs. I figured that lots of people keep those things together and switched on the light to take a look. They must've been your Aunt Kate's, eh? Are the discs in the case? I hate it when I carry around a case and find that there's no disc inside. So embarrassing."

"This one still has the sticker sealing the case. She never watched it. *Scarecrow and Mrs. King.* I'd completely forgotten about this show, but I absolutely loved it when I was a little girl. Bruce was my first serious crush. Actually, Lee Stetson was. So dashing. And clearly so smitten with Amanda, even though he wouldn't admit it to himself. I saw that attraction even as a child. They were a wonderful couple."

"You and twenty million other little girls, swooning. Okay, that settles it. We'll watch *Scarecrow.* So your aunt was a fan, too? Did she have many DVDs?"

"No, not many. Not that I know of, anyway; there's lots of her stuff in the house that I haven't gone through yet. I'm surprised that she never mentioned these. But I've realized that most of my visits these past few years were spent doing chores for her, as fast as I possibly could. Not just enjoying her company. Maybe she was saving the shows for me." Claire experienced a spasm of guilt and sorrow in her chest, which made breathing difficult for a moment. "We could've watched them together, like we did her old movies on video-tape when I was a kid. She always seemed so healthy; I thought we'd have years ahead. Stupid to assume that. I just…didn't do much for my family and friends for a long time. That was one of the worst things about being so stressed. I didn't think I had the time or energy to visit people, send cards—things like that. I didn't think, period, I guess."

"Hey, this is an evening for feeling better, remember?" Margo gave Claire's shoulder a gentle squeeze. "Save the sadness, if you can, for a day when you haven't had a ghostly visitor yourself. You did the best you could then. Maybe now, you can do better." She dropped down on the couch. "Got a throw? It's actually cool enough to use one tonight. Fall's coming." Her voice was bright with the desire to change the subject and lift Claire's mood.

"Yes, thank goodness. Fall's coming. I hope it arrives early this year!" She slid the first disc of *Scarecrow and Mrs. King* into the DVD player, handed Marguerite the remote control, and fetched another throw for herself. They settled on the couch, glasses of Baileys in hand. The cats were already circling, scoping out their spots, and Lute plumped down between their two sets of stockinged feet.

"Let's have a toast," Marguerite suggested as the jaunty music of *Scarecrow* started up. "To new beginnings. And to fall."

"To new beginnings, fall, and friendship," Claire stated firmly.

"You and your revisions. Writers!" Margo spoke with mock weariness, then smiled and clicked her glass against Claire's.

CHAPTER 9

*T*he e-mail message came the next morning under the subject line "cuckoo clock."

Hi, Walter Henson called and left a message saying that you'd like to talk with me about the cuckoo clock that I sold him. Sorry I didn't answer sooner—I was out of town, and it didn't seem like an emergency. Would you like to meet over a cup of coffee? I'm usually available for a break at mid-morning on the weekdays.

Sincerely,

Sarah

P.S. Walter said that you were nice, but I'm thinking that a busy coffee shop might be best for both of us! How about Rudyard's on N. Wabasha?

The first part of Sarah's e-mail address, Claire noted, was "kindstranger27." That rang a tiny bell for her, but she couldn't quite make the connection. Noting that Sarah's message had come through only thirty-one minutes ago, she quickly wrote back and was relieved to get a reply almost immediately. Sarah was probably a smart phone user, like practically every other American who could afford such a phone. Feeling a bit wistful over her location on the far edge of popular culture, she typed an acceptance of the time and date Sarah had suggested—Thursday at ten o'clock—and sent it on its way. Today was only Monday, and she was eager to meet with this woman who might give her vital information, but pressing Sarah for a quick meeting would probably alarm her, and besides, the four days until the meeting would give Claire time to gather her wits and craft some questions. Not to mention finish painting the guestroom.

She clumped up the stairs in her paint-spattered tennis shoes, carrying a fresh roller cover, feeling warier than she had since moving into the house. The guestroom still smelled of latex paint and fresh plastic, and Scout's easel with its pristine pad of paper and the jar of water and paints occupied the same positions that it had yesterday. She raised the window that wasn't filled by the tiny air conditioner, thinking that any stray currents of air could be explained by the fresh, northerly breezes that had followed last night's rain. Drawing a deep breath, she whispered, "No offense, honestly," as she picked up the paint can and began pouring paint into a pan. It spun down lazily, folding over and over itself, a gorgeous, fluid orange ribbon that cascaded into the pan before dispersing into a thick pool at the bottom. Lovely.

A small thump on the outside of the door made her jerk, sending a splash of paint onto the drop cloth. A muffled, interrogative "Murr?" told her that it was Kipper, disliking being locked out of the room and wondering what Claire was doing in there, anyway. Lute's agonized whine reached her next. Tamsin, of course, was above all of that and was probably relishing her solitude downstairs, free for the moment from foreigners. Claire realized afresh how important her pets were to her, how much they helped her cope with life's shocks and disappointments. Including the shock of supernatural visitations.

"I'll be out pretty soon," she lied in her blithest voice that didn't fool anyone. "See you then!" She started on one of the pale tan walls that didn't carry the ghostly artwork, painting vigorously.

Gradually, the stiffness that came from fear eased, and she fell into a rhythm with paint and roller. This expanse was already looking wildly cheerful in comparison with the drab color beneath. She took a moment to step away, literally, and savor this small success. As she resumed work, her thoughts turned back to the hours she had spent with Marguerite the evening before. Her friend always made her feel better—lighter, more positive, more capable. Marguerite, she thought to herself, is a fine human bean, using Scout's phrase from his late toddler stage.

She pushed away the recollection of his frustration and anger to return to memories of the pleasant evening. The pizza had been delicious, and she'd only had to take one Tum to quiet the internal rumblings of acid reflux. Margo's thoughtfulness and concern had been touching. And she had to admit that she'd enjoyed the two episodes of *Scarecrow and Mrs. King* (the pilot and a slightly later episode that Margo had recalled with fondness) much more than she would've anticipated. Most of the TV series that she'd followed over the years had taken some time to find their characters and pacing, but SMK had been sure-footed from the start, balancing on the instant chemistry that crackled between the two main characters. It had held up well over the decades. And it displayed the same innocence and zest as the black and white movies that she'd watched with Kate. The two of them had talked about each episode over the phone, she recalled, Kate fully indulging her childhood crush. That's probably why Kate had purchased the DVDs—to ask Claire if she wanted to share them one more time.

The show had aired on Monday evenings, she remembered, at the same time as *Monday Night Football*, Greg's favorite. Their father was not a fan of TV at all and had limited himself to news programs and documentaries, with the occasional episode of *Cheers*, probably when the responsibilities of being a single father had overwhelmed him, she realized for the first time. They'd owned only one television set because he'd believed that children should be doing something more productive than sitting in front of a shifting screen. As an adult, Claire couldn't argue with that, but his past stinginess with the television had been hard at times. He'd also been scrupulously fair when squabbles about what to watch had sprung up between Greg and Claire, requiring that they take turns choosing a program if they couldn't agree on what to watch. (A video recorder had been out of the question; she didn't recall ever asking for one.)

Those "off" Mondays, with the excited calls of the sports announcers drifting up the stairs, had been maddening to her. The knowledge that she was definitely Missing Something had been so hard to accept then, and Claire felt a fresh wash of sympathy for Scout, shut out from supernatural adventures as firmly as Kipper and Lutsen were shut out of the painting project right now. Well, it was for his own good. The perennial excuse of rigid grown-ups.

She would sit in her grandmother's rocking chair, rocking and listening to the audiotapes she'd made of two or three SMK episodes once the rush of love for Lee and Amanda had engulfed her. The sound quality had been poor, needless to say, but she didn't care; her imagination filled in the gaps and scratchiness. Had she dreamed of a handsome stranger rocketing in her life, demonstrating his deep-down commitment and love for her by leaping onto the hood of a speeding car, dangling from the landing gear of a helicopter, or carrying her unconscious self down the winding stairs of a mansion? She must have. The show, she realized as she thought about it now, had been perfect for pre-adolescent Claire, with its theme of adventure and romance piercing the muffled normalcy of life. She had longed for that to happen to her, in whatever form. She'd have to find a way to ask Scout if he'd ever felt this pull—when he was talking to her again, that is.

Claire raised her head and resolutely carried the paint tray back to the wall with the lunar design. Best to get it over with, she thought sadly.

She carefully saturated the roller in the paint and stood up again, roller poised near the moon image. Her wrist was starting to ache from the unexpected, repetitive motion. It would take only a moment to cover this evidence of spirits and go on with her life, pretending that the "art session" had never happened. Yet the sleepy moon and stars, bold and golden-orange on their background of tiresome beige, looked so inviting. "Are you here?" she whispered. The curtains swayed slightly in the languid breeze, and the slinky plastic drop cloth rippled under her feet. But the sound of a distant, rattling lawn mower was all she heard, despite her strained effort to detect something more. She let the roller drop to her side, inadvertently marking her oldest jeans with a swath of "Burnt Sage" along the outer thigh.

Feeling both vanquished and strangely relieved, she gathered her supplies and slipped quietly out of the room.

As she scrubbed her hands in the basement sink, scratching off the paint splatters with her fingernails, Claire turned back mentally to last evening. There had been nothing in the bedroom just now, but last night...For the first time, she allowed herself to fully recall the slight shimmer she'd had glimpsed in her peripheral vision as she'd chuckled and beamed on the couch, the tantalizing scent of lime she'd noted, and the cool, airy fingers that had brushed her elbow, raising that tingle on the back of her neck. Marguerite, on her other side, had experienced nothing out of the ordinary, apparently. Claire had nudged Margo and inclined her head slightly, to indicate that Margo should look, but all her friend had done was sigh wistfully, "I know; he's stunning—absolutely gorgeous. Please don't tell Jason I said so."

Only Kipper, curled on Claire's lap, had reached out two paws toward the shimmer and stretched her toes, as if in tentative welcome.

ONCE SHE HAD CLEANED up and put away the painting supplies, Claire made herself a peanut butter and jelly sandwich, which she ate over the kitchen counter, took Lute for a quick walk in the shady neighborhood, let her fingertips gently scroll down the neck of sleeping Kip, and reached a friendly forefinger out to Tam, who had almost, but not quite, touched her nose to it. "I'll consider that to be the feline equivalent of an air kiss, Tamsin," she said, and then collected her gym bag and keys.

She'd decided that her walks with Lute and random chores really weren't enough exercise to keep her level of healthy brain chemicals up, and now that she had all this unfettered time and a community center membership, she had no excuse for not doing more. And perhaps adding some structure to her days would be helpful, too. Exercise in the mornings, chores and errands in the afternoon. And then, thinking again about the fun she'd had with Margo the previous evening, some time devoted to positive, charming books, shows, and movies should probably be part of most days. Didn't laughing create those healthy brain chemicals, too? She thought that she'd read that somewhere. Gosh, she was treating herself like a recovering…something. Well, who else was there to watch over her? She needed to be self-reliant.

The swim was as refreshing as before. She found that swimming was like lovemaking in the sense that although she knew that they both felt fantastic, there was no way to actually remember just how fantastic until she was immersed in the action, so to speak, whereupon she could think, Ah! This is what I've been waiting for. And of course, in the case of lovemaking, the wait was continuing to be a long one. Perhaps again someday, with someone who loved her… Come to think of it, maybe that experience was still ahead of her for the first time, ever. Her few serious relationships in had been…disappointing was the only word, to be honest. Each in its own way, disappointing.

Claire gave her wet hair a little shake as she exited the women's locker room and walked past a set of three people on a bench, every one holding a brightly-colored yoga mat that was rolled up like the morning newspaper, straps taking the place of the newspaper's rubber band. They were waiting expectantly, as if certain of a treat coming, glancing occasionally at the closed door of the studio across the hall, through which boisterous music and the instructor's shouts of encouragement could be heard. Claire's footsteps slowed, and she made tentative eye contact with a slender, gray-haired woman whose mat was magenta. "Yoga class, eh?" she managed to say. "I've read about it but never tried it. Is it hard?" What an inane comment, Claire thought. Why, it barely deserves an answer. Of course, it's hard. These people look like dancers, for goodness sakes! They've probably been doing yoga for years.

The woman smiled a genuine, friendly smile. "Well, yoga *can* be quite demanding, I guess, but this class is for all kinds of folks, so it's not too hard. The teacher is really good at giving instructions for the basics, and then for different levels upwards." She paused as if not sure that she'd made her meaning plain. "I had knee surgery last year, and I can do most of the poses. My knee lets me know when I'm about to go too far with anything."

"I guess I would need a mat of my own if I wanted to come," Claire heard herself saying. This was so unlike her. The idea that she might be possessed flitted through her consciousness. Do possessed people take a sudden interest in ancient forms of exercise and mindfulness? She turned the choke of suppressed laughter into a short cough.

"No, you don't need your own," the woman replied. "There are mats in there you can use. And a spray bottle of cleaner and paper towels, too." She squinted her eyes and screwed one side of her face upward, communicating perfectly to Claire her distaste at the idea of an unwashed yoga mat. "It's fun. Well, not exactly fun, but *good*."

The middle-aged, bald man next to her broke in. "I always feel great after yoga. Relaxed but completely alert at the same time. How often do you feel that?"

"Not often enough," Claire murmured, pushed her gym bag into one of the stacked cubbyholes near the door, and sank down beside the woman with the magenta mat. "You've convinced me. I'll give it a try."

SHE WAS RELIEVED to find that the studio wasn't redolent of overused sneakers, as she'd feared, but only of clean salt. The room, with its mirrored walls, fluorescent lights, and varnished floor, was almost cold, and several oscillating fans whirled calmly to and fro from their mounts up near the ceiling. She chose a mat from the rack near the wall, holding it with just her index fingertips and thumbs, and unrolled it in a discreet corner. She washed it twice with the available spray cleaner and fistfuls of paper towels, then settled down on it cautiously, crossing her legs in what she hoped was yoga style. The mat had a nubbly texture—to increase traction, she supposed. Noticing that the other students were barefoot as they stretched on their mats or sat waiting patiently, she removed her tennis shoes and socks and arranged them neatly, socks inside, each shoe on its proper side.

Thank goodness I wore shorts today rather than jeans, she thought. Who knows when I would've had the gumption to come to class for the first time another day? I probably would've chickened out. Look at me; I'm being spontaneous. The phrase, "Grasp the cosmic oyster while it gapes," the single thing that she remembered from an obscure novel by H. G. Wells called *Tono-Bungay*, rose unbidden into her mind. Well, yoga sounded like it could be a cosmic oyster. Cosmic, anyway. She spent the rest of the free time before class began trying to figure out which college course could possibly have included *Tono-Bungay* as assigned reading. This kept her mind off of her nervous apprehension.

The teacher turned out to be a woman perhaps ten years younger than Claire, fit but not intimidatingly so, dressed in layers of clothing—two singlets under loose over-shirt, baggy shorts over tights, and colorful socks which looked honestly tattered from wear rather than purchased in an already "distressed" condition. Her sandy hair was pulled back into a plain ponytail, like the one Claire often wore in the summer, and her smile was warm without being *too* friendly. "Too friendly" tended to put Claire's guard up. The instructor greeted the people gathered and sent a particular "hi there," Claire's way, making Claire like her immediately. Teachers should look like they want to be in the classroom, Claire mused, and then recalled the student who had told her during her grad school days, "You're the only teacher I have who smiles." That had been nearly twenty years ago. Had she smiled until the end of the most recent academic term? Well, she'd tried. But maybe she hadn't succeeded.

This young woman, who introduced herself as Molly, put a CD into the sound system. The airy sounds of Native American flutes came brushing out, reminding Claire of curling feathers. "We'll begin by standing at the top of our mats," Molly said evenly. "Close your eyes and focus on your breathing." Wanting to follow the teacher's instructions, Claire raked in a huge breath, overcompensating and feeling conspicuous, as if her belly were expanding like a balloon. She slitted one eye open to watch the instructor and the other students who were standing near her. Why, their bellies looked like balloons, too. Or maybe sails filled with wind. Yes, that was a better image. She wondered when she had last filled her lungs completely, as she was doing now. The process felt less familiar than it should. A feeling of giddiness reminded her to slow down, lest she begin hyperventilating. That was *more* familiar than it should be.

"In yoga, deep breathing is central to our practice," Molly was saying. "Inhale and exhale through the nose, and if possible, create a slight constriction at the back of your throat with each exhale, as if you are fogging up a window on a cold winter's night. This 'Ujjayi' breathing will help you to stay focused." The sounds of measured breathing filled the room. Claire kept her eyes closed and concentrated on creating the constriction, finding it difficult to keep from simply clearing her throat, although she liked the idea of the cold winter's night immediately. "If you're having trouble with the exhale part, think of it as 'Darth Vader' breathing," Molly added. Claire's eyes popped open in surprise, but immediately, her exhalations became sonorous and slightly raspy, like Vader's.

Breathe in, pause, breathe out. Hmmmmm. The sound of breath in a SCUBA mask. By Jove, she had it.

THAT FIRST YOGA class was dominated by Darth, even though Claire tried mightily to expel him from her thoughts. When she made an awkward triangle of her body in downward-facing dog, the thought of Darth, his cape flipped over his helmet as he stood balanced on his palms and tiptoes, rump to the ceiling, flashed through her mind. When she held herself in strong plank, her arms trembling from the unaccustomed exertion, the mental picture of Darth's black-gloved hands splayed out on a magenta yoga mat brought an unwanted smile to her lips. When she wavered into half shoulder stand, the sight of her bare feet against the ceiling was instantly replaced by polished ebony jackboots. Darth Vader doing yoga kept Claire in a state of intermittent amusement throughout the entire hour-long class period, easing her self-consciousness. For after all, she couldn't possibly look as funny doing yoga as Darth did.

The last ten minutes of class, Molly explained to them, would be devoted to lying motionless on their backs, eyes closed, muscles relaxed, feet tipped slightly outward, the right to the right, the left to the left. Claire decided that this would always be her favorite part of yoga practice. Sweat was slowly soaking through the roots of her hair, already damp from the pool. She felt her back sink into the mat, making contact. Her fingers curved slightly, like a bird's claws. "In Savasana, or corpse pose, we do nothing," Molly told them softly. "I will wake you when it is time."

The flute music fluttered over Claire's head, as soothing as the steady beating of wings. She kept her eyes closed and found that eventually, the impulse to open them faded. Her breathing slowed. In corpse pose, Molly had explained, the

Ujjayi breathing would be replaced by the normal type, and all the muscles would be allowed to relax. Claire let this release happen, snuggling her tired shoulders deeper into the mat. The realization that there were other people in the room gradually slipped away from her.

Initially, she thought that ten minutes seemed like a long time to lie still and do nothing. Corpse pose. Is this what it felt like to be dead? If so, the afterlife was surprisingly pleasant. At the instructor's suggestion, she imagined her body melting into the mat, the boundary between the two slowly dissolving. Of its own accord, her breathing slowed and steadied. Time passed, but how much, she had no idea. Under her eyelids, she saw constellations wheeling across the midnight sky, dark cliffs rearing up before the stars. She saw a flame dancing at the end of red candle's wick. She felt the pull of waves drawing her body smoothly up and down. She heard the sound of the sea, hollow, as if in a conch shell. Her chest dropped without conscious choice. Corpse pose was...

A voice broke into her reveries. "Begin to bring life and light back into your body by wiggling your fingers and toes," Molly's voice suggested gently, as if she knew she might be intruding.

Claire experienced a jerking sensation, like the kind that sometimes woke her. Dang, she thought. I was having such a good time where I was. But she obediently twiddled her fingers and spread her toes, enjoying the unaccustomed stretch. As she and her classmates rolled to their sides and then seated themselves cross-legged, hands on knees, Claire reveled in the sensation of feeling relaxed and energized at the same time, just as the nice man had said. And she realized, too, that her own silence was part of what she had enjoyed about the last hour. She had been utterly quiet and had followed someone else's lead to the best of her ability. It was restful, she thought, being a follower rather than a leader for a while.

Having found out from the woman she had spoken with earlier where she could buy her own yoga mat, Claire set out for home through the hazy afternoon. As she drove, the vents blowing on her cheekbones, she rocked her head from side to side and rolled it backwards, marveling at the lack of popping and crunching noises. She bounced once happily in her seat in response, but then unconsciously reached up to touch the furrow above her eye, finding it sensitive to even slight pressure. Could she actually still be holding tension in that newly-acquired wrinkle, three months after she had left her job? Claire frowned, her high spirits fading like a mirage.

Now her left eye was twitching. Pressing her fingers under that eye, she slowed at the sight of a crow in the road in front of her car, pecking at the remains of a poor, flattened squirrel. The crow turned to give her a measuring look as the car rolled forward, then hopped to the side of the road to await her departure. It appeared as glossy as onyx in the late afternoon light. Claire carefully avoided the pathetic corpse and drove on. In the rearview mirror, she saw the crow return to the middle of the road in confident leaps and resume its meal.

The twitching was increasing; it felt like the entire underside of her left eye was jumping. She pulled onto the shoulder, choosing a spot where dappled shade gave her some cover, and put the car in park, ready to allow some time for the ocular spell to pass. But the twitching eye was the harbinger of something deeper and stronger. Grief swelled up suddenly in her chest, pushing aside her heart and lungs, surging up into her now-tight throat and jaw. A sob wracked her shoulders, and then another, stronger yet, tore at her throat. Claire crossed her arms over the steering wheel, leaned her forehead against them, and gave herself up to the storm of sorrow and grief. The emotions bubbled up, hot and caustic and very potent. Her wrists were wet with tears and, and she feared, with snot, but there was no way to tell for sure. Her sobs had taken on a keening quality, as if she were lamenting some profound loss. She felt control spiraling away, as thin as a line of blue ink spinning into the distance.

A tapping sound jolted her head up. Through the smear of tears, she saw a concerned face peering through the partially closed driver's side window. Automatically, she noted the sun-thickened skin, graying hair, and thoughtful, dark eyes. Also the blue shirt with the cloth "St. Paul Police" patches sewn on the upper part of each sleeve, the radio clipped to the pocket, and the silver shield pinned to the chest. "Are you all right, miss?" he asked, concern and wariness both evident in his voice.

Miss. This man had called her "miss" instead of "ma'am." She gave him a genuine, though watery half-smile while she lowered the window and searched without looking for the battered box of Kleenex on the seat next to her. Ah, success. She swiped at her eyes and nose, hoping to capture at least some of the evidence of this embarrassing breakdown. Her lips felt simultaneously rubbery and tingly, and she heard a faint roaring sound from within her body somewhere. The twitching eye was now still, however. That was something.

"Yes, thank you, sir. I am...I just saw..." A silence ensued, during which the patient police officer waited. She gulped and continued on, doggedly. "I guess my life is little complicated right now. But I'll get better. I mean, it will get better. Really." Her voice had cracked on the last word. Blast.

He considered what she had said for a moment. "Well, I know what you mean. About life being complicated. We all have those rough patches. Some of us more than others. But, say, can I drive you home? Or is there anyone I can call to come pick you up?" His dark brow was crinkled with concern. What a kind man. And what horrors he must've seen during his time on the force.

Claire thought wildly about his question, came up empty. "No, there really isn't. Not in the area. But I can drive, honestly. My house is only a few blocks away. I'll just clean up a little here"—she waved the Kleenex to clarify—"and then I'll be right as rain."

"Well, okay. But I'm going to follow you, just to make sure that you get home without any problems."

She nodded, thanked him, carefully wiped her face and nose as he returned to his squad car, and shifted her car cautiously into "drive." A glance over her shoulder assured her that her escort was ready to go. Well, there was one bright spot here. After swimming, practicing yoga, and sobbing as if her heart were breaking, she would almost certainly sleep well that night.

CHAPTER 10

*S*he did sleep well. Nine hours, with only one weaving trip to the bathroom. What a boon to have experienced such heavy slumber. She marveled that there had ever been a time in her life when she'd slept that deeply every night. She had been eighteen, twenty, maybe, and she had succumbed to sleep then like a stone dropped into a lake succumbs to the water.

This morning, the weight of that deep slumber left her, paradoxically, feeling light, as if she had shucked something off and benefitted from her new-found freedom. Setting her cereal bowl aside on the cluttered table, she thought about the many Shakespearean characters who suffer from sleep disorders and about how in this way, as in so many things, Will was preternaturally knowledgeable about human nature. She had told her students, "If a character in a Shakespeare play can't sleep, watch out. That person is in trouble, or that person *is* trouble." Now she thought, I wonder which one pertains to me?

She felt stiff and achy from the yoga, with slender stitches of pain shooting up her back and sides when she turned, like taut lines of red thread, but the bodily complaints about the unaccustomed stretching and exercise were not as bad as she had expected. Perhaps the warm bath she'd taken before bedtime last night had helped loosen whatever was in danger of locking up.

Before entering the bathroom for her long soak, she'd created a sign using a page from Scout's tablet of art paper and her own set of multi-colored Sharpie markers. "Privacy, please!" she'd lettered neatly, and then taped the sign up on the outside of the bathroom door using blue painter's tape. And nothing had happened—except that she'd found no need to pick up the old copy of *Martha Stewart Living* that she'd come across in Kate's magazine rack and laid on the bathmat before running the tap. Instead of reading, she had almost dozed off in the tub. The well-worn blue terrycloth robe had felt like a hug when she'd slipped into it after the bath. She'd put that robe on again this morning since the temperature remained delightfully low, and now she was able to wear jeans, a t-shirt, and—ta da!—a light cotton hoodie. These simple pleasures reminded her that beloved autumn was coming.

After finding a pair of reading glasses amidst the books on the coffee table, she settled herself on the porch with her notebook and the clipboard that her father had given her: handmade of walnut and white oak in a checkerboard pattern. The wicker chair was uncomfortable, even with a throw pillow pressed into the small of her back, but the view of the enormous maple tree and the street scene beyond always pleased her, no matter what the weather or her state of mind might be.

She put the skinny reading glasses on and began to write. She had only gotten partway through her account of the "case of the turning pages" before Marguerite had arrived the other night, and of course, many events of a suspicious nature had occurred since then. As before, she chose to write as quickly and fluidly as she could, resisting the English teacher's urge to edit, ponder, and shape the narratives. What she needed now were the raw impressions and the major events before they began to fade in her mind.

Her memory was disturbingly selective these days. She often had to write down even the simplest task that she wanted to accomplish, knowing that it would probably disappear from her mental horizon if she did not, leaving her with no orange juice one morning or with cat pans that made her nose wrinkle in distaste, never mind the cats'. "To do" lists were a small price to pay to avoid both the frustration of trying to juggle tasks mentally and the self-disgust when all of the balls came thudding to the ground.

As before, she found herself enjoying the process of writing after only about ten minutes of scratching the pen across the surface of the paper. Both her handwriting and the content of her sentences became loopy, loose, and fluent. She felt a sensation of slipping deeper as she continued, like a single sheet of notebook paper that slides one way, then the other, in a current of air on its way downward. Layers of sleep last night, layers of written ghost stories this morning. What other layers would next appear, like those in rock cliffs, golden alternating with red and umber? Her pen sped on, not quite keeping pace with her thoughts and memories.

An hour later, she clipped the pen to the notebook's cardboard cover, thinking that she needed to develop a mid-morning ritual—like a coffee break without the coffee. Rubbing her wrist, she slipped inside again, trailed by Lute and Kip. Tam passed them and immediately jumped up into Claire's vacated chair, curling onto the warm cushion with apparent satisfaction. "Alone at last, eh, Tamsin?" she asked. "Well, you go, girl."

Muttering about the need for background info, Claire

took a seat at the computer in the study, flipped it on, and began browsing the booksellers' sites. She knew better than to attempt any kind of search relating to ghosts on the Internet. She would certainly get hundreds of thousands of hits, most of it nonsense. The Internet obviously contained a treasure-trove of information, but it was also completely indiscriminating, as she had frequently told her students, and therefore full of what she called "bilge." Anyone could post anything, and the subject of ghosts was certainly going to draw people who were, one might say, unusual. "That is, wackos," she whispered. After a beat, she added, "Gosh, I hope I'm not a wacko, too," and resumed her skimming of summaries and reviews. Finally, she chose two books to order, one a hefty tome that claimed to be encyclopedic in its accounts of hauntings, and, on the other end of the spectrum, a second, thin volume about ghosts of Nantucket. Maybe these books would give her some context. They should arrive by the end of the week.

Claire loved to anticipate and then receive packages, especially ones containing books. Just like the *Weekly Reader* books that she had waited impatiently for as a child. She remembered perfectly the leap of excitement she'd experienced at the sight of those books in neat stacks on her teacher's desk, an order slip dangling out of the topmost book in each stack.

And the books had been wonderful, most of them. She's read and re-read her favorites until the pages fell out in sections, creating miniature books that Claire bound together with large rubber bands. There had been disappointments, too, of course, like *The Ghost of Windy Hill*, a book that had enticed her with its title and let her down with its pat ending. No ghost had haunted Windy Hill, and the scientific-minded father had been right all along. No such thing as ghosts. The explanation for the supposed haunting had been thumpingly prosaic, although Claire couldn't recall at this distance of years just what that explanation was. Could there possibly be an equally logical explanation for what she had experienced in her new home recently?

Claire padded into her room, tucked the notebook away in the drawer of her bedside table, and began, belatedly, to make the bed. She picked up the terrycloth robe and slung it over her arm. Something—several things, actually—fell from a patch pocket and clattered to the floor. What in the world? She bent down cautiously to examine the fallen items. Three fine-point Sharpies—scarlet, bright orange, and brown—lay scattered across the old planks. Slowly, she gathered them up, arose on her slightly creaky knees, and spread the markers in a fan shape on the bed's thin summer blanket. Her hand gently explored both robe pockets and emerged with a yellow Sharpie from one pocket and two more in green tints from the other. She added them to the fan, making sure that the space between each marker was the same as she thought furiously.

These markers came from her set, no doubt. She had bought them last August to use at work, thinking that choosing some school supplies of her own would lift the sense of dread that was descending on her as the date of "all college" meetings approached. And she had brought them here to Kate's house in a box of office items earlier this summer and left them in the study. Since then, she had used the Sharpies just once: to make the sign last night. She had extracted only two markers for that job. And she had been dressed in her day clothes as she'd created it. The water wasn't even yet running into the tub, and the robe was hanging on a hook in her closet.

Leaving the markers and robe on the bed, Claire entered the hallway and stopped before the bathroom door. Her bare toes clenched on the smooth wooden floor. The curling sign was still there, held up by painter's tape at the bottom and top. "Privacy, please!" And the colors of the lettering were black and purple.

From the living room, the joyful sounds of the cuckoo clock marking ten o'clock skittered playfully into the hallway.

SUMMONING UP HER COURAGE, Claire decided to conduct an experiment that evening. Perhaps the phrase "set a trap" would be more accurate. But she would have to begin early; she wasn't about to deal with any supernatural goings-on once the sun went down. She actually checked the time for sunset in the newspaper, just to be sure her perception of when dusk arrived was accurate. Eight minutes after eight o'clock. Well, that would give her plenty of time if she started at six or so. And of course, it wasn't truly dark outside until well after sunset. Eight-oh-eight. That struck her as ominous, somehow.

First, she took Lute on a good long walk around a nearby urban lake ringed with late-summer wildflowers bowing in the breezes, after which she fed all three animals and tidied the living room. This last action was done out of nerves, pure and simple, but somehow, she felt more in control if the books were stacked on the tables and floor and the pillows neatly arranged against the arms of the mission-style futon couch. She even ran a dust mop under the couch and dining room table, which had nothing to do with her experiment but certainly needed to be done, nonetheless. (The pet fur clumped like tumbleweeds, swaying and traveling in the house's currents.)

After shaking the dust mop vigorously outside and returning it to its home in the basement, she had no more excuses. She would screw her courage to the sticking point.

She readied the DVD player in the living room, mellow with last light now, and rounded up the remote control devices. Satisfied that the scene was set, she retreated to the kitchen, made a large bowl of popcorn, and stirred melted butter over it. Hurrying lest she lose her resolve, she took a seat on the futon, picked up the remote, and pushed "play."

The lively opening music of *Scarecrow and Mrs. King* commenced. She tossed a few kernels of popcorn into her mouth and scanned the room surreptitiously. Nothing. Nothing unexplainable, that is. Lute, who was never too tired for a treat, panted hopefully at her feet. Claire cracked open a Pepsi and relaxed slightly. Maybe it would be just she and Lute in the living room tonight, watching TV like untold thousands in the city at this very moment. She felt an absurd sense of disappointment at this realization. Did she *want* to be haunted, for goodness' sake?

"Of course not!" she told Lute. "And popcorn is not good for dogs." He whimpered pathetically and let his crescent-shaped tail wag slightly, as if he were faint from hunger and unable to do more. "You just had your dinner, buddy. Honestly, you should go on the stage." Resolutely, she turned her attention back to Episode Two and to her popcorn dinner with its crisp, salty deliciousness.

Lute had wandered away, which was unusual when the bowl was still partly full. Normally, he begged until the last possible moment and then shot her reproachful looks for a good ten minutes after the final morsel was gone. She slid her gaze away from the screen, where Lee was fighting off a villain with a lawn flamingo, to Lute, who stood in the center of the living room rug, slightly to the left of the television on its console. His ears perked and he cocked his head, as if listening. One quick, sharp bark burst from him, natural and engaged. It was the his "ready to play" bark that she had heard so often, usually just before she threw his yellow tennis ball for him.

Claire clutched the smooth bowl but said nothing. The skin at the base of her skull was zinging, alert, and she felt her hair stir there. As she watched with half-closed eyes, Lute bowed gallantly, his paws outstretched and furry rump curved upward, another familiar play posture. His tail was wagging joyfully now, and his toenails ticked on the floor as he leaped lightly, twisting in the air. "Lute?" she croaked. Her fingers had gone numb, and she reminded herself to swallow the fear in her throat. He glanced over at her briefly, round eyes unconcerned, and then turned his focus back to his unseen companion. Oh, gosh. And she had asked for this— invited this, really. Well, maybe it was time to stop the DVD now and see if Lute's friend toddled off to…wherever.

Before she could arise from the couch, she felt rather than saw the flutter on her left, as if blinds were being rapidly opened and closed in a column of light. Puffs of frigid air tapped at her elbow, cheek, and ear. And in her mind, she experienced an unfamiliar scene, as clear as a new movie playing there. She saw a tiny room with shag carpet the color of old moss. A small, square television sitting atop a shelf made of raw two-by-fours and cinderblocks. On the screen, Lee was talking with Amanda about the case and the blue curtains that hung in their cozy kitchen, just as he was doing on the flat-screen in front of Claire right now. The hushing sound of evening traffic, punctuated by an occasional squawking horn, drifting in through an open window. A lava lamp undulating deep red. And she experienced emotions. Excitement. Appreciation. Envy. Hot envy, cutting through the other two, dominating the mindset of the person in the tiny apartment living room, watching *Scarecrow and Mrs. King*.

"Um, are you enjoying this, or not? Because I can switch

to something else, if you want." Claire's husky whisper surprised her.

The shimmers calmed to a pale, sunrise gold that reminded Claire of light on water, and the coldness beside her moderated into slightly cool. The scenes of the little apartment slid away from Claire's consciousness, like waves receding down a beach, and did not return. The envy quieted as well, leaving behind traces of pleasure and eagerness that Claire knew were not solely her own.

Sensing that all was well here, she glanced over at Lute. He lay on his back now, hind legs kicked open, forepaws dangling over his muzzle. Grunts of contentment, the kind he made while having his tummy rubbed, drifted to her from across the room. He wriggled his back more firmly into the patterned area rug and batted his paws lightly. "Okay there, Lute?" she called. He was too deep in bliss to even notice.

Claire popped a few more kernels of the now papery-cold popcorn into her mouth and chewed automatically. She felt rather than saw the glimmer, still next to her. The DVD played on, telling the story of Amanda and Lee facing danger together and getting to know each other, little by little. Claire blew out a long breath, wiped her chilly fingertips on a paper napkin, and crossed one ankle over the other, noting that stiffness had taken over her limbs from an hour of immobility. Well, wait until Marguerite heard about this. "Hey, Margo," she would say nonchalantly, "Guess who else is fan of SMK?"

OVER THE COURSE of the next few days, she finished painting the guest room, spent hours cleaning in preparation for her father and grandfather's arrival, and devoted the late afternoons and evenings to writing. She wrote about everything that had occurred, including the impressions that had clicked into her consciousness as neatly as slides on a screen. Her notebook was becoming satisfyingly full, she noticed. The Tuesday night's "viewing party" had been particularly intriguing, and she commented in her notebook on every part of it that she could think of, as if her experiences were agates that she could hold up in a clear shaft from a west-facing window and turn, then turn again.

For they were experiences, plural—of that, at least, she was certain. She had watched Lute having one sort of encounter while she herself had entertained the glimmer. Not to mention the glimmer's ideas. Or perhaps memories. She wondered if Lute had received some unfamiliar impressions as well. At half past eight, his pal had seemed to vanish, for Lute had gotten up, shaken his ears with a clapping sound, and trotted into the kitchen for a drink during the cuckoo's call, after which he had turned around three times on his cushion, as was his custom, and chewed on his red Kong toy contentedly. Within a half an hour, the glimmering presence on the couch had faded away, too, leaving Claire feeling as if she'd awakened from a skimming, dream-soaked sleep.

Her mind briefly touched down on the idea of *two* ghosts and then lifted off again.

Well, she'd always liked mystery novels, the kind with puzzle-like plots, no gore, and a conveniently unlikeable victim. Here was her very own mystery, complete with clues. This mystery involved no crime, as far as she could tell, but it did include a clock—a gorgeous, golden-brown clock watched over by intricate wooden owls. And tomorrow, she would find out more from the clock's previous owner.

SHE REALIZED as she walked through the door of Rudyard's Café at ten minutes before ten that she and Sarah had not included any information that would help them identify each other. She had left her bungalow early, wanting to be sure that she would have enough time, even if finding a parking spot were difficult, even if she got lost in her agitation. Even if her nerve drained away and she had to give herself a stern talking to in the car, breathing deeply and wiping her palms on a handkerchief all the while. The last was the only scenario that had actually transpired. Now, as she ordered a medium coffee ice crema and clutched her notebook, she heard her father's voice in her head, "It doesn't hurt to be early. Ever. If the meeting is important, show up at least fifteen minutes early."

The café had drawn a mixture of folks this morning, some reading, some manipulating phones, some composing on laptops, and some staring meditatively into the space just in front of their eyes. There were no booths, unfortunately, so Claire took the next best place: a table situated toward the back and against a low, dividing wall, giving her protection on one side, at least. She set down her cool drink and wiped some crumbs from the table before laying the mottled notebook beside it. But before she could open it to review the questions that she had prepared, a voice asked, "Excuse me, are you Claire?"

Standing next to the vacant seat was a tall, dramatic-looking woman in her early-sixties. Her crinkly brown hair was liberally shot through with strands of white and iron gray. She wore it in a loose twist, and her warm brown eyes looked down at Claire kindly through spectacles framed in turquoise and bronze. She was dressed in a loose, flowing blouse in vibrant shades of teal and red, and a skirt of basic black, giving the impression that she might whirl into a dance at any moment. Claire liked her immediately.

"Yes, Sarah, right? Please sit down." Claire half rose to shake, noticing that Sarah's fingers were dry, in contrast to her own. "Thank you for meeting with me today. I really appreciate it." They both settled in their seats, hands resting lightly on the table, as if this were a poker game in an old Western and the conventions must be observed if each person were going to trust the other.

"So, you bought the clock?" Sarah began, and took a sip of her hot, fragrant coffee. "I'm glad that it went to someone nice. After all of those years with it, I felt sort of attached. But I couldn't keep it in our apartment. Thin walls, you know. The neighbors would've complained." Her voice was pleasingly low and well-modulated. The phrase "pear-shaped tones" leapt into Claire's thoughts.

"Did you move, then, and that's why you decided to sell it?" Claire drew in a sip of her drink and was embarrassed by the tiny shrieking sound that the straw rubbing against the lid made. She felt her cheeks warming, which was an absurd reaction to such a tiny faux pas. Without waiting for a reply, she rushed on. "You didn't want to keep it and turn the lever for the cuckoo sound to the 'off' position, so it would stay silent?"

Sarah was silent herself for a moment. "You know, I honestly never thought of that possibility. Keeping the clock from ever cuckooing—that just didn't enter my mind. And it doesn't seem right, somehow. Do you think?"

"No, of course, you're right. A permanently silent cuckoo would be—oppressive, somehow. I've never silenced it, myself. Although one time…" Claire's thoughts turned backwards to that day when she'd had the morning migraine and had realized after she'd re-emerged that the clock seemed not to have sung for several hours during her pain. "It seemed to silence itself. Just once. Then it was fine."

"Hmm," replied Sarah noncommittally, and shifted in her chair. "It's a gorgeous clock, I think, with those owls keeping watch on top." She continued, leaning forward. "It was never hung up in my home, though. I've lived in the same apartment for years—we can't be bothered to move, I guess." Claire leaned in, too. "No, the clock hung at the place where I used to work, and when it closed down, the boss, I guess you'd call him, said that I could have the clock. Told me to take it, in fact. He never liked it." Her voice clamped down on the words, and Claire wondered if there were more objectionable attitudes in this man that Sarah was recalling. Her mouth looked pinched now with disapproval, and she met Claire's gaze challengingly. "I was afraid he'd just toss it out one day. But he didn't, thank God. Too superstitious, I suppose. That seems like an odd combination, now that I think about it. Unimaginative and superstitious, both. That fits him to a T, though. Bloody man."

Surprised, Claire drew back fractionally. "It sounds like you two don't work together anymore. That's good." She wanted to be diplomatic, but this conversation was not going as she'd expected at all. "Do you mind if I ask, um, what kind of business it was that you were both in?" She mentally shot through some possibilities: historic hotel or B and B, German restaurant, law firm…Art gallery?

"Oh, I thought that Walter might've mentioned it. It was a theater. The clock hung in the green room downstairs for decades, I think—before I worked there, even. The Luna Theater, just a few blocks away from here." She looked around the shop as if surprised at where she was. Her sigh was audible to Claire. "Of course, it's just a pile of rubble now."

CHAPTER 11

"Or maybe it's a vacant lot if they've carted the rubble away," Sarah continued, a sharp cord of anger stringing one word to the next. "To be honest, I can't bring myself to go by there yet. I drive blocks out of my way to avoid the sight. Poor Luna." Her fingers, which had been tapping erratically, stilled on the tabletop. Her strong posture weakened momentarily, shoulders rounding. "It didn't deserve that fate."

"Luna! Yes, I read about it in the paper. The theater company closed, didn't it, and the building itself was owned by someone else." Claire stopped there, not wanting to put into words what had saddened Sarah so deeply. The memory of a smiling crescent moon arose in her mind's horizon. Luna. She felt a sparkler of excitement and discovery, tossing out light first one way and then the other. How could that be mere coincidence? She deliberately composed her face into an attentive, neutral expression, to match what Sarah was telling her about the theater, but internally, her spirits danced and swayed.

Sarah ground out her next words. "Yes, the owners

wanted a parking lot. Or a parking garage, I guess, to be fair. As if we need more of *those* downtown, when we could've preserved such a wonderful old theater! And there were other acting companies interested in it—that's what really felt like a knife in the ribs to me, and to plenty of other people, too. The building had history. It could've gone on being a place where actors moved audiences, made them laugh, cry, feel something profound. But the owners didn't care. They weren't theater people, you know, and they just didn't care. It was hard enough to lose Luna, but to lose the theater building itself, too, was just—shattering." She drew in a raspy breath and ducked her head slightly. Wisps of hair slid forward over her jutting jaw, catching in her dangly, silver earrings, which reminded Claire of her father's more complicated fishing lures.

"I'm so sorry," Claire began, stopped, and finished her thought sincerely. "I'm so sorry for your loss."

Sarah lifted her face and smiled a wavering smile, her eyes full of tears. "Thank you. That's very kind."

They sat quietly for a few moments. The rattling of spoons in mugs, the rough roar of the espresso machine, and the tapping of laptop keys smoothed over the lack of words between them. Meanwhile, Claire's thoughts surged forward, making connections, darting down one avenue and then another. The clock was from a theater! She would never have guessed that, yet somehow, it made sense. There was such an aura of drama about it and whatever had come with it.

"Isn't it unusual for a theater to have a cuckoo clock?" she ventured. "I mean, didn't the cuckooing interrupt the performances, even in the green room? Although I have to confess that I'm not completely sure what a green room is, exactly. A kind of waiting room, isn't it? Did I just ask a bunch of stupid questions?" She felt a jab of something like anger that she hadn't gone beyond the normal boundaries that separate theatergoer from the realms behind the stage by doing something as simple as taking a backstage tour. Deplorable lack of curiosity.

Sarah had recovered her composure enough to take a sip of her cooling coffee in its heavy, cream-colored mug. "No, not at all. Most people, even theatergoers, don't know much about the green room. It *is* a waiting room of sorts—a room offstage where actors can relax before or after they go on to perform. Although maybe that's an oxymoron—the idea of a 'relaxed actor.' Bundles of nerves, actors, especially during performances, of course."

"And is the room really green?"

"Not usually, but maybe in the distant past, it was painted green to rest the actors' eyes after their time in the bright lights—the lime lights. There are a lot of theories floating around about the origin of that term, none of them an obvious frontrunner, in my opinion. But there have been green rooms in theaters for a long, long time—since the mid-sixteen hundreds, at least."

"Wow. I love things like that. Traditions so old that the beginnings are hazy." She paused, then took the plunge. "I was an English teacher, you know, and Shakespeare was my favorite class to teach. The students were self-selecting, so almost all of them were interested and up to the challenges. I only got that assignment a few times, though." She brightened her voice purposefully before Sarah could comment on that or ask any questions about her job. "Did Shakespeare have a green room at the Globe? And did it have a special clock?" she teased.

They chuckled together, yet Sarah's reply was serious. "The King's Men might've had a green room at Blackfriars or the Globe. No idea about the clock, I'm sorry to say. But traditions have to start sometime, right?" She seemed somewhat cheered by that thought, and Claire didn't want to say anything that would remind her that Luna had been razed and the clock was in her possession now. "I have to say that our cuckoo clock might not have been the wisest choice, practically speaking. I don't know where it came from. But people liked it. Felt it was good luck, somehow. A lot of the actors would reach up and touch the owls before they went on. Did you notice how shiny their little round heads look? Caused by decades of oil and sweat from actors' nervous hands."

"That's fantastic, Sarah! I feel honored to have it." Wondering if Sarah would think her a worthy recipient, she pattered on. "I mean, I know that I'm not an actor or a theater person, but I do love plays, especially Shakespeare's, and I appreciate what an art…I mean, um…" She trailed off, having lost her train of thought and her confidence together, sensing them swirl downward and disappear.

Sarah inclined herself slightly forward again, back straight, mouth and eyes earnest. "No, worries, my friend. I think that it was kismet that the clock came to you. Does it keep good time, by the way?"

"Well, yes, it does, actually, but don't you know that, after all of those years it hung in the green room?" Claire shifted in her chair, hoping that she hadn't misunderstood the question.

"Not really. Our green room was pretty well insulated, but it wasn't completely soundproof. You mentioned the problem of the cuckoo calling out during performances, and we dealt with that in the simplest way possible. The stage manager just stopped the clock during final rehearsals and performances—stilled the pendulum, I mean. Then he started it up again when the coast was clear. So the clock kept its own time. Maybe that became part of its good luck. That crazy, out-of-time quality."

"And did anything happen when you stopped the clock?"

Claire's face flushed warm with uncertainty and embarrassment. When she had let it run down, she had paid for her carelessness. And so had poor Lute. She still felt a stirring of resentment when she thought about the flapping tablecloth and atmosphere of anger that had met her upon her return to her home.

"Happen? What do you mean?" Sarah's dark eyes were watchful and curious over the rim of her mug. Claire, remembering her own iced beverage, bought some time by drawing her fingers down the length of the plastic cup in the condensation.

"Well, the clock seems to have come to me with some… personality attached." She breathed in for courage and described the evening's occurrences, being as brief as she could manage. "There have been other events. It all sounds crazy, I know." She stirred uneasily and picked up a napkin to wipe her hands. Scraps of white paper fell lightly to the tabletop.

Sarah's eyes had transformed into quarter-moon shapes, utterly focused and attentive, and her forehead wore shuttered lines that had not been there before. "Well, as my mother used to say, you could knock me over with a feather. That's a very strange story. The theater never stuck me as spooky, but I'm a practical person who's dealt with numbers and schedules all of my working life. Maybe I was just too busy at Luna to notice. My job was part-time, and I was always rushing to get it done and go to the other job I had then. I'm relieved to hear about what's been happening to you, though. Does that sound callous? It must've been frightening, Claire."

"Well, yes and no. I was frightened but also—hmmm—exhilarated at the same time. And even when that tablecloth moved so violently of its own accord and the anger was practically visible, I didn't get the feeling that the spirit or whatever" (she rushed past that part) "was wicked or venge-ful. Nothing like that. It was just…honked off! And I was sure that the anger was due to the clock being stopped because that's the only time it has blazed up, and the only time that the clock wasn't running since I brought it home. So I don't know what to make of the fact that your stage manager stopped it often. And there were no repercussions to that?"

Sarah shook her head. "Not that I'm aware of."

"I'm just stumped by that." They were quiet together for a couple of beats, thinking. Sarah let her gaze drift to the front window, unseeing and inward. It was Claire who felt a real-ization take shape and grow stronger. "But the situations are different, aren't they? In the theater, the clock-stopping was purposeful and temporary. Probably not that frequent, either, when you think in terms of months and years. In my house, it was the result of my forgetfulness."

"I bet you've been careful since then." Sarah offered, her lips quirking with amusement. They burst into relieved laughter together.

"Yes, I have been, believe me. In fact, I wind it more than once a day, just to be sure!" Claire led off another volley of shared laughter. The two women subsided finally, Claire dabbing the corners of her eyes with the twisted napkin. Recalling a reaction that Sarah had referred to earlier, she asked, "Why do you say you're relieved that the clock seems to be haunted?"

The older woman paused to think, and when she spoke, her words came slowly. "That wasn't very nice of me, was it? But I couldn't help it. Luna Theater was hugely important to me, and to lots of people. Losing it in that…wanton way was such a painful blow. I'm still grappling with it. Adjusting. Trying to hang on to the good stuff, you know? I don't want to lose those memories, ever. They're a part of me that I want to keep in touch with. And so hearing you say that something of Luna survived cheers me up. I hope that doesn't sound selfish, when you're the one who has to deal with… whatever it is that came with the clock."

Claire reached out to lightly touch Sarah's forearm through the filmy sleeve of her blouse. "No, it doesn't sound selfish. It sounds positive. I understand what you mean, honestly. And I think it's great that you want to keep the times you spent at the theater fresh, somehow. The past can haunt us, or it can keep us company, can't it?" She thought about Mr. Henson's relief at the idea that perhaps his wife's spirit still existed somewhere, even if he had no way to meet it. Maybe ghosts exist because the living need them, she thought meekly.

She remembered Sarah's email address, all of a sudden. "Hey, 'kind stranger'! I've been wracking my brains to make the association! 'I've always depended on the kindness of strangers.' *A Streetcar Named Desire*, right?"

Sarah's smile was shy. "Yes. I worked in administration at Luna, but I always wanted to be part of the action on stage. So now, I'm writing a play." She spread her palms in a charmingly frank gesture. "A happier one than any of Tennessee Williams's plays, though."

"Gosh, I'm relieved to hear that. Williams's work is so grim." They chatted on about Sarah's play, her upcoming wedding to her partner of ten years, and each woman's favorite authors. Finally, Claire posed the question that had been taking shape in her mind during the last few minutes of their conversation. "Sarah, you said that you never knew of any strange events connected to the clock when it was stopped in the green room. What about elsewhere in the theater? Any strange occurrences that you know of?"

"Well, yes, now that I think about it, I did hear about some odd events during the years that I worked there. Seemingly odd, anyway. It's hard to tell, really. So many people came and went through the building: actors, directors, stage managers, set builders, costume designers, props people, maintenance workers, administrators. And that's not even considering visitors and audience members! Let's say that a prop ends up in a strange place or goes missing for a while. Who can say for sure that one of those many people didn't absentmindedly move it? Or that someone was playing a little joke? Or feeling crabby toward the person it belonged to? There's a lot going on in a working theater. More than anyone can keep track of, believe me. 'Barely averted chaos,' the artistic director who was in charge when I first started working at Luna used to say. So to be honest, I never paid much attention to the stories or put much stock in them."

Sarah unhooked a strand of hair from a rattling earring and paused. Claire recognized that the other woman was considering her next words and waited. It had always been her inclination to leap into other people's silences, wanting to avoid the gaps in conversation, and now, she consciously held herself still and silent. Wait. Just wait, she told herself.

"Maybe the person you should really be talking to is that earlier artistic director I mentioned. He's retired now, but he still lives in the Twin Cities. I could give him a call, see if he would be willing to meet with you." A slight, indulgent-looking smile lifted Sarah's face. "He's quite a character, if you'll excuse the pun. 'Cranky' would be another word to describe him. I can't predict how he'll respond to my request. I wouldn't be surprised by a flat refusal. But let's think positively. I'll be as diplomatic as I can. If he does agree, would you like me to come with you? Smooth the way, if you know what I mean. It might be easier if I do. What do you think?"

"I think that's a great idea. Thank you, Sarah. Thank you for everything." She struggled on. "I know that this isn't easy to believe and that maybe you don't believe it. Thanks for entertaining the possibilities when you don't even know me. I don't feel so alone with all this now."

"Alone? It sounds like you're never alone! Not when you're home, anyway. But maybe we can get to the heart of this puzzle, eh?"

"Yes, maybe. I do want to understand more about what's been happening, so I can cope better. This leave of absence from my job was meant to be restful."

"And you don't want to just get rid of the clock? That might do the trick." Sarah set her mug down gently and left it alone on the table.

"No. I've thought about that, but the idea seems flat-out wrong to me. Wrong and cowardly." Claire's throat constricted as if a tiny hand were squeezing there, so the next words sounded choked off, even to her own ears. "It's time for me to be brave, if that makes sense."

"It does. Okay, then. No guarantees, but I'll make that call."

"Oh! I'm sorry; if this man agrees to see me, the meeting will have to wait a bit. My father and grandfather are coming into town tomorrow from St. Louis and staying until the middle of next week. I don't think I should take on something that important until after they're gone." She hurried on, pressing down her nervousness at the prospect of talking with a cranky character. "I'll need to entertain. And prepare for the conversation, too, I think. Come up with some questions."

"That shouldn't be a problem. There's no huge hurry, is there? I think it's nice that your dad and granddad are coming to see you. I like to hear about parents and children living together as older adults. As long as they get along, of course!"

"Oh, they get along fine, most of the time. But Gus and

Dad aren't father and son. They're father-in-law and son-in-law."

CLAIRE HAD FORGOTTEN how unusual the living arrangement of her father and grandfather must sound to people unaware of the family's past. Her dad had decided that he wanted a change, and Gus had volunteered to make the move with him, saying that David needed someone to look after him. Both had agreed that St. Louis would be an experiment for life-long Minnesotans.

Gus had been a part of Claire and Greg's lives since they were small children, sharing the role of elder caregiver with Kate. But he had lived a only a few blocks from the Brackens, while Kate's apartment had been in downtown St. Paul, a forty-minute drive away. Even before the loss of their mother, Gus had picked them up from school; made them snacks of popcorn and mini-pizzas; taken them to the park; taught them chess and backgammon; read them books that were beyond their years; and answered their questions about birds and animals, poring through his red and black Colliers encyclopedias when he didn't know the answers himself.

Claire had leaned back into him unselfconsciously then and continued to do so now. Her love for her mother's father was layered with respect, enjoyment, and trust. She knew from conversations with friends that some grandchildren lost the closeness they had shared with their grandparents once the children grew up. Or they lost the grandparents themselves. Just as Kate had been lost.

As she swung through her living room the next afternoon, plumping throw pillows and straightening placemats, she vowed fiercely to savor every moment of the days that Gus would spend as her guest. And to visit him more often in Missouri. Maybe in the winter or early spring...

She conveniently focused her thinking more on Gus than on her father, whom she loved, of course, but in a thornier, more complicated way. Three days with him once the two men switched households sounded quite daunting. How in the world would they spend their time?

Feeling abstracted, she put the newly arrived package containing the books she had ordered into the closet and stepped out on the porch to await Greg's arrival, leaving the comforting sound of ticking behind.

During the drive to the airport, they chatted about Scott's last days of summer vacation, Greg's job, and the seemingly constant state of road construction in the Twin Cities. "I'm telling you, Claire, you may not be getting out much these days to notice it, but the construction is just insane! I'll try my usual route to get somewhere, and when that doesn't work, I switch to another road, but that's all dug up, too! Where the hell do all of these orange cones and barrels come from, anyway? Are they shipped in from other parts of the country? Sheesh. It would be easier to mark the roads that *don't* have construction than to mark the ones that *do*." He blew out an exasperated breath, and Claire could feel his glance flicking over the side of her face. She continued to look straight ahead, figuring that too much sympathy would get him wound up even tighter.

"Well, the roads have to be fixed during the warm weather, and we don't have that much warm weather in Minnesota," she countered evenly. And I do get out. Every day, practically, she added silently.

"Tell me about it. Sixty-three degrees at four o'clock on the twenty-third of August," he plowed onward with his complaints, gesturing at the dashboard, from which the data came. "Where's global warming when you need it? I made Scott take a sweatshirt to his soccer practice this afternoon, and he'll probably leave it there when his mother picks him up. Crazy weather."

"I like it. And each day in summer that's not hot is one less day that can *be* hot, in my book. So there, big brother." Claire turned to smile serenely at him.

Greg fought unsuccessfully against an answering grin. "Yes, you always have liked it, haven't you? Do you remember that picture that Gus took of us on the porch swing the first day of school? You were about eight, skinny, with scabs on your face from having the chicken pox only a couple of weeks before. It must've been cool that day because you're wearing a jacket and long pants, and I'm dressed in a t-shirt and shorts, angry because I didn't want my picture taken. We looked like we were in different seasons!"

"We were, sort of. You were in late summer and I was in early fall. Kate kept that photo framed on her desk, remember? She said that it made her smile every time she looked at it." Claire felt touched that Greg recalled the photo, even if he used his memory to illustrate the gulf that had always existed between them.

"Yeah, I remember." His voice was low and scratchy—with sadness, Claire, thought, He sighed heavily and engaged the turn signal for the airport exit. "Kate. She's passed, and Gus is eighty years old. I'm kind of worried about seeing him, Claire. And Dad, too. They're old men."

"Greg, Dad is sixty-six—that's not old, not nowadays. We're lucky to still have him and Gus. Lots of my friends are already losing parents, never mind grandparents. And among my students, grandparents die like flies, especially when an essay is due! I always felt bad about that. My assignments seemed to have a toxic effect on those grandparents." She kept her expression serious, even when Greg chortled with laughter.

"You've got a warped sense of humor," he said, turning

into the darkness of the parking ramp. "Anyone ever tell you that?"

"Yes. You." And she rearranged her bag on her lap, casting her thoughts forward to the time when she would be with her father and grandfather again.

GUS LOOKED BETTER than she had dared hope, more upright, in fact, than when she'd last seen him five months ago. Loss had worn him down then, but he seemed to have sprung back up somewhat; his shoulders under a white Oxford shirt were almost square. As she hugged him, she drew in his familiar scent of Dial soap, Ice Blue Aqua Velva, and wintergreen. He squeezed her tightly, saying softly, "Sweetie pie! I'm so happy to see you." He cupped the back of her neck with one calloused hand and kissed her cheek resoundingly.

"Me, too, Gus! Thank you for..." She wanted to say, "Thank you for realizing that I needed to see you," but she felt that that would sound overly dramatic and probably raise her father's suspicions, as well, so she finished more tamely. "Coming. Thank you for coming."

"My pleasure, Claire-Bear. I was getting tired of St. Louis and anxious to see you and Greg and Scott. Grace, too." Claire warmed inwardly at the way he included Grace, suggesting that she was still a part of the family although her divorce from Greg was several years old now. Family had always been one of Gus's great joys. And he had many sources of joy, Claire realized. That talent for appreciation was one of his superpowers.

She stood beaming at him, one hand still on his shoulder, while he jingled the coins in his pockets. At her side, she realized that Greg and her father had stopped their backslapping embrace and were now waiting. "Hey, how about a 'hello' for your old man?" He spoke in a jokey, irritated tone, but Claire thought that perhaps a tinge of genuine annoyance lay beneath that. He held out his arms, and she wondered why that posture in him looked like a command rather than an invitation.

She stepped into his embrace. "Hi, Dad. Welcome back." He felt as wiry as Lute, and nearly as restless. His hug was quick and emphatic, like a brisk hit from a rubber stamp. She could almost hear the popping sound as they separated, and, with an effort of will, she resisted the impulse to look down at her torso to see if Mr. Bracken's red ink was now staining the muted tans of the plaid blouse that she wore.

Greg had grasped Gus's elbow and was shaking him lightly. "How about an early dinner, you two?" He hadn't discussed this with Claire. "You three, I mean," he added hastily, casting an apologetic glance at her. He looked happier than Claire had seen him in a long time, his expression open, even delighted. His cell phone chirped in his jeans pocket, and he reached back to turn it off without looking. "It'll be my treat."

$\mathcal{C}$ laire leaned back against the door until she heard the "snick" of the lock catching and then set Gus's suitcase down on the leaf-patterned living room rug. He had wanted to carry it himself, but she'd insisted, saying mildly that he was the guest here, after all, and that he'd just have to get used to the privileges that went with that. Privately, she thought that despite his upright posture, Gus no longer seemed sturdy enough to tote luggage up steps. Or, she preferred that he not do that on her watch, at least.

He was bending over to pet Tamsin, who had actually trotted over to meet him and was now leaning against his ankles, her head cocked to accept his caresses. Claire could hear the purr from her place by the door. Gus was crooning, "Tamsin, you beautiful girl, how are you? Is Claire taking good care of you, hmm?" A whimpering Lute half circled them in the throes of envy, wanting his share of Gus's attention but fearful of Tamsin's wrath should he venture too near. Her hisses and strikes terrified him still.

"Gus, I'm astonished. I try so hard to be friendly with

Tam, yet she'll hardly give me the time of day. You, she greets with a brass band and banners."

When Gus looked up, his eyes behind the aviator glasses were gleaming, their blue brighter than usual. "She remembers me, sweetie. She remembers my visits to Kate. And I think she might associate me with Kate, too. Who knows what animals can pick up on when a close relation of their owner comes into their home? Maybe the sound of my voice is like hers, or the way I move. My scent. Something."

"Well, Aunt Kate didn't wear Aqua Velva, as far as I recall, but maybe you're on to something. I'll try to deal with my feelings of rejection. It's nice to see her being so friendly with you, actually. I feel bad for her. She's waiting for the person she really wants, and that person never comes. I'm not even second best, or third best. She looks right through me." Relief seeped through her, surprisingly cool. It was tiring to experience Tam's disappointment and longing day after day, and telling Gus about the cat's attitude alleviated her sense of failure a little.

Gus's knuckles, smooth as river stones, rubbed gently under Tam's chin. "I know, sweetheart. I can imagine. Just be patient. She'll come around, I think. She's a loyal one, this girl. Kate set great store by her. And vice versa, obviously. But she'll come to you in the end. After all, you're Kate's great-niece."

That was so like Gus, Claire thought, as she took one of his mottled arms and tenderly helped him back to a standing position. He'd passed right over the fact that Aunt Kate was not her blood relation any more than he was. When she had learned as a little girl that his wife had been a widow with two young children and that one of those children had become Claire's mother, she had taken to her bed and sobbed. "You're not really my grandpa!" The hot tears had smeared her cheeks and wet the pillow in its daisy case under her head. She'd keened with grief and a sense of desolation, unable to catch her breath, her legs wildly kicking under the covers. He had stroked back the tangled dark hair, swept away the tears with both rough thumbs, and growled, "Claire, I promise you, I am your grandfather! In every way that counts. And you're my granddaughter, so don't you forget it! If anyone tells you different, you send that person to me, and I'll set him straight." He had lifted her up and hugged her so tightly that she'd gasped.

Now, the twilight sounds of crickets, like rafts of small bells shaken, and of cardinals commenting on the day drifted in through the casement window that Claire had forgotten to shut and lock before leaving the house. A curl of wood smoke from someone's chiminea wafted after. Lute danced sideways up to her, bowing and sneezing, and she reached out to give his muzzle a light squeeze and ease the jingling collar around his neck. "Hey, buddy, hey buddy, hey…" He scampered to Gus for some pats and greetings and then returned to Claire, panting happily. The more people in the house the better for Lute, in contrast to the wary cats. Kipper was nowhere to be seen, Claire noted, although she would probably sashay out later, acting like a benevolent queen greeting her public.

Gus had taken a place under the cuckoo clock, listening to the resonant ticking, fingertips extended to touch the chains. "And this is the antique clock that you told me about over the phone. I can see why you were so taken with it, Claire. It's…it's…" He shook his head at his inability to find the right word. "Really something else." Claire had described only the clock's external appearance, thinking that when she chose to tell Gus about its "spiritual attributes," it would best be done in person. His acceptance of her eccentricities has always been wide, but this story might strain even his willingness to think that she'd hung the moon. She would find the right time to describe the strange events to him. Unless a ghost decided to make its presence felt before then. She didn't want Gus frightened. But a soothing certainty that he would accept whatever happened rolled through her, as steady as a slow wave from the sea.

Echoing her mood, Gus said, "Claire, it's so good to be here, in Kate's home. In *your* home. Thank you for inviting me." He moved the Speidel watchband on his wrist slightly to one side. "And this clock sure is beautiful. I've never seen a cuckoo clock with owls on it before. I should know what kind they are, but I can't think of the name right now. Some kind of European owl, of course. Maybe we can look it up on your computer tomorrow? The other birds might be trickier to identify." He sketched a little "ta da!" gesture with both hands, fingers spread and then quickly curled together. "It's just nice to know, don't you think?"

Claire scooped up a wiggling Lute and laid her cheek against the top of his curly head. "Well, I understand the impulse, Gus, and I have fond memories of your Colliers Encyclopedias. But right now, I'm trying to...let go of needing to know and just meet with life as it comes. To be..." she thrashed after the word she wanted. "Flexible. Well, not quite 'flexible.' Like a tree that bends in the wind. Oh, what's the word?"

"Resilient?"

"Yes, that's it! Resilient. Thanks, Gramps." There was no discomfort in being tongue-tied in front of Gus. They smiled at each other, but Lute suddenly lurched in her arms, forcing her to bend so that he wouldn't have so far to jump. There was a briskness between Gus and herself now, a sense of shifting, like the page turning in *Puck of Pook's Hill.* "Would you like some tea and cookies? It's cool enough for tea, I think, and I have Fig Newtons. Are they still your favorite?"

"Still my favorite, sweetheart. And the tea sounds great." She linked her elbow in his and led him to the pool of light cascading down from the fixture over the round dining room table. Tam followed, her tail straight up, a little guardian for Gus.

WHEN CLAIRE ENTERED the kitchen the next morning, she found Gus already dressed in a seersucker shirt and navy chinos, washed and shaved, with the newspaper and a cup of coffee in front of him. He'd chosen her favorite Ten Chimneys mug from all the mugs in the cupboard, she noticed, as she leaned to kiss his soft cheek, redolent of Aqua Velva. "Good morning. How did you sleep, Gus? And where did you get that coffee? Did you send out for it? My, you must've been desperate, you java hound, you." She could tease Gus gently, knowing that he would return the favor soon if not immediately. She was reminded of the way that she and Lute would tug lightly on the same strap, he pulling her a few steps and then she pulling him.

Her grandfather curled both gnarled hands around the pale orange mug as if she might try to take it away from him. "Well, I hope you won't mind, sweetie, but I brought my own cone and filters and ground coffee. I'm not proud to say this, but I depend on that first cup in the morning. Plus, maybe just one or two cups in the afternoon. It's a long, long habit, and pretty harmless as habits go, I guess. I just have to stay away from it after dinner, though, or I spend the night walking the floor."

"Of course, I don't mind—in fact, I wish that I liked it myself! I think that I was the only grad student at the University of Minnesota who didn't drink coffee. It smells divine, but to me it tastes like...no offense? Minerals dissolved in hot water."

Gus burst into hearty laughter and gestured to the place across from his where a Fiesta tumbler filled with cranberry juice already stood, the ruby hue of the juice bright against the tumbler's chalky turquoise. "Well, different strokes. You're young yet, so there's hope for you." He winked at her. "I slept well, to answer your question. Better than usual, in fact. That's a very comfortable bed that you have—just the right amount of 'koosh.' And the cuckooing was nice to hear in the dark."

"The clock! Oh, Gus, I'm sorry. I meant to stop the pendulum or move the lever to the 'off' position before you turned in." She felt an uneasy stirring in her chest. Maybe she'd forgotten on purpose somehow, afraid of what the repercussions of stilling the clock would be.

"No worries, mate." She smiled and relaxed, wondering where he had picked up that expression. "I just heard the clock a time or two when I happened to be awake anyway. Old men have to use the bathroom during the night, you know. Several times. And I sat up once to spread out that extra blanket you left at the foot of the bed. It got chilly in the room all of a sudden—almost like there was a north breeze blowing. I found it refreshing, though. You don't find August breezes like that in St. Louis, I'm here to tell you!"

Except in haunted houses, Claire thought. She would have to tell Gus today. He needed to be prepared for spookiness. Yesterday's confidence about his ability to cope had vanished utterly. What if his heart were weak and the ghost came upon him unawares? Or what if he fell, trying to get away?

She felt a blade of fear unfolding, sharp and serrated. She herself had lain awake last night in the upstairs bedroom for what seemed like hours, fearful of what might occur there, knowing that the golden moon artwork smiled from its wall nearby, although she could see no trace of it in the dark room. The calm presence of Kip silhouetted in the open window and Lute breathing in his oval dog bed had gradually convinced her that there were no other "presences" in the room. At present, she'd thought wryly, and turned over on her side to sleep.

"What would you like for breakfast, Gus?" she said aloud, latching onto a different subject to buy herself some time. "I could make you an omelet or scrambled eggs. I have bagels and some honey wheat bread that makes nice toast, and cereal. Oh, and some fantastic-looking blueberry jam from Canada. I got it for Scott. It comes in a can." She shook her head slightly at the out-of-place quality of that final comment.

"How can I resist that? Jam in a can, and from Canada, no less. A person could write a children's book about that. Dr. Seuss material, I think. But here now, sweetheart, you sit and I'll make breakfast. You know how I love to cook with eggs." He stood up, a hand on the back of his chair. "Where's your fry pan?"

"It's in the cabinet under the silverware drawer." She cleared the lump out of her throat. "Gramps? I'm so happy to be with you again!"

AFTER BREAKFAST, they took a stroll around the neighborhood, admiring the old houses; the mature maples, oaks, and locusts; and the gardens, looking a little tumbled, but still bright with orange California poppies, purple asters, and intense yellow goldenrod nodding lightly in the breeze. The cicadas whirled a complement to the sunshine, which felt mild now that autumn was just a whisk away. Lute pranced ahead of them, only occasionally looking back to make sure that they were still accompanying him.

Then, while Gus settled on the porch with his newspaper, Claire fired off brief, encouraging email messages to Marguerite and several other friends from the college. Classes would start on Monday, and she wanted them to know that she was wishing them well. As she wrote, images from her own past career arose: packing and repacking her large leather bag to make sure that she would have the bulky stacks of syllabi and textbooks at hand the next morning, laying out her carefully chosen clothes, checking the class lists for names that she might stumble over in the morning and taking a stab by writing them in the margins the way she thought they might be pronounced. She drew in a shaky breath and clicked "send," her positive thoughts for Marguerite's first day rushing after this last message.

That accomplished, she brought up Google to find out the hours for Como Conservatory that day, knowing that Gus had enjoyed visiting it when he lived in the area. He had owned a nursery throughout his adult life and had always harbored a love of plants. As the page for the conservatory took its place on the screen, a sheet of pain sliced through Claire's head, bisecting it from the base of the skull upward to her brows. The familiar, dreaded dots sprang into her field of vision and expanded into paisley patterns, pulsing and growing, while the somber black shutters took their places on either side, leaving her only the front view. The sparkling coronet arose like a harsh, revolving sun and rolled upward. Saliva filled her mouth, despair, her soul.

She stumbled to the bathroom and then, remembering that Gus was using her bedroom, returned to the study and sank onto the daybed that she had purchased for Scout's visits. A low groan eased out of her chest, and she clamped a hand over her eyes, unable to block the light completely.

The slow clattering sound of the metal blinds descending reached her, and blessed dimness followed. She lay on her back, shivering and swallowing convulsively, elbows pressed to ribs. A light drape of fleece fell over her, and the shivering eased a bit. Some time passed, she thought—how much, she couldn't be sure. Through the shrieking sheets of pain, she heard water trickling and then felt the familiar pebbled texture of damp terrycloth across her hot forehead. A firm hand held it there while another gently smoothed the whole length of her arm. "Poor girl," her grandfather's voice breathed. "My poor girl."

Recalling the visitations she had experienced during other recent migraines, she tried to warn him. "Gus, there might be…" Her voice was clotted and thick. It trailed off to silence, the ideas she wanted to express unavailable to her.

"Don't worry, sweetheart," Gus whispered. "You just rest now. I'll watch over you and be here when you wake." Through the chaos of migraine pain and visions, Claire recognized the words as the same ones he had spoken to her when she was a child, napping at his house or her own. Those words had worked like an incantation then, and now, they still soothed. She nodded slightly and found his rough fingers with her own, giving them a slight squeeze. Gus. What would she ever do without him?

WHEN SHE FINALLY SURFACED FROM the depths of the migraine, having felt frosty currents stir her hair, she found Kipper snuggled next to her. The slight vibration of the tiger cat's purr reached Claire's ears, and she surveyed Claire benevolently with her sleepy, golden-green eyes. The washcloth draped over Claire's forehead was warm on the skin side and cool on the air side. She pulled it off, extracted her legs from under the blanket without rousting Kip, shuffled into the hall, crouched down, opened the small low door to the laundry chute, and let the washcloth slide. She remained in that position, sweat beading anew on her forehead. If she arose now, her head would surely split like a ripe honeydew. She was trapped by her own poor choice. And not for the first time. She laid her palms flat on the floor, considering her limited options.

Gus's feet in black corduroy slippers appeared in the gloom next to her. "Sweetheart, you're back amongst the living! Man, those headaches really lay you low, don't they? I hate to see you suffer like that. Give me your hand now." She clung to Gus and arose slowly, experiencing only a quick pounding sensation instead of the glass shards of pain that she had feared. She blew out her breath in relief.

They walked slowly to the porch, arm in arm, and Claire took a seat in a creaking wicker chair while Gus partially lowered the white blinds over the porch windows. He departed briefly and when he stood before her again, he was holding a glass of ginger ale out toward her. With ice. Claire reached for it numbly, averting her gaze from the bubbles rising, not wanting any reminders of the throbbing dots and splotches that had been her constant companions during the migraine.

She sipped and he sat in the chair next to hers, hands cupping his knees, watching the birds flitting from the maple's branches to the hanging tubular feeder. Every now and then, he shot a surreptitious glance toward Claire.

Her voice sounded even rustier than usual when she spoke. "Gosh, I'm sorry, Gus. That wasn't the way I wanted you to spend your first day here. These migraines just over-take me, and once one hits, there's nothing to do but ride it out. What time is it, anyway?" She had no idea where her watch was—hadn't worn it in days, she realized.

He consulted his Timex. "Half past two." The clock

caroled agreement. "How often does this happen to you, sweetheart?" he inquired carefully, as if controlling anger or grief. She noticed that he seemed unwilling to actually say the word "migraine."

"Well, it varies. Sometimes I can go several weeks without one, and then I'll have a bad patch...During the last couple of weeks, I've had three, I think." She cast her thoughts back. Had it been only a few weeks since the clock had come to her? Not that the clock had anything to do with her migraines, but its arrival was a definite milestone for her. BC and AC, "before clock" and "after clock." "Yes, three in the past two weeks. Blasted things." She shifted uneasily and set the glass of ginger ale on the linoleum floor, checkered in beige and pine green like an antique game board. "Where's Lute, Gramps?" She let her head fall against the curved back of the chair, perversely welcoming the scratchy sensation against her scalp.

He didn't let her change the subject that easily. "Outside in the backyard. Snoozing under the hydrangea, last I looked. What brings these headaches on? There must be some pattern?" His face looked tight as he leaned toward her, wild eyebrows knotted together and lips pressed into a line.

She sighed. "Well, I've only had them for a few years, and they've gotten worse in the last year or so. Much worse. This time off was meant to—get to the bottom of them." Her words slowed and elongated until they rasped. She dropped her gaze and pleated the loose material of her cream canvas trousers with a thumb and forefinger. "They come from work," she confided. "From my job. I just got so...I couldn't do it anymore. I'd have migraines before I left to teach, just before. When I pulled into the parking lot or stepped through the door. In my office during office hours. Several times while I was actually teaching." Her voice shook. "Some students had to get one of my co-workers to lead me away. I just couldn't function. At all." She closed her eyes against this memory.

"And now? You've been away from teaching since May, Claire."

"That's not enough time, I guess. I still get them. They've picked up lately, in fact, probably because of associations with the fall semester. That's what I think is happening, anyway. It's like my body doesn't realize that I'm not going back this year, and it still...protests." Claire had never told anyone this, not even Marguerite, who would certainly understand and sympathize. She cleared her throat roughly. "It's a weakness, I suppose. That's what most people would think, anyway." She fell silent, unable to say more.

Quiet reigned for a long moment while Gus considered what she'd said. "Well, I don't think of it as weakness. I see it as a warning sign—a huge warning sign. Big as a billboard. With lights blinking!"

"No blinking lights, please!" she interjected without thinking, and they both chuckled a bit. "Gramps, can we talk about this later? I just can't take any more right now."

"Of course, sweetie. Of course. Can you eat? Silly question. Yes, you can eat. But *what* can you eat? Whatever it is, I'll make it. You stay right here, and I'll bring it out to you. On a tray." His smile was hopeful, and she realized how much he wanted to help her.

"Maybe some crackers spread with peanut butter. Have you had lunch?" Her first attempts at hosting an adult family member in Kate's home was not going as smoothly as she'd hoped, to say the least.

"Yes, yes, I made myself a sandwich an hour or more ago. I was just reading out here while I waited for you to get over that danged headache." He waved a hand toward the small table, where her trade paperback copy of *The Land Remembers* lay. "And look what I found inside." He picked up the book and let it fall open on his palm where a piece of torn art paper marked the reader's place. "Scott is getting to be a good little artist, isn't he?"

The paper he held out to her carried the image of a smiling golden moon and stars, more detailed than the version on the wall upstairs, with much of the background colored midnight blue. Created, she was sure, with Sharpies.

CHAPTER 13

She waited until he'd returned with the plate of peanut butter crackers to begin the tale. "Ah, Gus? About the drawing. It's not Scott's, I'm pretty sure." Gus had been unable to find a tray, and she clutched the crockery plate he'd brought to her, bracing herself inwardly as if against unsettled weather. What if he didn't believe her? What if he thought she was crazy? Worst of all, what if he were disappointed that she could even entertain the idea of a ghost in the house? The possibility of losing Gus's confidence cleaved her tongue to the roof of her mouth. Carefully, she set the plate down on the little table. "That drawing is almost the double of one that appeared upstairs in the guest room while I was painting. Except that the upstairs one is bigger. Much bigger."

"Appeared? I don't understand." He had turned in his crackling woven chair and was searching her face, his expression puzzled. He licked his lips nervously.

She drew in a deep breath for courage, and the exhalation took the form of a sigh. "I think that the house is haunted now. That a spirit of some sort came with the clock. Maybe two." The air on the porch appeared to shake with her uncertainty and apprehension. She felt the underside of her left eye twitch, pause, and twitch again.

"Haunted, sweetheart?" he said, his voice hoarse. "That sounds serious. Tell me, please." He turned his chair so that it faced hers and leaned forward, fingers intertwined. A childhood memory of him holding his hands in the same way to show her the church, and then the steeple, and then the congregants flashed into her mind. Gus had always been religious in an unobtrusive, non-judgmental way. What would his response to this tale be? She must make sure that the benevolence, even playfulness, of her encounters came through in this story. And it was a long story, she realized belatedly—how could she tell it now, when she was still shaken and inarticulate from the migraine? Oh, this was not going well, not going well at all...

Inspiration rayed out. "Gramps, you sit, and I'll be rrrright back," she stuttered lightly. "Just wait here for a minute." She walked as quickly as she was able into the study, each step pounding her spine into the underside of her skull. She retrieved the mottled black notebook from her file cabinet and found her cork-soled Haflingers under the daybed. Ah, much better. These woolen clogs were as comforting for her feet as mittens on a cold winter's night were for her hands. The return trip to the porch could be somewhat speedier.

"I wrote down everything that I could remember about what's been happening here." She handed him the notebook and sank into her chair again. "You could just skim if you don't want to read it all." Her voice faltered. "There's a lot. And some of it is...mental, I guess you would say." She picked up the glass of ginger ale and laid it against her hot cheek and temple, hoping that he wouldn't think, she's acting "mental," all right.

He was already tipping the cardboard cover open, bending over the notebook. His fine silver hair, long enough to cover his shirt collar, still showed the faint marks of a comb. "I'll read every word," he said.

While he read, Claire got up again, thinking that maybe a picture would be worth a thousand words, and came back with her camera. She flipped through the photos as she waited, grateful for something to do. Marguerite and Jason, each with an arm curled around the other's waist, heads inclined toward each other. Lute, tongue lolling, four-square in front of the fireplace. Kipper peeking out under the hem of a curtain. A seated Tamsin, regal even as she held a hind leg skyward preparatory to bathing. Scout building a fort with Legos on her living room floor. The front of the house after she'd planted lime-green and burgundy coleus plants in the window box. A pale face in the window behind the plants.

Wait. Whose face was that? She pushed on her twitching lower eyelid, then found the button with fingers that shook to zoom in on the face.

The photo appeared to show a slender visage, maybe with a pointed lock of hair falling over the forehead, but in the deep shadows, it was impossible to tell for sure. She cast her mind back to the day that the picture was taken. She had planted the coleus the same afternoon she'd bought them and then snapped the photo but couldn't recall the exact day. A weekday, she thought, since she liked to avoid the weekend crowds as she ran her errands. Could it be Scout's face in the picture? No, the date stamp didn't jibe with his last few visits, she was sure. She exhaled deliberately and moved on through the queue.

The next photos showed the smiling moon that was

becoming almost familiar to her now. She'd taken pictures from several angles to make sure that she would possess a good representation of the artwork before painting over it. And of course, Claire had decided not to destroy it; the original still graced the wall upstairs. And it *was* graceful. If she overlooked its supernatural origins, the moon and stars prompted a slight smile every time she looked at them. She sighed. Life in Kate's house had certainly grown…rich since she'd brought that clock home. Maybe she should snap a few photos of the clock itself to see what they might show in addition to golden chains and pine-cone-shaped weights and carefully-carved wooden birds.

She glanced at Gus. Absorbed in his reading, he was wiping his forehead with a pale blue handkerchief, although the day was mild. Claire turned off the camera, closed her twitchy gray eyes, and waited.

She felt herself slipping downward toward a doze, jerking up into wakefulness only because Gus had coughed loudly. When she turned to look at him, she found that he was holding the notebook out to her as if he no longer needed or wanted it. "Well," he rumbled, "that's quite a story, sweetie. And reading your notes just reminds me what a wonderful writer you are. I feel like I'm right there with you." He rubbed his forearms vigorously. "Some of those descriptions gave me goose bumps," he added, voice fading. "Especially the story about the pages turning by themselves. Spooky—no doubt about it."

"You don't believe me." She spoke quietly, working to keep any hint of accusation out of her voice.

"Of course, I believe you, Claire! I believe you experienced some odd, odd things. I just don't know what those experiences *were*." He reached out for her hand, his feeling warm and raspy. "I'm sorry that I can't offer anything more than that. These things are just…out of my ken." He was holding her hand in both of his now, shaking it up and down gently, as one jostles a crib to comfort the occupant. His startled eyes searched her weary ones anxiously. "What do you say, huh?"

Claire felt the weight of disappointment settle over her like a heavy cape. He didn't believe her, would be of no help. She had counted on him, as she had during her childhood, and he had let her down. Then the logical part of her brain shook itself and spoke up for him. He had no frame of reference for what her notebook contained, and his personality, as accepting and loving as it was, had no place for the supernatural. He had worked all his life with plants: starting seeds in carefully-prepared boxes, digging in the soil, twining vines around stakes, tipping beetles into plastic buckets of soapy water, harvesting flowers and fruit. His years had been charged with the energy of nature, and energy that came from a source outside of that must seem bizarre and threatening to him. Supernatural? The natural world was super enough for him. Her tales of otherworldly events would definitely trouble him.

She laid her free hand on top of both of his and squeezed. "It's okay, Gus. I told you, and that's the main thing. I really feel that this situation is mine to deal with. It came to me, the clock. The clock and whoever tagged along—I brought them into my house. So I will figure out what's going on and what I should do. But I'm glad that you know. This way, if something happens, you'll be prepared."

Gus grinned, relieved. "Like a Boy Scout, you mean?"

"Yes, just like that." Claire slipped the drawing Gus had found into her notebook and laid that on the table next to the plate of peanut butter crackers, which were looking pretty good to her right now.

"And I'll tell you this, sweetie; if any ghost bothers you while I'm here, I'll tie a knot in its tail and kick it down the street." She had to smile more broadly at that, her lower lip pushed forward. "Oh, and Claire? I remembered the name of the type of owls that are perched at the top of your clock. They're tawny owls, common in Europe. That round head is the defining feature. The other birds alongside the clock's house—those I don't know, but I can find out, I'm pretty sure."

"Tawny owls. Thanks, Gramps. You're such a whiz with birds." In her mind, the owls oared through Black Forest darkness on silent wings, seeking prey. Every piece of information she gleaned about the clock was significant. And more would come to her if she were open to learning. Receptive. Feeling that she was sounding suspiciously like Yoda in this line of thinking, she gave herself a mental shake and reached for a cracker, noticing how the peanut butter glistened on the saltines from being out on the afternoon-warmed porch for so long, "Let's salvage part of this day. What're you up for this evening, Gus? And what would you like to have for dinner?"

THEY ENDED up walking Lute in the neighborhood, going out for their evening meal, and then stopping by the community center for a dip. Claire had told him about the center, including the large whirlpool, and he had brought his swimming trunks along to Minnesota, ready, he said, to aim those jets of hot water right at his lower back.

While he soaked blissfully, chatting with the tub's other occupants, Claire paddled in the large pool. She didn't have the energy for lap swimming, but the water felt divine after the migraine. She slipped experimentally just under its surface to slide through the wavering cones of gold that shone from the wall-mounted lamps, ready to immediately re-emerge if being under water caused her any pain. It didn't.

Relishing the cleansing sensation of the water sliding along her skin, Claire swam until her cache of air ran out. She reared her face up then, regretfully leaving the rippling, muted realm of water for the louder realm of air. She crouched low in the shaking water and swanned with cupped hands so that she continued to move forward with all of her but the upper part of her head still submerged. Swimming always made her feel better, she realized, and promised herself again that she would come to the community center for laps and yoga regularly. Once Gus and her father had gone home again, she would figure out a rough schedule, open to change as required. She couldn't imagine having a migraine in either the pool or the yoga studio. The two could simply not coexist, and that was worth recognizing.

THE PHONE RANG as she and Gus were finishing their tea and Fig Newtons a little past eight o'clock. They both jumped at the unexpected sound. "Maybe I should just go and see who that is," Claire said cautiously. She trotted into the bedroom and waited, hoping to hear a dial tone once the machine had said its piece. (She had decided to keep Kate's old-fashioned answering machine because it allowed her to screen in just this way.)

"Claire, it's Greg. If you're there, please pick up." She could feel her brother's impatience sparking through the answering machine's tiny speaker. "C'mon, Claire; I'm desperate here." He made a little huffing sound as if to underscore this point.

Cautiously, she reached out and picked up the receiver. "Desperate again?" she said lightly. "Honestly, Greg, this is getting a little...shall we say, familiar? If you need a babysitter for Scott, I wish you'd given me some advance warning."

"What? Ha, I knew you were there. No, no, this has nothing to do with Scott. It's Dad."

Claire's inhaled sharply. "Dad? What's desperate about Dad? Is he all right?"

"Yes, he's fine. Physically, that is. The question is, am I fine, and the answer is, 'No'! He's driving me crazy, with his probing questions and his toolbox. There's no place safe from him in the whole house. Do you know that he has learned how to fix plumbing now? Or so he says. He's been working on faucets that have nothing wrong with them, using Scott as an assistant. They're having a ball, but I'm worried about what'll come next. He has his eye on the dishwasher—claims that it doesn't sound right to him. Claire, it's brand new! It hardly makes a whisper." Greg's own voice dropped so low that Claire had to strain to hear him. "You have to help me get him out of the house."

"Well, you don't need me for that. Just let him choose someplace for you all to go—some kind of outing—and go there. The Twin Cities have more things to do than you can shake a stick at." She wondered if this last phrase was one she'd picked up from Gus recently. She liked the mental image of Greg waving a leafy branch at downtown Minneapolis, in any case.

"I *have* done that," Greg hissed, "and he's chosen the State Fair for tomorrow." Claire felt a sympathetic frisson rattle up her backbone. Greg hated the fair—said that it was hokey, crowded, and overpriced. He hadn't been there in years, to her knowledge. Neither had she, for that matter, but that was because it always began just a few days before classes at her college did, and she was too busy and anxious to make the trek. She didn't dislike the fair itself. Although there were more negatives in that mental note than she felt comfortable with. Didn't dislike…

Greg's voice broke into her thoughts, and it had that

imploring quality that he used to such good effect with her. "I thought that we could all go together: you, me, Dad, Gus, and Scott. Whadaya say, Claire? I'll owe you big time for this one. It's supposed to stay cool tomorrow, high of 71."

"Weeellll," she strung out the word to tease him a bit. "Let me ask Gus. It's his vacation, too, you know." She laid the receiver down on the nightstand and returned to the dining room, where she found her grandfather on the couch reading the less-favored parts of the newspaper. Tam was weaving around his outstretched ankles as if casting a web around him. He cocked his head while he listened to her describe Greg's invitation.

"The fair, eh? With all five of us? Well, I suppose there will be something for everyone, and I haven't been to a fair in years. Will they still have those fried cheese curds, do you think? I used to love those, and I've never had anything like them elsewhere." He shook the paper in mild anticipation.

"Yes, I can almost guarantee that fried cheese curds will still be available, Gus. Shall I tell Greg that he's on, then?"

"Yes, tell him that, why don't you. It will be fun to see the fair from Scott's perspective, won't it? A fair is like a dream come true for a six-year-old, I'm guessing. Remembering, actually." And his eyes grew distant with the memories.

Greg let her choose the time of departure with a great show of bowing to her wishes, and after a brief, second consultation with Gus, she offered nine o'clock at her house. "And you won't mind missing church?" she asked Gus anxiously.

"No, honey. I'm not what you'd call a regular churchgoer these days, even in St. Louis, and this trip is something special. Plus, wouldn't you say that going to the State Fair qualifies as a kind of religious experience? I know that some people would argue that it was." Tamsin was now standing in his lap, and he ran his palm along her back while she pranced in place near his knees. She turned to bump her head confidently against the curve of Gus's belly while he gently smoothed her plush fur down.

"Well, a pilgrimage, at least. The butter princesses revolving in that refrigerated case for all to see." A memory of people pressing forward to watch the artist carving the likeness of a young, parka-clad woman into a ninety-pound block of butter flitted through her mind. Gus hooted with laughter, prompting a sharp look from Tam, and Claire chuckled, too. Gus might not be able to help her with the ghost, but he was helping her be herself. And that was comforting.

GREG HAD BROUGHT tickets for the whole group with him: a perk from his employers, he said. The five of them trailed through the gates, pausing to have their tickets torn, joining a milling, multi-colored river of people who were participating in "The Great Minnesota Get-Together." Claire had always liked that slogan—it sounded friendly to her, and Minnesotans were not known for their warmth, truth to tell. Politeness, yes. Warmth, no. She just hoped that she wouldn't have to mingle too much with the other tens of thousands of fairgoers who had chosen this Sunday to experience cow barns, artificial trout pools, giant pumpkins, watercolor paintings, and a dizzying array of fried food, much of it served impaled on a stick. She recalled that one of her colleagues had boasted last year about getting a fried pickle on a stick at the fair. He must've been making that up, mustn't he? The last of her family group, she passed a food cart that offered fried Snickers bars and began to wonder.

Scout was hanging on to Gus's hand, pointing first at the fried candy bar cart, next sweeping his whole arm toward the animal barns, and then hopping energetically on both tennis-shoed feet together as if he were on a pogo stick. She felt her heart clench. He had greeted her politely when she and Gus had walked down the front steps of the bungalow, but with no real warmth. A true stereotypical Minnesotan, Scout, Claire thought mournfully. He clearly hadn't forgotten or forgiven her decision to keep him away from the interior of the house. Yet what other choice could she make? What sort of aunt would she be to risk exposing him to more ghostly encounters? She heard his answer in her head as clearly as if he had spoken the words: a dull aunt.

As she watched enviously, Scout pulled Gus carefully toward her father and grasped his hand, too. The three of them walked together, arms swinging, forming a barge that caused those around them to stop momentarily or veer to one side. Yet the passersby smiled at the sight of boy and grandfather and great-grandfather striding along together. For once, Scout was wearing a regular, striped t-shirt instead of a team-sponsored one, and his tan cargo pants were nipped in at the waist by a thick Western belt. He was addressing his comments first to Gus and then to her father, his expressions animated and obviously happy.

Feeling extraneous, Claire fell into step with Greg. His face was set, his posture, slumped. Squeezing his hand momentarily or throwing an arm over his shoulder was out of the question. Greg was not one for displays of family affection in public. That is, if he felt any affection for her. She sometimes doubted that he did, to be honest.

"Geez, what do people see in this pokey fair?" Greg was asking. He paused to scrape the sole of his Adidas hard on the pavement, leaving a toffee-colored smear behind. "It's even more crowded than I remembered. And the smells! And the overpriced food!"

"I read the attendance figure for yesterday," Claire offered. "It's printed in the newspaper every morning. Let's see; what was it now? Over 150,000, I'm pretty sure. Maybe 180,000?"

Greg threw up his hands and shook his head. "Crazy. Crazy! Hey, guys, guys," he called out, hustling toward the trio ahead. "We need to make a plan here. Including where to meet if we get separated. We don't want to wander around aimlessly like chumps." She heard snatches of conversation drifting back from Gus, Scout, and her father as they swung along: "Machinery Hill," "Horticulture Building," "Octopus ride," "cheese curds."

Claire paused in her tracks, letting the murmuring currents of fairgoers curve and sweep around her, wishing with all her heart that she had a sister, or a girl cousin, or a grandmother. Or that Great Aunt Kate had not left her as the lone female in their small family.

CHAPTER 14

*S*eated on a bench in the tossing shade of a locust tree, Claire dug her spoon into a dish of apple chunks slathered in caramel sauce and strewn with crushed peanuts. Much easier to eat than a caramel apple, this indulgence allowed her to sidestep the fair's messy "food on a stick" tradition. There was only so much a person could do to wash up with a Kleenex moistened at the rare drinking fountain. Even now, she experienced a slight cracking sensation across her cheeks when she smiled or frowned, as if a layer of sweat, dust, and grease had been laid down delicately on her skin by the summer breeze that purled over the fairgrounds. She removed the band from her ponytail, scraped her dusty hair higher on the back of her skull, and replaced the band. This was definitely going to be a two-shower day.

On her right, Scout munched happily on a Pronto Pup glazed with yellow mustard. On her left, Gus and Greg shared a bag of mini-donuts, hints of the minis' sweet, old-fashioned fragrance reaching Claire on the breeze. Her father stood nearby, wiping his fingertips on a pad of paper napkins. "I can at least tell myself that corn on the cob is a vegetable," he was saying to no one in particular. Rounding on Claire, he added, "And roasting probably retains the vitamins better than boiling, eh, daughter?" He offered her a roll of Tums after taking one of the tablets himself.

"Hmm," she sighed, peeling a tablet from the roll and passing it on to Gus. Her attention was snagged by the t-shirt worn by a blocky, fiftyish man who was passing by. It bore the silhouette of a walleye and the slogan, "Your bait sucks and your boat's ugly." She had to admit that she found the slogan funny, along with one on a shirt worn by a pre-teen girl with an auburn braid and a confident gait: "Yes, I'm a girl. I have a bat, and I know how to use it." Greg gave Claire a wide-eyed, mock fearful expression as that youngster went by; she deliberately turned away from her brother, back toward the flowing tide of humanity.

The fair was the premier place for people-watching in the entire state—no doubt about it. Observing the undulating waves of fair-goers all around her, she wondered if all the rest of St. Paul were eerily empty at this moment because its entire population was here on the fairgrounds, milling and gazing and grazing. She imagined silent streets under the late afternoon sun, malls echoing, supermarkets colorful with produce but utterly deserted, park swings swaying unoccupied and forlorn. She experienced a twist at that last image and turned to Scout.

"What's been your favorite part of the fair so far, buddy?" She needed to mend fences with him somehow. Maybe the day at the fair had softened his attitude toward her.

Having reached the delicate stage in eating the Pronto Pup where the stick was visible down the center of the cornmeal-coated hotdog, Scout was willing to pause and answer.

"Well, I'm sure that the Octopus ride *would've* been my favorite if anyone had took me," he replied pointedly. "But since no one would, I guess the alpacas. Can I have an alpaca, Dad?"

Greg snorted lightly and popped another mini-donut into his mouth. The bag in Gus's hand was showing splotches of grease, looking like unknown continents on the waxed paper. "In your dreams, pal. Those things are expensive. And probably a huge amount of trouble. Don't they spit like camels? And I'm sure it's illegal to keep them in the city. No animals with hooves allowed. Claire's got pets. You'll just have to get your animal fix from them." Scout shot Claire an accusing look but didn't mention his banishment from the bungalow.

She soldiered on. "The alpacas are gorgeous. Those long necks and big, soft eyes. Do you know who they remind me of? The Beatles in their early years. They have those tousled, fuzzy top-knots…"

Gus chuckled, a half-eaten donut pinched between his thumb and forefinger. His eyes looked a trifle weary. "I see what you mean, sweetheart. Your mom was partial to that Beatle John. She about drove us crazy listening to the Beatles when she was young. The songs from *Rubber Soul* repeated in my head all day long when I was at work, one after another; I couldn't get rid of them. I used to ask her why she even bothered playing the record since it must've been in her head just as strongly as it was in mine. 'Baby, you can drive my car…'" he sang in a quavering voice. His face softened. "Although I always liked 'In My Life.' Beautiful song." He shook the donut gently, ridding it of its outer sprinkling of sugar.

The other adults all quieted at this rare mention of Claire and Greg's mother.

"Earworm." Claire, Greg, and Gus turned as one to face David, Scout alone continuing with his snack. "Earworm. That's what songs that you can't get out of your head are called. It's a calque from the German term 'Ohrwurm.'" He cleared his throat uneasily. "Right. So Greg, what has your favorite fair thing been? I mean...Oh, you know what I mean." He stamped his feet in brown Rockport shoes and stuffed the wad of napkins into his back pocket.

"Oh, it's hard to choose among so many things: smelly cows, smelly horses, smelly chickens, really smelly pigs..." His gaze fell on Scout's bent head and he appeared to catch himself in his own negativity. "But I would have to say the tractors on Machinery Hill. Man, those are big suckers. They look big when you drive by them on the road, but to be right up next to them makes you realize how really huge they are. Gus?"

His grandfather was twisting the now-empty donut sack into a red and white striped spike. "Oh, the crop art, I guess. Just to think of the patience required to make an entire picture of a lion on the African plain using only different kinds of seeds: oats and wheat and barley, and so on. What an eye those..." he paused, searching for the proper term, "crop artists must have! Real imagination, that takes, to find everyday seeds and realize how they can be used to create something completely different. How about you, David?"

Claire's father answered without hesitation. "That demonstration of the antique printing press. Wonderful contraption. You don't see something like that every day. And that gentleman who showed it to us—what a passion for printing he had. He really knew his machine and his subject." David's voice warmed with admiration. "I like people who are knowledgeable, people who care about something."

"Did you notice that he had only nine fingers?" Greg inquired.

"What?" David was unmistakably startled.

"I said, did you notice that he had only nine fingers. He was missing the ring finger on his left hand. Only a stump there. Probably due to an accident with that so-called 'wonderful contraption.'"

"Oh, honestly, Greg, I think you're making that up." David's face was flushed now.

"No, David, I noticed it, too," Gus said regretfully. "Poor fella. Although he seemed to do fine with just nine fingers, the way he was snatching those fliers out of the press."

Scout, who had finished his Pronto Pup and was leaning forward and using the stick to draw rudimentary space aliens in the packed dirt at his feet, spoke without looking up. "Claire."

"Yes, buddy?" She answered absentmindedly, still thinking about the man with the missing finger and his beloved printing press.

"You haven't said what you liked best." The words were as even as Chiclets in an unopened package, yet Claire knew that they indicated a small gesture of rapprochement. She frowned in concentration, not wanting to spook her nephew by showing too much enthusiasm. The possibilities sprang up in her. The scarecrow whose head was an aluminum watering can. The immaculate Brown Swiss cows, each with a face as lovely as a doe's. The glass-fronted beehive, swirling with golden energy. The display cases of field corn, the kernels in the various sections all appearing exactly the same except for the blue or red or white ribbon that they bore. The enormous pumpkins sagging under their own weight, looking partially deflated. The quilts as glorious in their purples and greens and reds as shining chords from a pipe organ.

"That girl holding the goat in her lap. Remember?" She spoke only to Scout, nudging him slightly with one knee and elbow. The teenager had cradled the white goat tenderly, her pet's legs curled under and its eyes with their bar-shaped pupils half-closed in trust. "A girl and her goat. That was my favorite part of the day."

Scout carefully turned sideways on the bench and began to drape his legs over Claire's, his feet dangling. She lifted the dish of apples that she held in both hands and then let her forearms rest on his shins in their cargo pants. He had done this with her since he was a toddler, needing a rest or a break or a bit of comfort. A breath of gratitude and understanding eased out of her chest, so quietly that only Scout would hear.

"I liked the goat and the girl, too," he said, "just as well as the alpacas."

THAT NIGHT after Gus had gone to bed, she retrieved the unopened package from Barnes and Noble and hastened upstairs with it almost guiltily, Kipper and Lute leaping up the stairs in front of her. Despite the August warmth of the upstairs room, she noticed that her hands had grown cold as she slit the packing tape with a pair of scissors and that the emotion she was feeling was not the usual surge of happy anticipation that accompanied the arrival of books. It was more like dread, actually.

The encyclopedia of hauntings was a thick paperback with an ominous-looking cover that included a photo of an indistinct "something" on a dark stairway. "Probably re-touched," Claire muttered as she made the book's hundreds of pages flutter, spotting more black and white photos but not stopping to look at them. "This book," she told Kipper, who was chirping at her feet, "is going to be for another time." And with that, she shut it in the guestroom's small closet, closed the door, and wedged the chock underneath. "Just so *you* don't get into the closet and cause trouble." Kipper appeared as guiltless as ever, while Lute snuggled down on his bed after turning around three times.

While Lute began to fade around nine or ten o'clock each evening, the cats began to shine. Kip's greeny-gold eyes were alight with interest, and Claire put the empty cardboard folder that had enclosed the books upside down on the floor, tent-wise, so the cat could explore if she wished. Kip immediately dived under it, only her ringed tail showing. Claire turned back to the smaller of the two books. A slim trade paperback, its rust-colored cover showed only a photo of an old-fashioned door handle. Claire decided to give it a try.

She quickly prepared for bed, propped herself up against the headboard, pulled the crisp summer sheet up firmly, and began to read, reassured by the scuttling sound of Kip playing under the cardboard and Lute's snuffling snores from his bed near the wall.

Hours passed, unnoticed. Some of the stories raised the hair on Claire's arms and made her skin tingle with electricity, but only a few conveyed malevolence. She read about ghosts who walked, ghosts who argued, ghosts who played the piano, ghosts who peered in windows. The story about the ghost of a child who stroked a sleeper's hair elicited a nod of recognition, and so did the one about a ghost who pulled on people's toes. She wasn't alone! Others had experienced events as inexplicable as she had. Some had experienced events *more* inexplicable than she had, including the two young women who'd seen figures outside moving a long, rectangular box; for hours, the women had watched these figures, counting sixteen at one point, seeing them fade into runnels in the ground when the police arrived with flashlights and reemerge once the officers had left. Now, that would be something to experience. Who could even make that up? Claire mused. Finally, she slid into deep sleep, the book still clasped in her now-warm hands.

From the wall, the moon smiled at her from its sparkling net of stars.

.   .   .

HER LAST DAY with Gus passed pleasantly, taken up with the delayed visit to the Como Conservatory, a stroll around the small lake there, and a picnic in a shelter under the lushly canopied oak trees in the park. She half-expected to be struck down by a migraine because it was the first day of classes at her college; she'd even made sure that Gus had his driver's license with him before they'd left the bungalow in case he had to get them home. But nothing happened except that she and Gus chatted, admired the flitting birds, and ate egg salad sandwiches, bananas, and more Fig Newtons.

"Oh, Claire," he said as he popped the lid back on a Tupperware container. "I forgot to tell you before. I figured out what kind of birds are on your cuckoo clock. Aside from the tawny owls, I mean. It's a little hard to identify them without the color, of course, but I think I've got them pegged. The one on the right with the long beak and the tail that angles up is a European wren, I'm pretty sure. And the left bird is some kind of bunting, I think. I would guess a yellowhammer based on the range of the bird. And I noticed that the woodcarver tried to indicate the streaky plumage by creating patterns on the bird's breast and sides. He did a nice job, really." Gus smiled shyly at Claire. "I used your computer to look at European birds this morning before you got up. I hope you don't mind."

"No, of course I don't mind. Thanks for the info. A wren and yellowhammer. That's nice to know."

"It really is a beautiful clock." Gus shifted on the bench of the picnic table. "Whatever its background is." His chin dipped toward his chest. "I'm sorry that I can't be of more help with that."

"No worries, Gramps. Honestly."

"Maybe your dad could…" He let the sentence trail off.

"Well. Maybe." A scampering sensation raced up Claire's shoulders and nestled into the roots of her hair. The combination of Dad and the spirit world did not seem promising. But on the other hand, it would almost certainly be interesting.

GREG, Scout, and their father arrived at the bungalow with take-out Chinese food for dinner, and they all crowded around the dining room table that was really meant for just four, hopping up to fetch extra servings from the cartons on the kitchen counter. (David always liked the table to look "civilized," as he put it—free from containers or bags of any kind.) In the back yard, Lute yapped occasionally to remind the selfish humans that he was out there, being deprived of their company.

Scout's eyes were glinting with mischief and delight from his seat on the borrowed kitchen chair—he had succeeded in entering the forbidden zone. In fact, he was so busy glancing around in the hopes of seeing something supernatural that he didn't even bother to complain that he hated pork lo mein. Claire was grateful for small favors.

Claiming that he had to get Scott home in time for a phone conversation with his mother, Greg ate with what Claire considered to be unseemly haste. She wasn't even sure that Greg still had a landline, but she knew better than to mention that. The members of the two groups bid each goodbye rather self-consciously, and Gus thanked Claire for a wonderful visit. Then Greg picked up Gus's suitcase and they departed with Scout hanging onto his great-grandfather's hand, Greg calling back a reminder of their barbecue on Wednesday evening at his house. Claire watched them drive off, then returned to the living room and her father, leaving the door between the house and porch open so that the cats could come and go as they pleased.

Now it was just the two of them, with the clock ticking. Claire took a seat, planting her feet in their Haflingers flat on the floor. "Well, then." Remembering that she had to change the sheets in her own room so that the bed would be fresh for her father, she leapt up from the rocking chair, relieved to have a task to do. "Dad, why don't you rest or read or something while I put clean sheets on the bed you're going to sleep in." She knew that he wouldn't argue that this was unnecessary, that Gus was perfectly clean and had used the bed only three nights. David was as persnickety as she was about personal hygiene. She was already halfway across the room when she heard him clear his throat and arise from the couch.

To her disappointment, he was following her. "I'll help you," he said, sounding glum. Deciding that resistance was futile, Claire fetched some blue and white striped sheets from the linen cupboard and took the opposite side of the bed that her father had chosen. Wordlessly, they pulled off the current sheets, Claire lifting Kip down to the floor repeatedly after the cat had jumped up. "She thinks of the bed as hers, I guess," Claire muttered. There was no reply from David. They tugged the clean fitted sheet onto the mattress over the mattress pad and Claire tossed the flat sheet out. Once again, Kip jumped to the edge of the bed and then pounced to its center, commenting all the while, and took a seat.

"Let's lift this cat on the sheet," David suggested suddenly. "Like an Alaskan blanket toss, you know?"

Off Claire's surprised look, he explained further. "It's a traditional part of the spring whaling festival in Barrow. I saw it in a documentary. We won't throw the cat high, of course. Let's just try lifting. I think it will like being lifted."

"I don't know, Dad. Kip's never experienced anything like that before. My pets lead rather sheltered lives, really."

"All the more reason to give it a try." David was gripping the long side of the sheet tightly and holding it slightly up already. "My friend Rosa volunteered at a zoo, and she told me that every animal had an 'enrichment plan' designed by the zookeepers—activities that encouraged the animals to perform their natural behaviors, investigate things, exercise, and so forth. The tigers, for example, liked to sniff used straw from the camel exhibit and find the spots of perfume that'd been sprayed on the tree trunks. Even the hissing cockroaches had enrichment plans. This will be enrichment for your cat."

"I don't think that dealing with being tossed on a sheet is a natural behavior for cats, Dad. And what could be enrichment for a cockroach, anyway?"

"I don't know! Maybe they were given some envelopes so they could eat the glue off the flaps. Come on, Claire; let's just try lifting him. Look, he's waiting for something to happen."

"Kipper is a girl, Dad." Claire glanced down at Kip, who was still seated in the middle of the bed, whiskers fanned out from her pretty face, appearing rather expectant, it was true. "Usually when I'm changing the sheets, I just throw the blanket over her and she runs around under it like a wild thing for a little while. Then she jumps down and I finish with the bed. That's what she's expecting."

"Well, let's give her something unexpected." Claire found his set expression very familiar. His hands still held the sheet firmly.

"Okay, but if she's scared by this, I'm going to lower the sheet immediately, do you hear? Immediately." Gosh, Claire thought, I'm starting to sound like Dad, myself. He's been here alone fifteen minutes, and already, he's taking over. But she added aloud, "On the count of three, then. One, two, *three*." Claire and David each raised a side of the sheet smoothly together, lifting Kip about a foot off the mattress, leaving her crouched in a gentle indentation created by her own weight. She was facing Claire, and the eyes that looked up to find Claire's were as round as a cat's eyes can be, the pupils huge with amazement. Yet, Kip made no attempt to escape. In fact, she was lashing her tail excitedly

"Lower her on three," her father directed. "One, two, three." They gently let the sheet descend until Kip was seated on the mattress again. She sat up straight, meowing a question that sounded like, "Air? Air?" "See, she likes it." David's voice had grown fulsome with triumph. "Let's do it again. Ready?"

Claire bit back a smile and gripped her side of the crisp sheet. Maybe this visit with her father would go better than she'd expected. "Who is this Rosa, anyway?" she teased, lifting.

"Hmph," David's angular face grew slightly pink. "A friend, like I said. A… a nice friend. We met through shared volunteer work at the nature center. Look, this cat enjoys being airborne, whether it's a natural sensation or not."

Taking pity on him, Claire let the line of questioning go. They lifted Kip several more times, to her apparent delight, and then lowered the sheet slowly over the mattress. The cat waited a moment to make sure that the blanket toss was over and then scarpered out of the room, her hind legs slewing sideways as she took the corner of the doorway at top speed. Claire turned to get the pale green summer blanket from the bedside chair while David tucked in the sheet. "Claire, I think your other cat has gotten in here somehow," David was saying.

She turned back to witness the center of the sheet rising up over the center of the bed where Kip had sat only moments before, creating a bulb-shaped, air-filled hollow. Chills skittered down her arms, caused partly by the suddenly wintry temperature over the bed and partly by shock at what she was seeing. Effortlessly, her mind flashed back to grade school, when she and the other children had been given a billowing parachute made of silky material to play with in phys. ed. class. Following the teacher's instruction, a ring of children had tossed the parachute up, hustled underneath it, and then pressed the edges to the wooden floor of the gym and sat on them, the light material hovering over its supporting cushion of air, creating a mushroom cap that lingered for enchanted moments while the children oohed and ahhed inside.

This poofed-up shape of the sheet reminded Claire of that parachute. And she knew that Tamsin was not responsible. And then another image slid into place in her mind: sun-dappled sheets on a clothesline, pinned with wooden pegs, swaying in the breeze. And this was not her memory, she felt sure. Not her memory at all.

"How is she doing that?" David mused. "I wouldn't think that a cat could..." One hand cupped his chin with slender fingers and thumb, his classic gesture of perplexity or discomfort.

Claire almost ran the few steps to her father and took his arm. "She's acrobatic, that Tamsin. You remember Aunt Kate's stories about her exploits: pulling on the roller shades, leaping from one high piece of furniture to the other, always wanting to be 'top cat.' Say, I'm pretty thirsty, Dad, aren't you? Why don't you get us both some lemonade, and I'll finish up here and join you on the porch in a minute. And listen, I bought some beer for you, so you can make shandies if you want. So refreshing in summer, Marguerite says. Half and half, I think, is the right proportion." She was steering David toward the door and talking fast, trying to keep his attention. Oddly, she seemed to be succeeding. With only one more silent glance over his shoulder, he departed from the bedroom. But he was troubled, Claire felt. His shoulders slumped with uncertainty in the gloom of the hallway. He paused there for a long moment and then began walking slowly away.

Claire shook her head and returned to the bedside. The sheet was still doing an impression of an engaged parachute, swaying and rippling gently over the mattress. "Hey, you," she hissed. "This is my father you're performing for. He will not appreciate your presence one bit. In fact, he will not believe that you exist. So cool it, can't you? No pun intended." She resisted the urge to add, "You're going to get me into trouble." The sheet wavered, as if considering, and then gently fluttered down to cover the mattress. It twitched a moment and then lay still. "Thank you. Believe me, I'm grateful."

It took her only a few moments to finish making the bed, including tossing out a fleece throw to protect the blanket from cat hair since David was not used to it. She had to stop for a moment to burble with nervous laughter, palm clapped over her mouth, at the realization that a ghost had been playing with a sheet. Once she got herself under control again, she rubbed her arms vigorously to erase the goosebumps there, ran a shaking hand through her hair, and joined her father on the porch.

He was standing by the screened windows that ran along the front of the porch, facing outward, holding a glass of shandy down by his side. Although he wore light-colored summer clothes—khaki trousers and a pale yellow polo shirt —his silhouette appeared gray and indistinct. The racket of cicadas poured in through the screens, louder than the faint barks of Bilbo, the setter from across the street. When he heard her arrive, he turned to gesture toward her glass, which stood on the little side table. In the nearby wicker chair, Tamsin was curled and snoozing, her front paws crossed and hugged over her eyes. Obviously, she was deeply settled and had not moved for some time. Claire picked up the chilly glass of shandy. "So Dad," she said evenly. "How about a toast?"

His eyes, the same shade as hers, thinned suspiciously, but he held out his glass toward her, the other hand fisted in his trouser pocket. "What shall we toast to, daughter?"

"To summer visitors." And she raised her drink in the classic toast gesture without actually touching her glass to his.

CHAPTER 15

"*H*ello? Hello?" Claire said rapidly into the receiver of the kitchen phone, ready to hang up if no one answered immediately. Although she prided herself on being polite, she drew the line at listening to telemarketers, and she'd found that hanging up during the moment it took for the connection to be made was easier than trying to extricate herself once the dreaded person actually started to speak.

"Is this Claire?" a woman's voice inquired.

Deeply suspicious, Claire answered evenly, "Yes, may I ask who's calling?" Her father had drummed into his children at an early age to answer the phone with this level of formality, and the training had never worn off for her.

"It's Sarah." The voice tickled her ear with its familiarity.

"Sarah." Claire's mind scrambled to make a connection, failed, and then succeeded.

"Sarah! How are you? I'm sorry that I didn't recognize your voice. My father is visiting me right now, and he, and he…takes up all of my concentration." (The final sentence came out in a guilty whisper.)

Sarah chuckled. "I understand, and I remembered that

your folks were staying with you this week. I won't keep you. But I wanted to let you know that Roger answered. Roger McMaster from Luna Theater. He's the one I told you about, the artistic director who might know more about the clock."

"Yes, and what did he say?" Claire felt suddenly snatched away from her present, which was consumed with the question of how in the world she was going to entertain her father during the remainder of his stay, and catapulted into a future that would most likely include mystery, drama, and intrigue. How delightful.

"He said that he would meet you! Along with me, of course—later this week!" Sarah crowed. "If you're available, that is."

"Are you kidding? Of course I'm available. After Thursday, I'm free as a bird." She sighed with longing. Thursday. And today was only Tuesday. Was she a horrible person to be thinking this way?

"How about Friday morning, then. About ten? That was his suggestion. Why don't you come by my place and we'll ride together. I'll send you the address and all. I just wanted to set this meeting up right away if I could. You've got me really curious about the clock and its possible... inhabitant. Has anything else happened? Anything—you know —suspicious?"

"Yes, but I'll have to tell you on Friday. My father is waiting for me. We're going to the hardware store."

"Okay, then." Sarah sounded only a little puzzled. "Have a good time there. And look for an email message with my address later this week."

"Thank you, Sarah. Thank you so much. See you on Friday."

Claire replaced the receiver gently in its cradle, squared her shoulders, and strode off to find her father. He stood near the front door, examining the bubbles in the ancient varnish on its exterior. "Ah, there you are, daughter. I thought I'd lost you." And he turned to give her a slim smile.

BY TEN FORTY-FIVE, they were embroiled in the project. She clumped down the basement stairs after him, toting a cardboard box filled with planks, cylinders of screws and nails, carpet remnants, and hanks of rope. The murky coolness of the basement crept up around her ankles like an unwelcome tide. He had already set his box down on a card table and was looking for a place to hang the two trouble lights that he had purchased along with the building materials. "I can't believe that you had no trouble lights," he was saying, his voice sounding stretched because his head was tipped back. "Every homeowner should have at least two trouble lights. Along with a stepladder and some basic tools. You need to be prepared to make at least simple repairs here, Claire. I mean, bungalows are great little houses—homes were built to last in the twenties—but no house goes on indefinitely without problems developing. It's the principle of entropy. Things break down."

"I know what entropy is, Dad."

He continued on as if he hadn't heard her. "And you don't have the money to hire expensive repairmen when you're not working." He hung the second of the two lights on a strut-type object that was supporting a water pipe and directed a laser look at her.

"Yes, well, I thought I would get by with Marguerite and Jason's help." She set her box next to his. "And I have other friends who would lend a hand. And Greg." She added her brother's name belatedly. He had said that he owed her big time for her impromptu babysitting. Not that she really wanted to call in that favor.

Her father clucked his tongue as he removed items from

one of the boxes and laid them neatly on the table in stacks and clusters, according to the materials' nature. "Your brother has many fine qualities, but he is no handyman. And he would be the first to admit it. No, you need to be independent, Claire. Learn to make repairs on your own."

"Well, I did re-paint the upstairs bedroom," she argued, and then wished that she could snatch the words back. If he asked to see her work, questions about the moon and stars painted on the wall would no doubt ensue. Pointed questions.

"Yes, well, painting is a start. It's a good beginner's project. And satisfying because it can improve the appearance of a room so dramatically." He was placing a tan carpet remnant on top of a cream one, lining up the edges.

"Yes, the room is dramatic now," Claire added peaceably, surprised at the jingle of pleasure she was experiencing from having made this veiled comment. Was it healthy to feel, at forty-two, such a kick out of fooling her father? At this moment, her inner thirteen-year-old was stirring rebelliously.

"I got some good work done at Greg's house. Of course, most of it wasn't really needed. But it gave me something to do. And Scott an activity to do with me."

Claire knew that playing with children did not come naturally to her father. She recalled David sitting down to Monopoly and backgammon with her and Greg occasionally, and that was about the extent of their "play." Yet she didn't feel deprived, then or now. He had been consumed with his teaching job and with being a single father at a time when that was an unusual role. Play was for children then. Or for people with fewer responsibilities than he had.

He continued. "Scott and Gus will have a ball this week while Greg is at work, I'm sure. Picnics. Parks. Building competitions with Legos. The whole works." Was there a little bit of resentment buried in those words? Searching her father's handsome, lined face as casually as she could, Claire was unsure.

He pulled the printed instructions for making a "cat tree" out of his back pocket, unfolded them, laid them on the last clear space on the table, and smoothed them down tenderly. "I really think those cats of yours are going to like this. Ongoing enrichment—that's what it will provide them. You can put it in the sunroom against the north windows and they can watch the birds out the window, stalk each other, leap around…"

Claire didn't have the heart to tell him that the cats didn't interact with each other much. It was considerate of him to think of building a piece of furniture just for their amusement, and the project had given some structure and purpose to the day already. It was as if he were building something just by finding the plans on the Internet, suggesting the trip to the hardware store, and laying out the supplies when he could've sat back on her couch upstairs and waited to be entertained. Not knowing what to say or how to respond to her own sense of gratitude, she said gently, "That'll be nice for them, Dad. Thank you."

He was turned away, rummaging again in the box he had brought down the basement steps. Then he held something out toward her, still looking downward into the box. "Here. These are for you, daughter."

She took the object from him. It was a clear plastic envelope that held a hammer and three different sizes of screwdrivers. It occurred to Claire that this was one of the best presents he had ever given her.

"Oh, and you'll need these," he said gruffly, dropping two cylinders of assorted screws and nails into her outstretched palm. "For your new home. Shall we get started?"

She would never tell him that she already owned a hammer.

It took them just the one day to make the cat tree, with a lunch break for grilled cheese and tomato sandwiches, which David made with both cheddar and Swiss cheeses and served with sweet pickles and corn chips. He had chosen a modest design for the tree, consisting of a platform base, two support columns rising out of it, and another platform, rimmed this time, atop the columns. Its overall shape reminded Claire of the small hand weights she had seen in the yoga studio. The platforms and one of the columns were covered in tacked-down carpeting, the other column in scratchy rope that David had wound and then meticulously glued. "This is solid," he said, smacking the top of the cat tree with a palm. "It's no good if the whole thing tips over when a cat jumps up on it, right?"

"No good at all," Claire agreed. "It might hurt them as it fell. And even if it didn't, they would never use it again."

"Once burned, eh? Well, I'd give the glue until tomorrow to dry, and then we can take the tree upstairs and see how they like it."

"It may take them a while to get used to it," she warned him. "Days, even weeks. Cats are curious, but mine are also cautious."

"Well. If they don't hop on to it before I go, you can tell me about it when they finally do. It'll give us something to talk about." He was loading scraps of wood and carpeting into one of the empty cardboard boxes.

Claire sighed inwardly. She hadn't realized that their tele-phone conversations were as difficult for him as they were for her. A light blanket of sadness settled over her. "Here," she handed her father the other empty box. "For an immediate reaction, put this in the middle of the living room floor. They won't be able to resist."

"Won't they?" he replied, and she thought she detected a bit of hope in his voice. "Well, that's good to know."

THEY SAT in the living room that evening, drinking lemonade and watching Kipper batting one of her toy mice around in the box with as much vigor as a hockey player swatting a puck on a rink. David commented, "That cat has very nice detailing: the little stripes on her legs, the black fur on the bottoms of her feet, that light fur on her belly. Her markings remind me of a wild animal's. Why did you name her Kipper?"

"Well, the markings made *me* think of a fish's skeleton. And I was reading some British novel where the characters were always having kippers for breakfast. And cats like fish. I don't know; the name seemed to suit her, somehow."

"I believe," her father intoned, "that kippers are usually smoked herring. Although they can be smoked salmon."

"Well, 'Herring' didn't seem like a good name to me, Dad. She was such a cute little kitten, with a whippy tail like a piece of cord. And huge ears. I used to wake up at night to find her sitting by my head, waiting for me to do something interesting, I guess. Sometimes, she sat *on* my head." David chuckled politely and took another sip of his lemonade.

Deciding to risk something in the conversation, she added a question that had come to mind several times during the twenty-two hours that he had been staying with her. "Why didn't we have pets when Greg and I were kids, Dad? You seem so interested in them now. And we certainly would've loved a dog or a cat. I remember wishing for one on my birthday candles. Lots of times." To her surprise, her heart was thudding, hard. She usually took the path of least resistance with her father, not wanting to incur a flat stare, a lecture, or a bout of unwelcome advice. She wondered if they would ever be able to converse as two adults, as equals. This question might be an invitation to strife between them, again.

But his voice was quiet as he answered, imbued with regret. "Claire, I was barely able to take care of you and your brother, even with Gus and Kate's help. I knew you wanted a pet, but I just couldn't take on one more single thing." He was looking down, running a thumb over the rim of his glass, jiggling one leg nervously. The clock's ticking sounded steady and reassuring. She glanced up to admire again the vibrant carving, the warm molasses tones of the wood, the polished round heads of the tawny owls perched at the roof's peak. Claire wished now that she could've had a cuckoo clock just like it when she was a child, especially since there had been no pets in their house. It would've eased my loneliness, she thought, at least a little. Even if no ghost had come with it.

"I understand, I think," she replied slowly. "And now? Why don't you have pets now?"

"I do! Didn't I tell you? I have an aquarium with neon tetras and angel fish. Rosa is coming in every other day while we're gone to feed them. Pretty things, they are, and so serene. Having an aquarium lowers your blood pressure; did you know that? And Gus is always feeding the birds and building houses for them, so there's a lot of avian activity around the duplex. They're not pets, of course, but they brighten up the place. Even though they're outside and we're inside, of course. Anyway!" He slapped his hands down on his knees. "What do you say we visit that community center you've joined? I need some exercise."

· · ·

WHILE DAVID WALKED around the track that circled the gymnasium from the heights, Claire went to a yoga class. The break from each other will be good for both of us, she told herself. I'll join him on the track once this class is over. Forty-five minutes is not too long to leave him walking alone. She carefully unrolled her new mat and arranged it so it faced the front mirrors, angling it alongside a floorboard to ensure proper, forward-facing alignment. She'd chosen a long, golden-orange mat, much more cheerful than the dull black one belonging to the community center that she had borrowed during the first class. Who wants a matte black mat? she asked herself, pleased at this wordplay that no one but she would ever know about. The answer came to her effortlessly. Darth Vader, of course.

Afraid that she would burst into laughter if she thought again about Darth doing yoga, she seated herself in the classic cross-legged position, palms cupping knees, and considered her new purchase. The nubby surface of the mat made her think of the corn on a cob that her father had eaten at the fair, or perhaps of a cobblestone street in which each rounded "stone" was a smooth golden nugget. Yellow bricks, golden cobbles, a road paved with gold… Her thoughts wandered, and she allowed them their freedom.

One of the aspects of her current life that she most enjoyed was the spaciousness of her mind and thoughts. In recent years, her job had jammed its way into her consciousness insistently, nagging her, poking her, raking her with fear and uncertainty, popping her eyelids wide open at night as if they had been pulled by a wicked string. And she had felt helpless to control her own mind. She recalled Molly's soft voice during corpse pose at the close of her first class: "Let your thoughts be like clouds. Let them go." That advice, which would have been as impractical as "fly to Alpha Centauri" in the past, seemed remotely possible now. She would stretch and strengthen her creaky body, and she would stretch and strengthen her stiff, pain-wracked brain.

With that resolution, she sat up straighter on her new mat, dropped her shoulders away from her ears, tipped her heavy head backward, and finally closed her eyes, the better to envision a mackerel sky rippled with twilight shades of rose and cobalt. Or maybe just a plain, pale sky against which the clouds formed little contrast. That would be a start.

"I LIKE YOUR COMMUNITY CENTER," her father told her that evening over their dinner of French toast and scrambled eggs. He loved to make French toast and had a time-honored method that he was happy to tell any onlooker about in great detail. Claire was just grateful that he'd offered to make the meal, lifting a bit of responsibility from her.

She popped a forkful of egg into her mouth and chewed longer than strictly necessary. "Really? I mean, I'm glad you like it. I thought you might consider it to be a...a...an unnecessary thing." Rats, she thought. Another bout of "chase the word." I'm so *sick* of that. Under the table, Lute licked his lips loudly.

"An extravagance? A luxury?" he jumped in, too helpfully. "No, I think it's great. Lots of diversity in the activities, the people, the equipment. While I was walking, I looked down from the track onto that divided gymnasium below and saw teenagers shooting baskets, little children learning gymnastics, women in some kind of exercise dance class, seniors playing pickleball...at least, I think it was pickleball. I've never been quite sure what pickleball is. Anyway, everyone was moving, everyone was having a good time. It was nice to see all of that energy being expended in a positive way. How long does your membership last?"

The last question came so abruptly that Claire was caught off guard. "Three months."

"Three months? Why, that's hardly any time at all. Surely it would've been a better deal to buy a full year? That's usually the way those things work. The longer the membership, the more economical it is." He had laid his fork on the side of his syrupy plate and was staring at Claire, mouth pursed.

"I, I didn't know if I'd like it," she stuttered, "or how much I'd use it. And a full year is expensive." She swallowed hard and tried to muster an attitude that suited the adult that she was. "It was an experiment."

"And a successful one, I'd say! That's apparent already. Your shoulders weren't hunched up after the yoga class like they usually are. You stood up straight…for a while, anyway. And you can take Scott when he comes to visit, show him that physical activity is a normal thing for healthy people. I don't know that Greg is much of a role model in that department—he's looking pretty slack these days—and who knows about Grace. She's thin, but that's not the same thing as fit. Tell you what, daughter; when that membership expires, I'm going to send you a check to extend it. Will you let me do that? I'd like to."

Claire bit back her desire to say, "No! No, thanks. I can take care of myself." Surprisingly, she found another, contrasting response arising—"Dad, you're taking care of me! You noticed something about me to praise. Yes, thank you. I would be happy to receive your gift." Realizing that she could not possibly actually say either of these things to her father, she rephrased the second, benevolent one into something appropriately bland. "Thanks, Dad. That would be very nice. I appreciate it."

She watched as he slid himself forward on his chair to fetch a small black pocket calendar from his hip pocket.

"Could you please hand me a pen there, daughter?" he said, indicating the mug full of writing utensils next to Claire. His fingertips deftly flipped pages. "I want to make a note of that."

He also insisted on rinsing the plates and silverware for the dishwasher and cleaning the electric skillet, too. "You go relax or read or something. This won't take long. I like to be useful. Go on." And he made a shooing gesture with the hand that wasn't holding a sticky, chocolate-colored plate under the running tap.

Claire decided to give Marguerite a call from the bedroom and find out how her friend's classes were going. She was amazed, actually, at how little she had thought of that ship sailing off without her for the first time in decades, if she included her years as a student along with her years as a teacher. The timing of these visits was great, she thought to herself as she closed the door behind her. Even if having Dad as a houseguest is a tad stressful.

She punched in Marguerite's number, one of the few she knew by heart, noticing that Tamsin was reclining on one of the pillows, front paws outstretched, looking royal. "Hi, gorgeous," she whispered to Tam while the phone rang.

"Claire! How are you, you woman of leisure, you?" Marguerite's voice danced and teased.

"Leisure! You call having houseguests for five days straight 'leisure'? One of them being my father? My father, Margo. You've met my father, so you know what I'm referring to." The unfairness of this rankled immediately, requiring her to add, "Although I have to say that the visit has gone pretty well so far. Quite well, if only the ghosts would behave."

"Oooh, a ghost has shown up? Fantastic! Tell me about it, sister."

Claire launched into a humorous narrative of the ghost playing under the sheet while she and her father were making up the bed with fresh linens, prompting loud laughter from her friend. "A ghost playing with a sheet. What could be more appropriate?" Claire said in summary. "But seriously, I don't know how I'm going to explain any possible future supernatural occurrences. Dad didn't buy my theory that Tam was responsible, especially since she had obviously been asleep on the porch the entire time. If something else happens, I'm sunk."

Margo had tamped down her laughter enough to speak. "Why will you be sunk?"

"Well, because I won't have a reason that he will accept. My dad doesn't believe in ghosts, I'm pretty sure. He's a scientist, through and through."

"Then what do you have to worry about? The ghosts aren't your responsibility or your fault. They came to the house without an invitation, and you're dealing with them. That's it. You don't have to explain or convince or anything like that. I'd say, if something happens, it happens."

Claire let her friend's opinion sink in and waited for her own reaction to rise to the surface. Often, there was a delay in processing this these days, especially when she was dealing with other people.

"You know what, you're right, Margo. You're absolutely right. He's an adult, I'm an adult—he can deal with whatever might happen. And speaking of dealing with things, tell me about the beginning of the semester. How's it looking so far?"

They chatted for another ten minutes about faulty class lists, confusing school policies, and problems with textbook orders. "But there's always that surge of energy at the beginning of the semester, and I do like that," Margo added. "While it lasts. Which isn't nearly long enough. Where is my energy at mid-term time? Locked in a storage cupboard somewhere, I think."

Claire noticed that she herself felt an intense surge of relief rather than of energy. Safely out of the hurly-burly. "When you need a break in October or November, you come visit me, my friend," she said softly. "Right after your classes are over for the day. I'll make us both some tea, and we'll have cookies—homemade ones involving chocolate in some form. And I'll build a fire for us. A fire in the afternoon. Doesn't that sound heavenly?" And Marguerite agreed heartily that it did.

Then Claire reminded her friend that she and Jason were invited to the barbecue at Greg's house the next evening. After hearing Margo's assurance that they planned to attend, Claire said that she'd better return to her father, and they said their goodbyes.

When she reentered the living room, she found David crouched in front of the TV set, flipping through the DVD cases that were stored in a tiny plastic crate there, while Lute tried to lick his face. He was gently holding Lute off with one palm against the dog's shoulder. "Care to watch TV for a little while, daughter? Some of these discs are Kate's, aren't they? Maybe something light would be good this evening." He patted Lute absently while he turned a DVD case over to read the back copy.

Claire nodded, remembering how the ghosts had acted out during her last session with the TV. "Sure, Dad. You choose something, and we'll watch it together."

CHAPTER 16

*H*er father's choice was an episode of *Partners in Crime*, a BBC series from the early eighties based on Agatha Christie's husband-and-wife detective team of Tommy and Tuppence Beresford—Kate's discs. Claire seated herself on the couch next to David as the opening credits rolled, trying to monitor all parts of the room without arousing suspicion. The show was the same vintage as *Scarecrow and Mrs. King*, it featured a male/female partnership, and it was an adventure program of sorts. The ghosts were bound to be attracted to it. Realizing that she was holding herself in an attitude of iron tension, she concentrated on relaxing her shoulders, her legs, her clenched hands. She slipped into Ujjayi breathing, thinking that this would calm her mind. Her father turned to her and asked, "What's the matter? Are you getting a cold?"

"No, I'm fine. Just trying to relax."

"Hmph. Well, what is there to be nervous about, I'd like to know?" He clasped his hands together over his almost-flat stomach and settled back in the couch. "These types of shows always end well. That's one of their attractions, in my opinion. You don't have to watch them in a state of dread like you do so many current series and movies. You can be assured that everything will turn out fine. So unlike real life."

Claire's head swiveled at that last comment. Her father had always seemed in control of every situation that his life had flung at him. Even the loss of his young wife. Could it be that he sought out comfort, too? Forgetting about the ghosts for a moment, she studied her father's profile: the neck only slightly sliding into wattles, the prominent chin, the aquiline nose with a dent at the tip, the gray eyes so like hers (now fixed on the TV screen), the dark hair beginning to go salty at the temples.

"What?" he asked without turning.

"Nothing, nothing," she said hurriedly, slewing her gaze away from him. "I was just thinking about what you said. That's one of the great things about mysteries for me. The answer comes at the end and all is explained. In real life, you don't even know when the end is, usually. And so much is messy and uncertain."

"Hmm. You're probably on to something." He stirred uneasily, rearranging the square throw pillow that he'd placed earlier at the small of his back. "Let's watch now and talk later. We might miss some clues if we're chatting."

"Right." Claire subsided. Quietly, she waited for a supernatural event of some kind, sure that one would occur. But the only coolness came from the humming air conditioner, which made the dialogue hard to discern. Lute slept flat out on his side at their feet, undisturbed. The cuckoo caroled eight, with vigor. The floor lamp radiated bright light with nary a shimmer to be seen. Her skin was chilly, yes, but only from unmet anticipation. *Nothing doing*, she thought to herself. *And I was so sure they'd come. Well, this will be easier.*

But so much less exciting, another voice, perhaps not her own, sighed in her consciousness.

THE NEXT MORNING, Claire limped into the study, feeling an ache in her lower back and wobbliness in her knees from the unaccustomed exercise. For some reason, she felt more discomfort after last night's yoga class than she'd had after the first one. How discouraging. She recalled a robot Halloween costume she had constructed as a child with Kate's help that had consisted of cardboard boxes (various sizes) with holes cut in each end that she could slip her arms and legs through, plus one large box with hinges for her torso. Kate had strapped her in and sent her out into the darkness on Halloween night with Greg. The costume had made her walk stiffly as she made her way from house to house trick-or-treating, with Greg always ahead of her on the sidewalk, exhorting her to hurry.

Yet as an eight-year-old, she had been warm and solid and wiggly inside, ready to spring off in any direction. This morning, she felt like she *was* that costume, the boxes loosely strung together, with no one inside. Rattly. Empty. Ready to collapse at the slightest provocation.

This moment of gloom enveloped her before she was fully aware of its strength. Just because of a little stiffness from yoga, she told herself firmly. She disliked the phrase "buck up," yet felt that in this case, it might be good advice to give herself. At least she hadn't been overcome by wave after wave of emotion after this second yoga session, as she had been after the first one. She didn't know whether to feel grateful or disappointed about that. Her sobs would've been hard to explain to her father, certainly.

She turned on the computer, checked her email, and found a message from Sarah that reminded her of the time of their meeting at Sarah's apartment, provided her with the address, and ended with the phrase, "This is going to be interesting!" echoing her thought from the night before. Well, yes. And possibly illuminating. But more likely crushing. She'd have to snatch some time to compose a list of questions for the artistic director, Roger McMaster. Some tact and delicacy would be called for in this situation. Well, Sarah would be there, too, to help smooth the way between Claire and this prickly Roger. She wondered how anyone had the nerve to be prickly. It was tough enough to get along with people when you were shy and kind and overly accommodating, with porous boundaries.

Kipper ambled into the room, announcing her presence with a few comments and swinging her tail like a buccaneer swings a cutlass. Upon reaching Claire, she switched modes from piratical to childlike, rearing up with her front paws extended and an entreating expression on her dainty face. She always asked if she could come onto Claire's lap rather than simply jumping up uninvited—ever since she had made that leap and landed in a small plate of cottage cheese that Claire had been balancing, surprising them both greatly.

Once up, Kip thwacked Claire several times with that striped tail, engaged her soft purr, and settled down over Claire's thighs, paws tucked in demurely and eyes closed. Claire found that she could still reach the keyboard if she arranged her arms on either side of her recumbent pet. She bent to bury her face for a moment in the ticked fur of Kipper's sweet shoulders, which smelled of beeswax and bayberry. Who could resist such displays of affection from lovely Kipper?

Claire turned her attention to the mundane process of searching the Internet for baked bean recipes, having recalled in the middle of the previous night that she'd promised to make this dish from scratch for their barbecue that evening. The first recipe she found began with the instruction "place navy beans in a large bowl, cover with water, and soak overnight." The second said the same thing in slightly different words, and the third. "Soak overnight!" she lamented aloud to her cat. "I'm doomed!"

Lifting a protesting Kip against her shoulder, she got up from the computer and sought out her father, who was drinking coffee in the breakfast nook. (Gus had thoughtfully left the cone, filters, and the ground coffee for David, realizing that they wouldn't be needed at Greg's house.) She set Kip in the open window. "Dad, I need to make a quick trip to the grocery store today. To buy baked beans for the barbecue. If the deli doesn't have them, I'm going to have to buy canned. I'll probably never hear the end of it from Greg if he finds out. Who knew that you have to soak beans overnight before cooking them!" Her annoyance with herself for not finding a recipe earlier was strung through her words, making them edgy.

Her father pulled out the chair below the wall phone for her. "Okay, I'll come with you. I'm going to make a fruit salad. We need to have something healthy to counteract all of the chips and brats and pop and such. Don't worry about the baked beans. The canned kinds are much better than they were when you were little. And we can doctor them up. Do you have brown sugar and ketchup? I know that you have maple syrup." He gave her a sideways smile, as if they were co-conspirators. "Believe me, Greg will never know. And your secret is safe with me."

Claire sank gratefully into the chair. "Thanks, Dad. You know how Greg can get ahold of things and not let go of them for a long, long time. I have all of those ingredients except for the ketchup. And I can help you cut up the fruit. Working in the kitchen won't make a very dramatic end to your stay here, though. Once we get done, we can…" she searched mentally for possibilities. She found that she genuinely wanted to offer an activity or event that would please her father—for his sake rather than for hers.

"Daughter, just being with you is fine with me. That's special enough, believe me." Seemingly embarrassed over this sentiment, he ducked his head to take a sip of his coffee. He had chosen the pale orange Ten Chimneys mug, too, purchased after a tour of the Lunts' home in Wisconsin. What was it about that mug that made everyone choose it?

Claire pressed her lips together to keep her relieved smile from becoming large and thereby alarming her father. "Okay, then. The grocery store it is." After only a slight pause, she added, "My, that coffee smells good." This changed the subject as deftly as she was able with her current level of clumsiness. "Do you think I'd like it?" Claire looked around as if for someone else; she had spoken without any consciousness of doing so until the words were out, as open as a child's.

"Well, you like coffee-*flavored* things, don't you? So I bet you're ready for the real thing. With sugar and some half and half. Coffee might help ward off those headaches of yours. You sit, and I'll make some for you."

He hummed tunelessly as he heated water in the kettle, arranged the unbleached paper filter in the cone, set the cone carefully over the Gunflint Trail mug, dampened the filter, spooned in the coffee, and created a little shallow spot in the coffee's center. Claire waited, just as she'd been instructed to do, feeling her bad mood gently break apart and dissolve under the comfort of her father's concern for her. Geez, it felt good to be taken care of. Even middle-aged people need that sometimes, she told herself wistfully. It's not a sign of weakness, or dependency, or anything like that.

"Okay, come watch what I'm doing here." A divine scent arose as David slowly poured steaming water from the copper kettle over the grounds, letting the fluid column wet the burnt-brown coffee in its filter and sink into the hollow in the middle. The trickling sound of the liquid making its way through the cone made Claire's mouth water unexpectedly. She stood beside her father, listening to his stream of coffee-making instruction, which flowed along with the water from the kettle's notched spout. "Be sure that all the ground coffee is wetted. Pour in concentric circles. Slowly, slowly—that's the key. Patience makes a good cup of coffee."

"Who's Patience?" Claire couldn't help herself. He had set that up so beautifully.

"Ha, ha. Clever girl." Her father's voice held a hint of amusement and another of annoyance, twisted together like a multi-colored wire. "And of course, you'll need to buy coffee that's the right grind for a cone and filter paper like this. You can grind it yourself in the supermarket. Something between fine and medium is the best, in my opinion. And be sure to get unbleached filters since the bleach imparts a nasty taste to the coffee. Not to mention, you don't want to support the completely unnecessary use of bleach! Why use a harsh substance like bleach to whiten a piece of paper that's going to be dyed brown by the coffee anyway? Sometimes I just despair about the level of people's intelligence." He was staring into the cone, waiting for the last of the water to seep through the filter.

She peered, saw that the process was complete, and shook her father's elbow lightly. "Hey, you awake? Maybe you need this cup more than I do!"

Her father came back to the kitchen from wherever he had mentally traveled. "No, no, this one is yours. I suggest at least a spoonful of sugar since you're new at this. And don't be shy about using the half and half. Although how you reached the age of forty, including two years spent in grad school, without drinking coffee, I don't know…" He slid the mug gently along the counter toward her. Curls of steam arose from the rich, dark liquid within.

"Forty-two." Claire picked up a spoon and dipped it into the bag of sugar she had fetched from an upper cupboard.

"What?"

"I'm forty-two. And a half. I'll be forty-three in March."

"Well, of course you are. I know your age, daughter. I meant that forty is a kind of milestone, and if a person hasn't taken up coffee-drinking by then, she's not likely to, ever!" David frowned as if daring her to challenge that pearl of wisdom and picked up his own mug. "But you might prove to be the exception. As in so many things."

Claire added a generous dollop of half and half after the sugar, watched it disappear momentarily under the coffee's surface and then bloom up like a cast spell, stirred, and raised the cup to her lips. The sip she took was small, uncertain. The coffee might still be burning hot. It might be bitter. It might be caustic. But it was delicious, as she had somehow felt in her bones that it would be. Brown, deep, homey. A long-lost memory of her mother bending to let Claire sniff the ground coffee in a decorated blue tin that had once held caramels flashed through her mind, as intense as sunlight. "Ah," she sighed involuntarily. "Good save, Dad." And she took another sip of the coffee that he had made for her.

AFTER THE TRIP to the store and a quick lunch, they began preparations for the barbecue sides dishes, beginning with the baked beans. Claire had recalled seeing a crockpot in the basement and had brought it up and cleaned it carefully, thinking that it would be the perfect receptacle for both warming and transporting the beans to Greg's house. She opened the three large cans of baked beans—Boston variety, at her father's urging—and poured them one at a time into the crockpot. Tamsin trotted up from the basement and took her place at Claire's feet, staring up with a clear sense of entitlement.

David paused in his search for the brown sugar to comment on this. "Don't tell me that the stand-offish cat likes baked beans!"

Claire was holding a foil envelope of cat treats. "No. Well, I don't know, actually, since I never offered her any. But whenever I open a can, she comes hurrying in here and waits like that. I figure that Aunt Kate must've given her something tasty from a can, so if it's not tuna that I'm opening, I give her one of these little treats. And Kip, too, if she shows up."

"Claire, you realize, don't you, that this cat is training *you*! Honestly, who's in charge here?"

"She is, I guess. I mean, just in this particular situation. She's gone through so much—losing Aunt Kate, having to live with me and my animals, sharing a house that she must think is hers. I can't stand having her watch me, expecting a treat of some kind, and then disappoint her by offering nothing. And that's not the way to win her over, either," Claire added defensively. "Remember, I'm the one who has to live with her for the rest of her life." She bent to offer Tam the treat and then stroked the cat's forehead lightly with one index finger while Tam munched the fish-shaped morsel.

"She doesn't look particularly grateful," David poured ketchup into a large measuring spoon and shook it into the crockpot. "She's living here on a Claire Bracken grant, whether she knows it or not." He stirred the ketchup into the beans and added in a gentler voice, "Although I can see why you don't want to find another home for Kate's pet. She's pretty, too, with that blue-gray fur. Just don't let her gain the upper hand—that's my advice."

"Too late. How much brown sugar and maple syrup?" Claire washed her hands again and then plugged in the crockpot while Tam swayed over to the twinned kitchen windows, leapt lightly into the nearest one, and settled down for an afternoon sunbath. The muted sound of mourning doves calling added to the sense of drowsy, late summer well-being. David and Claire exchanged small smiles and got back to work.

Once the beans were warming, allowing the flavors of the newly added ingredients to meld, according to David, they began preparing watermelons, oranges, pineapples, and mangos for the salad. The bamboo cutting board he was using was soon swimming with pinkish juice from the melon slices he had stacked neatly upon it. He had chosen local watermelons from a roadside stand, thumping them and listening intently, and the melons cracked open under the knife, showing their ripe interiors blushingly.

Claire, peeling oranges, wiped the side of her cheek on her sleeve. An aromatic burst of juice had erupted from the orange as she'd pulled a spiral away with her paring knife, spraying her face in a fine mist. She could feel it beginning to dry into a tacky patch alongside her cheekbone already. "It'll be nice to spend some time with Grace," she started to say, but then stopped in confusion.

A low, irritated meow arose from Tamsin, drawing Claire's attention. The cat was standing now, back arched, leaning against the window screen and facing into the kitchen as if avoiding an unwanted caress. A ripple of apprehension and excitement raced through Claire. She licked her lips, her mouth suddenly dry. Someone had arrived.

Tamsin's eyes were slitted in annoyance, her tail slightly puffed, although not in full bottlebrush mode yet. As Claire watched, Tam flattened her ears against her skull. The plain, cream-colored curtains that were hanging on either side of her filled, flapped, subsided, and filled again, making a sound like a sail luffing. The curtains at the open window next to the one she occupied hung straight and still. Tam huffed and growled, then shot a paw out—bat, bat, bat. As quick as a prizefighter, she slapped at whoever had approached her. Claire saw nothing, but obviously, Kate's cat was dealing with pesky and unwanted attentions. Poor Tamsin, she thought. Another intruder to deal with.

Claire opened her mouth to speak, but before she could form a word, Tam jumped from the sill and stalked by father and daughter, stamping each foot audibly on the maple flooring, her bristled tail lashing. Claire and David wordlessly followed the path she had taken across the kitchen to stand side by side in the doorway, watching her march through the dining room, then the living room (scattering Lute), and finally the sunroom at the far side of the house.

She raked the sisal-covered post of the new cat tower with her front claws, taking possession, and then leapt to the platform, her gaze jumping from one sparrow at the feeder outside to another. Now that she'd left her visitor behind, her demeanor and actions calmed. Her tail twitched and flipped, normal-sized now. She chattered at the birds.

"Lookee there, Dad," Claire said, too heartily. "She likes the tower we built!" In the living room, Lute's furry rump was just visible under the couch, but Claire didn't draw her father's attention to her worried dog.

David turned to eye her, his face pale and slack with surprise. His whiskers showed up against the skin of his cheek unusually well, like iron filings on paper. Claire managed to think, he didn't shave this morning—he must really feel as though he's on vacation!

He returned to the windows and examined the curtains that had taken on a life of their own while the other pair had stayed lanky. Obviously, all four panels were made of the same fabric and subject to the same breeze or lack thereof. Outside, the insects' whirring zither-sounds, joined by the whooping call of a police siren, seemed to grow louder in contrast to the kitchen's silence. David let a curtain panel fall from his fingers and returned to the counter where he and Claire had been working a moment before.

Across the counter, watermelon seeds were freshly strewn, damp and dark. And the outermost slice of watermelon in the stack was riddled with holes, as if someone had poked out each seed with a quick and exploratory finger.

"Daughter," David thundered. "What the hell is going on here?" His face was now blotchy red and pink, almost matching the watermelon he was referring to. Hands on hips, David was an imposing figure of wrath, disbelief, and outrage.

Claire shrugged with deliberate nonchalance. "I really don't know, Dad. But I do intend to find out." After a beat, she added firmly, "After all, it is my house now. My responsibility." And she picked up the half-peeled orange and sticky paring knife and resumed her work.

CHAPTER 17

*C*laire set her plate down near the corner of the square, tippy table and took the chair next to Grace's, receiving a shy smile from her former sister-in-law in response. Greg had supplemented the classic picnic table in his expansive backyard with a card table and a flock of ribbon-style lawn chairs in order to make one long table that would accommodate all eleven guests. To his credit, he hadn't required that the three children—Scout and two of his friends from down the street—form a "children's table." The kids were interspersed among the grown-ups as they wished, forming an intergenerational group that warmed Claire's heart. She found herself enjoying the fact that all of her family members were sitting down to a meal together, and the friends who had joined them just made the gathering that much lighter and more festive. Friends kept the familial fireworks from flying since no Bracken enjoyed making a scene in public.

"Grace, it's so good to see you," Claire said, and left it at that.

"You, too! This was a great idea. Whoever it was."

Willowy Grace had a plate in front of her that held only a spring roll with its adjacent pool of peanut sauce, a chunk of cornbread, and some fruit salad. Grace used to have a more robust appetite, Claire mused. She spoke up over that thought.

"Greg's idea, I think. He wanted to get everyone together before Dad and Gus go back to St. Louis tomorrow." She shifted in her chair, then found herself saved from further awkwardness by David, who had taken his place at the head of the picnic table at Greg's urging and was now standing, plastic cup of beer in hand. Gus was the only one in the family to pray at gatherings such as this; the others toasted.

"To friends and family," he intoned. "May we always continue to learn and grow."

Amid general cries of "Hear, hear!" the guests raised their cups dutifully and prepared to drink. Greg's voice rang above the others, teasing and affectionate. "What's that, the official toast of teachers? How about the rest of us mere mortals?" Laughter greeted this statement as people stirred, leaned forward, and picked up utensils, already eyeing their entry point into the meal: brat or baked beans or coleslaw or what have you.

David glowered at his son. "Well, maybe it is, or should be! After all, there are a number of teachers in this group. And everyone could benefit from the sentiment." He took a seat in a royal blue captain's chair and tossed a small chunk of cornbread into his mouth, gesturing that everyone should begin as well.

Scout piped up. "Grandpa's a teacher, and Marguerite, Dr. Lu, other Dr. Lu..." (His friends' parents were both professors at different private colleges in St. Paul.) He faltered. "Claire? Are you still a teacher?"

She felt her face flushing. Good question...

Gus, across the table from Claire, jumped into the breach.

"Of course, she is, Scotty. Think of all the things she has taught you through the years. That alone makes her a teacher."

"Then so is Mom, and Dad, and you, Grandpa Gus. And Han, who taught me how to play backgammon, sort of, and Liling. She taught me…"

"My point exactly, grandson," David interjected smoothly. "We're all teachers and all students, really." He sought out Claire's eyes and smiled only with his eyes, letting her know that he was supporting her from his place at the head of the table all the way to her seat alongside its foot.

"So how is the sabbatical going?" Han and Liling's father asked her.

"Excuse me?" She froze, her plastic fork hovering over the largest compartment of her plate. The sound of Marguerite's laughter, followed by Gus's and Jason's, floated by her. They were clearly deep in their own conversation, so there would be no help from that quarter.

Dr. Lu spoke again. "Your sabbatical. How is your work going?"

"Oh, I'm on a leave of absence, not a sabbatical. So there's no work. No academic work, that is. Although there is a topic that I've begun researching informally." You are such a fraud, Claire told herself. Ghosts have nothing to do with your teaching and never will.

Dr. Lu drew back, embarrassed. "Of course, of course. I just assumed from what I was hearing… Stupid, really, to make that assumption." He straightened and grasped the edges of his plate lightly, as if to find ballast. "I hope your time off is refreshing for you."

She smiled mechanically to let him know that she hadn't taken offense. Sabbaticals, usually available to a college-level instructor every seven years, involved a break from teaching but work on some kind of research project that would enrich the person's teaching. They were also paid, although not always the full salary, depending on the school and the seniority of the person taking the sabbatical. She had taken one sabbatical but absolutely could not have waited for the next one to withdraw from the classroom. A leave of absence was unpaid, but the leave-taker was expected to return to work when it was over, the job held for that instructor. She envisioned a book with a marker, holding her place. Yet inwardly, she shrank away from ever taking up that particular book again.

Well, there was no need to dwell on that. She had almost a full year of leave ahead of her. As well as two more paychecks because she had chosen to receive her salary year-round whether she taught summer school courses or not. She tugged her thoughts away from that subject and back to this evening, this gathering, this table. This slant of light nudging its way under a bank of clouds, peach below, dove-gray above.

Claire launched into her own meal as if this were her first food in a long while. The canned baked beans did taste better than she remembered, lifted up, no doubt, by her father's additions. She glanced up the table and saw Greg gather some beans from his stamped paper plate and pause, listening to Liling on his left. The utensils were made of a bluish, translucent plastic, and the brown and golden beans actually shone through the bowl of the spoon in the mellow light of six o'clock. He popped the bite in his mouth, nodded energetically at the little girl, and gestured with a shrug of his shoulder toward his son on the opposite side of the table.

This is ridiculous, Claire thought. Waiting for some kind of judgment from Greg, which will probably never come. Upset by a stray remark from a perfectly nice professor, who is the father of my nephew's best friends. Man, I've got a lot of work to do... She began sawing at her bratwurst, the serrations on her plastic knife scoring the paper plate with long, angry-looking cuts. The jangle of voices and laughter were getting on her nerves now, causing a sense of futility and discouragement to lap higher, up against the base of her throat now. You need to get out more, she told herself disapprovingly. A simple barbecue with family and friends shouldn't cause this kind of reaction. She wondered mournfully if she would ever be able to hold onto a buoyant mood for more than twenty-two minutes or so.

The piece of bratwurst in her mouth seemed too tough to chew and swallow, but she persevered, finding that a sip of lemonade reactivated her saliva and allowed her to move on to the fruit salad that she and her father had made. Brats were just not friendly to nervous people like herself, she decided. She had visions of sausage segments skidding across the white paper tablecloth and into the lap of some unsuspecting person nearby. Of knocking over a bendable cup of lemonade into the bowl of potato chips in front of her. Of choking on a stubborn bite, drawing the concerned, embarrassing attention of everyone at the barbecue.

Who needs ghosts to create images? She wondered silently. I can create my own visions of things that have not happened—all small dining disasters, apparently—without even trying.

Vowing to redirect her attention to others, she turned to Grace. "Did you enjoy the wedding?" she thought to ask.

"Pardon me?" Grace's fair skin appeared milky in the thinning light of evening.

"The wedding you went to earlier in the month. When Scott was with me. It was in Wisconsin, wasn't it?' She felt a flash of amazement that so much had happened to her in such a short time. Why, she'd had the clock in her home only a day or two then.

Grace paused. The warm breeze ruffled her silvery-blonde hair, which was cut fashionably short. "Well, it was a lovely wedding in itself. Another Realtor that I've known for years was the bride. I'd never met her fiancé, but he seemed nice. They looked so happy together, beaming after the ceremony was over, lighting candles, feeding each other cake, so gently. Dancing alone while everyone watched." In a burst, she added, "But weddings make me sad, to be honest. The people getting married don't know what they're getting themselves into." Her voice had a scratchy quality that Claire had not heard before.

She blinked and spoke quickly to cover up the surprise she felt. "Well, I see what you mean. But maybe that's where a leap of faith is absolutely necessary." Of course, Grace's marriage had not lasted, yet she'd always seemed like a positive person in her own quiet way. Not bitter about her divorce, unfailingly civil and accommodating with Greg. And wonderful Scout had come of her marriage. Claire could not now imagine the world without Scout. He filled up so much space for a small person.

Jason spoke up. "I hope I'm not intruding, but I couldn't help overhearing you. I read once that if you went to a lawyer and said, 'I'm thinking of entering into a legal contract with another person that will make me equally responsible for all of her debts, even if I didn't know about them,' the lawyer would tell you to run like the wind. I've always remembered that." He smiled to soften his words and stirred his baked beans in their compartment.

Marguerite chortled. "That's so romantic, honey."

Jason gave her a wide grin. "Well, I'm just saying…People get desperate and settle for 'good enough' in a relationship, which doesn't turn out to be 'good enough' at all. Or they can get swept away by the romance, marry too quickly, and live to regret it. Of course, that's not everyone's story, thank God.

It's certainly not mine! Marrying you, Margo, was the smartest thing I've ever done."

Marguerite waggled her fingers at him, mollified, and then blew him a little kiss. "Sweetie!"

"All right, you two," Gus chipped in. "Stop right there before you give the rest of us indigestion. I agree with Claire. Hitching your life to someone else's takes a lot of faith. And like you said, Jason, it can cause a world of unhappiness and grief. And not just for the obvious reasons: you find out that you're not suited for one another, or that your spouse hasn't been faithful—something like that. There's the grief that comes when that person is taken from you. Too soon, taken from you." His blue gaze shifted from one person to the other; Claire felt its light touch on her face and shoulders. Gus had lost his beloved Milly in a car accident on icy roads when she was only in her mid-forties. She'd been drinking. Claire could barely remember her. And as for her own mother... Don't! she told herself. Don't let yourself travel there.

Gus was speaking again. "Sorry, sorry! I don't mean to throw a shadow over the party. I just mean that you can't let fear of loss keep you from taking chances, including getting married." His knobby hand reached over the table to squeeze Grace's smooth one. Seconding Claire's earlier thought, he added, "And you got Scotty out of the deal, eh, Grace?"

She jogged his fingers up and down a bit before letting them go. "Not to mention you, Gus! And Claire and David. I have no complaints, believe me. Scott is amazing." For a moment, she appeared as if she had more to say. But then she plucked up the spring roll from her plate and swished it through the peanut sauce, seemingly intent on thoroughly saturating its stubby end. Whatever her final thought had been, she had decided to keep it to herself.

Hmm, thought Claire. There's a story there. No doubt

about it. Maybe she'll tell me one day. And she vowed to invite Grace to something. Lunch or tea, whatever wouldn't be alarming for either one of them. They had never been close during Grace's marriage to Greg, yet ironically, now that the marriage had ended and Greg no longer hovered over them, Claire had the sense that maybe they could be better friends.

Claire felt for a moment that a haze had been swiftly cleared from her vision. Han leaning sideways to speak with Scout, Rose Lu explaining to Gus how she and her husband had made the filling for the spring rolls, Kang Lu joining the tale-telling to remind her of the first, disastrous time that they had attempted the recipe together, Grace getting a pen from her purse and jotting the recipe down on her napkin despite her attachment to her iPhone, David and Greg laughing at Liling's joke, Jason and Marguerite conversing in the joshing, shorthand speech that couples use with one another—they all looked lustrous, intense, brightly colored. Like people in a play whose every utterance was charming or funny or touching.

She was lucky to have them, she realized, and yet, some of them she scarcely knew. What was she waiting for? She was forty-two. Her life was half over. She had a new home, a year off. Some money in the bank. A fascinating mystery to pursue. Impetuously, she patted Grace's back and tipped her head to touch her sister-in-law's, receiving a gentle side hug in return.

Claire picked up her own spring roll, noticing the pinkish shrimp just visible through the tight, translucent rice paper. The slight chilliness under the breeze brought a whisper of autumn to the summery table. Time to dig deep, she promised herself.

. . .

THAT EVENING, after her father had gone to bed, she sat at the kitchen table and wrote about what she had witnessed with him earlier that afternoon. She was confident that Tamsin had been annoyed rather than frightened, and that her behavior would've been the same if a mortal like Scout had petted her without permission. The cat had recovered her composure quickly once she'd left the offending entity behind by sauntering into another room.

And those curtains filling and receding while the others hung still. Claire shivered slightly at the memory and wrote a description that was as accurate and as complete as she could make it. Then she fired off questions on the paper. Was that movement of the curtains undertaken deliberately? Was it some side effect of the ghost's presence, like a strong gust that often sucked the curtains inward against the screens just before a thunderstorm? Was the coldness that Claire had experienced and that many people in the book about Nantucket ghosts had commented on something that happened during every supernatural visit, or only some? Was it an effect that the ghost controlled? ("I don't think so," she wrote in parentheses after that query.) And what in the world was the ghost trying to accomplish by poking the seeds out of the slice of watermelon?

"I think he was playing," Claire wrote. "He wanted to play with Tamsin, and when she wouldn't cooperate, he turned his attention to the watermelon. He's not evil or destructive, just naughty." Feeling that this last word wasn't quite accurate, she added another. "Cheeky."

She blew her bangs off her forehead, tapped her fat Dr. Grip pen on the notebook, and added another observation that had just occurred to her. "I didn't receive any mental images, like I have so often in the past." She recalled telling her literature students, "Look for what's *not* there that you might expect, as well as what *is* there." Yes, that lack of images must be significant. "Why is this?" she jotted down. "Was I too far away? Was it the presence of my father that kept the images at bay?" (No, because he had been there when the memories, or whatever they are, of the sheets blowing on the clothesline had come to mind.) The scent of lime that she had noticed before was absent, as well. "Did the ghost want this encounter to be different from the others?"

She waited, pen in hand, for the next idea to come to her. When it did, she wrote it down slowly. "I need to differentiate between the two spirits, I think. Because I'm sure now that there are two."

She reached for a yellow highlighter and a green one from the mug next to her elbow, then began flipping back through what she had already written, dotting the description of each encounter with yellow or green in the left margin. The pages of *Puck of Pook's Hill* turning, the reassuring caress along her cheek, the phone being taken off the hook—all were green. That ghost was taking care of her in some way in these events. The Sharpies in her pocket, the painting of the moon and stars on the guestroom wall, and today's goings-on were yellow, the actions of the mischievous ghost. Some of the events were less clearly identifiable. Who had flapped the tablecloth the night she had let the clock run down? Probably the green spirit, but she didn't know for sure. And who had been petting Lute while the other spirit watched *Scarecrow and Mrs. King* with her? She hesitantly marked the ghost with Lute, yellow, and the envious one with her, green, mainly because the yellow ghost had been interested in Tam, so it seemed likely that he had wanted to interact with Lute, too. The sheet incident she left unmarked, although she was leaning toward yellow.

"Is that right?" she asked aloud, the last word cracking. "Am I getting warmer?" She gripped the arms of the chair, and waited, straining to capture the least shimmer of light or currents of air.

The only response was the clock singing out from its perch on the living room wall to mark the hour of eleven. No wonder the surface of her eyes felt granulated. And she hadn't yet come up with any questions for cranky Mr. McMaster. Tomorrow would be taken up largely by her father and grandfather's departure, and the appointment with the artistic director was the following morning. Well, she'd find some time tomorrow to consider what she wanted to ask Mr. McMaster. I hope he'll talk with me, she thought. I hope he doesn't bite my head off. And I hope I don't stutter too much!

With that, she slapped her notebook shut and call-whispered, "Lute! Bedtime, pal!" The scrabbling and jingling sounds approaching from the dining room were reassuring. She would've been a lot more scared about the supernatural guests in her home without Lute and the cats' company. "Just another benefit of living with pets, right, Lute?" she crooned when he appeared carrying his red Kong, eyes already sleepy. "It'll be three against two, I guess, once Dad and Gus go home." Although, truth to tell, she didn't feel that the ghost were opponents, really. No, not opponents at all. More like... troublesome housemates.

SHE AND DAVID sat in the living room the next afternoon, waiting for Greg and Gus to arrive. Her brother had volunteered once again to drive them all to the airport to make David and Gus's four o'clock flight to St. Louis. Scout had gone home with Grace last night after saying goodbye to his grandfather and great-grandfather. He had hugged them both hard, said, "Come back soon!" frowned, and scuffed his Croc-shod foot in the bland grass to keep from crying. The prospect of first grade beginning on Tuesday was making him emotional, Greg explained after Scout and Grace had departed in her Prius. Although really, no explanation was necessary, Claire thought. Scout loved his grandfathers and was sad to see them go. Wasn't that enough to prompt his mood? Now, remembering that leave-taking, she turned Greg's comment in her mind like she would turn a stone under a lamp and found a more positive side to it: he was being sensitive to the anxiety that his son faced about starting "real" school and making allowances for it. Good man.

David checked his watch again, drawing Claire's attention, then sat up straighter on the futon couch and slid one slender hand around his face as if to check whether he needed a shave. "Well, daughter, this has been a fine visit. Really fine. Thank you for the invitation and for everything you've done while I've been here. Much appreciated, believe me."

"It was my pleasure, Dad. I'm glad that you could come." Claire purposefully had not made it clear whether the "you" referred to both Gus and him or to David alone. (She loved English, including its ambiguities.) And she *had* enjoyed her time with David as well as with Gus. As was so often the case, the thing that you worry about and brace yourself for turns out fine, she mused, and instead, you're blindsided by something you hadn't even imagined. She had realized this during her final years of teaching, and instead of bringing her a sense of calm acceptance—a sunny, "que sera, sera," mindset—it had only fed her anxiety and dread. For good reason, apparently. A quiet student who'd occasionally come for help during office hours had gone on a rampage one day in class, shrieking and swearing after receiving a low score on a ten-point quiz. Completely unexpected, that outburst had been. Claire had given the sailor blouse she had worn that day to Goodwill even though it had been a favorite because she knew that she could never wear it again without recalling the onslaught of rage and profanity directed against her.

The golden cuckoo's bold announcement of half past one swept these thoughts away. "Your brother's late," David muttered. He shifted uneasily, causing Lute to glance up from his place on the rug. Finding a pet hair on his navy polo shirt, David tried to brush it off, to no avail. Apparently, it had knitted its way into the fabric, requiring him to find its free end and tug it out. He laid it carefully on the armrest of the couch. The clock ticked in its tidy, reassuring way, and David latched onto it with his somber gaze, seemingly grateful to have an object to talk about. She was surprised that he had waited until now to refer to it. "Gus mentioned that you'd bought a cuckoo clock. You don't see mechanical clocks very often these days. In fact, you don't even see analog clocks much, never mind the kind that runs on weights and gears and springs. Does it keep good time?"

"Yes, quite good, as long as I adjust it to compensate for humidity. The leaf on the pendulum slides up and down."

"Ah, I understand. During humid times, the pendulum expands and becomes slightly longer, causing the clock to run slow." Lute yawned hugely, making a brief whining sound at the yawn's acme, then flopped on his side and abandoned himself to sleep. "You're aware, aren't you, daughter, that the origins of the cuckoo clock are murky? Very murky."

"Really. News to me. How do you know that, Dad?"

"Oh, I did a little research on them when I found out you had gotten a Black Forest clock. Just out of curiosity. There are several theories about their invention, one having to do with a Bohemian traveler bringing a cuckoo clock to Bavaria in the mid-sixteen hundreds, and the other having to do with a man named..." He trailed off, thinking hard. "Well, I can't remember his name. But he wasn't even born at the time the first known written reference to cuckoo clocks was made, so that theory has fallen into disrepute. And there was no tradition of wooden clock making in Bohemia at that time, either."

"So where does that leave us?" Claire asked, bemused. She admired her father's questing mind, even though the quests he chose were different from her own.

"In the dark," he admitted, examining a fingernail. "It's even possible—probable, according to some sources—that the first makers of wooden clocks tried to replicate the sound of a rooster crowing or a cow mooing rather than a cuckoo calling. But they couldn't get those sounds right, so they settled on the cuckoo." His glance flicked up from his fingertips toward her rocking chair.

Claire chuckled. "Well, the rooster's crow, I can understand. It's another bird, after all, and crowing is cheery. It would get your attention. But a cow mooing? And a tiny cow figure popping out from behind a door? I just don't think that would've caught on."

"No, you're probably right about that. Instead of being something that many tourists bring home from Germany, a cow clock would most likely be a rarity seen only in obscure museums." He cleared his throat with a light growling sound. "As I see it, the 'take away' from that story is, those first clockmakers were flexible. When one thing didn't work out for them, they tried another. Maybe another after that. And voila—or however you say that in German—they ended up with a wonderful invention. A classic!" He gestured in a circular "come on!" manner. "Flexibility and resilience are so important in life. Don't you think?"

Claire felt her love for her father spreading behind her ribs, finding its way outwards. If you knew how to read him, he was a wonderfully supportive parent. "Yes, I do, Dad. I think you are absolutely right about that."

As Greg drove them to the airport, David in front and Gus in the rear with Claire, a brief silence descended. "Is someone meeting you at the airport in St. Louis?" Claire finally asked.

"Yes, Rosa is coming. I believe." The back of David's neat head looked a little self-conscious, somehow.

"That's nice," Claire relied neutrally, and let it go at that.

"I'm thinking of moving back to the Twin Cities, you know," David continued. "I haven't made a firm decision yet, but that's the way I'm leaning. What's your latest thinking on that issue, Gus? Are you ready to return to the frozen north or no?"

Claire felt that she must've done a double-take at this announcement, her chin jerking in toward her chest and her eyes widening. She'd had no inkling that either her father or grandfather was contemplating a return to Minnesota. She turned to Gus.

"Well, I'm still thinking through it," he replied, drawing the words out uncertainly. "There's not much holding me to St. Louis, I guess. I like it all right, but the winters aren't any better than the ones here, in my opinion. They're warmer, for sure, but that means ice, and ice is worse than snow, in my book. And you two are here, and Scott, of course, and Grace. Old friends. Old haunts." He stirred uneasily at that word and cast a worried eye on Claire. "I'm inclined to come back."

"So am I," David announced. "It's settled then. Missouri was an adventure, but Minnesota's home."

"Whoa, whoa," Greg interjected, and actually slowed the SUV he was driving to match his words. "Is that how you decide things? It seems like an awfully important decision to make so quickly. What about the duplex?"

"Oh, the duplex is rented, as you know," David said airily. "And the lease is up in the spring—April, I believe. Perfect time to move. That will give each of us time to sort through our belongings, pack, give things away. I don't have that much, really. How about you, Gus?"

"No, not much. I still have boxes in the basement that were never unpacked in the move to Missouri. Two years is enough time to be sure that I don't need whatever is inside."

"What about Renee?" Greg's question sounded slightly strangled. This situation is slipping away from his control, Claire thought.

"Rosa," David corrected, slightly deflated. Noting this, Greg glanced over at him hopefully. Claire felt a wash of sympathy for this unknown woman. "She's a fine person, and I value her friendship. But," he continued in a stronger voice, "she can come visit. The flights from St. Louis to Minneapolis-St. Paul are really quite reasonable, especially if you can be flexible about your travel dates. And there's always the Internet. Email and FaceTime!" he concluded triumphantly. "Son, surely you wouldn't object to having your old man and your grandfather back in their native land."

"You make the Twin Cities sound like the Old Country or something," Greg sighed. "Of course, I would like you both to move back. And Scott would be over the moon to spend more time with you. I just didn't want you to rush into anything. Act in haste and then regret it later, you know?"

Claire was beginning to take pity on Greg and spoke up to deflect attention from him, as she had when he was a teenager in trouble with their father for staying out too late or getting a poor grade on a geometry test. "We were just talking about this last night, weren't we, Gus? Margo and

Jason and Grace and Gus and I. We started talking about marriage and the conversation expanded. To risk-taking in general."

David spoke up again, softly now. "I just think it would be good to have the whole family together again. It's time for that. Weather, cost of living, taxes—what are those compared with seeing your own flesh and blood regularly?" Claire wondered if he were thinking of Kate as he answered his own question, spreading his palms under the windshield. "Nothing, really. Nothing whatsoever." And he leaned forward, placing his hands firmly on knees, as if to speed the passage of time.

CHAPTER 18

"Sarah, wait a minute," Claire said, but she had hesitated a second too long before speaking, and Sarah was already pushing the doorbell, which produced the classic "bing-bong!" sound from within the depths of the house. The older woman made an "I'm sorry!" grimace and shrugged her shoulders. Blasted stutter, Claire thought, and took a half step back so that she stood partially behind Sarah. A curl of discomfort in her midsection made her think longingly of the small bottle of Tums that she always kept in her purse. The damp breeze stirring under a blank white sky was better than nothing.

The door swung open, and Claire summoned up a stiff smile that she worried might be scary in its inauthenticity. The foreign scent of "other person's house," always different from house to house and especially noticeable during the first visit, reached her. She let Sarah take the lead as the greetings between her new friend and Brian McMaster commenced. Coward, she told herself sternly, and waited for her moment to shake the hand of the man who had retreated into the foyer and waved them in.

He was only about her height, she realized as they shook, and little bit stooped, as if from lack of exercise. His salt-and-pepper hair was clipped and curly, and his dark brown eyes behind half-glasses examined her with a dismaying mixture of intelligence and curiosity. He wore canvas trousers, a plain white Oxford shirt, and a tan cardigan. "Welcome, Ms. Bracken. Won't you two come into the living room and have some tea with me. I try to stop what I'm doing for tea and a snack at around this time. Without the snack, I get crabby. Or so my wife says." His voice was crackly and appealing, like a salt glaze on pottery.

The room he gestured them into was comfortable, with casual furniture and many books lined up properly as well as stacked sporadically on tall shelves. Claire resisted the urge to snoop and instead perched on the edge of an armchair upholstered in worn, tufted fabric the restful green of elm leaves. Only then did she notice that the couch under the front windows was already occupied. Two slender heads arose from two sets of outstretched paws. Greyhounds, one lion-colored and the other a burnt-black shade.

"Oh, what beautiful dogs!" she exclaimed, leaning toward them unconsciously. "Are they rescued track dogs?"

Mr. McMaster had taken his seat beside them, reaching over to toss the paw of the tawny one gently up and down and then encircle the muzzle of the dark one with his large palm and hefty fingers. "Yes, they came to us together, when Raffles was two and Tag was three. That's typical for track dogs. A five-year-old racing greyhound is considered an old man." He continued gazing sideways at his regal dogs, affection for them evident in his softened expression. "They didn't even know how to get into a car or climb a flight of stairs when we first got them. Track dogs live in crates when they're not racing, you know. Let out four times a day for exercise and raced every fourth day. Otherwise, their life is a metal crate." He turned back toward Claire and Sarah. She felt his anger over his pets' stunted early years. "Do you have dogs, Ms. Bracken? You seem to know something about greyhounds."

"Please call me Claire," she managed to get out without a quaver. "I don't know much about greyhounds, only that they tend to be calm, although people often expect them to be high-strung, like thoroughbred horses. And that you should never let them off the leash except in fenced areas."

"Right on both counts. These two spend a lot of time on the sofa, but when we take them to the dog park—watch out! And they're also prey-oriented. I don't think a squirrel or a rabbit has dared to set foot in our backyard since the hounds came to live here." He chuckled.

"My dog is a tireless hunter, too. He's a terrier mix, and quick. But he's never caught anything that I'm aware of. He always gives himself away by barking like a madman before he even begins the chase. Just can't resist, I guess." The dark hound, Tag, jumped gracefully to the floor, approached Claire, and leaned confidingly against her knees. She reached out for him, slowly so he would know what she was planning, and she and Mr. McMaster exchanged the slight smiles of animal-aficionados as she smoothed Tag's forehead and the extra-soft patch of fur at the base of each fragile ear. The homely smell of warm dog arose from him.

"You didn't have dogs when you were at Luna, Brian, did you?" Sarah asked. "I never heard you mention any." Claire had nearly forgotten about Sarah in her rapt interest in the greyhounds. And she'd forgotten to be nervous, as well, she realized. Animals always made her feel more like herself.

"No, I was too busy then—away from home too long. Anne was working full time, and I was working—well, much more than full time. You remember how long the hours were, especially right before an opening night. Life for a dog in our house would've been nearly as bad as the crate." His voice took on a grinding quality. "I missed out on a lot during those years. I wouldn't trade them for anything, of course, but once you step away from that world, you realize just how much went on outside it. Crazy-busy, Luna was. All theaters are, really."

"Yes, I think you're right—Luna *was* a world unto itself," Sarah offered. Both of them quieted as they recalled the theater where they had worked for years, Sarah's tenure overlapping that of Brian.

He roused himself from his reverie after a moment. "Hmm, let me get that tea before we get too deep in conversation. I'll be right back. Please make yourselves comfortable."

He departed for the kitchen, leaving Claire to continue the process of furthering her acquaintance with Tag while Sarah talked softly to both of them. "Brian's wife was a graphic designer before she retired. She used to come to every first night and sit in the back row. Said that that was the only place in the theater that he allowed her to take! He wanted her to come, but not make a big deal of being there. Close, but not *too* close. I always thought that that was the ideal relationship between married people. I've even mentioned it to Alicia. She agrees that we'll need to maintain some healthy space once we get married." Sarah gave a little shiver and rubbed her forearms. "It's only two and a half months until our wedding date." Startled by that realization, she added. "God, we have a lot to do before then!"

Claire smiled. "I'm sure that it'll will be a lovely wedding. Tell me about your plans."

They were still chatting about cake options when Brian returned bearing a tray loaded with an old-fashioned brown crockery teapot, a bowl of sugar, a tiny milk pitcher, three heavy cream-colored mugs, a plate of shortbread cookies, and some scarlet paper napkins. He set the tray down on the coffee table and called the dogs into the hallway, placating them with fresh rawhide chew pieces, white as bleached bones in the gloom, which he'd extracted from his pocket. "I know; our dogs are spoiled. But after what they went through in their first couple of years, we figure that they have some catching up to do. Do either of you want milk or sugar in your tea?"

All three settled back, each with a mug of steaming tea and a shortbread, which looked extra pale against the scarlet of the napkins. "Brian," Sarah began, "We're hoping that you can tell us something about the clock that used to hang in the green room. He Who Will Not Be Named offered it to me right before... before the end of Luna." She hurried on. "I took it because I didn't want it to end up in some trash heap but decided to sell it to Walter Henson because I really had no proper place to hang it. And Claire bought it almost right away." She beamed briefly at Claire as if the younger woman had done something remarkably clever. "The clock has been behaving somewhat unusually since Claire hung it in her home." Brian shifted his gaze expectantly from Sarah to Claire.

Claire's newly relaxed mood twisted upward again. Show time. She made an embarrassing gurgling noise over a sip of tea, swallowed audibly, and launched into speech, feeling like she was being flung by a trebuchet into danger and uncertainty. Brian McMaster had been very pleasant so far, but who knew what would come next? "Yes, well, the clock. It's a beautiful piece of work."

Brian waited, and when nothing else was immediately forthcoming from Claire, he said with a light snap of impatience, "I suppose. If you like that sort of thing. I never paid it much attention, to be honest. I know that some of the actors took a shine to it and used to touch it for good luck before going on stage. But surely you had more on your mind than the superstitions of actors when you and Sarah asked about meeting with me." This last sentence was not a question.

He took another shortbread, and Claire thought that maybe that would keep him in a good mood. She carefully placed her own half-eaten cookie and its napkin on the coffee table in front of her. The fragment of shortbread looked roughly like the state of Minnesota, she noted. Her list of questions was in her purse, and she would appear pretty foolish if she were to retrieve it under Brian's impatient gaze. She had only a vague idea of the questions now. I should've studied my script, she thought sadly, but I didn't have the time. She would have to improvise, doing her best under the circumstances. Just as when she had somehow left important lesson plans in her office and realized it only as she stood in front of a roomful of expectant students. This time, though, she could sense Sarah willing her to succeed from across the room. She could hear the muffled sounds of the greyhounds chewing and snuffling over their pieces of rawhide in the hallway. Acid reflux clawed at her throat.

"Yes, well, ever since I've hung the clock, my house has had some strange occurrences in it, and I was wondering— did you ever get the sense that Luna was haunted?" Oh, lord, that was much more abrupt than she'd intended. Yet maybe that was the best tack to take, anyway. It would save this man some time.

He grew suddenly still, face impassive, hands curved protectively around his mug. Any goodwill that she had generated through her interest in his dogs retreated back toward him and then evaporated, leaving the room's atmosphere dry and sandy. "Haunted?" He paused, then chuckled without mirth and took a small sip of tea. "Maybe you don't realize this, Claire, but almost all theaters are thought to be haunted." His voice and mien were impersonal, and she remembered some of her colleagues whose classrooms she had glimpsed from the hall as she walked by. They protected themselves by taking on this calm, slightly distant demeanor. Very few teachers, least of all Claire, could fault them for this tactic. They were protecting themselves from anger, from discord, and even from a connection with a student that might end in hurt feelings or misunderstandings. And now, Claire was in the student's seat with Brian as her instructor, whether he liked it or not.

In addition, it occurred to Claire that Brian was taking up this role of friendly dispenser of theater lore as he would a mask. What lay behind the genial mask, she had no idea. "And these ghost stories are not surprising, really," he continued, glancing away from her to the bookshelves across the way. "Theaters are usually old buildings. Oftentimes at least one actor or staff person or audience member has died in them, and sometimes, many people have shuffled off this mortal coil in a given theater, just because of the sheer number of people who pass through them. Why, 'the Scottish Play' alone is held responsible for I don't know how many deaths." His smile was grim. "And actors are such hams, really. They would definitely stay in the theater where they performed if they could. That's why we always shine a ghost light at night, after the performances are over."

"What's a ghost light?" breathed Claire. Her fingertips had grown pale and chilly, and not only because of the roaring air conditioner and cooling tea.

"It's just a plain incandescent light bulb on a portable stand. With a cage around the bulb, like a trouble light. Every night, the last person in the theater—usually a stage hand—turns on the light and sets it up in the center of the stage. It's left burning all night long." His eyes and voice were slightly wistful now, as if memories of Luna were working on him the same way they had worked on Sarah at the coffee shop the week before.

"Why? Why is the ghost light there at all?"

"Practical reasons, to start with. Modern theaters are designed to keep natural light from making its way in. All of the light on the stage comes from artificial sources. That means that a dark theater is *dark*—pitch dark. Cave dark. The ghost light is needed to prevent accidents. Anyone in a theater at night without it could easily trip over tools and sets—even fall into the orchestra pit, if there is one."

Sarah offered a comment, her voice teasing. "So the ghost light is really meant to keep new ghosts from being created, right Brian? Keep all of the employees on this side of the Great Hereafter."

He answered her smile with a slight one of his own but then returned to Claire, serious again. "Well, yes, but that's not where the name comes from. He shifted in his chair and pulled the two sides of his cardigan together over his modest paunch. "You have to understand that theater people tend to be a superstitious bunch. Athletes are the same, I've heard, and that makes sense to me, because actors and athletes are both performers. High stakes performers. And with performance comes stress, and that leads to superstition. Good luck charms and rituals and the like.

"A dark theater is unlucky because it's dangerous, and it's also unlucky because if it's dark during the time the performances usually take place—afternoon or evening—then the play has closed. And nothing is worse to an actor—or a director, or an artistic director—than having a play close prematurely. The ghost light keeps that darkness from taking hold. From taking hold of the theater itself or the people who work there. Actors love the light."

"I see." Claire realized that she was "seeing" only because of the light that Brian was offering her, and she felt grateful to him for sharing it with a naïve stranger. His attitude toward her wasn't warm any longer, but he was addressing her questions seriously. And that was more than he would have needed to do, even as a favor to Sarah.

"And there's also the folklore," he rumbled on, "that the ghosts who inhabit a theater need the light so that they can perform on stage after everyone else has left. We give them"—he spread his palms upward, fingers slightly curled —"a chance to act again, at night, unmolested by the living and uninterrupted by whatever takes place in the theater during the days and evenings." He paused. "If you believe in that sort of thing. I'm not sure that I do."

OH, my. Claire had skimmed her informal journal of supernatural events in preparation for composing the now-forgotten questions, scanning the paragraphs that caught her attention, including the one that described her first supernatural encounter, when the pages of Kate's book had turned on their own and unfamiliar images had arisen in her own mind. Images of dainty lights outlining bare tree branches, unfamiliar purple flowers, and fair hair teased into elflocks, while a flute spun out a single strand of song. Her intuition rose up and handed her the answer as if it were a rolled parchment tied with a green ribbon. These images, artful and delicate and lovingly crafted, came from the stage rather than from real life. From a play in performance.

The play was *A Midsummer Night's Dream*. The images had focused on the fantastic appearance of fairies, on enchanted woods lit by fireflies, on magical purple flowers. And the book that had prompted their appearance had been *Puck of Pook's Hill*. Kipling had taken the character of Puck from *A Midsummer Night's Dream* and made the elf his own, just as four hundred years earlier, Shakespeare had taken the same character from English folklore and recreated him for the *Dream*.

She sucked in air and black dots jigged in front of her eyes. Not a migraine, please, not now, she prayed, and no hyperventilating, either. She reached forward to set her mug down, almost missing the edge of the coffee table as she did so. "I think that at least one of the ghosts that came with the clock is an actor rather than a staff person or theater-goer." Her voice grew stronger with the next thought. "In fact, I'm certain of it." The flute melody still swayed in her memory like a rope made of mist. She almost laughed out loud in the delight of finding this connection, in the surge of energy she was feeling. The black dots had utterly vanished. Looking from Brian to Sarah, she said, "The ghost is an actor who played Puck in the *Dream*. Do you have any idea of who that might've been? I mean, who that *is*?" She hastily described that first, fateful meeting, stammering a little and glossing over the images she had experienced in just a few sentences.

Silence followed for a long, long moment. Sarah was twisting her engagement ring and shifting uneasily in her chair. Then Brian spoke, his voice clipped and formal, his expression impassive. "Ms. Bracken, do you know how many people, both male and female, played Puck in Luna? That theater was built in 1922. *A Midsummer Night's Dream* is one of Shakespeare's most popular plays, and it was staged at Luna literally dozens of times. And let's say that this ghostly actor *had* played Puck and was drawn to the book because of the title. How can you be sure that the production of the *Dream* that he or she acted in was even staged at Luna? Hmmm?" He raised his eyebrows and gestured his impatience. "You've described a ghost that gets into the minds of the living. Into *your* mind. That sounds like a scenario for a movie—a not-very-good movie, frankly. And it's probably too much for even superstitious theater folks to swallow. I don't mean to be impolite, but I have to give you my honest opinion." He looked over at Sarah and directed his next words to her, dismissing Claire. "Shall we talk about something else now? How is that play that you're writing going, Sarah? And when are you going to give a draft to me to read?"

Claire felt her shoulders tighten and her stomach lurch. She stared downwards at her interlaced fingers, breathing fast. How disappointing. How embarrassing. How deflating. Then a flash of bright anger coursed through her. How rude!

CLAIRE AND SARAH regrouped in Mears Park, not far from Sarah's apartment in Lowertown. With its artificial but lovely stream meandering through a corridor of genuine ferns, flowers, and slender silver birches, Mears was one of Claire's favorite spots in St. Paul, but today, she was still sputtering with anger and could not appreciate it. The clouds appeared lower and more sodden than they had earlier this morning, their undersides rumpled and threatening like an old, inverted mountain range at the end of winter.

"I know that Brian McMaster is a friend of yours, Sarah, but that was, that was—not the way a host should treat a guest!"

"I agree. Honestly, I do." Sarah, dressed today in a flowered top and wide-legged slacks, crossed her ankles and plumped her soft, ample purse of plum-colored leather on her lap. "Brian is a 'work friend,' not a 'friend friend.' I mean, he was my boss there, and there's still a bit of that power differential between us. And we certainly used to butt heads occasionally at Luna. He sometimes seemed to hold me responsible for being the bearer of bad news when the theater was struggling. Remember, I warned you that he might be prickly!"

"That wasn't prickly. That was downright rude. I *hate* to be dismissed. He acted as if I were dense. Dense and superstitious. And foolish." She tacked on the last phrase and stamped the toe of one shoe on the brick pavement, then the other. Was this how her students had felt when they thought she had passed over them? She swallowed against the nausea that arose in response to her question. Talk about a power differential. In a moment, Brian had pivoted, treating her first as a promising student, next as a dunce. The control was all his. He had done this on purpose, she was sure, but had she behaved the same way in her classrooms, consciously or unconsciously? It was so difficult to maneuver through a whole roomful of people, each with his or her own preferences, talents, weaknesses, and expectations. And having control over others had never settled easily around her shoulders, as it seemed to with some of her colleagues. Yet she had never been consciously rude, as Brian had. Had she?

Sarah's voice scattered her thought. "Well, I'm with you on that. He *was* rude. He's not king, though, is he? No matter how much you like his dogs, he's not the boss of you." This elicited a chuckle from Claire, despite herself. "And listen. Did you notice that he failed to answer your question?" Sarah pushed back a strand of wayward hair and waited.

Claire froze, considering.

"You asked him straight on if he knew who this Puckish ghost could be. His response was all about the many actors who had played that role and about what a foolish question it was." She frowned, thinking. "Say, have you ever seen *All the President's Men*?"

Claire blinked at this. "Well, yes, I have. It's one of my father's favorite movies, actually. We watch it if we're together around the Fourth of July."

Sarah gave her a sharp look at that statement, her brown

eyes canny. "I'd like to meet your father someday. In *All the President's Men*—"

"Ha! It was a 'non-denial denial,' wasn't it? Rather than answering the question with a solid 'no,' Brian made a lot of statements about hauntings in general and mine in particular. Statements meant to make me mad, make me back off. He just, just…slipped away from me!"

Her friend nodded. "Without answering your question. I think he knows, or at least has a good idea, who this ghost is. He's not going to say, though. At least, I don't believe he will. He's a stubborn man, Brian. That quality served him well when he was artistic director at Luna. It helps to be a bit of a bulldog in jobs like that, especially in regard to grants and funding. But he can dig in in other ways, too. And he was digging like crazy by the end of our conversation today. Remember, I know him—have known him for years."

Claire felt a light spritz of drizzle on her head and bare arms. She swept her gaze around the park, noticing for the first time that some of the birches that arched over the stream were tossing leaves of yellow-gold among the green in the rainy breeze. The shower skittered down the brick pathway, hustling fallen leaves before it, their stems making a scratchy sound. A few larger drops of rain were leaving dark ovals on her trouser legs; she could feel their dampness against her skin. The clouds looked ready to settle in and rain steadily all afternoon. Sarah was rummaging in her bag, presumably for an umbrella. It was the first day of September, Claire realized. "Well, okay for Brian McMaster," she said, chin jutting. "That just means that I will have to work harder at investigating myself. I don't need him."

"That's the spirit," Sarah said, and popped open a black umbrella to shelter them both. "No pun intended."

CHAPTER 19

It was mid-afternoon when she returned home. She dropped her bag in the mudroom, kicked off her damp shoes, slipped into her clogs, and immediately popped open a can of tuna from the cupboard, finding both cats underfoot faster than she thought it would be possible for them to scent the fish in a modest-sized house. She gave them each a taste on saucers, put Lute outside with a toy that contained a rattling dog treat, and continued on with the tuna salad on toast preparations, adding capers to the tuna along with the mayonnaise, as her grandfather had. She was so hungry that she didn't wait to find the kitchen scissors to cut open the bag of Classic Lays chips, instead pulling recklessly on either side of the crinkly bag and ripping it lengthwise, sending chips, like large, blond pieces of confetti, flying up into the air in a gentle spray. They landed lightly on the counter, across the floor, in the sink—one particularly large chip dropped into the furthermost slot of the toaster as if drawn there by a tractor beam.

She stood next to the counter, torn bag still in one hand, her head hanging and her earlier confidence leaching away.

Outside, the rain still fell in steady, silver rods; she could hear it spattering on the back steps and gurgling through the gutter above the sink window. The cats had vanished, finding secret nooks in which to nap away a rainy September day. Lute was probably in his favorite haven under the raspberry canes, gnawing at his toy and keeping fairly dry. And here she was, alone in a dim kitchen, surrounded by potato chip fallout, lashed by hunger.

She sighed, placed a handful of chips from the devastated bag on her plate next to the toast spread with tuna salad, and made her way to the table in the breakfast nook, trying and failing to avoid the fallen chips on the floor. Crunch, crunch, crunch. She took a seat and picked up the first triangular piece of toast.

A zing of electricity, like that associated with lightning and ozone, raced along both arms, met at her spine, and zoomed upwards, alerting the skin under her ponytail. She shrugged her shoulder blades involuntarily and clutched the toast so tightly that the bread crust between her fingers became dough again. Coolness enveloped her, a slab of fresh, chilly air with definite boundaries. She took a stunned moment to feel refreshed by it and to set her toast on the plate once again. Then came the sound—a dry rattling like November leaves scuttling before a stiff breeze. The unbroken chips on the floor, she noticed stolidly, had come to life. Ten or so, near the refrigerator, were stirring, becoming a small crowd of chips that met, conferred with one another, and then separated again. A few stood up on their edges, reminding Claire of meerkats on sentry duty. The sense of motion spread across the maple floor. The path of broken pieces that she had inadvertently made remained inert, but almost all the other chips were now quite lively, twirling, tapping, even bowing to one another.

Claire pressed her lips together to make sure that no

sound escaped them until she was ready to speak. This scene was…dramatic. Chips gone berserk. Yet really, who could be afraid of potato chips?

She found her voice at last. "Hello. You're not the Puck ggguy, are you?" (She'd started to say "ghost," but not wanting to risk offending whoever was inspiring the chips to dance, substituted "guy" instead. Thank God for that catch-all word in American speech.) A small herd of chips gathered in front of the table at which she sat, continuing their milling movements.

And images came to her mind. The wheel of a bicycle spinning along a sunny sidewalk. A plastic model of an X-wing fighter on a coffee table. A book held open with slightly grubby hands. The cuckoo clock, seen from below, the cuckoo bird emerging to bow and call, just as it was bowing and calling two o'clock in her living room, right at this very moment. A purple and yellow Whizzzer top spinning over a beaten hardwood floor.

She parted her lips to speak again, making an unintentional smacking noise because her mouth felt both dry and sticky, like sand in glue. She cleared her throat and prepared to try once more.

And then, across the room and right in front of the entryway to the dining room, the air took on substance. It shimmied. It shivered. It swayed in a way that should not be visible to any mortal soul.

"Ah," Claire's voice cracked. "You're both here. That hasn't happened in a while. Um, welcome. You're the Puck actor, right?" The shimmers swirled afresh, becoming denser, taking on deep blue and oyster-gray shades, rounding into a form that Claire thought approximated a human—a human comprised only of light and spirit. She could make out a featureless head, a slim torso, and amorphous limbs. Her lower jaw dropped down, like Scrooge's when the ghost of

Jacob Marley first appeared to him in the production of *A Christmas Carol* she'd attended years ago. She remembered how that spirit had shrieked, and felt a flash of gratitude that neither of her ghosts shrieked. Her ghosts. Such familiarity with these two when she didn't even know their names or much of anything about them. But she would. She vowed that to herself and experienced a sparkling shower of anticipation at the thought.

The drumming of the rain outside suddenly shifted into a rushing torrent of sound. Claire dragged her eyes away from the ghost to the window on her left. The rain had undergone its own transformation, from light shower to deluge. The harsh, impatient barks of Lute on the back stoop punctured the rain's ongoing roar. Her dog's rough coat was naturally water repellant, but it would not keep him dry in this cloudburst. Claire stood up briskly, felt her vision immediately darken, then put a hand on the back of an adjacent chair to steady herself. The chips were still milling and the figure at the dining room entryway was still swirling, quite striking in its opalescent blues and grays. She had the impression that he was watching her without eyes—a thought that caused a lance of fear to strike sideways though her chest. Her face flushed hot and then immediately subsided into clammy-cold; perspiration glazed her forehead, upper lip, neck. Rivulets slid down either side of her nose. She gasped and lowered her own eyes to the path of crushed chips—the fallen ones that did not move.

Lute, however, was waiting for her to let him in, and he roused her from her frozen fear. His barks had a shrill note of the frantic in them now.

"I, um, have to let my dog in now. Excuse me, please." She arose and tiptoed as best she could on wavering legs across the floor toward the mudroom, watching the unbroken chips scatter in front of her, presumably to regroup behind. She recalled how schools of minnows had parted and streamed away from the prow of a red canoe as it glided through the shallow water of Lake Harriet, her father steering from the stern. Having reached the door without crushing a single chip, she was keenly aware that she was turning her back on supernatural activity, something she had never done before. But Lute needed her—that was that. She picked up the clean, faded towel that she kept on top of the recycling bins for drying his feet, opened the door, and crouched down to envelope a wriggling, panting, smelly Lute. She started to stand with him in her arms, but he was too quick for her, and it was impossible to get a grip on him while he was within the folds of the loose towel. He sprang out of her embrace, trotted the length of the tiny mudroom, and paused at the threshold to the kitchen, surveying the scene.

The chips danced, the visible ghost revolved, faded into mist for a moment, and then re-formed into dense, cool fog. Apparently astounded, Lute kept still except for his head, which turned as he took in one set of jigging chips after another. He looked up at the blue-gray ghost across the room. This prompted him to whine and shiver, and his hackles rose over his shoulders. Was the whine from fear or desire, Claire wondered? Yes, the supernatural had once more risen up in his new home, and now chips were moving on their own. But they were *chips*—and Lute loved chips. His whole body trembled from indecision.

Then he leapt into the room and began snatching up chips as fast as he could. They fled from his predations toward the edges of the kitchen cabinets under the counter and finally collapsed, defeated. Claire could hear his teeth clicking together as he crunched down this unexpected bounty, scampering to the right and left, calling on the long-buried instincts of a terrier in the midst of a whole flock of prey animals. "Oh, Lute…" Claire almost whispered. "I hope that this doesn't make things worse." She raised her eyes fearfully toward the gray-blue ghost. Rather than swirling, he was now shaking. In anger? In frustration? In fear? His head was tipped downwards and directed toward Lute, seemingly following the little dog's energetic hunt.

She noted an additional drop in temperature as if a north wind had entered her kitchen. Wisps of frigid air found their way to her from the ghost's place in the doorway and fanned against her sweaty cheeks and the top of her tingling head. She hugged her arms across her chest, bracing for a wave of anger from the ghost that did not come. Her breath charged out in a small frozen cloud, as it did when she stepped from her doorway into December. The ghost was fainter now, and still vacillating, with pulses of brooding blues alternating with the gray shades that reminded her of a wintry sea. Lute was now actually standing immediately in front of the apparition, his attention having been caught by the flickering movements, apparently. He looked up at what seemed to be the ghost's head and barked sharply, tail up, hackles down. The ghostly form vibrated in response, twirled once more, and then drew in upon itself and dissipated.

The scent of lime drifted past her.

Claire called Lute back to her, noticing that warmth was returning to the kitchen. After wiping her palms and face on the dry side of the towel she still held, she knelt to pat Lute and reassure herself that he was all right, both mentally and physically. He licked his lips appreciatively and groaned. Crumbs of potato chips still clung to the fur on the bridge of his muzzle.

Claire was a newcomer to supernatural events and had never experienced a ghost in all her life until two weeks ago. Most of the visits she had witnessed since bringing the clock in the house had not consisted of any manifestations at all, but rather of actions that couldn't be explained in a rational way. She was no expert on otherworldly beings, surely. But when she mulled over the appearance of the gray-blue spirit just before he dissolved, shaking in the doorway, it occurred to her that he might have been laughing.

SHE WAS WRITING FEVERISHLY in her notebook late that afternoon, yellow and green highlighters at the ready, when the phone rang. Wanting to capture this most dramatic of ghostly visits while its impressions still thronged in her mind, she glanced up only for a moment, and then kept on writing, her pen flowing over the paper like a small boat riding ocean swells. From her place at the dining room table, she could hear the answering machine pick up and then her own brief outgoing message play. Next the caller's voice spoke, a woman's voice that sounded familiar, yet Claire couldn't quite place it, nor could she make out exactly what the speaker was saying. With a gusty exhalation of annoyance, she snatched off her reading glasses, flung her pen down, and stamped into the hallway and toward the bedroom.

In a rush, a moment of near-panic suddenly assailed her. Was it Rosa, calling to say that something was wrong with Dad or with Gus? Wait, if her father were ill, Gus would call himself. But if Gus himself were injured or ill, she could imagine her father wanting to pass on to someone else the difficult task of relaying the news, and Rosa might be prevailed upon to agree. Twenty different scenarios of grief and desolation shot through her mind, seemingly all at once. Stop fretting, just stop, she told herself as she passed into the bedroom. Everything's fine, great, wonderful! Maybe.

At close quarters, she recognized the voice on the recording as that of her sister-in-law. She had expected gloom and instead received a welcome, albeit unexpected, phone call from Grace. She decided to pick up, whether she lost her train of thought as a writer of ghost stories or no. Life was for the living.

"Grace! I'm here. Sorry I didn't answer sooner. I was… involved in a project so it took me a little while to get to the phone."

"A project, eh? You're turning into such a homeowner, Claire. And I remember very well how many projects a house generates. Sometimes they seemed to me like dandelions; no sooner was one taken care of than another one sprouted up. Never-ending work, houses are." She chuckled. "Although as a Realtor, I really shouldn't be focusing on that, should I? I should be always positive and ready to talk about all the satisfactions of homeowning rather than the difficulties."

"Yes, I'm lucky that I have so much time to devote to the house right now. I would've felt…" she searched for the coltish word that just eluded her. The pause grew uncomfortably long.

"Overwhelmed?" Grace suggested gently.

"Well, 'inadequate' is the word I was trying to come up with, but 'overwhelmed' will do. As it is, I feel only inexperienced, which is better than the other two, I think. And you're right about the satisfactions. I love having my own home." Fearful that this might touch on a sore spot for Grace and wanting to change the subject, she asked, unimaginatively, "Say, how are you, Grace? And how is Scott?"

They chatted for a few minutes about Grace's work, including the current overheated housing market in the Twin Cities, which actually made her job harder, and then about Scout. "First grade," Grace lamented. "How can he be old enough to go to school when I remember starting first grade myself so vividly? I insisted on wearing the new jumper that my mother had bought me, even though the temperature must've been eighty-five that day. I came home exhausted and soaked in sweat. I'm sure that I must've made a great impression on the teacher—a cross, stubborn little girl with pigtails and a bright red face."

Claire could picture this perfectly. Grace would've been one of those slight, elfin children that sturdy Claire had looked upon with wistfulness as a girl. "I always wanted to wear my fall clothes, too," she offered mildly. "But over-dressed or not, I loved going back to school. The pencils, the box of fresh crayons, the three-ring binders—what is equivalent to those for adults?"

"Maybe a new app," Grace offered. "But that's not really the same, come to think of it. Well, we have our memories." Her voice was a little sardonic. "And the stories that the kids tell us when they come home. I seriously think that that's why some people have children—to live through the kids, remake a rough time in their own lives into something positive."

"Hmmm," Claire hummed, noncommittally. She had decided some years ago that commenting on parenthood when she herself was childless showed the worst kind of hubris. It would be like pontificating about being an astro-naut—who could understand it without going through it oneself?

So she'd kept her mouth shut, even when students had told her, "My mother thought that my essay was really good!" It would certainly have never occurred to her to consult with her father about her college grades, and if she had complained to him about one, he would have told her to work out the issue with the teacher herself because it was none of his business; she was responsible for her own educa-tion. And he had been right about that. "Well, I hope that Scott likes his teacher," she said, picking up the thread of the conversation with Grace again. "And that she—or he—chooses good books for the kids to read. Those early books are so important, I think. Although Scott has access to lots at home."

"But not *Mike Mulligan and His Steam Shovel*! He keeps talking about it, and when I offered to buy it for him, he went quiet and said, 'That book lives at Claire's house. I don't think it belongs here.'"

"Oh, Grace, I'm sorry! I told him that he could take it home..." She trailed off, not wanting to add that he had chosen to leave the book at her house and feeling guilty that he had been effectively banned from both bungalow and book.

"It's okay, Claire—honestly, it is. I'm happy that he's so close to you. And to David and Gus, too. It takes a village, right?"

After a moment spent considering her own small family and Grace's even smaller one, Claire thought that Scout's village was tiny and that the homes were widely dispersed. "So!" Grace continued brightly. "I have to leave in a few minutes to show a house, but I was wondering... Would you like to get together on Sunday? I thought maybe we could go to the farmers' market, have a quick bite afterwards. Something like that. A day together, to catch up." The final words trailed off, the last one all but inaudible to Claire.

She launched into speech herself. "I would love that! I thought myself of inviting you to do something and just haven't...put the plan into action yet." She rushed on, shifting the focus to Grace's invitation so that it wouldn't seem as if it took a lot of effort to spend time with her sister-in-law. "Which farmers' market would you like to go to? There must be one up your way."

"Yes, there is, but I was thinking of the St. Paul market. It's really the best one in the Cities. It's even gotten national attention. Named one of the top twenty in the country, or something like that."

"Really? I had no idea." Claire hadn't been to a farmers' market in years and had never made it to the one in downtown St. Paul, even though it was only a ten-minute drive from her new home. Shopping at regular supermarkets had seemed easier since they had long hours and vast parking lots. "That sounds like a lot of fun. What time sounds good to you?" And immediately, a memory of the golden cuckoo bowing and calling nine times floated up from her subconscious, the image as vivid as that of a living bird arising from a sunlit meadow.

GRACE TURNED BACK at the pavilion's entrance to make sure that Claire was ready to follow her into the milling marketgoers. Her grin was slanted and happy, and even though Claire was not fond of disorganized crowds, she returned Grace's smile with a genuine one of her own. "I'm right behind you, girl," she said. "But maybe we should decide on a place to meet—just in case we get separated." Claire was twisting one of the straps of her purple backpack and tipping her head from side to side.

"The market isn't *that* big, Claire. We'll find each other, no problem. But I'll tell you what. If you put that backpack on, I'm as sure to see you as if you were wearing a homing beacon. I've never seen a backpack in that particular shade."

Claire considered its vibrant color as if for the first time. "I got it in high school. Purple was my favorite color then. I'm pretty sure it was a birthday present from Gus."

"Ah, Gus—he would know to give you a pack in your favorite color and be able to find it in a store somehow, even though a purple backpack must've been unusual. And before the Internet, too. The man is a marvel. He has such a sure touch with people."

Claire agreed as she slipped the straps over her shoulders

and snugged them tight. "Yes, Gus is a rare gem. I miss him already. Dad, too," she added, and to her own surprise, realized that this was true. "They would both love to be here with us right now, wouldn't they? Maybe I'll take some pictures and send them on. Luckily, I remembered my camera. At least, I think I did." She rootled through the purse's contents while Grace waited indulgently, hands in the pockets of her twill jacket. "Here it is!" She held it up in triumph. "Ready when you are, Grace." And the two of them eased into the current of humans, each set on procuring fresh, homegrown veggies on this crisp fall day.

CLAIRE FLIPPED through the photos with Grace as they sipped their lattes and waited for their meals at a neighborhood restaurant that had been well reviewed in the newspaper. She held the camera sideways on the table so that they could both see. "Look at those squashes, Grace—just look at them! They were so beautiful with the morning light on them. The deep gold ones, the reddish-orange ones, the striped orange-and-green ones. I never knew that there were so many different kinds of winter squash. And the woman who worked at that booth told me that this is just the beginning—that there will be more varieties of squash as well as pumpkins next week or the week after at the latest. I can't wait to get a pumpkin. Maybe two." Claire gazed fondly at the photo, thinking that she would definitely send it on to Gus because it was her favorite from the many she had taken.

"Well, I can see you're a convert to the market already. Isn't it nice to actually talk with the people who grow your food, maybe even get to know them a little? That woman, Carol, threw in a couple of squashes for free, just because you were so enthusiastic, I think." She sipped her latte. "This is delicious, too, by the way. Made by someone who knows her way around an espresso machine."

"Amazing. I'm in a mood to be amazed today."

"You saw the market at its best, I think. In September, summer and fall overlap; you can still buy tomatoes, red peppers, raspberries, maybe even sweet corn, but at the next booths, the vendors are selling squash, Indian corn, bouquets of Chinese lanterns, potatoes, apples…"

"Oh, the apples," Claire sighed. They both grew ruminative over their memories of the fragrant apples proudly displayed in draw-string bags and bushel baskets and labeled with those evocative names: MacIntosh, Honeycrisp, Summer Red, Cortland, Wealthy, State Fair. "I'm going to have to clean out my fridge to make room for what I bought. No loss there, I guess. Say, have you always been this interested in local food, Grace? I feel like I should know, but I'm sorry, I don't."

"I've gotten more interested since Scott's gotten older, I guess. Kids love junk, but if you give them fresh food, they'll eat that and get to like it, too. Especially if it's slathered in butter or melted cheese." She looked impish. "Don't give me that look! They can handle the dairy products—need them, even. I remember another Realtor telling me about her daughter. The mom only gave her skim milk, bare broccoli, broiled chicken, things like that. And the daughter started stealing her classmates' lunches! Poor kid. She never had any treats. I hope she doesn't have an eating disorder when she grows up."

Emboldened by this, Claire set down her wide latte cup in its saucer and said, "I was a little worried about you at the barbecue, to be honest. You hardly ate a thing."

Grace picked up her fork and tested the tines with her fingertips. "Oh, you know how it is. Sometimes, brats look like the best thing on the planet, and sometimes, you just say, 'Ick.'"

Claire burst out laughing. "I understand. After a few bites of mine, I was thinking along those lines myself. Greg over-cooked them, and they were—how shall I put this delicately? A teensy bit dry."

"It was a very nice barbecue, though, and Greg must've gone to lot of work to put it together," Grace hastened to add. "Cleaning up the house and mowing the yard, buying paper plates and plastic silverware and all." She set her own fork down gently alongside the serrated knife, making sure that they were even with one another. Claire thought, what a kind person she is. She doesn't want to criticize Greg, even over something as unimportant as his grilling abilities.

"Is Scott with him today?"

"Yes, today and Monday. Greg had tickets to a Saints game for this afternoon—one of the last of the season, he said. I hope that Scott doesn't come home with another jersey. They're good quality, of course, but I'd like him to wear some non-franchised clothing once in a while. Something without a logo, you know what I mean?" The late morning sun had found its way through the nearby window and poured over their table; Grace's pale face was lit up like an angel's from a religious Christmas card.

"Definitely. Greg does love professional sports. Always has. We used to fight about what to watch on TV when we were kids; he always wanted the football game."

"Tell me about it!" Grace opened her mouth as if to say more about that, but her attention was suddenly captured by the sweep of a shadow outside; Claire had noticed it, too. "My God, look!" Grace's voice squeaked. "There are horses going by outside!"

Claire jumped up and half-stood, leaning and twisting

over the table to peer through the window and see for herself.

Two horses sauntered by, their riders St. Paul Mounted Police. The horse nearest the window, a bay, was massive with wispy feathering above his hooves; he strode slowly along the sidewalk, his head nodding, each of his steps a decision made. The mare on the far side was as bright as a new penny, delicate, with pricked ears over alert eyes and flaring nostrils. She danced lightly sideways until her rider corrected her course in some unobtrusive way. Each horse wore a yellow-green reflective breast collar and straps around all four fetlocks. The distinctive "clop, clop, CLOP!" of their shod hooves meeting the asphalt reached the women even through the window. The riders sat perfectly at ease, chatting together, gloved hands holding each rein separately, the golden stripes on their navy uniform trousers appearing extra vivid in the autumn sunshine.

Claire and Grace watched the horses' progress until only the swaying rumps and swishing tails, along with the officers' blue backs, were visible. Then the women turned simultaneously toward each other. "Did you see that, Grace? Did you *see* that? Horses right outside the window! Wasn't that the coolest thing?"

"The coolest. Absolutely." And Grace offered her palm for a gentle slap of shared triumph. Instead, Claire shook it firmly as if they were meeting for the first time.

THAT NIGHT, Claire made the rounds of the bungalow's ground floor, shutting and locking windows and snapping off lights. Lute paced along with her, his eyes already sleepy. Dimness leapt forward from the room's perimeter with the loss of each lamp's light, a shadowy pool that gradually deepened into near-complete darkness. The sound of ticking was steady and reassuring to Claire, like even stitches in a quilt, she thought as she wound the cuckoo clock. Last of all, she paused in front of the Tiffany-style floor lamp that stood next to the futon couch. Its light showered down over the floor and rug, a warm bell shape casting a spell of comfort over the dusky room. Her fingers dropped from the slender chain that controlled the lamp without pulling it. "Okay, guys," she whispered. "All yours now."

CHAPTER 20

*C*laire wanted Scout to know that she was thinking about him on Monday, the day before he started first grade—"the real deal" where school was concerned, to use his own phrase. She recalled Grace saying that he would be with his father until Tuesday morning, when Grace would meet them so that all three of them could go together to Scout's classroom. She wished that she had thought to send him a card with animals in which she could've written her good wishes, but it was obviously too late for that now. He had no email account, being only six. The only option left was to call him.

She punched Greg's cell phone number into the wall phone in her kitchen, nervously squeezing her ponytail as she listened to the burring ring tones. After four, Greg's message boomed out, causing her to hold the phone away from her ear. "This is Greg. Leave your name and number and I'll get back to you." No softening "hi" or "thanks." But honestly, why should she expect Greg to be soft?

She stammered her message, holding the receiver with both hands. "Hi, Greg, it's me. Claire. I was just calling to…

to…tell Scott that I'm thinking about him. That I'm sure first grade will go fine! That there's no need to be nervous, but if he is, that's fine, too! Everyone is nervous on the first day of school. Including, probably, the teacher. So please be nice to her or him! Okay, see you soon, I hope." She bit her lower lip in frustration at the ridiculous, rambling message that she had left and could not retrieve. "Bye." And she clapped the receiver onto its hook and leaned on the table, breathing hard.

There would be no response. Leaving a message for Greg was like sending a radio signal into the darkness of space. Unless she saw Scout in person and asked him about it, she would never even know if her nephew had received her good wishes, garbled as they were. Well, she'd tried.

Automatically, she heard Yoda's voice in her head when he was exhorting Luke to have confidence in his own abilities. "Do. Or do not. There is no 'try.'" As a young person, she'd thought this was oversimplified. Now, in middle age, she thought it was a truth condensed, as potent as the last cider of October.

"CLAIRE, I really want to meet these new friends of yours," Marguerite said as she zipped her rust-colored sweater, leaving only the collar of her turtleneck visible. The late afternoon sunshine was mild, but the teasing breeze had a bit of a snap to it. Claire rearranged her grip on the handle of Lute's retractable leash and stole a look at Margo, wondering if she were resentful. But no, of course she wouldn't be. Her friend's face was as serene as it was possible for a teacher's to be after a long week that had included, according to Margo, some conversations with "difficult students," one discussion centering on plagiarism. In Week Three of the eighteen-week semester.

And Margo was one of the most generous people she knew, without a possessive or mean bone in her body. "Well, okay," Claire ventured, keeping up with Margo's energetic stride, "but you've already met Grace. And she's not a friend; she's my ex-sister-in-law. Former sister-in-law—that sounds nicer." She gazed ahead at Lute scampering along the path through the prairie grasses, which bowed and whispered before the tugging wind, each segmented stalk banded in shades of blond and amber and wine-red. It was lovely to walk the land surrounding this nature center, especially this windy prairie hillside. Tamarack trees grew by the little lake, their needles turning golden now in autumn. She had not come here during the years that she had worked at the college, although it was only a ten-minute drive from the huge school parking lot. Seemed a world away, though.

Margo was speaking again in her slightly scratchy voice that carried—a teacher's voice, Claire thought. Her own voice has lost that forced quality, she noticed. "Grace may be a former sister-in-law, but to me, she sounds like a present friend. A new friend, along with Sarah. That's great, Claire!"

No, Margo definitely wasn't resentful of these people who seem to have sprung up in her best friend's life overnight, like mushrooms: Grace the smooth-capped type the color of moonlight, and Sarah an exotic lilac variety with frills. Still, Claire wasn't eager to host again after the long period of having houseguests. The prospect of a dinner party, for example, set inner alarm bells clanging madly. "I'm not sure what kind of gathering I might have…Any ideas?" she asked cautiously. Why was Margo pushing this?

"Something completely simple and straightforward, like a potluck. I would host, but you're centrally located. Plus, your house is *much* more interesting than our apartment. You have to admit that." Her grin had a mischievous curve.

"My house," Claire groaned. "You know about the ghosts,

of course, and so does Sarah, but Grace doesn't. Not unless Scout spilled the beans."

"You and your beans—you're fixated on them, you know that?" Margo jostled Claire's right arm gently.

Claire had to chuckle. "All right, all right. You got me there. Did I tell you that Tamsin has decided that she likes baked beans? *Loves* them, actually. I was sitting on the couch eating some of the leftovers from the barbeque, and she caught one whiff, climbed onto my lap, and practically pulled the bowl out of my hands! Licked the juice off my fingertips. She is coming right along, I think."

"Good. You can socialize her further by exposing her to more people. How about next Friday? I'll come over early, right after I'm done with work, and help you clean and straighten up. In fact, I could do all of that while you sit on the couch, eat bonbons, and provide direction."

Claire chuffed with poorly suppressed laughter and then grew serious. "What about Grace? I really do think that I should tell her that I'm inviting her to a haunted house, don't you?" Claire felt the pull and sway of uncertainty once again.

Marguerite plucked lightly at her own lips, considering. "Yes, I do. But you could tell her through writing—an email message that will go along with the invitation. I know that you feel more comfortable writing than talking sometimes."

"Sometimes! Try, 'All times.'" She called Lute back to her and gave him a treat from a Ziploc in her pocket for coming so promptly. "But you know, now that you mention this little gathering, I realize that I've been wanting to tell Grace about the ghosts, get her perspective on all of this...activity. I'll have to summarize, of course."

"I would say something like, 'Just so you know, my new house is haunted,' and leave the next step to her. She can ask for more details, ignore it, beg off, whatever. Although I hope she doesn't beg off. I really would like to get better acquainted with her. Maybe we could all be friends, eh?"

"Maybe." They walked in silence for a long moment, Claire noticing the slight give in the earth under her boots from the recent rains, the skittering sounds of insects among the high stalks, the scent of warm grass in cool space. "That would be nice, actually. And I could use as much help as possible with the ghosts. They're getting more brazen, for sure. Both of them."

"This seems like an obvious question to ask an academic person like yourself, but have you thought about doing some research? Looking into the history of Luna Theater, for example?"

"I have thought of that, and I probably will do some research." She tried to infuse her words with confidence and a sense of purpose. "But right now, I feel like I should figure out what's going on myself, through my interactions with the ghosts. I don't know why, exactly. It just seems that I should be doing primary rather than secondary research."

"Okay, my friend," said Margo doubtfully. "Like I've said before, you really are brave."

"I don't feel brave. More curious than anything. And I've got the animals with me at home all the time. They're like barometers for supernatural activity, so I know if anyone extra is around. You should have seen Lute snatching up those chips in the kitchen!"

"Wild. Say, is that a new harness he's wearing? It has nice broad straps."

"Yes, I just got that for him on Monday. I thought it would be more comfortable than a collar on walks, especially long ones like this, when he's running back and forth." She paused. "I think he looks like a superhero in it. Maybe because it's red." At that moment, Lute turned back to gaze at the women, wanting to make sure that they weren't too far behind, it seemed. The wind stirred his brown and white fur, the brown patches appearing ruddy in the swathes of golden evening light that played upon the prairie hilltop. His narrowed eyes were sharp and black and glittering, and the straps that enclosed his furry chest and sides blazed scarlet.

The two women stopped to admire him. "Red is definitely his color. And doesn't he know it, the handsome rascal," Margo said.

CLAIRE WROTE AN INVITATION TO MARGO, Sarah, and Grace that same evening, thinking that she might lose momentum if she didn't act quickly. "It'll be a potluck," she typed, "and anything you care to bring will be wonderful. I'm going to make some soup, buy loaves of crusty bread, and pick up a bottle of Baileys Irish Cream for dessert." She hesitated and tapped out, "Turning the calendar page to September means that autumn is officially here! I hope that we can celebrate that together and get to know each other a bit better in the process." Would that sound strange to her sister-in-law, a woman she had known, at least superficially, for seven years? She highlighted the phrase "get to know each other..." in blue and deleted it, then added, "and have some good conversations and fellowship." That was worse yet—so hokey-sounding. Delete, delete, delete, followed by a lengthy pause for consideration. "What should I say?" she asked Kipper, who was washing her whiskers from her place in the doorway.

Claire dropped her fingers over the keyboard again. "Turning the calendar page to September means that autumn is officially here! I hope that we can celebrate the changing of the seasons together by enjoying each other's company over a simple but tasty shared meal." That was better. She added, "RSVP by Wednesday, if that's possible, so I know how much bread to buy," and then typed a smiley face. :). The DIY emoticons were vastly preferable to the pre-fab ones, some of which were downright alarming, in her opinion. She clicked "send."

Oh, blast—she had forgotten to mention that the bungalow was haunted. And she really needed to warn Grace about that. Hastily, she cued up another email message to all three, typing "P.S" in the subject line. In the body, she wrote simply, "It seems that my new home is haunted, but to paraphrase Bullwinkle Moose, 'They are friendly spirits!'" Send. Now, all she had to do was wait for replies from Grace and Sarah. For all Sarah's helpfulness, she'd told Claire that she was ambivalent about the possibility that ghosts even exist, so Claire didn't think that she'd be hesitant to come to the bungalow. But how was she going to explain the yellow ghost and the green ghost to her practical sister-in-law? Well, she'd figure it out at the time, if Grace accepted the invitation and if the subject even came up. "Too many 'if's' to worry about yet," she told Kipper, then shut down the computer for the night, switched on what she now thought of as her "ghost light," and began to prepare for sleep.

To her surprise, acceptance messages from all three women, each copied to the other two guests, were awaiting her the next morning. "Thanks for the invitation, Claire," Sarah had written. "I'm looking forward to it already!" "Yay, Claire—this sounds so fun! It'll be great for all of us to spend some time together. Girls' night for grown-ups—with Baileys for sipping," came from Marguerite. Claire opened Grace's message last and with some trepidation, thinking that she'd better prepare herself for long explanations of the P.S. she'd sent. But the message read, "Count me in! Gotta dash," with a little hugging emoticon following her name. Attached was a photo of Scout wearing a Saints jersey and holding the straps of a dinosaur-patterned backpack, his hazel eyes round and vulnerable.

CLAIRE WAS GETTING into a loose pattern of exercise in the mornings, followed by errands, chores, and finally, lunch. In the afternoons, she worked on the house, read, and wrote in her journal, with a pause for coffee around three. She found herself enjoying the ritual that her father had taught her, including the pinwheel of half-and-half in the sweetened coffee and the melodic "ting!" when she gently tapped the spoon against the rim of the mug after stirring. The coffee smelled divine, and it was pleasant to warm both hands along the sides of the mug. She could feel herself relaxing afresh every day over this new tradition.

Some days varied from this pattern, of course, but generally speaking, she found the structure helpful. Comforting, even. Random hours increased her feeling of hollowness, while a pattern sketched into her days filled in some of the empty spaces. She worked steadily on Kate's home—sorting, cleaning, and arranging—and dove into her writing eagerly. Nothing of a ghostly nature had happened recently, yet she wasn't disappointed. The house still seemed occupied by persons aside from herself and her pets. She felt that she could almost hear their whispers and glimpse their sweep from room to sunlit room as she wrote, considering and reconsidering in her notebook what she had experienced with them.

Her writing was becoming less self-conscious, which pleased her. She had been silent on paper for a long while, and the irony of years spent trying to teach people how to write effectively while she herself wrote almost nothing, effective or otherwise, did not escape her. "I felt as if I were growing more and more quiet," she put down in her notebook, "my voice fading and my own writing dwindling down to blank pages."

Blank pages were inviting now, lovely spaces in which to consider, capture, and characterize the spirits she sensed around her. She was convinced now that the "yellow" ghost was a child, a boy child who pulled pranks with Sharpies, painted on walls with his fingers, played with his food, and pined to make friends with her pets. And the images that had been projected into her mind supported this hunch: the possessions, snacks, and activities of a child. Who was playing inside the canvas tent she had envisioned? His identity remained teasingly elusive. She couldn't explain exactly why she thought that this ghost was male—he just had that male vibe. And after spending so much of her childhood with her father, brother, and grandfather, she believed that she could recognize a boyish quality when she encountered it, even when it was generated by a spirit she had never seen.

The "green" ghost was an adult, she surmised, although probably a young one. This idea was based only partly on her belief that the part of Puck was usually played by a young person, male or female. The "green" ghost was old enough to empathize with her migraine pain, even try to soothe it, but young enough to be boiling over with envy as he watched Bruce Boxleitner playing the role of Scarecrow on television. Boxleitner had been in his early thirties when SMK first aired, she guessed, so perhaps the ghost was about the same age. "Was he envious of another actor playing a prominent role on TV?" she wrote. "A role that he wanted?" But she softened this statement as she spoke aloud, "Did you wish you were playing Scarecrow?"

She waited, glancing around the dining room where she sat at the round table and then beyond to the living room. Kipper was snoozing on the futon couch, all of her edges neatly tucked in like a Parker House roll, while Tamsin kept guard in an open sunroom window. From under the table, Lute sneezed and poked her stockinged foot with his snout.

No answer.

"All right for you!" she called out. "You're holding the cards now, but someday, you'll show up again." Silence. "Won't you?"

AT YOGA CLASS on Friday morning, she grunted and lifted her feet, first one and then the other, balancing on her sitz bones, arms outstretched at her sides, palms up, as if imploring clouds to rain. Her stomach muscles trembled with the effort of holding her body in this boat pose as she breathed hard through the nose, the exhalations rasping loudly enough to be heard by those around her. She didn't care. Glancing at her reflection in the wall of mirrors in front of her, she was surprised to see how small her bare feet looked, their soles perpendicular to the floor. How do I walk around on those tiny things? she wondered. Her feet were sized eight and a half, not small at all as women's feet went, yet the thought of all of her weight and height balancing on these fragile, tear-drop-shaped appendages astounded her. She felt a deep sense of gratitude that her body worked so well. She was lucky. She was astonishingly, profoundly lucky. What were migraines, acid reflux, panic attacks, and occasional insomnia compared to bones and organs and skin that formed a framework, allowed her to move from place to place, digested her food, let her see her own reflection in these banks of mirrors? She needed to hang onto these inner reflections while viewing the outer ones with humble thankfulness.

Yoga seemed to encourage reassessment, at least today. During Warrior Two, she held her arms out in front and behind at shoulder level, leaning into her bent right leg while the left leg stretched behind her, nearly straight. She thought that in the forward mirror, she looked ridiculous, like a lumpy, awkward, overgrown child playing Ninja. But when she directed her gaze to the side mirror, remaining in the same pose even though her arms longed to fall at her sides, she saw a powerful woman dressed in black, expression stern, arms straight and strong, ready to do battle if needed. She resolutely put aside the idea that she was awkward and lumpy and reached for the idea that she was strong and capable—Warrior Two, poised and ready to launch herself forward.

GUS CALLED LATER that same day, and she smiled into the receiver at his voice and took a seat at the kitchen table, dropping the Swiffer she'd been using to prepare for the gathering with her friends that evening.

"Is it still hot in St. Paul, sweetheart?" he asked, easing into their conversation as if it were a shady pool. "It's hot as blue blazes here. And I know how the heat bothers you."

"No, Gus, it's really starting to feel like fall here. Cool mornings, that soft, gentle feel to the air during the day, nightfall coming earlier and earlier. I haven't run the air conditioner or fan for days—maybe a week. I'm loving the quiet!

"Oh, I know just what you mean, Claire-bear. We're still dependent on the AC here, whooshing away every ten minutes, but I look forward every year to turning all of those machines off in fall. The silence of the fans, I call it."

Claire's laugh was gusty. "That's so funny, Gramps! Where did you pick up that expression?"

"No idea. Made it up myself, I think. Although I never saw the movie, of course." He made a rumbling sound that radiated disapprobation. "As if the world doesn't contain enough ugliness without us using it as some kind of twisted entertainment."

"Yes, I remember that you would never let Greg and me watch the Creature Feature films when we were staying at your house on Friday nights. And those were pretty tame."

"Well, I suppose that people have always wanted to scare themselves a bit while not actually putting themselves in danger. Probably human nature. But there was no need to expose you to vampires and werewolves and the like when you were just a little girl and didn't really know what you were signing up for when you tuned in." He cleared his throat. "Plus, I had a selfish motive for keeping you away from scary movies."

"What was that?"

"I knew full well that you'd wake up crying at two or three o'clock in the morning from nightmares and I'd have to figure out some way to comfort you and get you to go back to sleep." His voice was rich, warm, teasing.

"You're right, Gus—I'm sure you're right. I was a fraidy-cat, even then."

"I wouldn't call you a fraidy-cat, Claire. But you *are* thoughtful. Thoughtful and impressionable."

She wondered if he were going to mention the ghosts and decided that she didn't want the subject to come up again between them. Not right now. She rushed her response. "Thanks, that's a nice way of saying, 'wishy-washy,' I think. Hey, speaking of cats, did I tell you about Tamsin and the baked beans?"

They chatted about the animals, the gardens, the maple trees in the neighborhood that were beginning to uncover their fiery oranges, vermilions, and coppers. Claire described a sugar maple whose crown was still vivid green except for one blazing branchful of leaves near the top. "It reminds me of a person with dark hair and one lock of silver in front," she said. "Just one lock."

"Like your third-grade teacher. What was her name? Johnson, Thompson, something like that?"

"Mrs. Swanson. She was great. She introduced me to *The Cricket in Times Square*, *All-of- a-Kind Family*, *The Saturdays*. What a joy to be the teacher who gives her students those books, and other ones, too, for the very first time."

"You have satisfactions with your students, too, don't you?" Gus asked gently.

Claire pondered for a moment. "Yes. Yes, I did. Some people really lit up in class, and that was exciting to see. Or made great strides in their learning. But they were so few and far between. Lots of students were neutral, just doing the minimum that they needed to pass the course and go on. That I could deal with. But so many were angry, frustrated, lashing out, and I couldn't really blame them for that, especially in the developmental writing courses. What were probably called 'remedial' courses in your day. Those students had to pay for courses that didn't even earn them college credit. What in their lives had prepared them for college? For the academic work and also the culture of college? Not much. That was tough for me as well as for them. Worse for them, of course. But we all had a sense of failure, I think."

This situation was so disheartening that she hurried onward again, wanting to put distance between herself and it. "And some were tough in different ways. I had one student, Mike, in a lit. course, year before last. He was confident, well-spoken, a good writer. He never missed a class, always sat in the front row. But I realized pretty quickly that he never read a single assigned reading. I suppose he'd just skated by in high school on his talents and his ability to bluff and thought that he could do the same in college. Such a waste. He was wasting his own opportunities." She felt a weight gather deep in her chest. "I can still see his face perfectly."

"Sweetie, you do your best in your job. I know you do."

"But I think that my best hasn't been good enough. Not lately. Not good enough for my students, and not even good enough for me."

"Claire, maybe you should talk with your dad about these things. I've got no experience with any of this. He does."

"It helps me to talk to you, Gus—truly, it does. You're such a good listener. I need to figure out what happened, why my job makes me feel sick inside and out. How to move forward, one way or the other. I'll talk with Dad, too, but right now, thinking about Mrs. Swanson in contrast to myself is helpful."

"Maybe when she started teaching, her hair was all black," he said, "and her disappointments gave her the white lock. You just don't remember the kids who struggled through the third grade. You were sailing then."

Claire took this in. "Could be, Gus. Could be."

CHAPTER 21

Grace, the last of the women to arrive, handed her dinner contribution to Claire in a low white cardboard box. "Sorry I'm late! A showing took longer than I expected, and the traffic was—well, you know how rush hour can be, especially when you're going from one end of the Cities to the other. Crazy-making. It's good to be here!" She exhaled with a soft "hah!" sound as if to rid herself from the after-effects of flickering brake lights, tail-gaters, and autumn dusk. Claire set the box on the buffet, popped the tape with her thumbs, and carefully lifted out a pie in a stamped silver pie plate, the pale sugary crust oozing a burble of blueberries through its center slits.

The three guests gathered around Claire, surveying the items that they had brought to share: a pumpkin pie, a Dutch apple pie, and a blueberry pie. "Well, this is going to be a great pot luck," Claire said heartily. "All pies, but no duplications. And we also have the soup and the bread. Plus cookies and Baileys for later."

"Let's call it a potpie rather than a potluck," Marguerite

piped up. "Don't you think? Maybe we should start a tradition—all desserts except for a light main course."

"Sounds good to me," Sarah added stoutly. "I love pie. And think of how healthy this meal will be, with such a range of fruits and vegetables."

"The box gives away my guilty secret: mine's not homemade. I bought it at Fay's," said Grace.

"Really? So did I! Their pies are scrumptious. It's a wonder we didn't bump into each other at the counter." Sarah clapped Grace lightly on the shoulder. "Maybe we should've car-pooled."

"Next time!"

Pleased at the mention of "next time" so early in the evening, Claire asked her guests to serve themselves from the three pies and then take a seat while she ladled the soup into Fiesta bowls. Crusty bread, aerated with large holes in its springy center, had already been warmed, roughly sliced, wrapped in a colorful tea towel patterned with maple leaves, and nestled in a wicker basket. In the center of the table, Claire had arranged ears of Indian corn and miniature pumpkins: white Baby Boos and orange Jack-Be-Littles. A honey-hued beeswax candle held its tiny flame gallantly in the middle of this autumn bounty.

She carefully set a steaming bowl in front of the women, two by two, bowls of turquoise, paprika, marigold, and brown. She gave herself the brown in case anyone objected to its somber shade, slipped into her chair, and tossed out her napkin. "Thanks for the pie, whoever served me," she said, noting the three slender slices already on a single plate off to one side.

"What kind of soup is this, Claire?" inquired Grace, dipping a spoon into her portion. "Pumpkin?"

"Squash! I made it with butternuts from the farmers' market." And she gave Grace a light shrug with one shoulder to signal that these were the same smooth, pinkish-dun vegetables that they had chosen together less than two weeks ago.

"What could be more fitting? This is just the perfect fall meal, including the delicious cider. I love being here, my friend! Thank you for inviting me." And Sarah picked up the little cream pitcher, now filled with molasses, and poured a tempting, twisting stream onto the surface of her soup.

Avoiding talk of careers and partners as if according to a pre-arranged plan, they got to know each other for the first time or deepened their acquaintance while discussing farmers' markets and favorite autumn foods, then, as the trust between them grew, moved on to memories of grade school, family trips, and board games. "We about drove my father crazy with the Pop-o-Matic dice attached to the Trouble game," Grace mused, taking tiny, shaved bites of her pumpkin pie. "Poor man. I think he was about ready to break a window and heave the whole set outside a time or two."

"Ah, the noisy games were always the best," opined Margo, "and the ones that weren't especially noisy could be *made* so. My brother could rattle dice in Parcheesi cup loud enough to wake the dead." She shot a nervous glance over her and pressed the last bite of her blueberry pie onto the back of her fork, moving it around the turquoise plate to pick up some extra crumbs of crust.

Sarah took up the chain of reminiscences. "Mouse Trap. Do you remember that one? Those crazy, crooked plastic stairs with all the odd accoutrements: a boot and a broom and a bathtub—hey, what's with all the 'b' words? Anyway, I saw that game again on display when the Minnesota History Center had their exhibit of toys a few years ago. Did you go?"

"Yes, that was a great exhibit!" Claire enthused. Then she added, more soberly, "Although it made me feel old to see my childhood toys presented as museum artifacts."

"Ouija boards," intoned Grace. The other three drew back in alarm that was only partially pretended.

"No talk of Ouija boards!" Sarah exclaimed. "When I was in high school, a woman who was supposed to be a psychic came to speak to our psychology class. She told us never to use Ouija boards because they can conjure up evil spirits. And I never did." She shuddered and rubbed her forearms in their mint-green sleeves.

"I did," Grace replied. "But I'm sure it was my little brother who was moving the plastic indicator. Planchette, was it called? Even so, I don't think I'll ever repeat the experiment now that I'm middle-aged and much more fearful than I was then. Especially not in a house that's already haunted." She leaned forward toward Claire, hair shining almost silver under the chandelier, fingertips up on the table's glossy surface, and said, "Okay, Claire—spill! I've been consumed with curiosity ever since you sent us that email message."

Claire could feel Sarah and Margo turn toward her from their seats on her right and left. The clock ticked steadfastly on, and Lute, who was locked in her bedroom, let out a distant, yodeling cry.

She sighed. "Well, it started when I bought that clock. I'm certain that the ghosts came with it." She brightened the tone of her voice and picked up her plate and Marguerite's. "But hey, let's have dessert, shall we? I used a recipe from the paper to make ginger cookies with chocolate chips in them. Who wants coffee and who wants tea? Not forgetting the Baileys for a final course. We can move to the living room later for that."

Grace chuckled. "Okay, Claire. Dessert it is. But then ghost stories. Your ghost story, yes?"

. . .

ONCE THEY WERE SETTLED around the table again with the tin of cookies, clean plates, and mugs of coffee or tea, Claire picked up the thread of her story, beginning with the turning pages of *Puck of Pook's Hill*, and moving on to what Marguerite called "the early highlights": the supernatural reactions to Claire's migraines, including the phone receiver she'd found off its hook, the kitchen tablecloth flapped in anger after she had let the clock run down, and the SMK "viewing party" during which one ghost had interacted with Lute while the other one had, by design or accident, shared some of his memories with Claire. The women listened carefully, asking for occasional clarification, leaving their drinks and cookies untouched at times. Only Margo had heard all of these stories, and Grace, of course, had heard none.

"Things have been pretty quiet here just lately," Claire said apologetically, "but they were lively enough while my dad was here. The ghosts seemed drawn to him in some way, maybe because he's fun to rattle. Though come to think of it, one of the most dramatic incidents happened just before my dad and grandfather arrived." The story of the paint might just be enough to drive the women from her home, she thought mournfully, imagining Grace and Sarah jumping up and asking for their jackets, thanking her too hastily for a lovely evening. "Scott was here for that one."

She swallowed, trying to work up some moisture in her suddenly-dry mouth. What would Grace's reaction to this story be? Her own son had witnessed a ghost's artistic endeavors. The memory of the moon and stars appearing on the wall via those pads of hovering paint still made the hair on Claire's arms and scalp stand at attention. Yet Grace should know what had happened—should've been told immediately, Claire realized with a sickening internal lurch.

"Did Scott see a ghost here?" Grace asked, her voice even but with a needle of steel imbedded deep within it.

"No, no, definitely not. But he did see something strange. I'm sorry; I should've told you about it right away." Hesitating and searching for the right words more than had been typical for her lately, she briefly described the wall painting that the younger, mischievous ghost had produced. "The clock came from a theater called Luna—Sarah's former employer—and the design is obviously a reference to it. Scott didn't seem frightened. In fact, he was delighted! And then really honked off at me when I took him to the bookstore right away and told him that from now on, we'd get together in places other than the house." She paused and then went on, slowly, her voice not more than a whisper. "I don't think he's ever been so angry with me." She was afraid to ask, "Are you angry with me, too?" This evening, as well as the farmers' market outing with Grace, had been so enjoyable. She'd felt a click with her former sister-in-law in a way that she never had when Grace and Greg had been married, as if they could be sisters, of a sort. The area under her left eye began to leap and tremble.

And this lovely circle made up of women of different ages, backgrounds, and personalities—would it dissolve after just one night, never to re-form again? Perhaps her tenancy in Kate's cozy house, a place she loved and claimed as her home, would end up isolating her unless she found a way to rid herself of the ghosts.

Grace hitched her shoulders up and then let them fall level. "Scott's over it, Claire. His anger at you, I mean. He came home from that day you spent at the fair talking about your alpacas, your goats, your apples in caramel sauce. He had an absolute ball with you and David and Gus. He loves spending time with you. And I know you always take the best care of him that you possibly can. Greg palmed him off on you that day you painted, am I right?"

"Well, yes. I told him that it wasn't a good time for me to

babysit, but he said he was desperate. I have to admit that I was thinking of the painting job rather than the ghosts when I hesitated, though. Being haunted was unfamiliar then. I certainly wasn't expecting anyone to show up for Scott." Not wanting to sound like she was making excuses, she hastily added, "But I should have considered the possibility."

"Just do what you planned with Scott—meet him outside of the house for now. He's busy with school, soccer, his friends. He may still complain a little about missing out on the action here, but he'll ease up on that in time. He's not a grudge-holder, generally speaking." The words, "like his father" hung in the air, unspoken.

Claire let out a breath that she had not realized she had been holding. "Thanks, Grace. I'm so, so grateful." Her throat tightened, and she lowered her eyes against the tears that were rising up there. "Dealing with ghosts is completely new to me." She chuckled self-consciously, aware of how odd that sounded. "Kind of challenging, actually."

"And you thought you were going to have a nice, quiet year to regroup, didn't you, Claire?" Margo offered. "Haunted when you least expected it. Isn't that always the way."

"Can I see the photo of the image that appeared on the wall?" Sarah inquired, digging around in her capacious bag for her glasses.

"Sure. I'll get the camera. Or you can see the original, if you'd rather." Sarah's hands stilled in her purse, and the eyes that she turned toward Claire were large and startled.

"Hmm, the original. That's on a wall in an upstairs bedroom, right?" She pulled her gaze from Claire's face and directed it toward the stairway entrance next to the buffet behind Claire. The door was ajar, and the darkness on those stairs was complete at nine o'clock on an autumn evening. "The photo will be fine!"

. . .

WHILE THE GUESTS passed the camera from person to person, peering and shivering, Claire took up her story again. "I know that I should do some research about Luna since Brian McMaster shut me down, see if I can find out who these ghosts might be. And I still plan to do that. But it's such an intriguing mystery that I feel compelled to keep working on it on my own. I'm really enjoying writing about my experiences and theories, for one thing. I haven't written so much since I was in grad school. And despite this recent quiet period, the ghosts are becoming more forthcoming, as if we're all getting used to each other. Why, when that sheet bloomed up while I was getting the bedroom ready for my father, I almost laughed out loud! It was so playful, so unthreatening. And that ghost is just a child. I...I... find myself feeling sorry for the little guy. He plays pranks, yes, but he's stuck at being seven or nine or however old he is, forever. You've got to feel a bit sad about that."

"What about the older one, the one with Bruce Boxleitner envy?" Marguerite asked. "He sounds seriously scary to me. He was angry the time that the clock ran down, so he flapped the tablecloth. He appeared as a semi-solid blue fellow in the kitchen. And he gets into your head, Claire. Don't those memories that belong to someone else creep you out? Am I going to come visit someday and find that you've been..." she lowered her voice and laid the camera on the table, "*taken over* in some way?" Her freckles appeared darker than usual across her cheekbones.

"No, Marguerite, no. Really, *no*. The images from him and the little boy are perfectly harmless, just snatches of their lives, I think. I don't believe that the ghosts are even sharing their memories on purpose; it just happens. And I wouldn't be surprised to know that the sharing goes both ways. They certainly seem empathetic, or at least sympathetic, when I have migraines."

"How have those been lately, by the way?" Grace asked.

"Better! I still have them, but they're less frequent and somewhat less strong. The most recent one, about a week ago, only lasted two hours, and it didn't even make me throw up." Off Sarah's frown, she added, "That's an improvement, believe me. This year away from teaching has been good for me already, and it's only the middle of September. I love Aunt Kate's house—fixing it up, taking care of it for her, and also making it my own. Reading. Exercising. Spending time with my pets. Writing, as I said. And interacting with ghosts! I'm thinking out loud here, as you can probably tell, but they're a different kind of enigma from the ones I've been dealing with at my job all those years. Honestly, I find them less scary than some of the people I've had to deal with."

"I hate to be 'living-person-centric' here," Marguerite said, "and I realize that I'm playing devil's advocate. Well, maybe not, considering that we're talking about ghosts, and I'm not advocating for them." She shook her head as if to rid herself of confusion. "Why are you being so patient with them? Whose name is on the deed to this house, after all? Kate left the house to you. Not to these spooky guys. They weren't even on the scene when you moved in. They could be considered—well, I suppose 'pests' is probably too strong a word. Still, they're uninvited. Definitely uninvited."

"Yes, uninvited. I can't argue with that. Still, they're intriguing." They all paused to think about this.

Sarah broke the silence, shifting in her chair and laying her napkin beside her plate with an air of finality. "Well, I have to ask—what do you think will happen when Halloween rolls around?" She widened her eyes in feigned terror, and they all burst into laughter.

. . .

CLAIRE CROUCHED by the fireplace and loaded logs over the kindling that was already crisscrossing the grate. "I hope I'm remembering this right from Brownie Girl Scouts. I got a merit badge in fire building. Perfect for little pyros like me."

"Be sure that the flue is fully open," Grace said. "Do you mind if I take a look?" She used the flashlight in her cell phone to peer up the chimney, creating a harsh white glow on her face. "Looks okay to me except for this blackened area down here. Did you have a sweep come out?

"Yes, yes, Grace. You and your flashlight. The chimney is fine. Clean as a whistle, in fact." Claire brushed the stray bits of bark off her hands over the rough pyramid of logs and kindling that she had built. "And by gosh, this wood must be plenty dry! I think it's been languishing in the woodbox for years. Get back, Lute. Could you hold him, please, Margo, until I get the screen in place? I don't think he's ever seen a fire before." She struck a long fireplace match and carefully applied the flame to the birch bark that formed the bottom-most layer of the gathered fuel. It caught, spurted, spread. The fire began to crackle and spark, tossing warmth onto Claire's face. She smiled. Then frowned. The fire sank into death and darkness. "Well, I call that odd."

"Maybe you need a refresher course in fire building?" Margo joked, holding onto a wriggling Lute from her place on the futon couch. "After all, it's been a few years since Brownies."

"Ha, ha, very funny, you young whippersnapper. No seconds on Baileys for you. Just watch this!" She struck a second match and quickly lit the bark and twigs in a host of places, creating a constellation of glowing gold points that snapped and popped. Again, the fire spread beautifully through the dry fuel, softly lighting the interior of the fire-box. And again, it sank into oblivion, all at once, as if purposefully snuffed.

Claire remained in her crouched position, holding the long fireplace match with its blackened tip, a magic wand of sorts.

Sarah cleared her throat and said in a small voice. "Um, does anyone else have the sense that this might be…well, sort of uncanny? Because I've seen a lot of fires lit, and not one of them has burned brightly, happily, and then gone out all at once, all over. Like someone has thrown a switch."

"Well, I have to admit that the same thought occurred to me." She searched the air around her for flutters, saw nothing of the kind. "Maybe three times is the charm." For good measure, she added, "Guys, could you please let the fire burn? We would really like to enjoy a nice fire while we sip our Baileys and chat. It's a chilly evening." Recalling the ghosts' coldness, she went on. "You can take my word for it. Okay?"

She tucked additional birch bark and maple twigs under the logs, struck the last match, and touched it to the kindling. Light, crackling, glowing flames. The larger pieces of kindling ignited, and the oak splits would be next. "Ah, there we go. Thank you." Claire replaced the fire screen carefully, scooped up Lute from Margo's arms, and sank in the rocking chair with him between her knees, smoothing down his tangled fur. Tamsin emerged silently from the shadows and seated herself in front of the screen, eyes closed in bliss.

"Ah, that's more like it," Marguerite stretched her feet in their paisley stocks toward the fire. "This is such a treat, my friends, don't you think so?" She sipped her Baileys delicately.

"Claire, why are the flames blue?" Grace asked. "Those logs aren't the chemical kind, are they, that make colored fire? No, of course not. They're good old oak and birch. I saw them myself." Her words were hushed.

The flames were dancing blue. The color of cornflowers,

September skies, clear lake water. The pulsing movement was that of normal flames, but the color was bizarre. A surge of welcome filled Claire's chest.

"'The lights burn blue. It is now dead midnight.

Cold fearful drops stand on my trembling flesh.

What do I fear?'"

Sarah was the one who had spoken. "From *Richard III*. The scene before the big battle on Bosworth Field. It was an old superstition, even in Shakespeare's day, that when flames burn blue, it means that ghosts are nearby."

The room was quiet except for the soft snapping of the fire, sounding like a flag rippling in a brisk wind. Lute whined, struggling to free himself from Claire's grasp and approach this unfamiliar source of light and sparkling blue warmth. She let him go and he trotted forward, detoured around Tam, and sank down on the rug. Claire could see the reflection of the blue flames leaping in the sides of his dark eyes.

So. The gang was all here.

"If the older one's an actor," Margo offered in a quavering voice, "he would know about this blue flame thing, probably. From being in the theater. Even if he doesn't know it from being—you know—a ghost."

CHAPTER 22

By early October, Claire's migraines had calmed even more, seeming to her like toned-down versions of the bright, vicious headaches that had overpowered her life for months and years. The scintillating circles still flashed and rolled in her brain, but they reminded her now of twirling sparklers rather than of brutal crowns that cut as they revolved. The ghosts always made their presence felt somehow during these migraines, offering her the sensation of fingers trailing across her forehead, the quick peeks at a memory that was not her own, the muting of sounds around her. In these ways, they comforted her and kept her company while she was afflicted.

The pain was strong but bearable. She felt humbly grateful for this development and believed that health and a sense of wellbeing would be within her grasp in time. She chose not to think beyond this mellow autumn season, and when concerns about the future shuddered into her mind, she remembered what her yoga teacher had said: "Your thoughts are like clouds, let them go." Easier said than done, of course, but her ability to shunt unwelcome trains of thought off to seldom-used sidetracks was developing, too.

At Margo's urging, she gave herself tiny little pats on the back for these accomplishments. The rewards she bestowed were simple. Walks with Scout through the leaf-tossed streets of her own neighborhood, along the Mississippi River gorge to the west, and through the prairie paths of Tamarack Nature Center. A cup of coffee and an American teacake at her favorite bake shop, notebook open on the café table in front of her. A visit to a pocket-sized mystery bookshop in Uptown Minneapolis, where the owners greeted her with kindness, reading suggestions, and inquiries after her health, and their mixed-breed border collie with a few tail-thumps on the floor. A swim at the community center in the evening, the twilit sky a tender, aching shade of starry blue when she emerged—a shade she always thought of as "Maxfield Parrish blue." The sight of Tamsin and Kipper in the same yellow window when she returned home, waiting for her.

As the weather chilled and sharpened, she thought again of her childhood autumns, which from this distance seemed redolent of apples and spicy dried leaves and wooden pencils. She recalled eating still-warm caramel corn at an autumn carnival; choosing pumpkins with Greg and Kate from rough, blazing stacks of vegetables that trailed tidbits of vine; admiring ghost decorations turning in the breeze on a neighbor's porch. She remembered running home after school and finding Gus and Kate washing the front windows and fitting the storms on. Kate would ask if she wanted to apply the Halloween clings of merry jack-o'-lanterns, witches silhouetted against harvest moons, fiendishly happy bats, loose-jointed skeletons, black cats prowling. All of these memories, burnished and missing whatever rough edges the reality might have possessed, conveyed to Claire afresh the pleasurable shiver of childhood fear and anticipation that she'd experienced as Halloween approached.

Maybe, she mused as she looked across the Mississippi at the mosaic of copper and bittersweet and coral foliage, holding Scout's slightly sticky hand in hers, she'd been longing for ghosts all her life, without realizing it, and that's why the two from the theater had come to live with her.

She wrote ruefully about all of the autumns she had missed. The Halloween decorations left in the boxes, the cards unsent, the sweatshirts left on the closet shelves, her apartment looking the same in October as it did in July, the food the same, only the cardigans and corduroys coming out eventually. She had felt so overworked and overwhelmed that she'd caught the leaves' fall colors only in snatches; then the branches were suddenly bare and rattling. "Like Sally and Linus," she wrote, "I had missed it, and a whole year would have to pass before I got the chance to see those colors again."

She knew that this had been her own fault, her own responsibility. She could've left the student essays stacked under the table on Saturday morning and taken Lute out for a long jaunt, halved a squash in the evening to reveal its flesh the color of buckskin and its scent like that of a pumpkin but milder, and served it baked for dinner, each scalloped half holding a pool of melted butter and two grindings of pepper. Instead, she had graded every day but Sunday while the trees gave up their brilliant leaves to the wind, eaten sandwiches and cereal for dinner, and ignored the harvest fare.

"I felt as if I had to work that much in order to get everything done, done even reasonably well," she wrote. "I could be a poor teacher and have a life, or I could be a better teacher and have no life outside of school." She thought about that statement and added, "No *satisfying* life outside of school, that is. My colleagues told me that they spent just ten minutes per essay, no more, or that sometimes they graded an entire stack in one go. That they took under two hours to grade twenty-five essays. Or waited two weeks to begin grading. I just couldn't do that. So where does that leave me now?" Blank space followed this question, and she closed the black and white notebook and went outside to harvest the Chinese lanterns that were growing amid the raspberry canes, thinking that the intense red-orange "lanterns" arrayed along the stalks did indeed look as if they were lit from within against the still-green foliage.

She luxuriated in having the time to take on tasks that had forever been falling off the end of her mental "to do" lists. She wrote to old friends who lived in other states, peppering them with questions about their lives. She also wrote a long, heartfelt letter to Kate, telling her how much the gift of the house, the funds, and the cat meant to her and how thankful she felt for Kate's warm presence in her life. "I miss you, Aunt Kate," she wrote. "I'm sorry that even when I was with you physically in those last years, I was sometimes absent mentally." She crossed out "sometimes" and replaced it with "often." The pen moved across the paper slowly. "If I had the chance to make different choices now, I would." When she was satisfied with the letter, she recopied it and pasted the final version into her notebook.

She decorated her living room with a motley collection of Halloween decorations that she'd gathered together over the years: a pop-up haunted house that her mother had bought for her when Claire was younger than Scout was now; a cardboard skeleton that Greg had called "Tingly Bones" and pretended was speaking to him, to Claire's consternation; a small plastic pumpkin with a missing handle and a sheepish grin. She hesitated over a ceramic ghost figure with a slight potbelly, its shrouded arms up in the classic "boo!" position. Would it give offense to the spirits who had come with the clock? Well, she hoped not, but she decided that the ceramic ghost had languished in a shoebox and tissue paper long enough. "I got this when I was in grad school," she said aloud as she placed it on top of one of the built-in bookcases that separated living room and dining room. "I remember that it cost five dollars at a craft sale. That was a lot of money to me then, and I almost walked away from it. I'm glad I didn't; I've never seen anything quite like it since. Cute, isn't it?" There was no answer. The late afternoon sunlight tilted in through the western windows and fell, a fine, glowing gangplank, on the floor in front of the bookcase. Kipper looked up inquiringly, her ears pink and translucent, motes floating over her head. Claire smiled and continued decorating.

She came across a gift that a student in her last Shakespeare class had designed and constructed for her: a miniature stage only about twelve inches long, complete with a trapdoor, a railed gallery behind the stage, and gathered red curtains hanging on tiny dowels. The student had been one in a million, a whiz at music, math, and physics and an excellent lit. student as well. And a genuinely nice person. Where was she now? Claire had no idea, but the memory of that young woman's enthusiasm, intelligence, and thoughtfulness soothed Claire as she gently manipulated the trap door and set the four accompanying finger puppets—Hamlet, Ophelia, Gertrude, and Claudius—in a row across the front of the stage. Carefully lifting the whole ensemble, she carried it across the room and set it on the end table. Maybe the sight of it would encourage her to think about students like Melanie, and thereby counterbalance the grief and sense of failure she felt in regard to so many others.

As she swept through the living room that evening, she noticed that Hamlet was now perched on the gallery behind the stage, while Claudius, with his mean eyes and golden felt crown, was emerging from the trap door. Ophelia and Gertrude were embracing on the stage itself.

"Whoa," Claire said. She perched carefully on the front edge of the couch, feeling her hands dampen and chill and her breath catch lightly in her throat. Tingles flowed over the top of her head to her eyebrows. Silence. Stillness. Then, as she watched, the Hamlet puppet hopped from one side of the gallery to the other. Claudius disappeared altogether under the stage. The tiny trapdoor swung down over him, and Ophelia left Gertrude to stand firmly on top of the trap.

"Yes," Claire said. "It's best to keep that Claudius under control. He's a mean one." Gertrude swept forward from the backstage area and joined Ophelia. "Good, two women are always better than one, I think. And Hamlet is probably considering just what he should do next. Typical. I've always felt bad that Ophelia and Gertrude aren't able to support each other better in the play. Ophelia could certainly use some more women in her life, and so could Gertrude, come to think of it. They could've been like mother and daughter." The Gertrude puppet's long arm went protectively around Ophelia's shoulders. At that moment, Claudius's head came rearing up through the trap, throwing both women off their feet. (So to speak; as finger puppets, they had no actual feet). "On, no!" Claire's exclamation of dismay was genuine. "He's back again!" The Hamlet puppet leapt from the gallery to center stage below and began dueling with Claudius despite the fact that neither puppet possessed a sword. They bashed arms furiously, Hamlet driving his wicked uncle stage left.

She eased herself back in the couch to survey the action and watch the child ghost play, just as she had watched Scout play so often in the past. Of course, a child who had come from a theater would enjoy manipulating a diminutive stage and actor-puppets. A puff of January drifted over her face and stirred her loose hair. Her breath frosted. She shivered eagerly and welcomed the images: legs in breeches and white stockings pumping up a metal spiral stairway, dazzling lights overhead, an uprush of music from an orchestra pit. A boy actor, just as some of Shakespeare's original actors had been boys. Amazing. He was here with her, right this moment, moving the puppets to tell his own story. Remembering a performance of *The Winter's Tale* that she had attended several years ago, she whispered joyfully, "'Go, play, boy, play.' That theater's all yours."

Vanquished, Claudius dropped to the oaken floor below the theater, prompting Hamlet to hold up his arms in triumph.

AFTER WRITING about that encounter in as much detail as she could muster, exulting in the new information she had obtained and the tenuous connection she had made with the boy, she found herself drifting onto other topics. "I've noticed that I'm choosing to wear hoodies almost every day," she noted, "and wondered why. They do offer some shelter if it's needed, since I can always hide in the hood. Then I realized that these tops and jackets are clothes that I would never wear to work. I wouldn't wear wild socks, either." She looked down and rotated her right foot clad in magenta and violet. "It's good to be able to wear what I want instead of what the job demands. Although, of course, I know that people wear what the job demands every day. A uniform of sorts." She remembered how her father had always retreated to his room and changed his clothes as soon as he came home from work every evening, even though the khakis and button-down shirts that he wore to school looked perfectly comfortable to her. She hadn't understood his need to change clothes then and hadn't thought to ask him about it. Now, she felt she understood without asking.

.   .   .

THE GHOSTS WERE UNUSUALLY active that week. Four days after the puppet theater came to life, Claire was washing the hardwood floor in the sunroom, on her hands and knees with an old, damp towel. As she bent her head to give the shining boards a final swipe, a storm of frigid air descended on her, as distinct as a sudden squall. She could almost see snowflakes whirling in front of her eyes, blizzard-blown. She gasped, felt the cold air sting the inside of her cheeks. Then the memories and emotions that did not belong to her arrived. Pacing, pacing, in a cluttered room, panic crawling up the throat from the gut. A counter strewn with stubby sticks of makeup, a battered box of Kleenex, cloudy water glasses, greeting cards. The room was dim, but the expansive mirror was rimmed with golden bulbs, casting lights and shadows down. The sound of retching, throat-clearing, gurgling. A part of Claire was able to articulate a wish: "Look in the mirror so I can see your face!" Her wish was not granted. Instead, she saw tall leather boots striding, struts and ropes, other actors scuttling off stage. She heard the rustling of their dresses, like autumn leaves in an evening wind. Nausea, saliva filling the mouth, the black thought, "I can't do this! I can't!" filling every crevice of heart and mind.

She lifted her head. The brittle October sunshine angling through the windows illuminated her hands that were flat on the floor. She flexed her fingers gently. "That must've been so hard," she said aloud. "To have stage fright like that, with the audience waiting for you to perform. Feeling sick with dread, realizing that you *had* to go on. I know what that feels like, actually. Really, I do."

She wrote, "Feeling that actor's fear, I realized that I had been struck with stage fright, too. Or performance anxiety— whatever you want to call it. First I felt sick just on Sunday evenings, with the weight of the week to come on my shoulders. Then on Monday mornings, too. Then every morning. Always, those reactions would fade in time. Okay, I thought; at least I'm functioning when I'm actually at work and teaching. Next, the nausea started to sweep over me when I would I enter the college building, or a migraine would strike when I took hold of the handle to an outside door, as if it were electrically charged. Finally, I felt sick the entire time, morning and night, at home or at school." She forced herself to write the next words, "Retching. Throwing up." And the final sentence for the day, "At last, I knew that I couldn't go into a classroom one more time. So I left." She shut the notebook, laid the pen crossways on top, and asked the thin air, "So what happened to you? What happened to you, my friend?"

CHAPTER 23

$\mathcal{H}$er father called a few days later to tell her that an old friend and colleague of his, Ed Hurley, had died, and that he was flying into the Cities for the funeral the day after tomorrow. "At first, I figured I would just think about him here, honor his memory by planting tulip bulbs or something like that. Then I realized that I needed to attend the funeral. Wanted to come, I mean. For him, for his family. For me." His voice sounded heavy with grief and far away, even though Claire knew he was calling from a phone tethered securely to the wall in his St. Louis duplex. Her heart ached for him.

"Of course, Dad. I understand. Would you like to stay with me? I could pick you up at the airport, and you could borrow my car for the funeral." She thought a moment and then actually spoke the words that she wanted him to hear. "It would be good to see you."

"Thank you, daughter. I would like that. I'll see about the plane ticket right away and let you know the times. Talk to you soon."

. . .

THE DAY of the funeral was chilled by a north wind. They walked with Lute by the lake after lunch, admiring the rippled ranks of clouds that led straight over the bucking waves and beyond, a path north to Duluth, it seemed. After David had set out for the funeral in Claire's car, she began to prepare a special dinner for him, thinking that some comfort food was called for. She heated Tater Tots, browned grass-fed beef and mild onions, measured cheddar cheese and Worcestershire sauce, and stirred seasonings into cream of mushroom soup. The windows misted and the kitchen warmed and grew fragrant with the elements of Tater Tot Hotdish. Lute was so engrossed in the possibility that she might drop some savory morsel that he could barely tear himself away from the kitchen when the sound of the front door opening reached them. Finally, he pelted off to greet David and then trotted proudly ahead, a canine advance guard, as David entered the kitchen.

"What smells so delicious? Holy smokes, you're cooking! Will wonders never cease." Dressed in a black suit, white shirt, and somber blue tie, David looked like an elder states-man, Claire thought. He kissed her on the cheek as she stirred the soup, leaving a hint of Ivory soap scent behind when he stepped back from her.

"I thought I'd make a hearty dinner for us both," she offered shyly. "The recipe came from the Internet, but it originally appeared in a church cookbook, like the ones that Gus used to have. It's cool enough today for an old-fashioned Minnesota hotdish, I thought." She looked down and revolved the spoon in the seasoned cream of mushroom soup once more. "How was the funeral?"

"Sobering. Ed was only seventy-three, you know. He'd been retired less than seven years. Heart attack, while he was hauling brush at his cabin up north." David shook his head regretfully. "The funeral was sad. Joyful, too. A lot of his former students came, and his colleagues, like me. The place was packed. The stories people told..." He ran a hand roughly through his hair, and Claire thought he might be working to keep more emotion pushed down.

She took his forearm, the unfamiliar fabric of his suit slightly scratchy against her fingertips. "Why don't you change into more comfortable clothes and I'll finish this up and make us both some coffee. The hotdish needs to spend a half an hour in a moderate oven. Whatever that might be. I need to google it."

David offered her a wintry smile. "Three-fifty, daughter. A moderate oven is three-fifty." He shook his head in disbelief. "First, coffee, now hot dish. What will you serve me the next time I come?"

"That," she replied, knocking the soup that clung to the bowl of the spoon back into the saucepan, "remains to be seen."

THE HOTDISH WAS SO DELICIOUS, with its uppermost layer of melted cheese and shredded potatoes, that they both had seconds. Then David set the plates to soak in the sink, and they returned to the table. Claire would've liked to light one of the beeswax pillar candles but was afraid someone might turn up to manipulate the flame, so she set the cold candle on the buffet as if she were making room for mugs of black Irish tea and the frosted pumpkin-shaped sugar cookies she had bought for him at a neighborhood bakery. He picked up his cookie, snapped it in two, and said, "Ah, I remember these. They were your favorites around this time of year. Kate used to get them for you as you a treat."

"Yes, I did love them. My *favorites*, though, were the cupcakes with orange or chocolate frosting and the little plastic Halloween decorations stuck into the top: black cats and skulls and witches and that. But I remembered that you're not really a cake person."

David laid his cookie down. "Family. They know all of your secrets." Father and daughter sipped tea and crunched cookies for a moment. Then David cleared his throat, preparing to speak about something important, Claire realized. "I'll miss Ed, even though I hadn't seen him in years. Miss knowing that he's still in the world, still in Minnesota, radiating…decency and kindness and fairness. He was a fine teacher and a fine colleague. He helped me many times through the years, and I'll always be grateful for that."

"I know what you mean. My colleagues are the best—the best. Well, almost all of them. There are a few I wouldn't want to share a desert island with."

"That Marguerite is a rare gem, isn't she? Such a lively person. She must be a dynamo in the classroom. That's an especially valuable trait to have when your subject matter is —how shall I put this—not the most dramatic."

Claire smiled. "Yes, Margo is great. She's my best friend, no question. It's so good to be able to tell someone anything you want and know that it will be accepted. That *you'll* be accepted. Including your most embarrassing teaching moments: the clunkers, the mistakes, the frustrations. I would never tell a non-teacher some of those things for fear of being labeled a whiner or an incompetent. Most people think that being a teacher is a walk in the park."

"Well, depends which park that is. The Everglades, maybe, with swamps and quicksand and *gators*." He furrowed his brow ferociously and then let it relax. "Along with beautiful birds and flowers and such," he added. "Let's not exaggerate."

Claire laughed easily at his metaphor. "That is so accurate, Dad. I think that one of the hardest parts of the job is how unpredictable it is. 'One day you're a diamond and then you're a stone.'"

"You must've done something right with the student who made that miniature theater for you. Such nice work—I'll bet it took her hours and hours to construct that."

"Yes, but she was one out of—oh, I don't know how many. And you know what? The same week that she gave me that, a different student wrote a long email message to me that contained veiled suicide threats." Claire felt her stomach knot and roil in response to this memory. Yet somehow, she wanted her father to hear it, so she continued the story as he stirred uneasily in his chair, his gray eyes watching her. "She wasn't threatening to kill herself if she got a bad grade— nothing like that. She was just…full of despair, and I was the one she decided to confide in."

"What happened?"

"Well, of course, I called the counseling office right away. She needed a mental health care professional, not an English teacher! I forwarded her message to a counselor and then went to talk with him. And do you know what his response was?"

David swallowed visibly and shook his head.

"He said, 'Since you're the one she reached out to, you're the one who has the best chance of getting her to come in for help. She may be just bluffing, anyway. Students do that sometimes, to get attention.' Just bluffing! And what if she weren't? I wrote to her and waited for a reply. Didn't sleep at all that night, waiting. I was so scared. Terrified that she wouldn't write back or that I had said the wrong thing and set her off. She did finally agree to meet me at my office the next day, and we walked down to the counseling office together. She was in the hospital by that afternoon. She was cutting herself, Dad. Her arms and legs were covered in knife wounds, I found out later. That's why she always wore long-sleeved shirts." Claire found that her hands were twisting the cloth napkin into a tight spiral. She dropped it abruptly, a red pool by her plate.

David's lips were pressed into a thin line and his voice was imbued with iron. "That counselor's response was completely irresponsible, daughter! Who was he to judge from that distance whether she was serious in her threats or not? It's not your job to deal with suicidal students--that's not your training! You didn't sign on for that."

"No, I didn't." She looked up at her father's handsome, concerned face, shrugged. "But that's what I have to deal with. I loved being a student, and I thought that being a teacher would be a grown-up version of that. It wasn't. Not often, anyway."

"I should have shown you more of my own problems and challenges, I think. I always tried to do my work at school, or when you were with Gus or Kate, or outside playing, or asleep—anytime except when you could see me. I wanted to protect you from my work, let you be a child who wasn't weighed down. I thought you had enough to deal with. Maybe I should have been more open with you about my profession, so you could go into it, if you chose to, without illusions."

She covered his large, clenched hands with her smaller ones and squeezed them. "Dad, you did the best you could in a hard, hard situation. You were right to protect me. And Greg. Our childhood was as secure and light as it could possibly be under the circumstances. Okay? You three were the adults and you let Greg and me be kids. I didn't need to hear about the discipline problems and disappointments that you dealt with every school year. Every week, probably. I made my own choice of careers, and I'll deal with the effects of that decision. I'll be fine. Really." Surprising herself, she actually believed this reassurance.

David folded her fingertips in against his palms and nodded. "Just be sure that this job is worth it. Because no amount of financial security is more important than health. And a sense of well-being. You hear? There are always options. Always."

"Thanks, Dad. Thanks for saying that. And for listening."

THE WIND SWUNG around during the night and was blowing from the south, mild and almost summery, by morning. Claire wanted to take her father to a park for a long hike, but David insisted that they use the early part of the day to wash windows and swap the screens for storms. He really did want to help her ready the house for winter, she could tell, and since the old-fashioned storm windows were heavy and cumbersome, she was grateful for the assistance. Not all of the windows had screens installed, luckily, and they went to work on the ones that did. She cleaned the large panes in the storms with Windex and an old t-shirt, and he removed the screen windows and lifted the storms to hang them.

As they worked, he gave her a brief lecture about the benefits and drawbacks of this old style of windows. Claire let the words flow over her, focusing on her simple task of making the glass in the storms shine, and adding a noncommittal "hmm" occasionally. They left two of the screen windows in place, one in the front of the house and one in the back, so she could get some fresh air during these last weeks of October, which might contain more backward-looking days like this one.

"But don't forget to put those two storm windows in!" David exhorted her. "The windows themselves will take a terrible beating during the winter months if you don't. Not to mention driving up your heating costs." He glared at her as if she were planning to defy him.

"Okay, okay. I promise! Remember, this is my house now, and I've grown attached to it. I'll take good care of it." She smiled to soften her words. "After all, it will be here longer than I will, most probably." Would she join the present ghostly inhabitants when she "shuffled off this mortal coil," Claire wondered idly? Well, that would be one way of finding out who they were, what their stories were. Why they haunted.

"Hmph. No need to get morbid," David grumbled. "Hand me that Windex, will you? I see a streak here." And he gestured toward the glass that already gleamed and tossed back reflections of clean sky and high clouds.

THAT EVENING, as her father was absorbed in the new issue of *National Geographic* in the living room, Claire noticed the sky through the double-paned glass of the back door. Only the merest sliver away from full, a misty, rose-gold moon bobbed above the treetops. To Claire, it looked plump with autumn, its dappled surface appearing to undulate like prairie grass under the press of wind. "That's really something," she said aloud, swallowing hard. Beautiful sights like this huge moon moved her in a way that she could not articulate. She realized that she had the time and energy to notice quotidian pleasures these days, to stand and look as she was doing now, unhurried and appreciative.

Someone had joined her. Tendrils of chilly air curved lightly around her cheekbones and forehead, feeling like a gentle embrace. She placed one tingling hand over the top of this ghostly touch, feeling the coolness sandwiched between her warm palm and forehead. "Hey, there," she whispered. "Isn't that a gorgeous harvest moon?"

· · ·

THE GHOSTS KEPT a low profile during the night and the following morning, their only action being to puncture each yolk of the four eggs that David was cooking for breakfast. Beyond a baffled look and exclamations of surprise that the yolks would break in a pan while covered with a lid, he didn't offer much response to this. "Broken yolks. Well, in each life, a little rain must fall," he muttered as he slid the eggs onto their plates. "Do you have any hot sauce, daughter? I like just a dash on my fried eggs."

CLAIRE GAVE him a real hug before he took his place in the wending security line at the airport, standing on tiptoe to lay her cheek against his for a moment. "I'm sorry that it was a sad event that brought you north again, Dad, but it was good to see you." She grasped his arm lightly. "Thanks for all your help with the storm windows." Impulsively, she added, "And for the talk. You know, the one about teaching." She dipped her head, feeling her left eyelid begin to twitch and not wanting her father to see.

"Claire, you can talk with me anytime about whatever's on your mind. Teaching. Careers. Finances. Whatever." He cupped the back of her head gently with his palm. "Just promise me one thing."

"What's that?" Claire risked a quick glance up, thinking that he wouldn't notice her jumping eyelid in that brief view.

His own frost-colored eyes snapped. "Call me from your landline." And with a bark of laughter, he waved her away from him.

THE DAYS TUMBLED one over the other, blue, red, orange, gorgeous. Claire watched the peach-colored blush in a rustling maple gradually deepen to scarlet, scuffed through freshly-fallen leaves as bright as golden coins, listened to their dry brethren as they skittered away before the gusty wind, and chose pumpkins for the back steps that sported pale blond vines twisting from the stems. Had there ever been such an autumn in her life, or was the difference just that she had the time and the energy to notice? Both, she thought. Still buffeted by headaches, grief, and uncertainty, she breathed deeply during the intervals between these troubles, promised herself that she would relish every shred of this banner autumn that she could, spent hours outside every day so that when twilight fell, she was able to smell the fresh, cold air on her jacket and in her hair as she stepped inside to light lamps, feed animals, and cook her own dinner.

On Thursday, in the midst of raking the back lawn, she decided that she would plant tulip bulbs, knowing that the blooms' color would be as welcome in April as the leaves' shades of sorrel, sienna, and ochre that she was enjoying now. She hurried inside to get her purse and car keys, wanting to buy the bulbs and get them in the ground that same afternoon before she lost her energy or the soil hardened against her digging. She would buy a new trowel, too. And maybe another bag of bark mulch to spread around the purple asters that grew next to the garage—something dark to set off their dainty, star-like flowers.

An hour later, she walked up the curving path toward the back door, netted bags of tulip bulbs swinging from one hand, her sparkling keys from the other. Her feet slowed, pattered to a stop.

The screen in the east window was torn wide open.

CHAPTER 24

*C*laire dropped the bags onto the grass and lunged for the back door, fumbling to fit the key into the lock. She was calling before the storm door clicked shut behind her. "Lute? Kipper? Tam? Where are you? Come!" Her voice shuddered and cracked. Oh, God, the cats could've escaped as soon as that screen was torn; they could be terrified, lost, dead by the side of the road. And Lute? He probably wouldn't have jumped out of the window, but what if he had? What if the intruder who'd punched through the screen window had hurt him? A sob burst out of her throat, tearing it painfully. This was her fault, all her fault. She'd forgotten to shut and lock the window before leaving home, and her carelessness had left her pets vulnerable to a criminal.

Immediately, the familiar spots of a migraine rose up like predatory fish and began to swim across her vision, growing ominously. And she had to be able to see, had to be able to search the house for her pets.

A vague white figure appeared in the doorway to the dining room, down low. Was it one of the ghosts, manifesting itself in traditional form? She heard panting, followed by the ticking sound of toenails on hardwood. Paws were planted against her knees, and a cold damp nose brushed her knuckles. "Lute, thank God." She sank down to hug him, hard, and he licked her cheeks, which were already wet, she noticed. "Are you all right?" She cupped his head, ran her hands over his ribs and then along his skinny terrier legs. He didn't wince or pull away. Okay, then. Okay.

The migraine's spots had expanded into fireworks, each twirl throwing out sparks that sliced. Taking hold of Lute by his collar, Claire fumbled her way to the breached screen, slammed the window shut, and locked it. But what if the cats were outside and came home, only to find the portal that they had taken blocked? It was worth the risk for the moment. She released Lute and stumbled into the dining room, grabbing whatever she could for support and a sense of location: the edge of the buffet, the backs of the dining room chairs, the top of the eastern-side bookcase. "Kipper? Tam? Come. Please come." She tried to keep her desperation pushed down, thinking that it would frighten the cats away from her. Her teeth rattled together and her legs were leaden. Don't hyperventilate, she pleaded with her own traitorous body. Don't pass out. Don't have a panic attack. Please, just don't.

Like most cats, Kipper came only when she wanted to, usually when she thought that a treat was in the offing. Claire wracked her pain-drenched memory to recall a single time that Tam had come when called. Usually, Claire didn't press the matter and chose not to call her at all. But today... couldn't they come to her when she so needed to find them?

"Mrrr?" Someone warm and furry brushed against her ankles. Again, she knelt, slowly this time, and stroked the cat that had approached her. "Kipper?" Yes, it was Kipper, with upstanding, rather rough fur instead of Tam's plushness, Kipper's high meow rather than Tam's low, scratchy one.

"Good girl, good girl. Where's Tam, eh?" Claire picked the cat up and embraced her. Kip felt sturdy in her arms; a light purring reverberated through the cat's chest.

Claire still couldn't see much through the migraine's whirly-gigs, couldn't think clearly through the pain. Yet, she knew that she needed help. With Kip in her arms and Lute trotting at her heels, she made her way to the bedroom and called 911: "I've been robbed!" Next, letting her index finger recall the pattern, she tapped out Marguerite's cell phone number. She counted the rings and prayed that Marguerite would be available to answer. Prayer answered. "Margo, I need help. Please."

And her friend reached out, concerned, reassuring, utterly trustworthy. "I'll be there in ten minutes. Hold on, Claire. Just hold on."

SINCE MARGO WAS COMING from campus, she arrived before the police. Claire still hadn't found Tamsin, and her story of what had happened was jumbled and incomplete. But Marguerite, holding both of Claire's icy hands, understood what needed to be done. She guided Claire to the couch, brought her a can of ginger ale from the fridge, and wrapped one of her palms around Claire's brow and the other around the back of her skull, pressing hard. "Will you be all right here while I look for Tamsin?" The buzz of the doorbell made them both jump. "It's the police, Claire. Can you…"

"I can talk with them. Just find Tam. Please, Margo. Find Tam." Claire heard her friend explaining in a low voice to the police officer what had happened. The ocular explosions going off in Claire's brain were as intense as ever, as was the sheering pain. Her stomach was beginning to roil. She took another taste of the ginger ale and waited. Needling sensations in her right fingers began to probe up her arm. Oh, no. This migraine was going to be a monster. Again.

She felt someone sit beside her, saw only a dark shadow through the migraine's aura. "Miss, I'm Officer Jackson. I'm sorry to disturb you when you're sick, but I really need to talk with you as soon as possible, and your friend told me that your headaches can last hours or even a whole day." His voice was gentle, considerate.

She nodded numbly, fists jammed against temples. "Yes, please…just go ahead."

"Okay. I understand that your house has been broken into. Also that you can't see well right now and that you're in a lot of pain. Tell me, was there a television and maybe a DVD player on this console in front of us?"

THE KIND POLICE officer asked questions and Claire stuttered her answers, unable to enumerate all that had been taken. She swallowed again and again, fighting the nausea and taking tiny sips of ginger ale when she felt able. Her mind formed some coherent thoughts, even in the midst of the onslaught. What if Tamsin is lost? Kate trusted me with her pet, and now I've lost her. She'll be so vulnerable outside, and so frightened. Images of Tam hiding under a car or beside concrete steps, ears back, eyes huge, brought out a broken sob. She clamped her fingers over her mouth to forestall any other sounds from escaping and tried to concentrate on what the officer was saying.

Lute approached, and she felt him lean against her legs. She stroked the side of his face to calm herself.

Footsteps. Margo's voice from across the room. "Claire, I found her! She was crouching in the lowest shelf of the bookcase in your office. Behind the poetry volumes. I could see her eyes shining out from where she had hidden. She's okay. Just a little scared, I think."

Claire's shoulders slumped and relief poured over her, through her. She hadn't failed Aunt Kate or Tamsin utterly, although this tale might've had a very different ending. The animals were all right...that was all that mattered. The screen could be repaired; she would never, ever leave a window open again when she wasn't home. She would research home security systems... Hot fury burned away the relief. That bastard who had broken in! How dare he enter her home, scare her pets like this, steal her TV and DVD player and who knows what else...

Margo spoke through her diatribe, her voice washed with regret. "Sister, the robber took the cuckoo clock."

WITH MARGO'S HELP, the police officer was able to create a preliminary list of what had been stolen: the TV and DVD player, some DVDs, her camera with all of the photos from recent months, a metal Big Ben bank full of loose change. And the cuckoo clock.

Officer Jackson wrote this all down, including a detailed description of the clock given to him by Marguerite, seemingly unsurprised by its inclusion on the list, saying that the robber probably took it on a whim. "Who knows why someone is attracted to a particular object? I've known of some odd things taken: a glass frog, a pair of women's cowboy boots, a jar of aggies, a black fedora. People can be unpredictable."

Don't I know it, thought Claire mournfully. Where were the ghosts? What would be their reaction to having their home stolen? She hoped that they wouldn't be terribly upset. She felt a heavy cloak of dread settle over her at the thought of losing the clock, then snatched at the sliver of possibility that it would be recovered. Officer Jackson had told her that he would contact the local pawnshops and antique stores and forward the clock's description to the owners. Walter Henson would recognize the clock immediately, of course, if anyone brought it to him. Her thoughts raced, caroming from one side of her splintered mind to the other like hot bolts of energy. Perhaps she could create some other kind of home for the ghosts while they all waited for the clock's fate to be clear…some kind of shelter for them. Seemingly out of nowhere, she recalled seeing a picture of an accent light shaped like a cabin, three-dimensional, the walls root beer colored, the windows a shade brighter, glowing cozily. A lamp like that could serve as both a refuge for the spirits and a ghost light. If she could order one right away, it would probably be here in…

Officer Jackson interrupted her plans. "Ms. Bracken, I hate to hit you while you're down, but I really have to say this. What you did in entering the house before the police arrived was very dangerous. What if the perpetrator of the robbery had still been here? That situation could've been much more serious than what we have here: a few pieces of electronics and an old clock missing."

Claire's chaotic head dipped toward the haven of her clammy hands. She couldn't even get being a robbery victim down right.

ONCE OFFICER JACKSON HAD LEFT, Margo helped Claire into the bedroom, spread a fleece blanket over her, and left her in peace. Claire heard her murmuring in the living room and guessed that she was calling Jason in as a reinforcement. Kip leapt lightly up on the bed and nestled against her side, kneading the blanket. Automatically, Claire gently disengaged her claws and waited. The ghosts had always come when she was under the influence of a migraine, maybe out of sympathy, maybe because she was halfway between her world and theirs—out of her rational mind, at any rate. She waited, eyes squeezed shut, tears sliding silently out of the corners of her eyes into her tousled hair, breathing into the pain, angry that her home had been violated in this way, grateful that the animals were safe, frustrated that the ghosts hadn't protected her and themselves in some manner. "Why didn't you scare them away?" she asked aloud and waited. For her toes to be pulled. For unfamiliar, yet comforting visions to slide into her suffering mind. For a hand to be laid across her brow.

She waited. Again, fear poked its spikey fingers into her consciousness, intertwining with the migraine symptoms. Even with her eyes closed, she knew that the air around her was empty and still. "Where are you?" she croaked. "Guys? Give me a sign here, won't you? It's been a rough day. For you, too, probably. But we need to stick together. We belong together, you know? Your two and me and the animals."

Silence. Empty, eerie silence. And still she waited, stroking Kipper until the cat fell asleep. She clamped her lips together so tightly that her incisors cut into the tender flesh on her lips' undersides, cleared her throat, reached out with her thoughts for the young man ghost and the child ghost, willing one or both of them to return her gesture. Nothing. The room was neutral, quiet, still. Through her eyelids and her pain, she felt rather than saw that twilight was falling. Lute trotted through the doorway, shook noisily, and retreated, probably to ask Margo to feed him his dinner.

Hours passed. Darkness enveloped the room. She heard the radiator in the room tick as water circulated into it and then smelled the hot, homey smell of radiators that work. The front door opened and shut, and the low voices of Margo and Jason reached her.

Claire had to admit to herself what she'd suspected from the moment she had been left alone in this room with her jarring pain, blazing visions, and tattered soul.

The ghosts were gone.

THE NEXT MORNING, Jason installed the storm into the window that had been breached and left for work, promising to drop off the busted screen at the neighborhood hardware store so that it could be repaired. The two women sat in the breakfast nook, drinking coffee and talking.

"I should have known as soon as you told me that the clock had been stolen. The ghosts didn't just come with the clock; they were attached to it somehow. It was kind of a home within a home for them, I think. Remember that time that I let it run down? The older ghost was furious with me. But I thought that they would—save themselves somehow. I was even angry with them for not scaring the crap out of the robber and driving him away." She sniffled and reached for a Kleenex from the box on a seldom-used chair. "I think I'm coming down with something," she told Margo miserably.

"Maybe he took them by surprise, somehow," Margo ventured. "They live a pretty safe life with you." She frowned at what she had just said, pulled the sleeves of her sweater over the backs of her hands, and added, "Using the term loosely, of course. A visit from your father has been about the worst thing they've experienced since you got the clock, it seems to me."

"Yes, that's probably true. Although I think they had fun with him, ultimately. The boy did, anyway. The older guy kept a low profile while he was here. Damn!"

"What?"

"I'm going to have to call Dad and tell him what happened. What happened because of my carelessness." She swallowed down the uprush of breakfast and shifted uneasily in her chair, then ran her claddagh pendent on its golden chain.

Margo reached out across the table. "Claire, please don't start tearing at your fingernails again. They've looked so nice the past month or so." Startled, Claire clenched her hands in her lap. "You're going to be fine. Call your dad when *you* want to. It's all up to you. Remember?" She smiled encouragingly.

"That's the problem," Claire ground out. "I don't feel up to anything." She thought for a long moment. "Except smashing the face of the person who broke into my home."

Margo didn't exclaim in surprise. She didn't rebuke her friend for the violent speech. She didn't say, "You know you don't mean that." Instead, she said, "I could do the same, my friend. I could do the same."

AFTER MARGO HAD LEFT to teach, wearing the clothes that Jason had brought for her in an overnight bag, Claire called her insurance agent and then wandered around the house aimlessly, searching for more empty spaces that should be filled by her possessions, wondering which objects and pieces of furniture the thief had violated by his touch. At least he didn't take any of Kate's things, she thought to herself, pausing in front of the empty console. Not even the *Scarecrow and Mrs. King* DVDs. I guess I can watch them to my heart's content now. Once I get a new TV and DVD player, that is. After the dramatic events of her first "viewing party," she hadn't dared to pop another of the discs into the player, although she had been gathering her courage in recent weeks to do just that—maybe with the support of her friends. Too late now.

She flumped onto the futon couch, disturbing Tam, who had finally emerged from her haven behind the books of poetry earlier in the morning. The cat meowed in protest and put out a steadying paw as a person might take hold of a gunwale on a rocking boat. "Sorry. Sorry, Tamsin." The cat accepted Claire's light caress without flinching and gazed at her with shuttered eyes. Claire continued speaking aloud. "Maybe this is a blessing in disguise. I couldn't bring myself to get rid of the clock to find out if that took the ghosts out of the house, as well. I just couldn't do that. And now, the clock is gone, through no fault of my own." She hurried on. "Well, at least with no conscious decision. I didn't *mean* to banish the ghosts. Had no idea that accidentally leaving the window open would result in their... disappearance. So I'm free of them, without any guilt attached. Right?" Tam's green gaze was calm, inscrutable.

Without meaning to, she glanced up at the empty wall where the clock had hung. The lack of ticking was louder than the actual ticking had been, and the wall looked utterly blank and bereft.

She thought about the spirits individually. The boy who played with food, liked the animals, painted smiling moons and shining stars on her guestroom wall. Was attracted to a homemade toy stage and its puppet-actors. Then she switched her focus to the young man who reached out kindly when she was in pain, felt envy about the performance of another actor, and battled stage fright, just as she had, in her own way, battled stage fright in the classroom. She thought about their company, their mystery, their engagement with her home.

She didn't know their names or how they had died or why they haunted. She was just beginning to understand their nature, and her own, through her journal writing. They were her puzzle box, with the secret latch that would open the door yet undiscovered. She missed them. She wanted them back. They were her ghosts.

IT TURNED out that a cold *had* been lurking somewhere in her body and now was wrapping its tentacles around her, squeezing out whatever energy and ambition she might have otherwise summoned up. For several days, she occupied the couch and then the bed, the bed and then the couch, sleeping the heavy sleep of the NyQuil-taker. She coughed and sneezed and drank lemon-ginger tea, cup after cup, and nibbled Malt-O-Meal from a spoon. Her throat ached, her bones ached, her head ached, and her heart ached. Why would a person grieve the loss of a pair of strangers who were already deceased? They had scared her and complicated her life, moved into her new home without an invitation. Yet she missed them dreadfully. In her black and white notebook, she wrote about the day she'd bought the clock. "I think that they chose me. They wanted me to pick the clock, meaning that they must've sensed some kind of connection between us. I remember the prickling feeling at the back of my neck, a sensation that I've felt in their presence many times since then. And I heard the sound of applause, saw a spotlight, and felt happy and hopeful at the prospect of taking that clock home. They came to me." She paused, lifted her reading glasses to dab at her eyes, and continued writing. "And now they're gone." Period.

SHE ANSWERED the phone when it rang because the caller might be the police with news on the theft. Or it might be one of her circle, and she didn't want anyone coming over and risking infection to check on her if she didn't pick up.

When Grace called, she thoughtfully asked if Claire needed any groceries or supplies, and if she wanted company.

"Thank you, Grace, that's so kind of you, but no, not just yet. I have the animals, after all. I've even been going out for walks around the block with Lute. And that little bit of exercise and fresh air has been good for me. The cats are always ready to hang out, too. Tam perches on the back of the couch and Kipper snuggles up. The insurance claim is moving along. So we're all fine here. Really fine. How are you?"

Rather than answering that question, Grace offered one of her own. "You miss the ghosts, don't you? I know you do. And Claire? If you get them back, I think it would be fine for Scott to stay at your house again. He really wants to. If he's not afraid, then maybe I shouldn't be, either. And when you think about it, isn't this just another way to be inclusive and respectful of others? Maybe this is the new frontier: acceptance of ghosts." She sighed heavily. "Anyway, I just wanted you to know that. And also that I hope you find out where they are and rescue them. If anyone can do that, you can. Okay?"

The resulting constriction of Claire's throat sent her into a paroxysm of coughing. "Thank you, Grace," she finally wheezed into the receiver. "You're the best—the best sister-in-law ever."

"Same back. Now take care of yourself, you hear? Scott wants to come visit you by the weekend. And although I would send him to your house if it were haunted, I won't send him there if it's still full of germs. Bye!"

Claire hung up the phone and stretched one stockinged foot out to Lute, who sniffed it politely. "You want to go on a walk, hey, Lute? Let's go a little farther this time, do some leaf-peeping in the neighborhood. I need to shake this cold and get on with things, like planting the tulip bulbs I bought. And visiting Walter Henson at the antique store."

CHAPTER 25

The next afternoon, she slipped into an insulated barn jacket that was heavier than the weather required and drove toward Walter Henson's shop, timing her visit so that she would arrive about an hour before closing. She hoped that she would find him alone, and she did.

In response to the chirp of the door alarm, he turned from the bookshelf he was dusting. The fluffy blue Swiffer on its plastic handle sagged toward the floor as he recognized her. "Ms. Bracken—Claire—it's good to see you. Please sit down." He gestured toward the table that they had used the last time she had come. "Are you all right?" His wild brows beetled as he watched her make her way to a seat. He took the place across from her, the chair creaking under his weight. "I saw the description of the stolen cuckoo clock, and I knew that it was mine, of course. I mean, yours. I've never seen another clock like that one. That's such a tough thing, being the victim of theft. Shakes a person to the core, more often that not." He pulled at his fleece jacket so that one side overlapped the other and crossed his arms.

"Yes, the break-in is hard to deal with," Claire almost

whispered, protecting her voice. "I'm sick about losing the clock. I really, really loved it." She drew in a deep breath, gathering her strength to articulate the worst part. "There's more. When the robber took the clock, he took the ghosts with it. Apparently. Because they're not with me anymore."

"Ghosts? So there was more than one?" His mild blue eyes searched her face for clues.

Claire nodded mutely.

"Let me make us some tea. I'll be right back." He patted her shoulder as he passed by, and paused, clearing his throat. "I'm sorry, Claire. I'm sorry for your loss."

THEY TALKED the entire hour until closing and more, the shop slowly darkening because Walter didn't leave their conversation to turn on one of the many lamps in the shop. He listened to her pared-down story of the recent spectral activity in the bungalow with interest and sympathy, asking careful questions about her reaction to the goings-on. He seemed to want to respect her privacy at the same time that he longed for more information about the ghosts. Their mugs held only little pools of cold black tea by the time Claire reached the day of the break-in. "So you see, it was all my fault for leaving the window open," Claire said huskily. "I feel so guilty for that. I was worried about my pets being lost at first, but now, I think about the ghosts. Where could they be? Are they all right? Are they confused and frightened, especially the boy? I don't think he's very old. And I miss them, myself." She tried to put into words her sense of loss. "They were so intriguing. I miss the excitement and mystery they brought to my life." She swallowed hard, her throat raw, feeling the sorrow and guilt heavy in her chest. She couldn't draw a deep breath due to their weight.

"May I speak frankly to you?" She nodded mutely. "Yes,

you made a mistake by leaving the window open, but you're not to blame for the break-in. The robber is. You did something wrong by accident. The person who entered your house and stole your things made a choice to commit a crime. Those are two very different things. Please remember that."

"Thank you." Her voice was nearly gone.

"You're welcome. And as for the ghosts, I think that they can take care of themselves. And they're together. That's pretty clear. Safety in numbers, I always say." He rubbed his right eye under his glasses as if weary. "I am holding out hope that you will meet up with them again one day. If not here, than in…whatever world we will all inhabit in the future." This elicited a small, surprised smile from Claire. He rumbled on. "And if you are reunited with them here in St. Paul, would you do me a favor?"

"Of course, Walter."

"Ask them about Helen. Ask them if they know her. The chances are slim that they do, but you never know." Without waiting for a response, he arose and set off into the shop's dim caverns at a near trot, leaving Claire to consider what he had said. It had never occurred to her to ask the spirits about Kate. She felt that her beloved aunt was no longer accessible to her except in the most fundamental ways: in her own memories, her past, her bones.

She heard the sounds of Walter's scuffing footsteps approaching. He set something large and bright in front of her. It was the grinning papier-mâché jack-o'-lantern that had first brought her into the shop. She looked up at the shopkeeper's sad face, pale and sagging at this unflattering angle. "I'd like you to have this," he said. "It won't replace the clock or the ghosts, of course, but it's something. Something for Halloween. Please take it."

Claire reached out, feeling the dry, crackling surface of the papier-mâché under her palms. The leering jack-o'-lantern was as hideous as she remembered. "Thank you, Walter. Thank you very much for your kind, thoughtful gift. I'll treasure it, believe me."

"You're welcome. Just don't light a candle in it, whatever you do!"

ONCE HOME AGAIN, she placed the jack on the built-in-bookcase that the cats didn't jump on, before struggling out of her barn coat and dropping it on the couch. She had been honest when she'd told Walter that she would treasure his gift. Already, the jack-o'-lantern looked more like a bright orange Kermit and less like a monster. It's all in the perspective, she thought as she made her way into the study, Lute at her heels, and took a seat in front of the computer. Her fingers dropped onto the keyboard, lightly. She brought up the Google search box and typed, "Luna Theater St. Paul." Then she clicked the mouse, sending the search into motion.

216,000 results. Her hands clenched into fists and then relaxed. She rolled her head back, which sent her into a spate of coughing. Of course, she had expected this. The Internet released a torrent of information with a search that general. And she doubted that any of it would actually be pertinent to the time period she was interested in. The memory she had shared with the adult ghost of watching *Scarecrow and Mrs. King* in his apartment was a solid clue to his era as an actor. Quickly, she found the date that the show had premiered: October 3, 1983. The episode he had been watching was the next one, airing the following week. The Internet was in its infancy in 1983 and so was unlikely to contain the information that she needed. What this situation called for was a really good library and a skilled reference librarian. Lute scratched at her foot, requesting some attention. "That's one of the perks, Lutsen, of living in the capital of Minnesota: libraries like you've never seen." She leaned down to stroke the little dog's ears, then stilled, considering. "Do you miss your spirit buddies, eh?" she asked him. "They were enrichment for you, weren't they? Definitely enrichment."

"YOU WANT to find newspaper articles about a local theater from 1983?" The reference librarian from the George Latimer Library in downtown St. Paul had a slight Eastern European accent and an energetic air about her. "Our online indices are not going to go back that far. We'll have to use printed versions. Come with me, please." Claire trailed after her, hitching a zippered canvas bag over her shoulder. She'd brought supplies in case this quest turned out to be a lengthy one: her black and white notebook, pens, and a wrapped Salted Nut Roll.

The librarian halted before a shelf of blue volumes, each labeled, *St. Paul Dispatch Pioneer Press Newspaper Index*. The oldest volumes were actual bound books, but the newer indices were enclosed in plastic binders. She ran a finger along their spines, stopping on the binder for 1983. "Here you go. You might want to take a seat at an open study carrel; these books are heavy, and the print is small. You should be able to find any article referring to a theater under that theater's name. Then you'll need to write down the article's date and page number and take it to one of my colleagues in the room across the hall. That's where the microfilms for these old newspapers are kept." She lowered the volume for 1983 carefully into Claire's waiting arms.

"Thank you," Claire said. "You've been very helpful. Could you please pass me the volume for 1984, as well?"

Once she'd chosen a carrel against the wall, Claire extracted her notebook and a pen from her bag. Then she pulled the heavy volume for 1983 toward her with icy hands and flipped it open. Her heart was jumping wildly with suspense, so she purposely slowed her breathing, telling herself, calm down, just calm down. This is not time for a migraine. I'm researching, that's all.

Her fingertips were so damp that they turned the pages easily. The print was, indeed, very small. And she had forgotten to pack her reading glasses. Damn, damn, damn. She bowed forward, concentrating, her breath puffing out despite her earlier resolution to stay calm. There! The heading she'd been searching for: "Luna Theater." Below were the titles of perhaps seven or eight articles; her gaze swept down the column, trying to read them all at the same time. Articles that listed the plays chosen for the upcoming season, provided reviews, described renovations—but nothing stood out. Her heart pounded on, undeterred. She could always return to these articles, but maybe 1984 was the year she was looking for.

Of course! It wouldn't be 1983; the adult ghost was alive and well in October of that year, leaving only three months unaccounted for. Nineteen eighty-four or after would be much better bets. She clapped 1983 shut and snatched up 1984.

The pages rattled as she swiftly turned them. She swallowed hard, ignoring the pain she still felt in her throat. "Luna Theater," with a longer column underneath. And the title of the first article rose off the page for Claire and rang like a handbell. "Fire at Luna Theater Takes Two Lives."

"That's it," she breathed aloud. "That's got to be it." She scrawled the title of the article, the date of publication (Feb. 2), and the page number on the only paper she had, a fresh sheet of her journal. Then she hastily packed her gear except for the journal and slipped the two blue volumes in between their sagging compatriots on the shelf. Her bag jostled against her shoulder as she hurried across the hall.

Mercifully, a librarian sat at the desk near the window. "I'd like to see this article, please." She held the journal open to him. "And if you could show me how to use the microfilm, I would be so grateful."

He retired into a back room briefly, then returned with the spooled microfilm in hand, threaded it into the machine that projected it, and found the proper page for her. She sank down in front of the glowing screen, her eyes jumping over the whole article as if it to take it straight into her mind without actually having to read it.

"Fire at Luna Theater Takes Two Lives." Two photos swung open windows into those lives. The first showed a handsome man, his straight hair cut in the feathered style popular in the eighties. He smiled into the camera, confident and happy. His eyes crinkled at the corners. The caption read, "Matthew Vaughn, aged 33." Claire dragged her eyes to the other photo. A boy, solemn, a lock of dark hair falling over his forehead, features still somewhat unformed. He was looking over his shoulder, as if called back from play. "Edward (Teddy) Brewster, aged 9."

"Hello," Claire whispered. "Hello, you two. Matthew and Teddy." She tilted toward them unconsciously until her nose almost touched the illuminated screen. Her vision blurred suddenly, the images dissolving behind water. Sadness over the deaths drenched her from the inside out, leaving her as chilled as if the ghosts swayed beside her in the library.

She forced herself to read. The suspected cause of the fire was a faulty space heater left on during a rehearsal for Shakespeare's *Much Ado About Nothing*. Matthew had been playing Benedick, Teddy, the Boy. They had died of smoke inhalation. No one else injured, and the theater only moderately damaged by smoke.

Claire rocked back in her chair as if she'd been struck. She thought about these two lives snuffed out by a stupid accident: someone's carelessness or forgetfulness, like her own with the unlocked window. She thought of the grief that those deaths must've engendered in their family members, friends, colleagues. She thought of the distinctive personality of each of these two people, never to be found on this Earth again. Such brief lives they had had, much briefer than Claire's, even if hers were to end this very day.

Unbidden, she remembered a young student who had used a wheelchair due to a paralyzing accident he had endured long before he'd taken her writing class. There had been a drill for an active shooter each semester, and she had talked with her students about how she would jam a jacket under the door from the inside to keep the shooter out, how she would place her chair next to the door so that she could bring it crashing down on his head if he did manage to get inside, how they should overturn desks to create a barricade and duck down behind it. The young man in the wheelchair had said to her bleakly, "If he gets in, I'm screwed." She'd tried to reassure him, but neither of them had been convinced. They'd all known that a shooter could come, had come into many classrooms and schools, from grade schools to universities. They would all be utterly vulnerable, trapped in a classroom with only one way out. Teaching held so many perils for her now, so few joys.

In the library now, she breathed aloud, "I quit."

THE DISCOVERY OF THE GHOSTS' identities felt like a clarion call, and she didn't want to mull it over alone. She called Margo, Grace, and Sarah from the shelter of her car and asked if she could treat them to coffee at Kiffles and give them an update. Margo and Sarah snatched at the invitation and the three of them settled on four o'clock as the meeting time, giving her forty-five minutes to get home and take care of the animals before heading to Kiffles. Her call to Grace went to voice mail, but Claire's cell phone rang a moment later while she was poised to put the key in the ignition. Grace sounded crushed when she heard the plans.

"I can't, damn it," she almost wailed. "I have an appointment that I absolutely cannot break. But listen to this idea. I'll give you a call this evening, about eight, and you can fill me in then. And how about Scott and I stop by to see you tomorrow after lunch? He has the day off from school, and he wants to bring you a pumpkin and a card he made for you. Would that be okay?" She sounded harried, and Claire could only imagine the frenzied day that Grace was having. She felt honored that her sister-in-law had squeezed a phone call to her into it.

"Yes, of course; that'd be great. Talk to you then."

The three women found a booth toward the back of Kiffles and slipped alongside the sticky table, Claire on one side and her expectant friends on the other. She passed out copies of the newspaper article to Margo and Sarah and willed herself to be still as they read, concentrating on the fragrant steam from her coffee and the warm mug she held. They finished reading at almost the same time, their heads coming up together.

Sarah spoke first. "My God, how awful. Two lives lost at Luna. This was long before my time, of course, and even before Brian McMaster's, although I think he must've known about this tragedy, Claire. He was holding out on us when we met with him, in my opinion. He may have known more about the...activities at Luna than he let on, too. The moved props and cold drafts and such. He plays his cards close to the vest, that Brian." Her lips were pressed into a frown of disapproval. "I would think he could've been more open with a friend."

"He was no help, was he, with his 'non-denial denials,'" Claire replied. "Well, I take that back. His lack of info helped me to focus and keep on task. Anger works in me that way sometimes. Sarah, how long before the theater was scheduled to be knocked down did the other artistic director give you the clock?" Belatedly, she wished she'd chosen a milder phrase to describe Luna's end, but Sarah didn't flinch.

"Not long at all. Maybe two or three weeks? The last of the props, costumes, and furniture had already been carted out. The green room was completely empty aside from the clock on the wall and a few stray pieces of trash."

"Ah, that's what I wondered. Because if the ghosts had been haunting the theater for over thirty years and then real-ized that it was going to be demolished, they might've attached themselves to something familiar that they thought would be taken somewhere else. Somewhere lively. The props and scenery and so on—who knows what would happen to those? Or maybe the ghosts just couldn't believe until the theater was empty that their home was about to be destroyed."

Sarah said, "*I* couldn't make myself believe it—why would they do any better?" The next words tumbled out in her excitement. "And the clock became a house, a home for them, don't you think?"

Claire nodded. "When your home is in danger and there's no way you can protect it, you look for a new home. If you're resilient, that is."

Margo had been listening, wide-eyed and silent. Now, she gestured toward the small blurry photos of Matthew and Teddy in the article. "Or maybe they thought of the clock as a lifeboat, at least at first. I can just imagine this man saying to the little boy, 'Come on, kid; we're going.'"

Claire thought about the elder ghost's anger when she'd let the clock run down. Was he protecting a child in his charge?

"I can picture that, too, Margo," she whispered hoarsely. "Poor souls."

"GOSH, pal, that's such a great card. I love it! Thank you." Claire bent down to give her nephew a tight hug.

"No problem. I made it for you last week after soccer practice and homework. Mom said those come first."

"That's his own message," Grace chipped in quickly. "I suggested, 'Feel better soon,' but he wanted me to write, 'Sorry you lost the clock.' So I did."

"The message and the picture you drew are perfect, buddy. Since I never got around to taking photos, your drawing is the only picture I have of the clock, too. That makes it all the more special." She sighed and then corrected herself by saying brightly, "Shall we walk now?"

The weather was overcast and blustery. The trees were showing some of their bones now, the leaves tossing fretfully on the tips of twigs and the grass and sidewalks underneath swathed in shifting flocks of the still-bright fallen ones. The frequent rains of the last two months meant that the newly-fallen leaves were flexible rather than crispy, like scraps of supple fabric in shades of cinnamon, paprika, cayenne, and saffron. The two women and the boy scuffled through the drifts as they walked, Claire and Grace each holding one of Scout's hands, Lute scampering on Claire's other side. Their breaths hung white in the damp air. Every now and then Scout let go to run ahead and capture a spinning leaf before it landed or pick up a particularly colorful maple one.

Jack-o'-lanterns already occupied some porches and front steps in preparation for trick-or-treating in two evenings. Grace pointed out a huge, menacing jack that held sideways in its mouth a small, terrified looking one.

"Oh, poor thing," Scout said, and he meant it.

"Well, the little guy's not been swallowed yet," Claire offered in consolation. "He might still escape. In fact, I feel sure he will. What do you think?"

Scout came back slowly to slip his hand in hers. "I think he will," he replied, doubt in his voice. "At least, I hope so." Claire squeezed his chilly fingers, touched by his concern for the little jack-o'-lantern, until he took off again after a twirling leaf.

"I hope so, too," Grace added, seemingly as an afterthought. She appeared a bit distracted today, thinking of her work, perhaps, or of Greg. Or perhaps of something completely unrelated to Claire. Other people were always unknown on some deep level, she thought, as I am to them. The decision to quit her teaching job, she kept to herself, wanting to shelter it until she was sure it had taken root.

No more teaching, ever. For the first time, she let herself consider what that life might be like. She would need some other sort of job, of course, with its own gremlins to plague her—no job was free from stress and difficulties. But what if she found work that centered on writing? I could do that, she thought with wonder. I'm sure I could. From someone who had mournfully let her chief talent dwindle, she had transformed into a woman who exercised her talent, cultivated relationships, took care of herself, stood up straight. While she'd written page after page describing the haunting of Claire Bracken, fascinated by the ghosts' mysterious nature, she'd felt as if she were a strong horse running. The ghosts were gone now, but her writings about them and the renewal she'd experienced were both still with her. She would write for her job and for herself, she vowed, and go to work at both tasks without the doubt and dread that had been her cringing companions for so many years.

What a relief. What an unutterable relief, to be free from a role that made her sick, soul and body. Claire swiped the dampness from her cheeks with both hands but didn't stop walking, still lit up by her visions. Lute's feet made a pattering sound beside her. Grace was talking on her cell phone, she sensed, falling momentarily behind.

"Look, a Dumpster!" Scout called out, and ran toward it. "I saw one of these taken away by a big truck on our street the other day. It was cool. And noisy."

With an effort, Claire pulled her mind back to her nephew. His scarlet jacket looked like a banner on this gray day, against the dull metal of the Dumpster. The house that the huge bin stood in front of was going up for sale soon, she'd heard from a neighbor. The owners were probably in the process of clearing out their junk before moving on. Good for them.

She squinted. Something gold hung down over the lip of the lidded Dumpster, near Scout's shoulder. The wind swept over them all like a tide, twisting the golden line, shaking out glitters along its length, making her spirits leap up, hopeful and alive.

She rushed to the Dumpster with Lute and flipped its heavy lid backwards.

On a heap of discarded carpet lay the clock, one of its chains dangling outside the Dumpster and the other snaking from sight inside. The wooden crosspiece that normally held the watchful owls over the roof's peak lay askew, partly detached from the clock, and the owls' dark eyes were filmed with dust. The maple-leaf pendulum was snarled in the rust-colored carpet. Only one of the pinecone weights was visible.

Claire released a shuddering breath and reached for the

clock, lifting it gently, gently. The words, "Please, please, please," beat in her mind. She waited, hands trembling. Felt the hair bristle at the nape of her neck and along her outstretched arms. Heard Lute's bark of welcome. Detected, finally, the faint, sharp scent of lime.

DISCUSSION QUESTIONS

My hope is that *Clockwise* is a thought-provoking book as well as an enjoyable one. Below are some questions that I wrote to facilitate book club discussions, chats with friends, or individual musings. If the questions prompt a connection or two between the book and your own life experiences, I'll be delighted. To print or download the questions, just go to:

www.SusanBordenWriter.com/conversations

1. What glimmers of strength does Claire display in Chapters 1-5 despite her ill health?

2. What are the earliest hints of supernatural activity associated with the clock?

3. What does Scout's visit to Claire's home in Chapters 4 and 5 suggest about their relationship?

4. What roles do Lute, Tamsin, and Kipper play in the book? Would you miss them if they weren't included?

5. Does the friendship between Claire and Margo prosper mainly because of their differences or in spite of them? Why do you think this?

6. What new doorways does Sarah open for Claire?

7. In what ways is Kate still present in the book despite her passing before it begins?

8. Readers meet Gus and David via the phone before these characters actually appear in person. Do any aspects of their attitudes and behavior surprise you once they arrive in Minnesota?

9. Does Gus's inability to help Claire with the clock's mystery alter your opinion of him?

10. What does the trip to the fair reveal about Claire's family members and her relationships with them?

11. What indications do you see that Claire's health is returning?

12. What significance do you see in the telephones and phone conversations of *Clockwise*?

13. How do Claire's mealtimes change over the course of the book?

14. What's your reaction to the story Claire tells her father about the troubled student who was cutting herself?

15. In what way is Claire haunted by her experiences as a teacher?

16. How much responsibility do you think Claire should shoulder for the robbery?

17. In what ways does her second meeting with Walter, the owner of the antique shop, bring up new perspectives? In what ways does it echo their meeting on the day that Claire purchased the clock?

18. How does the theme of accidents relate to the last chapters of *Clockwise*?

19. Which of the possibilities for the ghosts' connection to the clock (Chapter 25) seem most plausible to you? Why?

20. Does the book have a happy ending, in your opinion? Why do you think so?

ACKNOWLEDGMENTS

Writing is such a solitary activity, yet I think that without a ring of supporters encircling the writer, not many books would get past the wishing stage. I am very grateful for the shining constellation of people who helped me in more ways than they realize.

Heidi Bailey encouraged my forays into writing fiction before I even had an idea for a novel, and she continues to cheer for me from afar.

Kelly Donahue and Susan Diekman were the first readers of *Clockwise* and the first people who wanted to see what happens next to Claire. Their engagement gave me hope for the book's future.

Nancy Mulvey, without reading a word, convinced me that *Clockwise* deserved my time and energy even during a bleak period in my life—*especially* during that bleak period.

Pat Pyle read the whole manuscript and, with her eagle eyes, found errors that I couldn't spot.

Ruth Hoffman, Beverly Jergenson, and Pam Biladeau have been my dear friends and comrades for many long years.

They are always quick to ask, "What's going on with the book?," bless them, and to believe in me.

Nancy Heitmeyer, Vicky Moore, and Donna White expressed their confidence and offered encouragement at key times.

Family members accepted my rather sudden change of careers without a murmur.

Dale Bengston kindly shared his knowledge of the intricacies of marketing in support of *Clockwise*.

Jennifer Brunk offered her thoughtful perspective on the website design as well as valuable ideas for improving it.

The book of hauntings that Claire reads late into the night is *Nantucket Ghosts* by Blue Balliett (Down East Books, 2006). Of all the collections of ghost stories that I have read, it's the most mysterious, intriguing, and gracefully written.

The line, "One day you're a diamond and then you're a stone" in Chapter 23 comes from "The Bug," a song by Mark Knopfler on Mary Chapin Carpenter's beautiful album *Come On Come On* (Columbia Nashville/TriStar, 1992).

And finally, my husband, Pete, generously and patiently lent his own artistic talents to the publication of *Clockwise*. He also shared the book's creation from the sidelines and felt happy that I was happy as I typed away. Du bist die große Liebe meines Lebens, Schatz.

ABOUT THE AUTHOR

 Susan Borden is a long-time Minnesotan who loves the cold. She has a master's degree in expository writing from the University of Iowa and a Ph.D. in English from the University of Minnesota. After many years of college teaching, she quit her job and, to her surprise, plunged into writing fiction. She lives in a cozy old house with her husband, tiger-striped cat, and three cuckoo clocks. *Clockwise* is her first novel.

For more about Susan Borden and her writing, visit:
www.SusanBordenWriter.com

instagram.com/susanbordenwriter

CPSIA information can be obtained
at www.ICGtesting.com
Printed in the USA
BVHW030250111021
618663BV00006B/293